D0423419

VOICES
FROM
HOME

NEIL CAUDLE

VOICES FROM HOME

G. P. PUTNAM'S SONS • NEW YORK

Copyright © 1989 by Neil Caudle
All rights reserved. This book, or parts thereof,
may not be reproduced in any form without permission.
Published by G. P. Putnam's Sons,
200 Madison Avenue, New York, NY 10016.
Published simultaneously in Canada

The text of this book is set in Baskerville.

Library of Congress Cataloging-in-Publication Data

Caudle, Neil.
Voices from home / by Neil Caudle.
p. cm.
ISBN 0-399-13421-2
[1. Stepfamilies—Fiction.] I. Title.
PS3553.A934V65   1989   88-36575 CIP
[Fic]—dc19

Printed in the United States of America
1 2 3 4 5 6 7 8 9 10

For Caitlin and David

The author is especially indebted to
Abigail Thomas for her counsel and encouragement.

PART ONE

A CHILD'S BOOK OF COLORS

1

She carried a word to her father. *Chicago*. All the way down
from School Hill, as she walked to the small-engines shop
where he worked, she was moving her tongue on the *chi* and
the *ca,* closing her lips on the *go* like a trap: *Chicago*. The word
was all edges and action; she wouldn't know what it meant till
she saw it take hold in his face.

Now she was crossing an apron of gravel, striding from
afternoon glare into deep, oily shade. And there was her father, lifting her over the tillers and mowers, setting her down
on the clean, hammered steel where he spread out his work.
While he was under the bench lamp, the light seemed to cling
to his hair and his clothing; when he stepped back in the
shadows, it settled and flowed like a skirt.

Libby said, "Momma get up with you yet?"

Her father was bathing a saw chain, lifting it out of the black
gasoline, inspecting the cutters and points. "Up with me for
what?"

"I better wait." Her gaze wandered off to the shelving and
bins of spare parts in the depths of his bay. When she looked
back at her father, he was wearing the chain like a necklace,
wiping his hands on a rag.

"You been to school looking good as all that?"

"Daddy, hush." Then, for the occasion, she added: "Just
because you think I favor Momma."

He didn't rise to the subject of her mother.

"You do so. You said me and her were on the small and
pretty side."

"I reckon that's right. I reckon that's the side you're on."

His hips squared around to the workbench; his bootheels
slid back a half-step on the slab. This way his body was canted,
and his hands could swing easily down to the parts of the saw.

The toe of her shoe pecked lightly at the back of his knee. "You got ants in your pants?"

Libby stopped kicking. "No."

"You got a date later on?"

Libby slid down from the workbench and stomped on the toe of his boot; it was steel-reinforced. "Daddy, you're a *mess*."

"Well?"

"No, I ain't got a date."

"Don't say 'ain't.' It's ignorant."

"No, I have not got a date."

Libby walked over the slab to the soft-drink machine and leaned with her forearm against it, letting her fingers drift over its face as though finding her route on a map: *Chicago*. The heel of her hand brushed the 7-Up button; a bottle dropped into the chute. Every school-day afternoon her father's coins were in the mechanism, waiting for her pleasure. He had told her 7-Up would have a better taste if money never showed; he was right.

She swigged from the bottle and spun with her heel on a dribble of oil, catching a glimpse of the owner, who watched from behind the glass door to the showroom, partly obscured by decals. Libby stopped spinning and lowered her bottle to collarbone level. She didn't want any owner around to eclipse what she'd come there to say.

The owner laid one little fist on the glass, as though ready to shove his way into the shop. Nothing came through but the pink in his fist.

When she saw him turn away from the door, Libby spun on the ball of her foot, letting her hair toss and fly.

Her father raised the bar of the saw like a gun stock, sighting the chain slots for true. "You about to bust or something?"

She kept spinning.

"You going steady?"

Libby stopped spinning and teetered a little. "Daddy, hush."

Her father assembled the saw, one hand fishing the parts out of gas, the other one screwing them down. "What's got you so full of yourself?"

"Who said I was?" She was scuffing the sole of her shoe on the slab. "I need to leave pretty soon."

"Come go to supper with Buddy and me."

She didn't respond.

"What was all this about your momma? You got some news?"

The front of his bay was open to the street, the door rolled overhead, and she looked out to see the owner backing away from the lot in his car.

Her father filled out a cardboard ticket and wired it to the handle of the saw. "Tell me something. You approved to be in here?"

"What?"

"Man said this morning his insurance won't cover you in here, unless you're approved."

"Who, Mister Small?"

He grinned and said, "Mister *Small?*"

"That's his name, ain't it? It says 'Small Engine Sales' on the sign."

He was still grinning. "You always did have a literal mind."

She licked the 7-Up taste from her lips; there was something like gasoline in it. She set her empty bottle in a crate and said, "I better go."

"What's the big terrible rush?"

There was no answer.

"You going to tell me this news now or what?"

She looked at him. "Oh yeh. I almost forgot. We're moving."

The shadows were roaming his face. "Who is?"

"Me and Momma and them."

"Where to?"

The question cleared out of the air, so there was nothing but fumes. She said, "Chicago."

He blinked, that was all.

She said, "Somewhere outside of Chicago. I forget where. Anyway, it's real close to Chicago. So you might as well call it Chicago."

There was a slight upward curl in his lip—the first pass of

anger—and the lines hardened near his eyes—defiance. But
neither expression would hold. He was looking away, out the
door, to the street, as though searching his way through ad-
justments of light on the mountains, the patterns of late afternoon. He was seeing something out there, and she didn't want
any part of whatever it was. She wanted him back with the
mowers and tillers and fumes in that bay. She wanted his
anger around her like powerful hands on her ribs. She wanted
his steadfast and furious action. She would go after that anger.
She would go after him over and over again with that word,
until it worked, until it meant something other than this.

"I can't believe it," she said. "*Chicago*. Can you? And we get
to live in a brick house. And I'm getting a car."

He looked her over, as though she had just then arrived. "Is
that what your momma said?"

Libby nodded. "Miles is going to make good selling paint
because his brother owns the store. I've got to have me a car
because the school is ten miles off. And Miles says his
brother's paint business is ready to take off, and if it does take
off I get a new one. But even if it doesn't take off, I can find
me one used."

"What does your mother say about it?"

"She was planning to call you about it. She thinks it's fantastic. And I can drive her places in Chicago."

"You just relax. Nothing's settled till I think it through."

"We're leaving in a week. We're going to sell Miles's car and
rent a truck, and he's going to buy himself a better car when
we get to Chicago."

"You've got a lot to say about the cars."

"What of it?" She tossed her hair, and it hung straight by
her cheeks. "Besides, you ain't got a thing to do with it.
They've got custody."

"Say 'haven't got.' Don't say 'ain't.' "

"Okay," she said. "Haven't got, haven't got, haven't got. I
can say that one more week."

"Go on, then. I've still got Buddy home to nag about his
'ain'ts.' You'd better go and get your packing done. He's
coming by. We're going to supper."

Libby picked up a small wrench and dropped it on the workbench. It clanged. "Let me have a cigarette."

"You're too little to smoke."

"Then I'll buy my own."

"Fine."

She walked toward the soft-drink machine and bumped the toe of her running shoe against the plastic crates of empty bottles. Setting her right sole against the stack, she snapped her knee straight; the stack crashed and the bottles rolled in wide loops toward the floor drains. She began to kick the bottles, launching them against the wall, the bench, the shelves. They were breaking all around. They were dashing under mowers, spinning like small glass animals chasing their tails. Libby sprang after them, kicking, clenching her fists, her long hair swinging in her face. She danced among the shards as people do in dreams when underfoot the floor has come alive with crawling snakes.

When she finished, her brother, Buddy, was watching her too. He was propped against the workbench, staring. "What's the matter with her?" he asked. Buddy was shorter and squarer than his father—his father's shape compacted. His hair was longer, and it curled behind his ears. But he had his father's cleft chin, with the left lobe slightly smaller than the right, a feature that made one profile seem rather weak, the other rather strong.

"Says they're moving to Chicago," her father said. "All four." He lit a Camel and replaced the pack in his shirtfront pocket, where "Jake" had been stitched on the fabric in red.

Buddy nodded. "I saw Momma while ago."

Libby could feel the glass under the soles of her shoes.

Buddy said, "What are you going to do about it?"

"It's up to her," her father said, waving his cigarette in no particular direction. "If she doesn't want to stay here, nothing in the world will keep her."

"And if she does?"

He didn't say.

"And if she does decide she wants to be here, nothing's going to make her go, is it?" Buddy asked.

"What do you care?" Libby said.

Buddy began to pick up the bottles, whole ones first, arranging them by brand in the crates. She watched him. The bottles had not been this way when she kicked them. She couldn't remember an order at all, only various sizes and tapers and colors of glass. Now they were being arranged.

Buddy dropped the broken pieces in a cardboard box. "What about Miles?" he said to his father. "Miles in Rapid Falls is bad enough. Miles way off with her—away from you and me?"

"Does he ever come around you, babe?"

"Course he does. We live together, don't we?"

He winced. "You know what I'm talking about."

"He might," she said after a while.

"I will know if he tries, won't I? The minute he tries? Won't I?"

She went to him and fished his cigarette out of his fingers, dropping the ash on his leg. He lit another one. Buddy found a broom and began to sweep the smallest bits of glass into a pile. "We'll need some money for all these that broke," he said.

Libby leaned against her father, watching Buddy. Buddy's broom was sequined. Her father put his arm around her, cupping her elbow in his hand. "Let it go," he said.

2

Momma packs and Miles carries to the truck. They are moving somewhere outside of Chicago. I don't have to go. So I sit on a box full of songbooks and wait. We used to sing out of these books whenever I asked her. I can't see what use they'll be in Chicago.

Miles carries all of our breakables out to the truck. "Jailbait," he says. Nobody hears him but me, because of Momma in the kitchen cleaning out her cabinets, and Grandma Whitley hooting in her bedroom. Grandma Whitley is a witch to me. She is only good for watching game shows.

"Stonewall Jackson! That's the answer! 'There stands Jackson like a *stone wall*.' " She likes to shell her peas and yell. She's not shelling any peas today, though.

Miles comes back inside. I say, "What did you call me?"

"You heard me. Ain't that what you are? Why else would you tell such a lie about me to your momma?"

The ceiling is gray with a big yellow stain in the middle. That's where the roof used to leak when we got a hard rain. It reminds me of seeing their mattress when Miles hauled it out to the truck.

Miles likes to talk in a whisper about half of the time. He wants to know if I truly believe he is stupid enough to be messing around with a jailbait like me.

I say, "You're fairly stupid."

"Why don't you go in there and tell your momma the truth?"

I refuse to answer him.

He says, "And while you're at it, you can go tell that daddy of yours too. Tell him, before Miles Downey dips his brush, he sees to it the can's been stirred good first. And if he don't believe it, he can ask your momma."

So I go, "She doesn't care about you anymore. She'd rather have Daddy smelling like licker than you smelling like paint."

He just grins and carries Momma's china horses to the truck. I hope he drops the whole box and it breaks every leg off her horses. I bet he can't even hold down a job in his own brother's store, once they get to Chicago. I bet he has to start scraping dead paint off of houses again.

Grandma Whitley goes to nagging the TV. That's how she wants to be lecturing me all of the time. It can get on your nerves how she goes on like nothing is changed. She barely knows we're alive.

The screen door slams. Miles is back. "Give me what you're sitting on," he says. When he grins down at me a few black hairs slip off his bald spot, and he mashes them back on his head with his palm. I slide off the box and sit cross-legged on the floor, which is already down to just wood.

I go, "Why don't you shut up and leave me alone?"

"Why don't you go in the kitchen and tell her the truth? Not that she ever believed you in the first place."

"I'm staying, ain't I?"

"It might be she believed you. Then again it might be she knows how you lied. It's easy to turn loose of a liar."

"Maybe she ought to wonder about you awhile longer."

He carries the box to the door and turns around. "Far as I can see, this time tomorrow I'll be up there in Chicago with your momma. You'll be down here. That how you like it?" The door slams behind him.

Miles thinks since he married Momma he can be in charge of me. He can't be in charge of me. He can't touch a hair of Daddy.

Here he comes again. I go, "You think you're so smart. I prized that nail out of my window. I prized it out every night. And then later I just worked it right back in to where you couldn't ever tell I'd been gone."

So he's looking right quick down the hall like he might be ready to go check on that nail. Then he grins down at me like he figures I'm lying. I wasn't lying. Nobody keeps me nailed in when I'm truly in love. When I'm in love I am very determined.

Grandma Whitley goes to hissing in the bedroom. She sounds like a pot boiling over. "*Succotash! Succotash* is a dish composed of corn and lima beans!"

Momma comes in from the kitchen wearing yellow rubber gloves and looking better in blue jeans than I ever did.

Miles heaves her up by her waist and near about bumps Momma's head. "Set me down, Miles. You think I'm a box of plates?" He sets her down on the hamper where we used to put our dirty clothes. You can tell what kind of a scabby person he is deep down. Places on him crack and turn this ugly purple color like a pine knot. Like his elbows are purple as pine knots and rough so I can't stand to see how they're next to my momma.

Momma says, "Look what I found in my recipes drawer."

She's got report cards and pictures and things people keep for some reason. Like all their different memories. Miles puts his hands on the pictures and says to me, "You always had the same hair? This hair looks yellow to me in the picture."

Momma decides she can look at me again. She says, "No, it was always the same. Butter and honey, I'd call it."

I'd call it more like the color of brown paper bags.

Miles keeps on reading the papers. "This one here's about colors. Says right here 'A Child's Book of Colors.' Somebody wrote 'Elizabeth.' That's not much of a handwriting, Lib."

"Give that here."

"Just hold your horses a second."

I stare at cracks in the floor and my hair wants to fall in my face.

Momma says, "I remember those colors, don't you? I remember you were just five, maybe six. Remember? And you came home from church? And you about cried half the night?" Momma looks at Miles. "Then we found that little paper book inside her Bible. And Libby thought we wanted her to take a bath in sheep's blood. Wouldn't even hear any different."

Miles turns the pages. "I don't see nothing about sheep's blood. I just see black, red, white."

It makes me want to throw up how he's putting his hands on our personal papers.

Momma says, "It was either Libby's imagination or that poor old soul Miss Cook. I never imagined a child could get so worked up about five words and three empty pages."

I guess this is how she gets me back, showing him that book. She knows I'd rather be dead.

The TV is blabbering on about something, but at least Grandma Whitley finally shut up. Maybe she's snoozing again in that rocker, with her lips curling back like a pony's when somebody tickles his nose. She thinks her job is to scare people off from their sins. Which is the same as that Old Lady Cook, who gave us those colors in Sunday-school class and said be sure not to fan them in the service. I asked her where were the words in this book. She said it was a book of colors, not words. Marcus said black weren't no color, and she pinched his ear. Miss Cook said that black was the first color ever, like dark on the face of the deep and the night before day. It was like all of our souls before we took a bath in the blood of the Lamb. Leona said, "Yuk." Miss Cook said Leona better ask forgiveness. I was afraid of Miss Cook. I was afraid of her mustache. Daddy said a mustache was the kiss of death on a woman.

Miles hands the book back to Momma and carries our ironing board out to the truck. The cover still shows where I burned it real bad with the iron. I did that on purpose one day. It was deliberate. The screen door bangs shut. Momma goes through pictures of us by our cars.

"That first blue Fairlane with you in diapers. The candy-apple-red GTO with Buddy's broken wrist. Your daddy in the Mustang with me on the hood. Seems like that's what our memories amounted to, a selection of cars."

"Don't get started, Momma."

"I'm not. I cried all I care to last Wednesday night."

Her eyes want to act like they're looking ahead to the future and not seeing all of this dust that is swarming around.

She says, "Back before last Wednesday night, I wouldn't have left you here in a million years."

"Just forget it."

"You know it?"

"Forget it. You're just moving, is all."

"First you were saying you'd rather be dead than leave your daddy. Then you said you would rather be dead than leave your brother. Then it was your friends you couldn't stand to leave. So I guessed maybe you liked some boy, because I don't know about any of your friends. Do you have a friend? You do? You said you just couldn't stand to leave your school before the year was over. So I knew you were dredging things up. Then you said you'd rather be dead than to move. But I know you better than that."

"Let's don't get started again."

"Then when you said what you did about Miles—"

I know she wants me to look at her face but I won't.

"After that, things turned as clear as a bell."

"Like what?"

"You're a young woman now, Libby. Fifteen years old. I can't believe it's September already and you are fifteen. But you are. And I have tried and failed to keep you from your father's ways. It's too late to try anymore. That doesn't mean I stopped loving you. I didn't. But you know, I had to let go. It's another rental house, where we're going, not even as big. Miles has aimed us at a new life. I see that now."

"That's all the reason you changed?"

"Changed?" She laughs so deep in her chest it just barely comes out. "I never changed in my life. I'm still the girl your daddy saw waiting behind the dugout when he whipped off his catcher's mask and came charging back for a pop foul. He never caught that ball, either. Did I tell you that?"

"You told me. But see, Miles is the trouble. See, Miles is the one that—"

"Never mind that, Libby. I see the right thing. I've had enough divorce. Miles is good to me. He is. I know he looks around, but most nights I find him in bed. Unlike your father." She pulls off the rubber gloves and unties her scarf. Buddy gave her that scarf for Christmas. It's the most confusing scarf I ever saw. It has every color you can imagine, but still it's green and shiny, like her eyes. She smooths the scarf on her leg.

"You know I dreaded to sign you over to your father. Custody. I hate that word. It sounds like you're under arrest. I wouldn't have done such a thing in a million years, before last Wednesday night."

"Why did you, then, if you hate it so much?"

The screen door slams. Miles says, "You know good and well why she done it."

Momma says, "Miles."

But Miles has to always keep running his mouth. "She did it 'cause you got your daddy mixed up in it all. She signed you over to him so he wouldn't come after me. I said, 'Let him come on.' "

Momma's not paying attention to him. She's getting ready to answer my question.

"I don't know whether it was because I thought you lied or because I thought you didn't. Either way, I saw things for the way they are. What would you have done if I had made you go with me?"

"Run away. I would just come back and live with Daddy."

She blows her breath with her mouth barely open, like somebody fogging up glass. "That's what I thought."

Miles carries kitchen stuff out. This time the door doesn't slam.

"So what if I lied about Miles? So what if I did?"

Momma looks me straight in the eye without saying one word. That means she's waiting to hear what I'm trying to say.

"Daddy said did that man ever come near me and I said he might. And I said he probably would if we stayed in the same house together. And especially if we moved off a long ways away. And that was the truth. So that's why I said it."

She shakes her head very slow like she's sick of my lies. That makes me mad. I go, "You just assume he's so perfect but what if he's not? You ever think about that? And what about Daddy? You can't just drag me off someplace and make me forget about Daddy. What about him?"

Momma looks straight at the ceiling, like she's concentrating on the stain. "Your father's not finished being himself."

"I don't care what you say. I love him."

She looks at me. "Of course you do. He spoils you. Scares the living daylights out of you. Squeezes you and won't let go. You've got his engine grease mashed so deep in your school clothes it won't ever wash out." Momma stops looking at me, and it seems like her thoughts wander off. "And he can do things. Make things look easy. If he could just handle himself like he handled those pitchers. You know it? If he could just handle himself like he handles a horse. You ever seen him with horses?"

She thinks about it a second and straightens her back like it's sore up and down from the packing. "But where was your father the night you went sledding down the Etchethsons' driveway and split your head wide open on the culvert? He was in a certain trailer over in Sinksboro. And here comes

Buddy, lugging you up to the house, your little head dripping blood on the snow."

"I remember that. I forgot about Buddy."

"It was a long time ago."

Miles picks up the floor lamps and carries them out like a couple of ski poles. There's just a few more boxes and Grandma Whitley. The furniture all went out this morning when Uncle Bob was here to help. The screen door slams. "What's that?" Grandma Whitley screams from her room. "This is the noisiest bunch I ever care to know! Can't I have a single quiet minute?"

Momma gets up from the hamper and walks down the hall. "Mother, Miles has practically got us packed. Do you need to do anything before we leave?"

"Don't bother me." Grandma Whitley is mad she has to move in the middle of her game show. She's mad they put all her mahogany furniture in Bob and Betsy's basement. "I'm ready as you are."

Momma comes back and sits down on the hamper again. I'm cross-legged on the floor. It's just me and her and some dust. She sips at a tall plastic glass of iced tea. "You want some of this?"

"Keep it."

Momma sets her tea down on the floor while she puts on her ring—the one with the ruby. "I never liked my name. Ruby. But your daddy did."

"You got a better name than Aunt Betsy."

Momma laughs and the echo sounds stranger than ever. "The thing is, Betsy will get you, just sure as the world."

"No she won't."

"My precious sister always did think she knew a better way to raise you."

"Daddy won't let her have me."

"Yes he will. Betsy will get you. Your daddy and that woman, that wife of his, won't be a family for long, not the way they carry on."

"They just argue, is all."

"They carry on. They carry on a sight, if you listen to your

brother." She looks at me square in the eyes, like she does
when she can't tell if I am in some kind of terrible trouble or
what. "What's going to happen to you, over there?"

The screen door slams. Miles says, "I'll tell you what's
gonna happen. They'll get to drinking and let her run wild."

Momma looks up at him quick. He goes out backward with
a box full of curtains, bumping the screen with his butt.
Momma looks down at her gloves and tugs at the fingers to
pull them straight out. "Now that my sister's got half of our
furniture packed in that basement of hers, she'll be after my
children next. You, at least. You see the way she was looking
you over this morning?"

"No." She makes me nervous with all this stuff about Aunt
Betsy.

Momma laughs at me again. "Now Lib, you mean you don't
want to live over there on School Hill in that nice brick house
with a full basement and eat tuna casseroles and go to church
three times a week?"

"No." Why does she think that's so funny? I don't like the
way she's picking loose threads off the edge of that little cloth
cushion on top of the hamper. I tell her Miles is probably
going to sell a lot of paint in Chicago and things will calm
down a good bit.

"Miles." Momma blows her breath all at once. "God knows
where he's taking me." She's working too hard on that ravelly
cushion. Before long there won't be any thread left on there
at all. After a while she says, "It looks like he's about got the
house empty." She shakes her head for a minute. "You know,
I don't have a present for you, Libby. Not a single thing."

"I don't care."

"Bob and Betsy paid that deposit on the truck."

"I don't want a present."

"Buddy would. Buddy likes presents. Maybe I'll send him
some little something from Chicago. When he got out of that
reform school, I gave him that little silver knife. Remember?
It was a big joke. He loved it." Momma's rolling her head
around on her neck like there's a sore spot back there somewhere. "Look after each other, Libby. He needs more looking

after than you. He's a nervous boy. His daddy keeps him confused."

"He's a lot better here lately."

"That motorcycle. Nothing would do but that his daddy give him a motorcycle. That's when his trouble started. Buddy's not coming to say good-bye, is he?"

"Him and Miles would just fight about something."

Miles comes to the door and says, "Ready?" He says, "See you, Lib."

"See you."

Miles says for Momma to bring Grandma Whitley out with her. Momma tells him not to forget Grandma Whitley's TV. So he comes in after it, and pretty soon I hear them arguing back there in the bedroom. Grandma Whitley yells at Miles for yanking the plug by the cord. He rolls the TV past us on its little cart and slams the door. After a while he cranks the truck and lets it idle. It's just me and Momma again.

"Is your daddy coming after you?"

"Soon as he can."

"I don't want to just leave you here in this empty living room."

"It won't matter where you leave me."

She pulls me off the floor by my arm and hugs me once, that's all. There's a good bit of strength in her arms. She is still the best-smelling person I ever smelled. Momma lets go of me. She opens the hamper and drops her scarf and gloves and the pictures inside, but she lays the little book in my hand. "I don't think that's the kind of memory I want to move after all," she says. Momma picks up the clothes hamper and carries it outside. The door slams hard enough to make me jump. I am by myself in this empty room when I hear the witch's slippers coming down the hall, smooching her heels. And of course she is dragging that rocker behind her.

"I have something for you," she says.

"I don't want your stupid rocking chair."

She loves to fold her arms across her saggy boobs and laugh at me, real hateful. It makes her scalp turn red, like somebody's been pulling her hair. The witch turns her rocker around and sits down. I'm standing over her, waiting. "Not the chair, Elizabeth. It's the only stick of mahogany they've left me. But at least I'm going, hey? Still part of the family, hey? No sir. My gift's not furniture, it's a thought."

"Why don't you get in the truck? You're holding them up."

"Momentarily, dear. The thought is 'watcher.'"

"That's the stupidest thing I ever heard."

"Be still! Listen! For every living soul there is a watcher. She is always there a-watching, but you can't see her. She can figure you out. If you try to hide a filthy act, she knows it."

"You're the only watcher around here," I say. "You spy at me through the curtains. You listen on the other phone. You go through my things."

"And I found a little something, didn't I? Something to smoke?" She wags her finger. "I had half a mind to take it straight to the sheriff."

"You don't have half a mind."

That old woman must be trying to prove I'm right, because her eyes wander off like she's going to sleep. Finally she gets up. "If you do too many filthy things, your watcher snaps you off—sssnapp! She goes away."

"Leave me alone."

She grabs the back of her rocker for balance and stands up. It gripes me, seeing her wobble. "Good-bye, Elizabeth." She drags the rocker and shakes her finger at me from the door. "You wait. I'll get twice as many channels in Chicago than you ever thought of getting here."

Her finger is crooked and red as a pokeberry root. Pokeberry root is a poison. Buddy tried making me eat some one time. Then he was scared when I swallowed a bite, and he shoved his finger way down in my throat so I puked it all up.

I sit around on the floor with my mouth to my knees and my feet in my hands, hearing Miles winding the gears down the road in their truck. After third, I can't hear anymore. That means they're out on the bypass and gone.

I turn my feet loose and reach in my blue jeans to pull out my lighter. I lay the Child's Book of Colors facedown on the floor. That means the last page is up. It is supposedly white like your soul once you're saved. I set the edges on fire and watch how the pages curl back when they burn. White and then red and then black. They burn a circle as big as my face on the floor and go out. This is my black place. This is somewhere I've been.

3

"Along about July the boys'll bust the cover off their baseball. Wrap the string up tight with black electric tape and let 'em whack it whopsided till the tape snaps loose and flaps and the ball sails loopy and goes ss-zz-ss-zz when it flies."

Jake Lampert lit a Camel and let his children, Libby and Buddy, imagine the sound of the ball: a wind through the mountains in winter.

"Now if you was to round up ever' one of those whopsided September baseballs, and drop 'em down together on the ground where they could soak up rain and sag and freeze, and if you happened to be looking down like God, then you'd see the way the mountains were that time it wouldn't snow."

That was years ago, when Jake and Ruby and Libby and Buddy still occupied the small frame house across the creek from Baughtown. Buddy was the one who begged to hear his daddy tell about the time it wouldn't snow. He'd been told it was the only winter he had been alive when Libby wasn't. He sat cross-legged on the floor by his daddy's recliner and said, "Why wouldn't it snow?"

And if Lampert wasn't on his way somewhere that night, and if he'd had a little something to drink but not too much, he would answer: "If you ask your momma, she'll say the good Lord was too worn out from making Buddy and didn't have the strength to muster a snow. It's a terrible chore to make a

Buddy. But if you're asking me, I'll say He didn't want to cloud His thoughts while He was dreaming up a Libby."

Libby balanced herself belly-down on the footrest of her daddy's recliner, kicking her feet like a swimmer. "Tell Parker's Ride," she said.

Then Lampert teased them: "Huh? Wha? Eh?"

"Parker's Ride!" they squealed together.

"Oh yeh. I remember. That was the winter Parker Wilson decided he would be the first boy ever to die of English smack-dab in the middle of math."

Libby and Buddy mimicked their father's laugh, a slow, audible pant with a jutting chin and squinted eyes.

The story of Parker's Ride, as he told it, began with the question of speed: "What's the fastest hill you ever saw, on a sled or anything else?" Libby and Buddy knew the answer. They were already feeling the wind on their faces, their skin and bones dissolving into pure acceleration.

School Hill Road was fast. It descended from the high school straight and steep for half a mile toward the lower grades. Near the junior high, five yards from a row of classroom windows, the road banked hard against a guardrail and veered off sharply right, leveling toward Main Street and the grade school's parking lot. Several nights each winter, when there was snow enough, the Rapid Falls police closed School Hill Road to cars. They cushioned the guardrail with bales of hay, set smudge pots in the intersections, and lit a bonfire in the high school's crescent drive. The road sloped north and held the snow all day while cars packed two hard sets of tracks. At night the tracks froze solid as milk glass and rippled with the hellish flickering of the smudge pots. That was where the brave ones dropped their runners, where the speed was honed and brilliant, faintly nicked by bits of gravel in the snow.

Down the softer edges came the families, careening down in stacks toward amazing spills. Buddy rode one sled alone. Jake would steer the other, with Ruby and Libby above him, whipping them side to side. He could never feel the slight relaxing of his load when Libby tumbled from the top. But

Ruby could and, as they reached the curve, would turn to see her daughter in a pink-fuzzed car coat, running down behind.

At the bottom Jake would whoop and face the slope. "That's the way to spend a hill," he said. They earned it climbing. At the top they found an orbit around the fire, a rich and glowing time between the earning and the spending. After four trips, maybe five, Ruby gathered Libby up to go. They searched the faces poised like orange moons around the fire and saw that Buddy's face was gone. "Let him ride," Jake said.

Buddy waxed his runners with a candle stub and rode the hill past bedtime, until his feet were numb inside his boots and wouldn't let him climb the hill. Each new ride would promise something faster, keener, more enduring—an indelible momentum. He was always striving for a slight refinement in his line, a tighter arc around the curve.

The high school looked north to Virginia and south to North Carolina, and in that part of the Blue Ridge children studied both states' histories and the snow came every year. Every year except the one when Buddy was alive and Libby wasn't. That December the children of Rapid Falls wore on their skins the chalky grime of regular attendance. They longed to drop their runners down for cleansing speed. In the neighborhoods on either side of School Hill Road, the lawns seemed permanently olive.

Early the first school day after Christmas, a boy from one of those neighborhoods pushed his new bicycle all the way up to the top of School Hill and climbed on. As Lampert told the story of what happened next, his children saw all that Parker saw—the blur of silver spokes, the pavement plunging downward, the nearing curve, the lighted classroom rising, desktops gleaming in a neat array like maple candy. Reflexively, Parker kicked the pedals to engage the foot brakes of his older brother's Schwinn. *"English,"* he said, as if shaken awake. His hands contracted on the grips, missing one brake. Three fingers caught the other. The bike stood on its front tire and shot him over the guardrail, across the fifteen feet of vacant alley, into a long, long dream of flight that plunged him headfirst through the splintering panes and mullions into the lighted room, where his body struck with such force that it drove one corner of a desktop through a twelve-inch crater in the classroom door. Parker died gazing into the thin, bluish face of his mathematics teacher.

"And that," Lampert said, "was how Parker Wilson got to be the first boy ever to die of English smack-dab in the middle of math."

Lampert's version of the story contradicted others, not so much in its particulars as in spirit, in its outright rebellion against the town's predominant view. Families from comfortable neighborhoods like those on School Hill had adopted Parker's Ride as a tragedy worthy of their town. It consoled them some to think that they had seen the worst, that nothing so terrible could happen again. But people in Baughtown, who never gave their children English bicycles for Christmas, did not necessarily agree. Most of them would tell the story only to instruct a child who wanted what he couldn't have.

Baughtown was not a town but the poorer side of Rapid Falls, a district of textiles and furniture-making lodged in the throat of the valley, backing a logjam of houses upstream. When Jake was a boy there, triple-A gables were already sagging in milltown; porch rails shed pickets like teeth. Children fought with sticks in the streets while their parents went inside from their yards, resenting each and every feature they had in common with their neighbors, belonging no more to the walls and space around them than to the battered aprons they pulled down from nails each day and lashed to their waists.

Each morning, while the black children collected on the dirt yard of the clapboard school, under the toneless hammering of its bell, Jake and the other white children of Baughtown had scuffed away to cross the business district and climb School Hill, where the new brick bungalows and ranchers and split-levels were going up on streets named not for Baughs or Vasses but for flora—Mulberry Road, Cedar Terrace, Dogwood Lane. They climbed side by side with children who had bicycles and dimes for ice cream and baseballs with covers year-round. In winter Jake would gaze out through a classroom window and see the coal smoke rising from his neighbors' chimneys, hanging over Baughtown in a bitter, ashen cloud, trapped by a phenomenon meteorologists call atmospheric inversion.

The Rapid Falls *Guardian* regularly reminded its readers of the Vass-Baugh Furniture Company's place as number-one employer, of its record of philanthropy. One had only to look at Vass-Baugh Park, claimed from a swatch of low land in a bend of Messer's Creek, and see the grassy ballfield and covered grandstand, "whose generous foundations enclose dressing space enough for eight-man football and nine-man baseball."

Jake Lampert was never impressed by Vass-Baugh's record of philanthropy, which he said smelled as rotten as the dressing rooms. "It got so foul in there they had to yank the toilets out and let us dress at home."

Libby didn't know so much about the town. She grew up thinking Baughtown's noxious glooms arose mysteriously from a sinister commingling of opposites—of clashing wills and incompatible natures, of wood and cloth, whittlers and knitters, whites and blacks, rich and poor. She got such notions from her father, who indulged himself in history only when it afforded a strong precedent for failure, and therefore either excused him or exalted him, or when it served to illustrate a lesson.

Until Libby was thirteen, the Lamperts lived together in a rented house across the creek from Baughtown, a house of inferior construction but, by the width of a creek, superior location. For the first eight years of that time Lampert was a mechanic at Vass-Baugh Number One. He was fired the morning after he followed a lacquer-room foreman home and beat him unconscious in the foreman's own front yard, with supper on the table. Libby's mother explained that her father was spending a month in jail for following his instincts.

After that he found another job, in the small-engines repair shop uptown. He drank some more and fought again, and Ruby, who was from a better place, asked him if that was how they carried on in Baughtown. It silenced him. He was proud of having put a creek between himself and Baughtown, an accomplishment he wanted always close at hand: "I can stand out on my steps and throw a baseball through the window of the room where I was born." When he said that, Libby wished he would.

In those days, Libby was glad to be home with her mother. Nothing they did required effort, not clipping the newspaper coupons or singing the hymns. They were the allies, the tenders of pleasure and calm in the uproar of men. Libby and Ruby would sit side by side after school on the painted wooden steps at the back of the house and drink coffee together. It was only half coffee, diluted with water, but it tasted remarkably good. They drank it from wide, shallow cups that had large, oval handles. Libby would bury one hand in the dense, burly boxwood that guarded the steps, feeling the heat amassed under its miniature leaves. The odor of boxwood was part of the flavor of coffee. So were the cool undercurrents of air drifting into the yard and the unsteady dimming of light as the sun settled into the mountains. Mother and daughter leaned back on the steps, their saucers in their laps, their knees in an unbroken line. Ruby would sip her way down to the last little syrup of undissolved sugar, and say, "I better go and start supper." And Libby would say, "I better get on my homework." But they lingered as long as they could.

The year Libby was thirteen her mother found out that Lampert was seeing another woman, and she stopped accepting the excuse of instincts. A year later they were divorced. Things were calmer but Libby was not. Her grandmother Whitley arrived to nag and persecute her. Later Miles, who painted houses for the landlord, came to paint theirs and came again to court and marry Ruby. Then two-fifths of the household was against her. And when Buddy wrecked a motorcycle he wasn't licensed to drive, began to limp and carry a knife, and was sent away to training school, it was half.

So Libby felt that her mother was always attending to the extra people, Miles and Grandma Whitley, people who didn't belong there at all. She would come home from school each day, arrive at the front door and stop, like a stranger, trying to remember whom she was there to see. Yes, there was a mother in there somewhere, but not enough of her to go around.

So she began to go to her father's garage, to watch him fix machines. She went every workday, except when it was raining or snowing, dropping her books on the hood of his Mustang, shuffling under the big double door he would roll overhead to have his air and watch her coming down from school. And that was where she liked him best—at work. She liked the way her eyes adjusted to him, in the deep, oily gloom of that place, as if he were new every time.

The garage was their place, where they became two new people, apart from the household and patterns of talking and touching they'd left in the past. It was the place where they exchanged their Christmas presents her fourteenth year. It was the place where they celebrated her fifteenth birthday. It was the place, that day in September, where she chose not to leave him at all.

For three days after she gave her father the news about Chicago, Libby hardly slept. As her mother began to pack and plan, Libby was forming a plan of her own. By the third night she knew what to do.

She had been out late that night, walking and thinking it through. When she opened the front door, she found her mother on the living room sofa. Ruby heard the door and sat up, her eyes blinking, unfocused. Libby said, "Momma, I need to tell you something. You're not going to believe this, but Miles—"

"Libby? Are you home?"

"—but Miles has been touching me places. So I had to tell you."

Ruby squinted at her, shading her eyes from the overhead light.

"It's the truth, Momma. I didn't want to tell you and get you upset but I thought I better go ahead and tell you since we were all getting ready to go off to Chicago and I didn't think I better go off that far away to Chicago with him if he's acting like that. So that's why I had to come out and just tell you."

Ruby was still blinking, still shading her eyes. She seemed

to resist coming fully awake, as though what she heard were a part of the fringe between sleeping and waking and she wanted to turn and go back from that fringe.

Libby said, "I guess it's kind of a shock but he's got this side to him that you can't see. He put his hands on me two different times and he said he would do something to me if I tried to tell."

Ruby's hand came away from her face. "I don't believe you."

"Momma, it's the truth."

"I *said*, I don't believe you."

Libby cried, hair falling into her face.

Her mother stared at her hard. Gradually, the stare came apart with the constriction of pain in her features. She was shaking her head, her hands gripping the edge of the cushion. "No. I'm not going to believe this."

Libby raged at her, leaning in from the waist, her fists balled at her sides. "You have to. It's true. Whether you want to believe it or not. And I'm going to tell Daddy. And I'm going to tell the law. And whoever else I have to tell. Until somebody makes you believe me."

She left Ruby hunched over the edge of the sofa, and went down the hall to her room.

Libby lay in her bed, motionless under the tumble and plunge of a pure, cold sensation. The sheets were frothing on her skin. The darkness and forms in the darkness were charged and electric. Her gaze darted through the room like a fish. She pictured her mother still gripping the cushion, the tension sustained in her fists.

What seemed like an hour later, she heard her mother's slippers in the hallway. She closed her eyes and pretended to be asleep. Her mother came in and sat on the edge of the bed. Libby could feel the compression and tension of springs in the mattress. There was no breath or noise. For that moment she wanted to feel her mother's cool fingers on her forehead. She wanted to wake up and have them both think it was only a dream.

The next day her mother left the house before anyone

woke. Libby never learned where she and Jake met, or the details of how their agreement was made. She gathered that Ruby had wanted to face him herself, to contain his explosion, absorb it. By the time Libby saw him again—two days later, in court—he was calm and composed. He didn't interrogate. He didn't even raise the subject. Ruby had negotiated this as well.

That was the day of the custody hearing. Her father had stood on the far side of the circular lobby, chewing the lining of his cheek as he did when he grappled with some problem of chain drives or counterrotating tines. Ruby stood alongside the opposite wall, gripping the straps of her purse as if she were heaving it out of hard ground by the roots. And Libby shuttled back and forth between her father and mother, not saying much or touching either one but maintaining an implied connection, as if she felt both the duty to sustain them equally and the hopelessness of doing so, like a mother who carries one damp cloth between the beds of two feverish children.

After a while she gave up pacing and stood apart, hidden from each of them by a four-sided column of concrete slabs faced with an aggregate of smooth, round pebbles. Over her, a skylight fixed its long, hot stare on the column's west face. Her cheek brushed the slab and lingered on the feel of sun-warmed pebbles set in concrete. She leaned there, feeling the column absorb her.

The courtroom opened, and they gathered at one side of the table, awkwardly, as if resuming a familiar pose after a long interruption. The table's sheen had been chemically dulled so that their reflections lay pitted and pricked with many shallow pores. She brushed a dab of moisture away with the heel of her hand and smeared a long, evaporating arc. When the questions came she saw her image quaver on the table, felt herself rattle like a husk upon the firm, insistent wind of whispered Yes-Your-Honors that carried her, steadily and irrevocably, from her mother to her father.

4

Rosco knows a place where we can hide his car and climb a logging road around the knob. We top the ridge about twelve-thirty, and under us the town is just a sprinkle of lights in the bottom of a deep black bowl. Sometimes if we're not in such a rush we'll stop and take a breather on a rock and watch the moon but we won't stop tonight for any moon.

Quick as we come off the ridge we're skidding down like fiends on leaves and under bushy places Rosco says are laurel hells and they deserve that name because of how they snarl you up and spook your butt and bust your chin if you forget to go bent over. Once we hit the steep we drop and go to crawling backwards on our bellies, grabbing us aholt of where a big rock split and gave those little snaky roots some running room. Maybe you would like to reach in there and feel those roots come squirming out the rock so cold and sweaty in your fingers. Maybe you would like to turn one loose and scream and have a heart attack before you ever once hit bottom.

Rosco says, "You're looking down," but I say, "No I ain't."

We keep working down the rock until we touch our feet down where the ground it piles up soft and leafy on the rock and tells us whereabouts we are. That's when we can go up straight and knock some dirt and dead leaves off ourselves and duck out through a patch of trees to where the sign rears up on five big rusted poles and blocks the sky. You can't read it from the backside. All you'll see is frame.

We come climbing through some crisscrossed X's where the sign is braced from underneath itself, and balance on the tip edge of a cliff they blasted when they built the Skyway View Motel. Skyway View's a perfect name for where we are because you get a higher view from here than any place around. In between the roof and where we're standing there's not anything but air.

Rosco says, "You're looking down," but I say, "No I ain't."

So I jump and I'm here. Then he jumps and we're both. This is our place, mine and Rosco's. You don't need to be here. You don't need to know about this wind and how this roof is slick and mossy every place and sloped to where it's hard to hold. You won't trust yourself to look and see a long ways down or up and see this sign keep heaving red a letter at a time. You'll slip off this place and die if you're not careful.

Rosco claims we've got our own tremendous sun. He likes rolling over on his back so he can spread his black self out across the roof like he could tan a face as black as his in all that red. He likes hearing juice go shooting through the letters. You don't want that racket in your ears. Every time the M comes on, a buzz goes up your backbone like a hornet up his hole. Then the O can make the roof boards go to flinching at your butt. Then the T is higher-pitched. Then the E swarms all around. Then the L goes crazy like some kids kazooing. Then the whole word burns together and it might as well be like the last big noise you hear before you die in the electric chair.

Rosco, he says people all around here sit up late at night to watch the sign spell M O T E L. He says they can't see us. He says even if they see us we're just ants.

He grabs my wrist and I flinch. He says, "You're scared." I say, "No I ain't."

I go crawling up these mossy shingles like some itsy-bitsy spider. I straddle over the peak and watch the other roofs go down like steps toward town. Rosco he can skip a rock off Building Three and if he hits it right that rock will ricochet off Two and hit way down on One. If I see him do it I start thinking I'll be bouncing down behind the rock, from roof to roof.

Rosco tightropes on the roof peak, over to the end. It starts to get on my nerves how he wants to keep taking these slow, steady steps and keep turning that color of red. I start finding lights I know in town, and that is hard to do because I have to get myself in rhythm with the letters. First I see red come around me like clouds and feel noise swarm down my neck like bees, and then I have to squint and think and get my breath because the next thing on my face will be the dark and still, and that's the time to see good.

M. Cars beside the Ford place that are mostly clean and used.

O. Street sweeper crawling along.

T. Church, where the steeple is lit.

E. Small's garage, with a dog shut up in there all night.

L. Rosco is lighting our joint. Leaving his clothes on the roof. He likes to take off his clothes at a distance.

M O T E L

Rosco hands over the joint. You can tell from the smoke this is some kind of dope. It has a shock to its taste like it's turning electric or something. He wants to know what I'm trying to do with my fingers.

Playing some pitiful game like they teach you in Bible school if you're a kid, which you are if you still have to go. Lace up your fingers and touch your palms.

O. My bracelet turns all shades of red on my wrist instead of just being its regular silver.

"Here's the church and here's the steeple, open it up and here's all the people."

Rosco's more interested in my buttons. My chest looks sunburnt on account of the L.

He says, "What a baby game," and so I grab aholt and show him what a baby game and he can almost fill the church. Almost.

Here's what I say to that witch and her Watcher. I say to go ahead, watch. Go right ahead and keep thinking I'll pay. Keep thinking I'll learn my lesson. I'm not going to learn my lesson. So if you despise a girl like me for riding places on the console of a 'sixty-nine Chevelle beside a man that makes you call him black, not colored, then you better just stay away from me from here on out. Because I'm going to do it again. Maybe you're just eat up with it. Maybe you've not ever been someplace where you could go a little wild and be more like yourself and have somebody good as Rosco love you. Once you find a place like that you keep it.

There never was any watcher. Just an old witch. If she came up on this roof and saw Rosco she'd melt in her clothes. And people like her claim that sex is no good for a person. They lie. For example, I'm a little nearsighted, not much. So when we head out on the highway late at night the tar-and-gravel's just a blurry cardboard color in the headlights. But soon as we've been on the roof I'm cured. There is something in the red. I'll be lying with the letters in my eyes, and every time another letter blazes we'll be bearing down like crazy. Then I want to close my eyes, they burn so bad. It burns like a fire around my eyeballs, burning all the crud off. And then I've got to close my eyes because the sign is blinding me and every letter's burning me and then it's me who's shining, me and Rosco.

So after that, whenever we start driving back to town, and I start looking through his windshield at the highway, every piece of gravel sticks out sharp enough to cut me. And that's what I call good for me. Rosco laughs at how I lay my chin down on his dashboard, watching gravel. I say, "Don't laugh, moron. Come tomorrow morning I'll just have my same old blurry eyes again."

I like to lie on my belly in moss and get cold. It's after two in the morning. That means the sign is turned off. I've got my best, sharpest eyes. I can see all the way down across town to the street where I lived. There's our same yellow porch light. In between the power poles. People already moved in there. It wasn't empty but less than three days. You'd think a house would need longer than that.

Rosco rolls over and feels of the moss. I like the looks of his fingers when they go to creeping out over the moss. I know those fingers will get me eventually. He rolls back over and looks at the sky and says how we sure need some dope. I say we still have to get ourselves down from up here.

Rosco says, "Maybe we'll float."

One thing I like about Rosco is, he'll let me talk once we've been on the roof. Most of the other times Rosco wants quiet. I like to wait till we've been on the roof before I ever say a whole lot.

"One thing I know about living in a trailer. It sure does have little windows. I had a time getting out."

Rosco likes breaking up pieces of moss and spreading it over his belly like fur.

"Daddy keeps saying his wife needs to stay at her mother's. I asked him when she was planning to come. He said a day or two maybe. I tried to get him to tell me if her and him had a big fight. Maybe they had a big fight about me moving in. Maybe she's chicken-shit of me."

Rosco says, "Ain't nobody chicken of you."

I throw some moss at his face but it blows.

Rosco says, "Careful."

"Daddy says we'll hit it off like we're sisters."

Rosco lays pieces of moss on his chest.

"I tell you what would be funny. What would be funny is her and me setting the table together. Then if she was to try and be nice, you know? And started to ask me these questions, like who are my friends? Then maybe I'd show her this picture of Tina. Maybe I'd show her this picture of you and me up on this roof. I wish I had me a picture like that. That would be all right."

When Rosco smiles it makes all of the strong places show in his face. He gets up and walks a good ways down the roof. He starts to pick up his clothes with his feet. He likes to hook his big toe under clothes and keep flipping them up. I like to watch how his clothes can fly up off the roof. He is the magic man catching his clothes.

5

The name of his woman was *Judith*, a sound with a long shank that curved to a barb. In the first months her father left home Libby carried the form of this name like a secret inside her. At the same time she began to dream about a dog named Jasper, a terrier mix she and Buddy had raised. Jasper was dead, killed by a car. The dream was part memory too, because Jasper had done all the things she was dreaming about him. Even his name in the dream was pronounced the same way she did as a five-year-old child: *Jap-ster*.

In the dream, Jasper was trotting to her from the bank of a river, but he didn't seem like himself. His ears were askew, his head was cocked funny, and his gait had an odd, sideways hitch. Something slender was thrashing behind him in the weeds, chasing him up from the bank.

Libby cried, "Daddy! *Jap-ster!*"

Her father knelt and pressed Jasper down on his back in the weeds. He opened his pocketknife and cut the filament line where it looped from Jasper's muzzle. He pried the jaws open and peered deep inside.

"No better sense than to swallow a hook."

Buddy didn't watch. He found a length of bamboo in the weeds and said, "Somebody left this so I can just carry it home."

Her father pinched the filament between his thumb and forefinger and drew it slowly away from the teeth of the dog. He seemed to be etching a line on the air. Libby tried forcing her breath through her own constricting throat. There was just enough room for a thread like the one he was pulling.

Out popped a small lump of bread tied to the end of the line. Her father dangled it between them. Jasper bounded up, sniffing the lump as it swung. Her father squinted at the soggy bread, and the knot it was tied in: there was no leader or hook. "Must've been kids down here making believe."

Jasper ran circles and yapped through the weeds. Libby ran chasing beside him. He nipped the legs of her jeans. Later she rode in the back of the Fairlane while Jasper curled up at her feet. Even the boat they towed home was the same in the dream as it was in her past.

But in the dream, when it came to the ride in the Fairlane, Libby felt as though she needed to spit. The feeling began as a tickle in her throat, then it touched her soft palate and curved on the blade of her tongue through her lips past her jaw. The tip of the cut end of filament line touched her collarbone. She knew she must cram this line back in her mouth and not speak. No one could pull out the line she had swallowed and not tear out her insides as well. There could be only one hookless line in the world. Jasper had found it. Then she woke from the dream.

What seemed to her to change most when her father left home was the house. People were the same but the places were not. The hallway was one moment dumbstruck, the next moment raging again with the sound of their coming apart: the concussion of skillet flung into the sink: the venomous outrage of grease: her mother insisting, "Why this *woman*— this *Judith*?" then her father's silence expanding, filling the hall like a surge of rapid water, and the sound of his saying, "I don't know."

His voice was only barely gone from Friday night when he came home on Sunday. This time he packed up his clothing and sat Libby down on the edge of her bed. "You'll be mine yet," he said.

Libby said, "What about Momma?"

"She wants a regular man, she can find her a regular man. Somebody steady as paint if she wants one. She wants some thrill off a man, she cain't hold him so strict by the book."

When he left, Libby discovered a rash of small amber stains on the ceiling and walls of their bath. Her mother tried to scrub them off. Water from the sponge traced a fine silver vein down the white underside of her forearm, branched in the creases of her elbow, and soaked through her blouse to her shoulder.

Libby said, "What *is* all that crud?"

Ruby said, "Your father liked to have a cigarette while he was shaving. That color goes up in the smoke. That nicotine color. It gets in your steam and it dries on the walls, the same way it gets on your teeth. Don't take it up." She stepped down from her stool, peeled off one blue rubber glove, and said, "Can you see them now?"

Libby squinted. "Yeh."

"We'll get it painted."

The bathroom was a place for hating in general, and for hating Judith in particular. Libby would smuggle a cigarette out of her room and sit on the toilet seat, making steam with the faucet, expelling her own little stains, imagining this woman, this Judith, what she said, what she wore. Or she would stand in the shower with hot water pelting her neck and mentally inscribe the words "I hate her" on every white or aqua tile that faced the enclosure, as though by completing this mosaic she might give her hatred form and substance, construct it around her like the walls of a small, impenetrable room.

The next year, when her father married the woman and settled for good the question of his ever coming home, the various guises of Judith, whom she'd never met, slipped away, and in their place came Ruby's. So Libby began again, with the uppermost left corner of the shower enclosure, to hate by inscription. And this hatred was more wanton and wonderful, as the hot quills of water lodged and bristled on her skin, because it plunged her deep in an electrifying jeopardy, in a solitary place where there was only danger.

Libby devoutly believed in the beauty of Judith. She imagined her mother and Judith together, their first encounter: Ruby ducking out of a cloudburst and into a florist's shop, or a jeweler's, where her father and Judith embraced. Her mother, whose hair and clothing had always seemed so simply and effortlessly tended, would by then have gone to pieces as the house had. She would tramp soggy and flat-footed in broken-down shoes and stained jeans, curlers in her hair, and—overcome by this vision, this goddess, this *Judith*— would crumple with envy and shame, would beg him to come on back home. But then it would already be, as was painfully clear to them all, far too late.

One day, as her mother stood at the sink paring apples, Libby crept up behind her, contorting her face in a lurid sneer and stooping hump-shouldered like a hag. Ruby wheeled, an apple peel coiled on her wrist. For a moment they stood sense- less, as if trying to remember who they were. Then Ruby gripped her elbow and led her briskly to the bedroom vanity bench, set her down at the mirror, and said, "Now make that face and see if that's a way you want to look." Ruby tried to play the hag herself, but her mouth failed to scowl and her eyes failed to sneer. Libby half smiled at the face alongside her. She wished they could live in the frame of that mirror, and never have to look directly at each other, or rise from that bench, or escape from the view of themselves side by side. But her mother was gone to her apples, and there was only the one empty face, a little too broad in the cheekbones, a little too thin in the nose. So Libby made the hag. It wasn't, she thought, any worse.

Every week the house went stiffer with age and distemper. Housepainters and televisions and grandmothers made it howl the wildest harmonics, as if there were no timbre left in the walls. And the voices from before, the sounds of herself, of her father and mother and brother, were all so enfeebled and wasted away that a single mote of dust, floating past a sunlit window, damped them out. She would walk down the hall, kicking at limp strips of varnish the floorboards were shedding, and echo the sound of her father.

She was a victim of hallways and bathrooms for more than a year, then she wasn't. The change began one June afternoon in the summer when she was fourteen. Libby had been sitting on her father's bench. He knelt among the rototillers, reading their bright yellow tags. Libby looked over his head through the door when a powder-blue Cutlass rolled up to the curb, some ninety feet away. She squinted to focus. The woman at the wheel of the Cutlass leaned out the near window. In the sunlight her long auburn hair seemed to burst into flame. Libby sucked hard at the Camel she'd been sharing with her father. She was certain the woman, who was peering from glare into shadow, couldn't make out the figures inside. A bracelet—a blaze of silver light—slid along her slender arm as she waved.

Lampert dismantled the tines of a tiller, his back to the door. He didn't turn or look out to the road. He didn't physically change in the least. But to Libby the wave from the woman transformed him, gathered him under its spell. This was the image she fixed in her mind: the long, tapering hand: the first finger lifted, the others curved inward, as if on a wand: the limber and musical path of her arm, a gesture like stirring the air.

The woman waved again, then hesitated, lowering her arm. The bracelet slipped down to the heel of her hand. The nails on her fingers were flickering. She drew in her arm and drove on.

Lampert stood up with the stone-blunted tines in his hands and dropped them clanging on the bench. He stood beside Libby, wiping his hands on a rag. They passed the Camel, sharing it. She kept her eyes on the place where the woman had parked. After a while she said, "Am I ever gonna come see where you live?"

He looked at her. "Last I heard, you couldn't hardly stand the idea."

"Maybe I changed."

"You can come on anytime. Talk to your momma about it."

"She'll just say no."

He shook his head. "Law says I got visitation. You just come on."

She didn't go right away, but she liked to discuss it. She liked the idea of conspiring with him against Ruby. She liked the idea of going with him to the home of this Judith, to see all her splendors, and Ruby unable to stop them. For a long time this much was enough—to come to his workbench each day and sit on its hammered-steel top, smelling the musk of cold oil and dry sod in his bay, where the bodies of mowers and tillers would squat on the oil-dappled slab like confederates around them.

After she began going to her father's garage, Libby was around her mother's house only to eat and sleep. At dinner one night, when Grandma Whitley began her usual complaint about the food, Miles stood at the head of the table and peeled off his paint-specked shirt. Grandma Whitley said the tufts of hair on his shoulders made her nauseous, so every night for a week he made her nauseous enough to leave the table and that way had quiet eating his supper. Grandma Whitley would take a tray of food into her bedroom, where she turned the volume of her black-and-white TV so high they had to scream to be heard. At the end of the week, Libby said to Ruby, "Do I have to eat around them?"

Ruby said, "Where do you think you will eat?"

"I'll get some money from Daddy."

"No you won't. You're never here as it is."

So Libby ate quickly and left. At first she went places where the young people gathered to gripe about having no places to go. When she bought a soft drink or some Winstons at the drugstore, other girls would smile and say, "How's it going?" But no one moved to give her space inside a booth, so she said, "Fine," and left. At the recreation center boys were nice to her, respectful. They knew Buddy. Some of them had hung around her father's shop, because he knew baseball and engines, and because smoking cigarettes there with him was a sober, exacting observance requiring few words and much manly style.

Soon she was walking with no destination in mind. She was just out to be out, with the vague but persistent impression that so long as she roamed through the town there was hope she could find what she sought. She didn't know what that was.

One night near the middle of July she climbed School Hill Road and then turned down a lane where the houses were large and set deep on their lots. She skirted the lawns, staying close to a fringe of white pines that ran north down the grade, and stopped a few yards from a basement where music was playing. A small part of the room was visible through a twin set of double-hung windows. There was music but nobody seemed to be moving inside. She stepped closer, venturing onto the grass, and could see almost all of the room. It was paneled, with a checkerboard pattern of tile on the floor. Dishes of food were on the tables, and glasses and cans here and there. But there were no people. The song finished playing, another began, and yet no one attended the stereo system. The house seemed to go right about the business of pleasing and comforting people even though all the people were gone.

Libby stepped back to the trees. She intended to walk in the fringe of the pines for their cover, until she could find her way to the road. She detected a movement back under the pines. What she saw first were the feet: twin pairs of running shoes steadily bunching the pine-needle blanket that covered the ground. Libby peered into the branches. The hand of the girl was in motion across the bare back of the boy. Her nails were pitch-black in that absence of light. Her bracelet rode low on her wrist.

Libby turned away and began to walk, hearing the girl whisper: "Wait. Wait, wait a second. I heard something. Was that somebody?"

Libby walked quickly the way she had come. Now that her mind was no longer on music, she heard the brief ripples of voices that seemed to be everywhere back in the woods. This was where all of the dancers had gone. The dance had gone into the woods.

She reached the pavement and crossed it and climbed a high, bushy embankment. Trembling, she sat in a cove of young hemlocks, smelling their branches' astringent perfume, feeling that she had just glimpsed a new realm in which she was an alien presence, a cipher, a dud. No wonder she didn't belong with the others. She had been walking the streets of the town and the halls of her school with the white crust of innocence on her. She was a fool to believe what her mother had taught her. There was no value in goodness. What had it gotten her mother? A housepainter and a live-in witch. Living had nothing to do with the tedious ritual surface of working and minding your elders and going to school. People led furious, passionate lives, lives she had only just glimpsed from the fringe. How could she have been such a sucker? Hadn't she seen her own father renounce both his home and his wife for the sake of his own overpowering passion—his Judith?

Now she understood why she didn't fit, why she couldn't speak in the language people her age seemed to use with such skill. The language was only a surface for deeper, unspeakable things. No wonder there was no place at the lunch tables for her. Certainly not at the tables of kids from School Hill. Certainly not at the tables of all the ferocious poor whites, who despised any sign of innocence or compliance. And certainly not at the tables where blacks seemed always to be fanning some smoldering secret to flame. She had been sitting at tables she knew were unclaimed. And that was what she was—unclaimed. Innocent, white, and unclaimed.

It rained for three nights and she didn't go out. When the rain let up on the fourth night, she left home in a hurry. She didn't go to School Hill or anyplace else she had been. She took the Messer's Creek Road where it broke from the town and descended the bluff into Baughtown.

A light rain was falling that night when she came to the bridge. She stood in the road by the creek for a moment, looking across to the dark, hooded shape of the grandstand. She carried a 7-Up with her, but she wasn't thirsty. She wanted the can in her hand, the contact with cool, polished metal. By the time she reached the near edge of the infield, the rain had picked up. She climbed the cinder-block steps of the grandstand to get out of the weather. As the rain became heavy, the lights of the town were diffused, blending and merging. Holes in the roof let the rainwater in, and the streams tossed around her like tinsel. She walked on the benches; her tennis shoes squeaked on the painted graffiti, glazed with the blowing mist. She kept her mind on the space just ahead of her toes. She was aimlessly looking for signs of a "Jake" or a "Judith," to find where they might have been carved in the wood. This was a test she had set for the world—whether it held in its lumber the deep, jagged hook of a J.

The rain did not stop right away. Libby sat down on a dry patch of bench and waited, damp from the splatter and mist. Her hair was wet down to the scalp and hung on her shoulders in ropes. She was cold. She pulled her legs up to her chest and sat with her feet in her hands.

The shriek seemed to come from a distance, a faint oscillating whine like a radio signal in static. Then it was lower and louder—a howl—and it rose in both volume and pitch. It was coming from a place in the road, where the darkness was thrusting a piece of itself into motion. Someone was howling and running, detonating puddles, then bounding straight up the block steps to the mezzanine aisle. There the runner stopped, panting, shedding rainwater over the planks, and said, "Wooo, get me outa this rain."

A woman—a very large girl—stood below Libby. She was black, with giant hands that dripped streams from their fingers, and a dense crown of glossy black hair from which water was seeping and feeding black rivers that ran on her cheeks and her brilliant white teeth. She said, "Who you?"

Libby didn't answer. She sat with her feet in her hands.

The intruder came up the six steps to Libby's level, and propped a great foot on the bench where she sat. The foot wore a mostly demolished black sneaker whose laces, though soaking and muddy, were meant to be pink. "Lemme see that drink a minute," she said.

Libby let her have the 7-Up, not so much because she was afraid—although she was afraid—as because it seemed to her that it was theirs together. She couldn't have said why that was.

There were others now, running and splashing through puddles, leaping up steps to the aisle. Three black young men. One of them, the tallest, said, "Don't hurt that little white girl, Tina."

Tina drained the 7-Up and set the empty on the bench by Libby. She said, "Look what I found. A monkey drinkin' 7-Up. See how she sits like a monkey?"

Libby let go of her feet. The others were laughing. The tall one said, "Don't let her catch aholt of you, little girl. She'll hurt you."

Tina said, "I won't hurt this monkey. I recognize this monkey. I go to school with this monkey. We never been friends in the day, though. You wanna be my night friend, monkey?"

Libby didn't look at her. "I don't reckon."

"Whooo-eeee," said one of the others. "She don't reckon."

Tina seized Libby under the arms, lifted her, heaved her back over her shoulder, descending the steps to the aisle, crooning, "Look what I got. Ain't she pretty? Look at my pet monkey!"

Libby's chin bounced against the small of Tina's back. Libby curled her upper lip and bit the flesh through soaking fabric. Tina dropped her on the planking. Libby broke her fall with one hand, rolled, and scampered backward on her knuckles, barking like a chimp. Then she stood up, a few yards down the aisle, tossed the hair out of her face, and looked at them, waiting. She had no idea what she was doing. She was not physically brave. It just seemed to her she was doing what she had been ready to do all along, that there was equipment in her she was ready to use.

None of them moved. The rain had let up to a drizzle. Tina said, "That monkey bit me."

One of the others said, "Whooo-eeee."

Tina stepped toward her, stood in her face. "How do I taste?"

Libby said, "Wet."

Tina raised her fist. Libby flinched.

Tina lowered her fist. "We goin' walkin'. You wanna come?"

"I reckon."

"You gonna bite me again, monkey?"

"No."

"Well, *good*."

Tina the Great. Tina the Ticket, who got her into everything, who admitted her where people didn't take a lot of pains being nice, where she was just another walker on the way to places secret, knowing in her blood and bones, as they did, all the gravity of secrets. Tina who, as Libby had watched her from a safe and unbreachable distance at school, stood tall as teachers and looked them in the eye and advised them what vile substance they should eat, and in what quantities, and for what duration.

Libby couldn't have said why she wanted to be with these people. They simply engaged that readiness in her. Maybe it was the danger she was ready for, the hazard of running with people whose lives and desires were as foreign to her as the lives and desires of a people from Mars. Because what could be more hazardous? She was the daughter of Jake Lampert. She was out loose every night down in Baughtown. And she was running with people whose skins were as black as a newly oiled road.

Libby and Tina walked almost every night. There were others who joined them from time to time—Chuck, the tall one, whom Tina had claimed for herself, and Leonard, Todman, Charlie, Raeford. Then, one clear night in July, about one in the morning, as five of them were passing an all-night market, a blue Chevelle pulled up alongside them, throbbing, and Todman called out to its driver, "Rosco, m'man, wha's hap'nen?"

6

Tina takes a joke too far and that's her only trouble. You would be amazed at how far Tina takes a joke. Whenever she decides to write a letter, she goes

> Dear Lib,
>   You monkey. Mr. Cunningham is fucking chickens. He's a chicken-fucking turtle-sucker and his pecker is an eel fish.
>   Love, Tina

Course, you can't get too bent out of shape about chicken-fucking when she draws those little circles for her i-dots. But Cunningham was pissed in English when he caught me cluck-ing and made me give the letter to him. That's how Tina got a blue note. She had to write a hundred times

       I must not commit obscenities to paper
       I must not commit obscenities to paper
       I must not . . .

. . . and on like that. It took her three whole sheets. The i-dot circles made three chains down every page.

She asked me, Was it deliberate? You would be amazed at all the words her daddy taught her. I said it wasn't a deliberate cluck. She looked at me funny and said, "Okay, you monkey." And if you think I'd cluck to get a colored girl in trouble, it's my business. It's my life. I'm not half as big as she is. She says, Can you fight? I say, Yes, but I'm a chicken.

When I'm bad to fight is when some girl goes behind my back and says something spiteful after she's been nice to my face. I mashed Kathy Loftwick's nose against her locker for telling P.J. Overham I was going to be just like the rest of my family. The only reason it got me in trouble was, she bleeds so easy.

Tina said I should've gave Kathy Loftwick some avulsed parts. Tina's daddy's got a lot of medical books, and Tina carried one to school about emergencies. It had color pictures showing people who were in some awful wrecks, and maybe had their bellies split so bad their bloody guts hung out, or maybe there's a fractured leg bone poking through the skin. That's what you call avulsed parts. And now when Tina asks somebody if she wants her parts avulsed, that girl knows ex-actly what she means.

And Tina knows the names of all the body organs. When-ever Old Lady Neft gets on her case she rattles off every organ in that woman's pitiful body and tells her how the cancer's gnawing and gnawing it smaller and smaller. Tina goes, "You're just lucky you're still breathing." That's how Tina got another blue note. And she never learned her lesson from the last one, either. Yesterday she wrote me four letters and never once stopped committing obscenities to paper.

Tina gets extremely excited about her daddy's medical books. People all the time are bringing her some pills to look up. If it's something good they have to give her one. So Tina's who can write your ticket. Tina the Ticket.

Let's say it's Saturday night. Her man Chuck's off waiting tables at the fish camp. Maybe Rosco's working second shift or maybe he just didn't get to call me. Because he loves me but sometimes he's busy. A lot of times he is. So then it's me and Tina. You can see her coming way off in her tight-white double-knits, and here she comes, those big teeth shining like vanilla Popsicles, and before she's close enough to touch you're smelling Tina's Prell. I guess a head like that is hard to rinse.

And when we're walking down the street the sky is black and steamy like the backseat window when you're inside loving, so close it makes you want to draw initials on it with your finger. Tina wraps me up and lugs me. She says, I just love your little bones. And then I get the wilds and frees, like Daddy says. Because there's nothing like Tina of a Saturday night.

And we ain't hurting nobody. We're just headed up Baugh Road, loving our bones. And maybe we've got stuff and maybe we don't. A Comet pulls up slow beside us and the guy goes, "Hey, hey, where's the party?" And Tina goes, "Hey, hey, what you holdin'?" And the Comet guy says, "Just my pencil." And Tina screams, "You moron!" Now there's Comet rubber scorching all the way around the corner. We head for the disco.

At the rec it's disco night for teens. Teens is what you call a crowd of seventh-graders and some eighth dancing their pitiful heads off. Tina's arms are folded. She licks frosted lipstick. She says, "Stand here by the door, and if you see a bloody scrap of junior majorette come skiddin' and floppin' this way, knock it down with your shoe." How does Tina know Belinda Tesh will be the only ninth-grade girl who goes to teen night? Dancing with the babies? All the heads are rocking

like the floor's a seesaw. All but Tina's. Tina's head is level,
floating on the seventh-graders straight across the gym. They
said Tina was too big for junior majorettes.

It's a dark gym. It makes you think you're off somewheres
late at night when there's this emergency. Maybe a drunk
plowed into a crowd of people and the ambulance is flashing
orange around and around. The disco has a flashing light that
sweeps across the teens and whips their heads around. All but
Tina's. And when the orange lights her up it's like a puff of
brown smoke on her hair. I can see her looking down at where
there's got to be Belinda. Tina waits until the record stops. It
was Michael Jackson, now it's quiet. People watch. Tina's echo
fills the gym up. "Did you call me nigger when my back was
turned?"

I can hear Belinda swearing that she didn't. She's a liar; I'm
the one who heard her. She just doesn't want her parts
avulsed. Tina raises one big fist. Belinda's hands fly up and
flap around her face like bat wings. She thinks Tina's going to
pound her. Tina doesn't. Tina laughs. What she says is way-
down deep and steady. It won't even echo: "Your name's not
Belinda. Your name's Tippy. Tippy Tesh. Come on, monkey;
let's us pop some talls."

And now Belinda's name is Tippy, because when Tina gives
a name it sticks. I don't think they'll want a majorette named
Tippy. And when she's old—just imagine. Until the day she
dies—imagine. Maybe she decides to run away and go to
Texas, where they never heard of Tippy Tesh. She grows up
and marries a man who's in the oil business, a man by the
name of Grover Pleats. Then she's Mrs. Grover Pleats. And
they have a bunch of kids that call her Momma Pleats. And
they grow up. And then one day she's living in this big house
made of pink bricks and the phone keeps ringing and it's
driving her to distraction because she's been trying to make
a Christmas Morning Coffee Cake and she's out of milk, so she
thinks she'll run down to the corner to buy a quart. And when
she pulls up she sees she forgot to change. She's got on her
broke-down, fuzzy-blue bedroom slippers that match her
ankle veins. But she says, I'll only be a minute, and she hops

out and leaves her white Eldorado running with the air conditioner dripping and a pink ribbon tied around the radio antenna showing people her first-born grandchild was a girl. And then she's inside cuddling a sweaty milk carton with the air conditioner blowing on a head full of wet curlers, and she looks down and sees her little pot trying to pooch through her brown pantsuit with orange flowers, and when she looks up there's a man in line in front of her who picks his sack of beer up off the counter and turns around and looks her up and down, and says, "My stars," all handsome in his necktie, "don't I know you? Aren't you Tippy Tesh from Rapid Falls?" Let her try and prove she ain't.

Tina's got connections at the Hop-Stop, so we get some talls and drink them down on Messer's Creek Road under a pine tree. And there's no use of me explaining how my deepest feelings feel about being under that pine tree, watching Tina chin the branches, burping little snootfuls of beer. I can really get relaxed. Tina finds a bird's nest she can touch. Arms like hers can reach up half a tree. She lays her empty in the bird's nest. "Tweet," she says. "Tweet-tweet." And maybe lots of people they will ride down there and screech about the litterbugs. But when I'm old and I come driving down that way I'm going to stop and see the tree where Tina hatched a Bud. It's not many roads that have a laugh as good as that.

Last night I made a prediction to Tina. I predicted that Judith would finally come. We were sitting in the grandstand. I said, "I bet tomorrow that woman I live with will finally come back from her mother's. Maybe I won't even recognize her. I never saw her but twice."

Tina said, "Take me home with you. I need to see."

"Shit."

Tina can grab holt of my neck in one hand so I can't hardly move. "You 'shamed of me, monkey?"

"Let go."

She did. She said, "You ever think about bringin' me home?"

"No. You?"

"My daddy don't allow me runnin' with no white."

I looked at her face and she was still grinning.

She said, "See, you and me despise each other in real life. We just like bein' the night friends and riskin' our daddies."

I looked at her. She just grinned and raised her foot in the air. "I feel somethin' in my shoe," she said.

She reached down under the arch of her foot, where she keeps all her dope in a plastic bag. She had enough for one thick joint. You can smoke dope with the Ticket and not even think about getting her germs. I don't know why that is, but it's true.

Tina said, "You miss your momma?"

I said, "She's not been gone but a week."

"That's not what I asked you. Do you miss her?"

"I reckon."

"That's what I thought. Give me that. How come you're after this dope like a fiend?"

I said it had a good taste.

She said, "Maybe your new momma'll like you too, in spite of your face."

We just had one little pinch of a joint when that deputy came. That's how I knew my prediction about Judith was right. New people happen in twos. That's been proved. It was in a magazine.

Tina said, "You better throw that away."

I didn't throw it away. I wasn't all the way stoned, but close to it. Sometimes it seems like my brain is determined to let something happen.

He came up shining his flashlight. He shined it down in the box seats. He shined it out through the chicken-wire net where the balls hit and roll till they drop out a hole. He lit a puddle beside home plate. He shined it up in the benches and right in our eyes.

Tina walked off a good ways and then stopped. He shined his flashlight against her and flipped off the switch. Then he came straight after me. I jumped the benches and climbed back as far as the wall. I set the roach on the edge of the wall and got ready to flip it way off in the weeds.

He shook his head and sat down. He didn't have on his hat, and I could see a place on the top of his head that was bald. He had a gun in his holster. I never provoked anybody with a gun before. It has a good bit of thrill to it.

Tina said, "Come on."

I said, "No."

She said, "I'm goin'."

I said, "I don't care."

She didn't go. She had to see what I'd do.

That deputy said, "Ain't you one of Jake Lampert's?"

I didn't say if I was or I wasn't.

He said, "Believe I seen you eating barbecue with him one night. At the fire station."

I thought, So? Daddy gets the sliced and I get the chopped.

That deputy said, "Went to school together with him. We used to come down here to the ballpark, back when he was on the team. You carved a bench with your name yet?"

I didn't answer. I figured it was illegal to carve.

He said, "Mine's down yonder somewhere, filled in with paint. And your daddy's too. All over the place. He didn't have to do his own carving. Mainly the girls did his carving. You know what I mean?"

I took a hit off the joint and laid it back down on the wall. Tina was standing there watching. I bet she was extremely impressed.

That deputy said, "I've just got one question. He a good daddy?"

I thought, What a stupid question.

"He was a pretty fair country catcher."

I thought, So?

He said, "I've got another question. What business you got down here around these colored people, smoking this junk?"

I said, "What colored people?"

He stared at me like I was funny-looking. I flipped the roach off as far as I could so nobody could find it.

He said, "You favor him some, you know it?"

That's all he said. He didn't even try to do anything to me. Tina got holt of my elbow and yanked it. She said, "You crazy?"

I said no.

She said they write down your name and keep track.

I said I didn't care what they wrote down.

7

The law had attached her to Baughtown, and that was a new kind of thrill. She liked the mark of that neighborhood on her. She liked the feel of it, wearing that stripe. She liked her night friends and all the risk in the night air around them, like fumes around lit cigarettes. She liked belonging. To Libby, a deputy sheriff was only the emblem of what they must all be against: unacknowledged authority. He was a stepfather nailing them in.

Libby knew where real authority lay. It was not in patrol cars or courtrooms or the well-tended streets of School Hill. It was there by the creek in Baugh's bottoms. It clung to the near side of death, drew its power from death, from the dead, from the blacks. It loosened the bonds of the people around her and set them adrift. She had learned this from her grandfather Lampert in Baughtown, one cold Sunday afternoon in November, when she was seven.

It was hot in his parlor. Libby, Buddy, Ruby, and Jake were sitting in spindle-back chairs in the front room, around the coal stove, a burnt-over stump of sheet metal that congested the air with its heat. The old man was in the kitchen. Libby dreaded seeing him come back into the parlor. She knew he was dying, and she preferred that he die out of sight, in the kitchen. She had overheard her mother saying to her father, that morning before church, "We *have* to go, he's *dying*."

Libby hadn't told her brother what she'd heard. She wanted Buddy to be the one in the dark, for a change.

The old man came in clinking four bottles of Pepsi. He used a church key to open the bottles and placed the caps color-side-up on a lamp table, so that they fit at the end of a winding, concentric mosaic of caps. The walnut veneer on the table had bubbled and cracked on the side facing the stove.

Libby was thirsty and wanted the Pepsi. At the same time, she was afraid of her grandfather, of the aspect of death about him, afraid of accepting the drink from his hands.

The old man said, "Ever' last pop-bottle cap on that table's a person what come here to visit. Not a one off a drink that I took for myself." He grinned at Libby. "There you are, honey. Have a nice, cold drink." She looked at the bottle, at him. His right eye squinted, enveloped in wrinkles; the left eye was cocked, with a noticeable wander, as though he heard whispers behind him.

"Thank you."

"You're welcome, honey."

She looked at her father and mother to see whether they would drink. They did, so she touched the bottle to her mouth. The barrel and neck of the bottle were sweating, but its lip was dry, the glass slightly grainy. The Pepsi was sweet.

The old man sat down in a chair by the stove. "Kindly dark in this house today, ain't it? Want me to switch on some light? My widder woman says, 'If you cain't keep it clean, keep it dark.' She brings me her rabbits to dress. Woman that squeamish got no use with livestock. I kid that old girl when she brings me a rabbit. I hold him by his feet and go, 'Ho there, buck, and be still. See if we can take the wiggle off your nose.' "

Libby looked around the room for any sign of rabbits, living or dead.

Her father set his bottle on the floor and wiped his mouth with the back of his hand. He half stood and shoved his chair backward on the linoleum, then settled back on the seat. Ruby, Libby, and Buddy all did the same. Their chairs had been inching downslope toward the center of the room, where the weight of the stove had deflected the joists.

The old man peeled a scab of hemp-colored cloth from the stove and dipped it into the coffee can. He draped it wet on the stove, where it hissed, exhaling a dank, woolen steam. He turned to Ruby. "I remember the first time you come here. You remember that, sweet pea?"

Ruby said, "Yes sir." Libby had never heard "sir" from her mother.

The old man turned to the stove. He stooped at the waist and inhaled steam from the rim of a two-pound coffee can. There was slack in the seat of his pants.

"Come here right after you-uns got married," he said, sitting down. "Went off and got married without telling a person. Up to that little Baptist church at Narrows. It's done been tore down to the ground."

Jake said, "She knows it."

The old man pitched forward over his knees, coughing, his body folding along an overworked crease in his gut. He recovered and said to Libby, "And you know what I ast him?"

Libby stared at him, afraid. When he coughed she thought for sure he would die. "No sir."

I said, 'What kind of good-payin' job have you got that you haul off so big and get married?' And you know what he said? Mechanic for Vass." He shook his head at the stove. "I never got that boy broke in just right. Young-un was headstrong. That's the main problem. I never did break him in."

Libby had no idea why this information was directed at her. She looked at her mother. Ruby was frowning into her lap. For a while her father's Adam's apple and her mother's fine legs were the only noticeably animated features in the room. Then Buddy began to drum his fist on his thighs.

The old man said, "Next they was settin' up house here in Baughtown with me and the niggers."

Jake said, "No. Place across the creek. You know good and well."

The old man got up and soaked the cloth in the can again.

The upholstery of his chair retained the impression of him in its folds. The fabric showed loosely stitched kinships of red: pink in the seat and the shoulders; rose at the skirts; a dark, oiled maroon where the back of his head would have lain. He draped his rag over an elbow in the flue, and sat down again, leaning into steam that unfurled near his chair.

He looked at Ruby. "I knowed your daddy. I ever tell you that, sweet pea?"

"No sir."

"He was from a better place than this. You was from a better place too. You gettin' tired of adjustin' yourself down to this knothead o' mine?"

Libby saw her mother look at Jake, but Jake had his gaze on the ripple of heat at the top of the stove.

"I never cared where a person was from," Ruby said.

"That what your daddy said about it, sweet pea?"

"He got to where he liked to go and see Jake play ball."

The old man snorted, expelling the notion of "ball" like a stray grain of pepper.

Libby finished the Pepsi and held onto the bottle. She wanted the smooth, solid feel of the glass in her hands. She felt a little queasy from the heat and the sweet Pepsi, and the effort of trying to understand what was happening to them. The old man seemed to be trying to whip them at something. Jake shoved his chair back again. Ruby, Buddy, and Libby did the same. Pushing away from the stove, they had opened the gaps among them. They could not have joined hands.

The old man spoke to Ruby. "Your daddy ever learn you the meaning of crotch mahog'ny?"

Libby looked at her father. Jake laid his hands on his knee-caps and squeezed. Buddy was far across the room, mostly obscured by the stove, its heat eroding his features.

Ruby flushed. "Is it—wood?"

"That's right. Sawed from the crotch of a tree where the grain burls up tight as the knot in that boy of mine's head." He brandished his fist toward Jake. It was large and ropy. Then he grinned at Ruby.

"Don't your momma—Miz Whitley—have a little bit of wood like that around the house? Some tables and sideboards and settees and such?"

Libby saw her mother nod.

"It's not nothing local about mahog'ny. Mahog'ny comes on a boat from Brazil. Ast you daddy how come him to buy it, with all of this local to choose from. Ast 'im was it on account of revenge."

"Revenge?"

Jake stood and dragged his chair another foot from the stove. He held the chair-back and raked a patch of linoleum with the toe of his shoe, as though he were tending the dirt at home plate.

"Me," the old man said, "I knowed better than go revengin' myself on a in-corporation. Right, boy?"

Jake said, "We need to go on in a minute."

The old man said, "What's your big hurry? You got big important things to do? Man sees the end comin' full steam ahead and he needs to explain a few things."

Jake's face was red. He looked as though he'd been spanked. Libby chilled. She felt her grandfather was trying to drag them off with him, away into death. She wanted her father or mother to grab her and run.

The old man turned to Ruby. Libby thought her mother was under attack. She was astonished that her father would stand back and just let it go on.

"Honey, you ever hear tell of the Baughs? Old man Smitty Baugh?"

"She heard," Jake said.

Ruby said, "I think he was rich."

"Rich? You reckon 'rich' is the word? I reckon 'rich' is the word. Then a-yonder comes a man named Vass. Tom Vass. You heard of him? You have? Well Tom says, 'Mister Baugh, can I please kiss your butt? And then can I please offer you some of these here hardwood shuttle blocks and bobbins?' "

Jake said, "Don't start that up."

"My house, ain't it? Bought and paid for."

Jake didn't answer. Libby had to turn in her chair to find

him. He stood in the hall door, half in the room. Libby wanted all of him back in the room.

The old man cleared his throat and, between the fits of coughing, told a story that Libby at first thought had come from the Bible. It made sense only as the Bible made sense: people long dead who, she assumed without question, would continue to doom this and every other Sunday of her life. It was the story of Tom Vass, who began his career sawing cross-ties for the railroad, married Smitty Baugh's daughter, then used her father's money to build the chair-making shop that would take over Baughtown and finally ruin the Baughs.

When the old man paused to rest, wheezing, in the midst of this story, Jake was pacing the back of the house, out of sight. Libby heard the unnatural sound of his voice in the long, hollow hall: "Those people are *dead*. All those Baughs and Vasses. They've *been* dead."

To Libby, this deadness of the Baughs and Vasses only assured them a terrible authority over the living. Here was her grandfather, not even dead but just dying, and yet so empowered by death as to cast them apart, to silence them, to strand her mother alone on her chair like a child, to dissolve her brother in the shimmering heat of the stove, to displace her father from his usual post at the center of power.

The old man sat back in his chair, wheezing.

Libby saw her mother shift forward in her chair and straighten her back, as if to stand. "Maybe you better rest. You better go and lie down. We took enough of your time up already. Jake? Don't you think?"

Libby listened for her father. He was somewhere deep in the house, out of range.

The old man waved his hand to dismiss the idea of his needing to rest. "Here comes the part that's concernin' your daddy," he said, eyeing Ruby. "You want to hear about him, don't you, sweet pea?"

"Not if you're tired."

"Your daddy." He grinned, shaking his head as though over some folly. "People all over this town knowed his story. Your daddy was what you call an accountant. I never knowed what one was till I worked half my life. Well, he set hisself down big and fine to a solid walnut desk at Baugh's."

Libby was watching her mother. Ruby's hands were loosely clasped in her lap. Every few seconds, her fingers would tighten, one hand constraining the other.

"Then your daddy goes off to war, and when he comes home, durn if the Vasses ain't done took over. Got all their own accountants, thankee just the same. So there he was, all that fine education, and nowhere to set."

Ruby stiffened in her chair. "My daddy was a fine man. He worked hard and did right by my sister and mother and me."

Libby rejoiced. *There* was her mother. Her mother, at least, could be heard.

But the old man went on as if no one had spoken. "You want to know how Harvis Whitley got revenge, sweet pea? Stuffed his house with the fanciest goods he could get. Crotch mahog'ny. Brung it in from Grand Rapids, Michigan. Near 'bout ruint hisself, makin' payments. Claimed he wouldn't have a stick of Vass for love or money. So honey, that's how you and your big sister come along, when you was girls. With Harvis Whitley's revenge and crotch mahog'ny." His laughter decayed into coughing.

Now Libby saw that her mother was angry. She saw this in the way her mother adjusted the ring on her hand. "I guess you—"

The old man stared at her. "What's that, sweet pea?"

Ruby had thought better of saying what she had begun. She glanced at her children, as if to make sure they were not in immediate peril. She looked into the hallway for Jake. Finally the stiffness went out of her posture. She said, "I guess I never thought to ask about the furniture. Why we had that particular kind."

The old man peeled the moist cloth from the stove and mopped his forehead and cheeks and the bridge of his nose. He inhaled the moisture from the cloth and lowered it into his lap, creasing its corners toward the center, tucking the folds. "Jake's momma died when he was right young."

"They know it," Jake said. Libby craned to find him. He was

near the door, hands in his pockets. It seemed that her father had appeared on command—the old man had finally spoken his name.

"Jake came along kindly late, after both of my girls was up purty good size. Jake had him three kinds of momma, there for a while. And then two. And then none. Both of my girls got some kids of their own. One bunch up at Hampton Roads and one up near to Tennessee." He squeezed the cloth in his palm, looking into the steam from the coffee can.

Jake said, "Why don't you get to the ending. Get to the ending so we can go on."

The old man's eyes didn't shift from the steam. He said, "There's a lot of people tell you Tom Vass built this town. What he did was run through a heap of good men and purty lumber. Then he brung the niggers in. Give 'em the school-house. Give 'em ever' house that come up empty. Put 'em in the rub room, rubbin' lacquer down with rottenstone and rags. They was some boys around that said weren't no harm in havin' colored in the rub room. But then you take a man like me, a white with twenty-some years on his lungs. And once he can't catch his breath, and once he can't make production—once that happens, he's gone. And in his place they stand the kind that stinks like rottenstone. And then we'll see what 'finish' means to Vasses. 'Finish' don't mean beans to Vasses." He looked at Ruby, tilting his bald head at Jake. "And now here he is a Vass mechanic."

"What I really do's play ball."

"Great day in the morning," the old man said. "You ain't outgrowed that yet?"

It took the old man three more months to die. But for Libby, her grandfather died when they closed the door behind them and fled his house that Sunday afternoon. In the myths she employed to make sense of what had happened, he died because they shut him in that house, like the witch in her oven. From time to time through the rest of her childhood, the image of the old man would rise against her, would almost overrun her with fear of his wheezing, of the heat in that room like the near edge of hell, of those "coloreds" whose smell, he had said, was like a rotten stone.

But she also remembered the thrill of escape, of leaving that house with her mother and father and brother miraculously restored to her, intact. She could feel, all the rest of her childhood, her feet sail that path from his doorstep, the cool air of November on her face like redemption.

8

Quick as I came up the hill to the trailer I saw that blue Cutlass of Judith's. It was parked right beside of his Mustang. So I knew my prediction came true. They were back in the bedroom when I came inside. They had the door shut and I could just barely hear talking. Mostly that low kind of talking, like Daddy. I sat around in the kitchen and waited. Buddy was gone or his drums would be making a racket. Buddy is always either gone or else playing his drums, one or the other.

I kept on watching the clock. Judith's got one or two things that make good decorations. For example, her clock is a banjo. It's shaped like one, anyway. It said five-thirty, or thereabouts. Nothing was cooking yet, so I figured Daddy was planning to pick up some chicken again. I was too nervous to eat right that second. I couldn't see what was taking so long.

I started thinking why Judith might hate me bad enough to stay at her mother's all week. I only met her one time, so you'd think it would take more than that to turn her against me. I figured maybe she can't take a joke. Maybe she hated my guts for that night when we went out to dinner.

It was right after my momma decided to move. Judith and Daddy and Buddy and me all went out to dinner. The first time I saw her I thought, Jesus Christ. I thought she was so gorgeous and built. Her sweater was cowl-neck and fit her exact.

I couldn't believe I was in the Red Wagon Family Restaurant with somebody gorgeous as her.

Daddy said it was high time we went out to dinner together. He called Momma from the Hitching Post Lounge at the restaurant and said it was high time. I had to make him because he didn't care to. That was while Judith was in the little girls' room. While we were waiting, Daddy leaned back on the old-timey hitching post. I said, "You better call Momma." He said, "I'm not a telephone talker." I said he had to call Momma or we couldn't eat.

He put some dimes in the phone and waited a minute and said, "I'm taking my wife and my kids out to dinner."

I bet she sounded tremendously shocked.

He said, "I've kept Libby away from her because you said we had to wait for things to get more settled. So now you're running off with her, and things won't ever settle any more than that. Will they?"

Momma couldn't say too much back about that.

"I'm taking them to dinner." He slammed the phone.

We didn't make one sound at our table till somebody came with our water and got ready to write. I wanted country-style steak just like Buddy. Judith said beef tips on rice. Daddy said he better have him some chicken livers. Then nobody talked till the salad bowls came, because of her being so gorgeous. Then we said how fresh the salad was there. Sometimes you can't find the words around somebody gorgeous as her. This lantern they put on the table was one of the old-timey kind that has a real flame, and the flame liked to flicker all over her hair which was better than auburn, and flicker all over her neck which was smooth as the side of an egg. I couldn't look at that hair and that neck without feeling amazed. I kept opening crackers and Buddy ate crackers and shredded the wrappers and we run through a whole lot of crackers right quick. I could tell how deep her and Daddy were in love by Judith's face blushing. They were so deep in love it's not funny. It was just obvious.

Judith kept acting like she wanted to talk but she couldn't find a subject. That's because I'm not much and my clothes are not much and so what can she say to a person like me? She says, "Let me see now. What grade are you in now?"

I told her ninth, and it looks like I could've at least found more of an answer than that. I sat around like a dunce and nobody said much. Buddy kept tearing those wrappers till Daddy said, "Stop." Judith was dabbing up crumbs from her melba toast and sucking them off of the ends of her fingers. When he said "Stop" she froze up with one vanilla-frost fingernail stuck to her lip. She looked at Buddy and saw him stare at his bowl with the shredded-up wrappers still stuck to his hands, and I guess she figured out "Stop" was for him. She had these long gorgeous vanilla-frost nails that can shovel up crumbs and look sexy and slick going inside her mouth.

The waitress came over with two country-style steaks and came back with the beef tips and rice and Daddy's livers. He started talking to me and I couldn't understand why he was talking to me with this fantastic woman around him. He said, "I have to order chicken livers whenever I go out to eat because Judith's momma never taught her how to fry."

"Jake!" Judith swatted at him and her body was in wonderful shape in that sweater.

Here she was, gorgeous, and Buddy can't look at her straight, but my Daddy starts grinning at me like we're on the same team against her and my brother. Which didn't make sense but that's how my fool brain wants to twist things around. He said, "What she does is fill a pan up with Crisco and dump the livers in before it ever gets lukewarm. So they sit there and go soggy waiting on heat."

"Jake!" Judith played mad but it was all a big act. Then she started talking to me like it mattered what kind of opinion I have. I didn't know how I all of a sudden turned into a person that people like her need to prove something to.

She said, "He knows perfectly well what my main problem is. My main problem is that Momma always told me not to heat the grease up high enough to where it smoked, because if grease ever once smokes it goes sour, you know it? But every time I look at a pan of oil, it looks like it might be fixing to smoke any minute."

Buddy cut all of his meat before he ever ate any. I like to cut mine a bite at a time.

Daddy was chewing chicken livers with his eyes closed, like he was in heaven. He swallowed straight at me and grinned. He said, "Here's what she does. When she sees they're about to go soggy, she cranks up the burner on high and scorches them good, so the drippings are too burnt for gravy. When she hears the smoke alarm go off she knows they're done."

Judith goes, "Lordy! One *time* that happened." She pretended to punch his arm.

Daddy kept talking to me and not Judith, which was so unbelievable I couldn't stand it. He said, "Do you think before you go off to Chicago you could teach her to regulate the heat?"

Judith goes, "Jake!" and he swallowed one whole so we all bust a gut. We got the crazies from laughing. Then Judith and Buddy started tapering off so I thought maybe I'd catch my breath and not die from a fit, but then Daddy stabbed one of his livers and stuck it up proud in the light from that lantern. So Daddy and me about croaked and the people around us were staring like they never ever had any fun in their lives.

So that's why I figured that maybe she can't take a joke. Maybe she can't stand the idea of me living around her, because of me laughing at how she cooks liver. Maybe they had a big fight about me moving in.

I sat there at the kitchen table till right after six. Then I finally heard somebody moving around in the bedroom. Judith and Daddy came out. She didn't look like herself for a minute. She looked like somebody drowned, except drier. Seemed like her face was a watery blue. Seemed like she breathed like her chest was still half full of water. She wasn't sure of herself on her feet. I wondered what I had done.

Daddy was wearing his work clothes. There was a long, oily smear on his T-shirt, in the shape of a lizard asleep on his belly. He laid his hand on the table. There was grease in the cracks in his skin and up under his fingernails. He said, "We have an announcement to make."

I looked up at his face. It was his same steady face that needs shaving. Most of the time if you see Daddy's beard after work then it means he's about to get thirsty.

He didn't smell like a drink yet. He didn't smile. He said, "Judith is pregnant."

9

"First let's get my file confirmed. Is the mother now gone?"

"The mother's now gone," Lampert said.

He and Libby were assigned to plastic chairs. He didn't use much of his. He pitched himself forward, right fist clapped to left palm, elbows on thighs, legs spread, weight on the balls of his feet, in a crouch so naturally balanced and composed that moving or replacing his chair would not have upset him. Libby, beside him, clasped the forward steel legs of her chair with her ankles and entwined its arms with her arms, so that she and the chair were entangled completely and could have been lifted as one.

"To—Illinois? Along with a grandmother and the stepfather?"

"Just outside Chicago," Lampert said.

"But not the brother?"

"Buddy stays with me."

Ramona Jetts didn't raise her eyes from the file. "Elizabeth Corey Lampert. Grade nine. C's and D's and one, two F's. Two? Fifteen unexcused absences—not a record but getting there. Fights. One fight. One fight? I have only one fight here. Known associations"—she glanced up—"we will have to touch on known associations."

Libby tightened herself on the chair.

"Custody to father. Adjudicated undisciplined minor. Are you clear on what that means?"

Libby looked at her father.

"We're clear on it," he said.

"Youth subsequently placed on juvenile probation for purposes of monitoring social behaviors and adjustment to the father's home." She laid the file open on her desk and gave them her attention. "Now let's review. When the mother requested the custody change, then the court was apprised of Elizabeth's record at school. We had a serious pattern developing there. And some reason to believe there were other activities we needed to monitor. So the judge sought our input and we recommended probation. Now then, that's the black-and-white. It's my job to see the human being begin to emerge."

"Here's my goal," Lampert said, inclining his head toward Libby. "Help this little girl be happy. That's how we get her straight and keep her straight."

Ramona smiled like a teacher interrupted by an intercom.

"Happiness is an issue we'll certainly address, while focusing on the gravity of juvenile probation. The court was reluctant to award custody to you in this case, Mister Lampert, in light of your record and that of your son, who is also of the home. And we don't seem to have a lot of knowledge about the stepmother—"

"Judith's pregnant," he said. "Libby's going to help her with the baby."

"The court prefers a more stable home environment. That is one reason juvenile probation was indicated in this particular case, and was ultimately made part of the custody agreement. The court felt that Elizabeth will need the support of our community-based resources."

Lampert sat back in the chair, tapped a pack of Camels on the heel of his hand, slipped one into his palm, and opened a folder of matches.

Ramona said, "Please wait until you leave this office."

The cigarette hung on his lips, still as the tail of a startled dog. He seemed to be waiting for some reason to humor her, aside from her figure.

Libby wanted him to light it. She had never seen him let one go unlit. She began to rub her palms on the knees of her jeans.

Ramona said, "Are there any questions up to now? What are your concerns to this point?"

Libby's habit was to wait that kind of question out by absorbing, ceiling first, the look of a room. It was a dropped ceiling, droning a cold dew of fluorescent light on their skins. Some of the acoustical panels crumbled at the edges like broken saltines. The walls of the room were of cinder block, painted a watery beige, and there was no window. The corner of a poster had sprung away from a small rectangle of foam adhesive and was curling into a powerful green sea overprinted with typography Libby knew she was expected to find inspirational. She wanted only to press the corner back or rip the whole thing down.

She wanted him to get her out of there, to settle her the way he had that morning, when she had climbed beside him on the granite steps to the lobby, the softly echoed stealth of their rubber-soled shoes padding up behind them like the sound of animals on rock. They had sat on an upholstered bench, facing four adults and a baby across the lobby. She was all nerves.

"They're staring," he said.

"Daddy, hush. They'll hear."

"They're staring because they think we're the people who deserve to be here, since somebody must deserve to be here, and Lord knows it can't be them."

"I don't care."

"I can make them stop," he said.

"No. Not here."

He slipped a folder of matches from the cellophane wrapper of his Camels, tore one match out, and showed it to her. "This is all I need."

"You're a mess."

"Do you know how a match is made? When they make a match they dip it in two vats. One vat's got combustibles and the other one's got liquid envy."

"Envy's not a chemical."

"Yeh it is. They found a way to boil it down and coat the matches with it. Did you ever know a person who could watch somebody strike a match without wishing he could strike one too?"

She laughed at him. He was comically hung over, red eyes sunk in a doughy face. He pressed the match to the back of the cover and said, "Keep one eye on the match and the other on the people."

"Okay," she said.

"Okay?"

"Okay." She pressed her lips into a firm line. He scratched the match. She heard it hiss and smelled the combustion. He inhaled the cigarette smoke and shook the match out firmly, as a nurse shakes down a thermometer.

"They're not moving," she said.

"Give the smoke a chance to float that far."

She imagined she could see the pale smoke drift across the lobby and settle on the people, animating them. A thick man whose belt was buckled with a nickel-plated marlin struggled up from a bench and hobbled into an alcove marked "Toilets." A young couple frowned as if his smell were a contamination and busied themselves with a pink-fringed wrapper until the baby wailed. A dark-faced man slumped near them in the corner grew sullen, stubbed out his half-smoked cigarette, and quickly lit another.

Libby pressed her face into her hand, her sleeve, her father's shoulder, but could hear herself anyway—a hard, hiccuping gurgle in that solemn public building. He could tickle her and that was better than Chicago.

"No questions?" Ramona said now. "Then let's get specific. Here's what I expect from you, Elizabeth: Report to me biweekly at a designated time. Curfew will be ten P.M. sharp. That means *home* at ten. There's a range of behaviors that will land you in court: fighting, truancy, running away, flagrant misconduct in school, and any violation of the law whatsoever. Clear?"

Lampert sat back in his chair and cradled the Camel in his fingers. Libby watched it, nodding.

"Good," Ramona said. "Those are the court's terms. I have three additional terms of my own. They are not in writing on the order and I would rather not be forced to go before a judge and put them there. I won't have to, will I? Number one: Do not associate with Tina Triplett. Number two concerns a blue Chevelle from Baughtown. I know whose name is on the registration. So do the police. Do you want that name appearing on a charge of contributing to the delinquency of a minor? So number one: Tina Triplett, off limits. Number two: blue Chevelle, off limits. Clear?"

"You said three," Lampert said.

"Three's a piece of cake. Libby joins our peer group for a weekly session at Mental Health. That's where we initiate her adjustment."

"How's that going to make her happy."

Ramona construed it as a question. She cocked her head and strummed the tip of her tongue on her upper front teeth, as if she'd been asked to describe her favorite flavor of ice cream.

"We create a supportive environment for self-expression. We draw emotions out where we can deal with them. We concentrate on breaking down communication barriers. This is what we mean when we say 'constructive adjustment.' "

Lampert rose and stood with his thumbs clamped hard on the plastic lip at the top of the chair back. "What I said was, I would make her happy."

"I appreciate your—"

"And all I need to know to get her straightened out is, number one, who drives this blue Chevelle, and number two, who's Tina Triplett?"

Ramona closed the file and laid it on her desk. "Elizabeth?"

Libby clenched the chair, constricted with the dread of both woman and place. The dread seemed to have been there all along, as constantly and audibly as the droning, cold-blue fluorescent fixture.

"Let's be realistic," Ramona said, raising the file in her hand. "We have at this moment, documented in this folder, patterns approaching delinquency. I expect that if we knew everything we would have to go ahead and say 'delinquent.' Wouldn't we?"

Libby didn't answer.

"If I have to put these people on your order then your father will have access to all of the pertinent information. Do you understand what I mean by 'the pertinent information'?"

Libby nodded. There was a vase of four carnations on the corner of the desk, set like a paperweight on a stack of forms. A few sheets were creased at the edges because they had ventured out beyond the rest. The sense of paper and carnations mingled so that she felt interchangeably in her damp fingers the cutlery edges of pages and the fine plush of carnation petals. She couldn't smell the petals but imagined they were scented like her mother's lingerie drawer, a small sachet tucked deep among the silky pinks and whites. She didn't want to think about that smell.

Ramona came around the desk and propped herself on the edge nearest Libby, as if to show her what it was to be Ramona: Ramona's womanly breasts; Ramona's rounded calves in fine, pale stockings; Ramona's glossy perm; Ramona's good new polished-cotton print.

Libby felt the denim slack across her own thin knees, her breasts just pooching at the T-shirt. She wiped her palms on her thighs and waited for her father to settle this, to get her out of there. He was behind her, moving near the door.

Ramona tracked him a moment with her gaze. "As for these associations, let's just call them magnetic influences that are gravitating Elizabeth into pressure-cooker situations she is not equipped to handle. Beyond that, let's just say that when you ask, 'Who are these influences?' you're raising complex emotional issues that I feel Libby should discuss with you at a future date, after we've laid some groundwork in our peer group."

She regarded Libby with a half-smile, as if they now had some pact between them, and said, in the tone of a matron who had dispatched some necessary unpleasantries and was now at liberty to help a young lady select her wardrobe, "Let's discuss your options, Elizabeth. Do you know your options?"

Libby nodded. "They're like choices."

"They're like choices. Exactly. We've discussed one choice you made without my input. I mean by that your father, instead of Chicago. Time will tell if you outsmarted yourself on that one. Won't it?"

Libby couldn't say.

"The misconception tends to be that fathers give more freedom. But the one thing I see every day, the one thing I drill into people's heads every day, is that license isn't freedom. My role is to look at this choice you've made in the context of the community, and when the community looks at this record, and this home environment—well, the community has to say, right off the bat, *high risk*."

Libby concentrated on the room, the sound of her father prowling its edges.

"Now, another option you might choose is to ignore the terms of your probation. The consequence of that choice is back to court. That restricts my options. I can extend your probation and put you into a supervised study hall. Beyond that, I can recommend placement in a therapeutic wilderness camp for six to eight months. I can arrange placement in a group home employing low-level behavior-modification techniques. I may decide the only way to go is training school. Those are *my* options."

"You sent her brother off already," Lampert said against the door.

"There's a certain amount of stigma attached to it. That's why I exhaust all of my community-based alternatives first."

Ramona slid from the desk and walked behind it to a bulletin board, where she tapped her ballpoint pen against a ruled page of handwritten verse mounted on construction paper. The page was already pen-specked.

"When this girl came to me she had training school written all over her. Then we got her into peer group. We got her out of pressure-cooker situations. We gave her creative outlets for her turbulence. We got her into tin-can art and potato art and detergent-bottle dolls, and then we turned her on to poetry. This is what we got." She tapped the pen more emphatically. "There's some raw sensitivity under the surface here. This is the real Patsy Edwards. And this is where I want to see you, Elizabeth, five or six months down the road.''

Libby stared at the page, half expecting the cow-faced gaze of Patsy Edwards to emerge. Ramona came back around the desk.

''You're more fortunate than ninety percent of the kids who come through here,'' she said. ''You have a pretty face that just needs some relaxing. Your verbal and quantitative batteries—those tests you took in school—have all been within parameters. We've got every reason to expect a productive life. I'm not here to be your opposition. I'm on your side. Keep me on your side, and I'll be happy. Okay?''

''Okay.'' Libby nodded into her folded hands.

''I'll be ecstatic.''

''Okay.'' She was an undisciplined minor with a pretty face, and her batteries were within. She was going to do what she knew how to do, get them out of there. ''I believe I'm ready to try hard and do better.''

Ramona said, ''That's as good a place to start as any. Now, I won't keep your father any longer from his cigarette.''

He left the office, moving fast, and Libby chased him at a trot down the hall and up the stairs toward the lobby, as he glanced into alcoves and offices, without pausing, apparently watching for some place to settle. Having been excused to smoke, he elected not to smoke, and flipped the Camel at a butt tray.

''Wait up,'' she said.

He strode through the lobby, past clerks, and down a hallway to the doors into the glare of an open courtyard where currents of cool air were insinuating themselves into the warm body of the autumn afternoon, and said, without turning around, ''In the car.''

He unlocked her side of the Mustang first, and she dropped into the bucket seat, watching him round the car.

The deputy passed on the sidewalk in his brown-and-tan twills, saw Lampert, and said, ''What're you doing up here today, Jake, marrying or divorcing?''

The deputy caught a glimpse of Libby through the windshield, and looked at his shoes, as if he might have stepped in something.

Lampert said, "Came over here two weeks ago to get custody of my little girl. Tangled us up with that woman downstairs."

"Jetts," the deputy said, grinning again, and then, in a voice that seemed to mimic someone old and daft: "Keep upwind o' hit."

Lampert wet a finger and held it in the air. The deputy's gesture was half wave, half salute as he left.

Lampert rocked the car getting in. He wrapped his hands high on the wheel, squeezing. Libby waited.

"You got something to say to me?"

She began to wring the tail of her T-shirt.

"She's just after me, that's all, just because of nothing. If people are going to make such a federal case out of me living here I should've gone to Chicago with Momma and them. And how come she can order us around like that?"

His upper lip tensed. She shut up.

He said, "You know what that place is? That's the law, in there. Once they get you in there, and get that writing on you, they can put you way off someplace I can't even touch you. I don't give a"—the heel of his hand hit the dash with a sound like the word he didn't speak—"about that woman. But you one time let me hear about you—"

"I should've gone. At least I wouldn't be on *probation*."

She let the word accuse him. He took several shallow breaths, each sounding as though it wanted to begin a sentence. Then he took a deeper one.

"All I care about is from now on. You be happy, and act right, that's all. What you did before was up to them, your momma and them, because you were under their roof. And I'm allowing for the way things were, with us split up. Just forget all that, and start off fresh with me and Buddy and Judith. A girl of mine knows how to act."

She spread the hem of her T-shirt across her lap. It was stretched and damp. "Her. What am I supposed to call her, anyway?"

"Her name."

"It's gross."

He shook his head, deadpan as a pitcher shaking off a sign, but she saw his lips test the syllables.

"What does Buddy?"

"I'm trying to remember. Nothing I can remember."

"I know the reason she went to her mother's. You had a fight about me moving in."

His gaze hardened. "She's got a bad case of nerves about being a mother. Acts like the world needs to stop so she can make a kid."

Libby cried a little, letting her hair fall over her face to hide it. He let go of the wheel and lit a Camel, smoked it solo awhile, and gave it to her half gone. She finished it and stopped crying, waiting for him to start the car.

He said, "You know what the best part's going to be? All those days like Christmas and Thanksgiving. Maybe you're supposed to go to your momma's for one of those, I don't know. I'll look it up. But birthdays I know for sure. Having my kids around me on my birthday. You know it?"

She nodded. He was fixed on something he saw through the windshield, something he seemed to watch for its motion alone. There were large, rounded bones in his face, and delicate creasings of skin in the hollows, tracings so splendid, like wandering paths to his mouth and his eyes, that she was imagining a pencil, gliding astray on his face, when he snapped to, and started his car.

Libby didn't go to her father's garage after the week she was placed on probation. She had been there only twice in the three weeks since her mother left town. She couldn't have described the difference, which was not so much in him as it was in the place, but going there now made her edgy. The machines that crouched around them no longer seemed like a band of confederates. The flavors of risk and gasoline no longer mingled on the lip of her 7-Up bottle. Her mother was gone, the occasion for confederacy was over, and she was anxious, because she didn't know what would take its place, or whether he would like her as well, now that she lived in his home.

Probation seemed first like entombment, then like a sentence of death. Later, during the second week, it was something that imbued her with romance and intrigue, like a curse or a bounty on her head. At school she told Tina that spies of the law were around her all day and all night. She intended to tell Rosco, when he next called—it had been more than a week since he'd called—that she would never be free, that he must try to forget her.

Each day, those first few weeks, she walked directly home from school, lugging more books than she would open, to the trailer Judith had hired someone to haul from Sinksboro to the crest of a clay hill across the creek from Baughtown. Buddy, who worked half-days repairing motorcycles, was often at the trailer before her, in his bedroom. She would cross the delta of gravel at the foot of the hill and climb the gullied drive to the yard, hearing the trailer boom, her brother inside, churning his sticks on the Slingerlands, a drummer within a drum. From the steps she would look back in the yard and see Judith slouched with a tabloid in the wheelless, engineless Fairlane her father kept in the yard, mashing an inky thumbprint to her cheek.

Libby liked the drumming. Inside, she sank to the floor and lay with her books on the bristling carpet, feeling things thumping around her, in the room where furniture and partitions could cease being themselves and become instead the manifestations of percussion. When it stopped she went to Buddy's door and saw on his face the coppery shimmer from his cymbals. He sat with the sticks crossed in his lap, staring without expression into the wall, as if the music had gone along without him and he could rest and listen to it progress far beyond his ability to propel it, hearing it steadily beating a path in the void.

When the wall was wall again, and Buddy himself, he dropped his sticks to the floor, slipped from the throne, and brushed past her as if she weren't even there. On his way to the kitchen, he dipped his finger into whatever Judith had been simmering when he drove her out with his drumming, smacking his lips on it, then hurtled away on his Harley, headed, as Judith said, "to God knows where, for God knows what, till God knows when."

It seemed to Libby her father had become awfully particular about the housekeeping. He insisted that things in the trailer be *right*. He wanted things "right for my kids." Trying to please him, Judith was constantly adjusting the furniture, experimenting with new recipes and table-setting arrangements, gauging his reaction, groping for the equation that would at last refine that elusive quality of family from the people and goods of their household. One morning she overturned a jelly jar full of coins on the kitchen countertop and, lunging for it, spilled a box of Froot Loops too, and didn't wait until everything had stopped rolling and scattering but chicken-chased the coins across the kitchen floor, cracking Froot Loops under her feet. Lampert laughed first, then Libby, then Buddy. Buddy's was the voice that stopped her, and she swung around, stunning them all with the swirl of auburn hair, her most beautiful feature, and outrage, her most riveting attitude.

Later that same day, Judith began a brief campaign to be pals with Libby. After dinner, she spread catalogues and magazines and books of baby names across the kitchen table.

Lampert said, "What's all this?"

Judith said, "Now you just go on where you're goin'. Me and Libby's got girl stuff to do." She beamed at Libby and said, in a singsong, as she counted on her fingers: "We've got names to go over. We've got baby things to go over. We need to pick out a cradle and find us a place to put it—we've got girl stuff to do. So just you go on."

Lampert went out and sat in his Mustang, listening to the radio. Libby wanted to go and sit with him. She lingered near the door, hoping to find a way out.

But Judith poured them both a glass of fruit punch and set the glasses on the table. She said, "Come sit here and let's think about names. I've got a feeling that we better start with a girl. What about 'Abigail'?"

"I reckon. Yeh, that one sounds good."

"Hmmm. What about 'Annabelle'?"

Libby said, "Are we gonna go through all of those letters tonight?"

Judith said, "Not if we find the perfect one. The one that's just perfect. What about 'Audrey'?"

A pickup pulled into the yard. When Libby looked out the window, there were two men with her father around the pickup, propped on the rim of its bed, passing a bottle. She could hear Jake's voice, and one of the other men laughing.

Judith worked her way down to the G's without finding the perfect name. Twice she took her fruit punch back to the bedroom. "I just need to find me a pencil," she said. The next time it was, "Wait, while I go to the potty." But Libby smelled the whiskey on her.

The third time Judith went back to the bedroom, Libby got up and went out. She sat in the Mustang with the window rolled down, listening to the men. She could not see their faces, but their voices were clear and resonant: a young man, an older man, and her father. They were debating the merits of some construction project. The older man was arguing for trusses—there was too much clear span to use rafters, he said. Lampert said trusses would block up the attic. He was in favor of rafters and two-by-eight joists. Lampert said, "Set you a beam and a flitch plate across 'er, right here." From where Libby sat, he seemed to be drawing the plan with his finger, perhaps in sawdust or dirt in the bed of the truck.

She didn't know why it pleased her to sit at that distance and listen to these men. She had no interest in construction. But there was a firm, easy rhythm in the ebb and assertion of their voices, a reassuring sense that the structure of things was intact, that her father was back at the center.

Later she heard one of them, the older, ask her father, "How you'n' that wife gettin' on?"

Libby saw her father shake his head. The other two laughed.

The older man said, "Them redheads—whooo-eee. You about got her broke in?"

The younger man snickered and kicked at the soil. The older said to him, "What's the matter with you, boy? That the kind of breakin' you'd like to be doin'? You think you're ready for that? Whooo-eee."

When the men were gone, her father looked into the car and said, "You and Judith get done with your girl stuff?"

Libby said, "Yes."

They went into the trailer together. Judith sat in the La-Z-Boy, watching television.

Lampert looked down at her, but she didn't meet his gaze. He said, "I don't want you drunk around my kids."

She stood up and staggered, furious. "What about our kid, Jake? *Ours?*"

He turned to Libby and said, "Get on to bed."

Soon after that, Libby and Judith stopped pretending to talk, stopped excusing themselves when they shouldered past one another at the bathroom door. Judith, Libby gathered, must be tolerated. She provided their place, the trailer. Judith: a form upon which odd pieces of clothing were assembled and haphazardly displayed, without effect, around the trailer. A stranger. A defective and almost powerless opponent, the source of her father's complaints. Judith stopped arranging furniture and refolding table napkins. She stopped prattling about "the little one." And so Libby believed that, despite the fact Judith was still sick many mornings and therefore presumably pregnant, the question of a baby had been argued and settled. Judith had lost.

10

You won't go to Mental Health unless somebody drags you. I had to wait where all the crazy people wait, and touch what all the crazy people touch, and look at magazines all ripped to shreds from crazy people's nervous habits. Plus that receptionist was shut behind her window like she didn't want my germs, and I had to spell my full name to her through a hole. There was only one good thing about it: Tina came.

But that's not what I said to my momma, because I couldn't start in to griping when it's long-distance, on account of how the person's far away and it costs money. So I told Momma I tried hard in Mental Health. (Because it's not like I didn't try. I tried right up to where Tina came in there.) And then I told Momma I thought Mental Health would help me be a lot better person inside. And Momma said, "Just do the best you can and stay out of trouble. Okay?"

It was Momma's first Sunday to call. She's been trying to get me for over a month, but she can't ever catch up to me on the phone. So we had to set us a regular time and be home.

Anyway, Judith about ruptured herself getting us ready. Judith claims she would never ever dream of coming in between a girl and her natural momma. She yanked the calendar off the wall and marked in every Sunday for the rest of the year, "Two p.m. Long Distance from Chicago," and circled it in red so nobody forgets and ties up the phone. Now we don't have any clean Sundays left in our calendar. We ate Sunday dinner early when we weren't even hungry so I could have my food digested and she could have the dishes done and wouldn't be banging them around in the sink when I was trying to talk to Momma. And Judith asked Daddy didn't we need to tell Buddy please not to be beating his drums during that time period, but Daddy didn't answer her. He was studying on something.

I don't see why I needed to go to Mental Health in the first place. One time Buddy he was delinquent, and he never had to go. You won't catch him someplace where they play a lot of violin music, like the dentist's office plays when they're about to drill your teeth. He would just say screw it, if there couldn't be some decent drums. He would rather get sent off. They put him in a place with a couple hundred colored people but he came out so you couldn't tell the difference. Except he was bigger and nobody better mess with him after he's been in there with those colored people. And keeping to himself. But that's how everybody's brother acts.

Another thing about a brother is, he won't ever in a million years admit when you were right. One time I told Momma that Buddy had my protractor in his room but he said, "You're a liar," real hateful. He swore he didn't have it, and Momma believed him, but I knew it was in his room. Everything is always in his room, but he keeps his door locked. He can't stand me going in his room. If I pop the lock open with a bobby pin and run away it drives him nuts. One time he wasn't home and I went in there and touched his stuff. I was amazed at all the stuff. Like this bird skull I thought was a spit wad until I got up close, and something's disgusting tooth, and dirty clothes, and dust from him sanding his drumsticks, and a bottle of clear fingernail polish he paints on the tips of his drumsticks, and pennies glued flat to his mirror, and hair on his comb, and all these crumbs from rotten food, et cetera.

It was one of those plastic kind of protractors that are hard to see once you ever lay one down. But I knew how to feel around and find it if Momma would just make him let me in his room. But she wouldn't make him, so I was going to fail my homework, and Buddy acted like so what. That was back when I still kept up with my homework. And what did he need with my protractor, anyway? Nothing, that's what.

After that he went to live with Daddy and then it was my job to go under the house for potatoes. And it was dark under there. And it smelled like a hole in the dirt. And I felt around in the dark for potatoes and at the bottom of the potato box were these soft ones leaking putrid juice and the other ones sprouting wormy feelers up my arm, and guess where my protractor was. Stuck to the box with potato juice. And I knew good and well what it was doing in the box, because it used to be Buddy's job to go under there after potatoes, and he would rather crawl all the way under a house than admit to my protractor. Which is how a brother always acts.

At least Buddy never had to go to Mental Health. You get sent to Mental Health and they've got ways to make you talk.

And once they start you talking they can tell right off if you deserve to be delinquent, and then the next step up from there is jail. Buddy went ahead and turned delinquent. At least he's got a license and a good-paying job. Which is more than me.

I had a long time to think of things to say to my momma because of Judith getting us ready ahead of time. It got to be one-thirty and we were all just sitting around in the living room, waiting for the phone to ring. Buddy was drumming his legs and making Judith jumpy. Daddy looked at Buddy's hands to make them stop. He said, "You going to talk to her too?"

Buddy said, "I don't know."

"You don't know?"

"I reckon."

Then I started thinking how irritating it would be to have three people hanging all over me when Momma called. I said did everybody have to be there. So Judith said she could go back in the bathroom and shut the door, and Daddy said he could go out in the yard. But I said why couldn't I one time have some of my own personal privacy. I tried to see how far the cord would stretch. It wouldn't stretch but just a little ways across the living room. So Daddy said he knew where he could find a longer cord.

Judith went, "Jake? On a Sunday?" She tried to make him stay home, but he ran off with Buddy in the car.

Judith watched the clock and said over and over how they wouldn't ever make it back on time. It was worse than sitting in the waiting room at Mental Health.

I had to sit beside Patsy Edwards, that cow. And I had to watch her punch buttons on that digital watch Milo Vickers gave her, and her going, "Group should be any minute now," like we couldn't wait.

But that was before I ever knew Tina was coming. It was just Patsy, Screech Nuchols, Amanda Whitt, and me in the peer group. Then Ramona showed up and started ordering people around in the waiting room. Screech was pissed. He said, "Why did we have to come here?"

So Ramona goes, "Why'd you decide to violate probation, Mister Nuchols?" She tried to make Screech look bad, talking sarcastic to his feet. She took up our cigarettes and said we couldn't have them back till after group was over.

So Screech goes, "I don't need no group. I just need a cigarette."

Ramona came over to me, after that. She likes to stand over people. I didn't look up. She said, "Elizabeth Lampert," knowing I hate my real name. She said, "You thinking good thoughts?"

I didn't say if I was or I wasn't. People were staring. I started hating that woman more and more.

She stood back in the middle of the room and pointed at all the people in the peer group. She said, "I don't want to hear word one from the receptionist about behaviors." Then she went off down the hall.

Amanda twisted her silver neck chain in a knot and tried to blink her eyes out from under eight tons of mascara. I don't like how makeup wants to look in Mental Health. Especially on some girl that needed two abortions up to now. It makes me want to wash her face.

Patsy had a lap full of poetry, and we were going to have to listen to it. It was Ramona's fault. Patsy was showing those poems off and bragging how Ramona told her that if you have a full figure then you needed to write some poems so people will respect you for your mind. And Patsy said Ramona told her to pretend she was different things lying around the house. So Patsy sits there and shows me her poems. "I Am a Pencil." "I Am a Piece of Paper." "I Am an Eraser." "I Am an Ink Pen." I asked her if she about had the hang of being office supplies, but Patsy just grinned. Next she'll write "I Am an Ignorant Dumbass."

I would like to see Tina write poems. Tina, she would tell Ramona where to stick her poetry. She would go, "Miz Jetts, do like it say on suppositories. Insert and permit to remain."

The thing I despise most about Mental Health is, you can't

tell who might turn crazy any second. I tried to buy a drink from the drink machine, and this old lady near about ran me over. She was creeping up on the receptionist in some of those shoes like the Pilgrims wore. And this old lady wanted to tell the doctor she was there on time, but the receptionist told her to sit down, so she sat in a chair and never even unrolled her newspaper. She just watched it like somebody was liable to smack her with it.

So we all sat around there and waited.

Then all of a sudden the Ticket walked in. She started hollering soon as she walked in the door. She said, "This here the peer group?"

She didn't act like she knew me or any of the rest of the peer group, which is typical. Half the time at school she pretends I'm not even there. Then about fourth period she'll say, "Hey, that you, monkey? I didn't reckonize your face in the day."

Anyway, Tina walked up to that window and smacked it real good so the woman shot up in her chair, and the glass went to shaking, and Tina screamed like it was a solid wall between her and that receptionist. She said, *"Hello?"*

And the receptionist said, "Yes?" real irritated.

And Tina said, "I've got a paper here says three o'clock!" And she crammed her paper through the hole, and that receptionist made out like Tina's hand was rancid and held the paper by one corner like a used-up snot rag, and said for her to spell her full name. And Tina goes, *"Trip*le-it! Trip-a-*lit*! It's on the damn paper. Says three o'clock."

The receptionist said for her to please have a seat in the waiting room, but Tina never did. She kept on walking around and around in that skirt that was some kind of print like the flags of all nations, and a turtleneck sweater with shoulder pads, making her look like she was all hot to tackle somebody, and I wondered where in the world she found all of those clothes.

So the receptionist kept telling her over and over to go take a seat. But Tina she grabs a good holt of the Pepsi machine, like she's getting ready to carry it off. Except she never had the money for a Pepsi, I could tell. So she peeked at the peer group to see if we had any quarters, but nobody was ready to turn loose of a quarter, so Tina slapped her hands flat on the glass and hollered, "What's the goddamn time?" and that receptionist knocked a stack of papers off her desk. And Tina was going, "Three goddamn o'clock. It's on the paper." And that receptionist was having a cow, and jumping up, and prissing off down the hall with Tina on her tail. And Tina was yelling, "His Honor sentenced me to this place. Three o'clock. Ain't *my* decision."

I thought that receptionist was running to hide, but she came back right quick and said someone would be with Tina as soon as feasible. So Tina goes, "I heard that before. Read that paper. Does it talk about three o'clock?"

The receptionist said for her to please take a seat. But Tina walks over to Patsy and me and props her big foot on my chair so her toes were stuck out the end of her sandal. Patsy is so scared of Tina. She didn't know it was all a big act. She thought the Ticket was going berserk. She about croaked when she looked at those toes.

I said, "How come you're wearing a skirt?"

Tina acts stunned and amazed. "What, this? This here's my Mental Health outfit. Makin' me look more mature. You think it does?"

I said, "No."

"How 'bout this toenail polish. I told Momma, Let me see your toenail polish. I'll put some age on these toes." She looked at Patsy and Patsy was so scared her chest had the quakes. Tina said, "You got a watch?"

Patsy that fork brain raised her hand and looked at this empty circle on her watch. That fork brain forgot to press the button. Tina goes, "Where's that thing's face?" She whispered it, like it might be a secret. Patsy that fork brain finally punched a button and lit some numbers up and they said three-oh-five. So Tina grinned and started charging the receptionist like a bull after red, and the receptionist, she won't dare look up, and she's cramming papers in a file as fast as she can, and Tina screams, "Time's up!" and runs straight out the door.

People just sat there. Then that old woman grabbed her newspaper and slipped her purse straps over her shoulder and stood right up and let her paper fall and smack the floor, like maybe the receptionist would like to make something of it. Then she was gone, and Screech said, "I'm gettin' outa here," and stomped out in his bare feet. Then Amanda turned loose of her neck chain. And Patsy stopped operating her watch and said she had a headache and better go lie down. And I wasn't going to be the only one in peer group, so I left too. And the receptionist just threw up her hands.

But I was there at three o'clock, and I've got witnesses.

Judith said for me to excuse her a minute. When she came back her hair was combed and I smelled mouthwash. She kept shaking her head at her watch and saying, "They won't make it back." Judith thinks she needs to be in charge of the time.

I thought Judith would pee on herself when it got to be quarter of. Then it got to be ten of. She said, "I told him not to try to make it there and back in thirty minutes."

When it got to be five of, Judith said, "Well, that's it. Buddy will just have to miss her." She was so disgusted. She said, "And next he'll try to carry us off to that horse show tonight, just like nothing ever happened." Then we heard the car skid up and they came running in and Daddy had wire around his arm. Buddy brought some tools. Judith said, "What are you doing? It's three minutes of!"

Buddy gave Daddy the cutters and Daddy went to cut the cord, but Judith said, "Jake! Don't you dare cut that cord! It's two minutes of!"

But he did. He cut it. Judith marched back to her bedroom and slammed the door. Daddy spliced in the new one, and wrapped it with tape, and said, "Come on." So I followed him down the hall, and the cord reached all the way back, and I sat on my bed with the phone in my lap, and he closed the door behind him, and it rang.

I said, "Hello."

She said, "Libby, it's me."

I said, "Hey."

She said how was I, and I said fine, and she said they had been missing me, and I said unh-hunh. And she told me Miles liked his job selling paint, and she was going to work part-time because of how expensive it was there, and Grandma Whitley joined a club for senior citizens, which she'd been looking forward to all week, and what was I doing. So I said we were having a ball. I said it looked like Judith was going to be my best friend, and her and Daddy were sweet to me, and took us out to eat a lot, and I was extremely excited about helping with the baby, and when I got my license I was going to get a car, and if she wanted to know something I really needed for Christmas—not this Christmas, but maybe the next Christmas—it was a calfskin cover for my steering wheel, because they feel so good on your hands.

She was fairly quiet after that. She said it was nice about Judith and Daddy, and how about Buddy, how was he doing? So I asked her did she want to talk to him. She said, "When we're finished."

Then we talked about probation and all, and I said Ramona was this woman with a lot of gorgeous clothes, and I wished I could be that gorgeous, and she was so disciplined you couldn't even believe it, and she really liked me, and she was going to help me express my feelings better. And Momma said that was nice. So then I tried to tell her about going to Mental Health with some crazy people, but she didn't really believe it, so I got a little ill about it, and said, "You don't know. You never had to be on probation around a bunch of crazy people."

After a minute she said, "Then tell me."

So I started trying to tell her about spelling my name through that hole, and that old woman and her Pilgrim shoes, but it wasn't realistic on the phone, which got me irritated.

Another thing that got me irritated was Daddy and Judith in the living room. They were whispering at each other. They were mad so the whispers were loud like a hiss. It's like that sound when you put a needle on the edge of a record, where there's not any song yet, but somebody left the volume knob all the way up, and the needle goes to hissing and popping, and here comes the song any minute, so you jump and jerk the needle up before it gets into the song and busts your eardrums all to pieces.

They ran Buddy off, as usual. I heard his motorcycle.

Momma said, "Libby, are you getting along okay? You don't sound like yourself."

That's when I said peer group would probably start making me happy inside. And it was a lie, but it sounded like something a person might say to her mother long-distance. So then I told her Buddy couldn't talk because he had to go someplace and he was sorry. She worried over me and Buddy some and said how she was missing us and loving us and all. And I said okay, and we hung up. And I sat there awhile on the bed until Daddy was gone, wishing I could call somebody. But you can't one minute hang up the phone from talking to your momma, and the next minute go to calling colored people. Not on the exact same phone.

Judith had a bottle of George Dickel whiskey out when I went in there, and she didn't say word one to me. She just poured some in a glass, like what was I going to make of it. So I got out of there, because Judith has a bad side. A lot of people have their bad side. They just keep it hid. And I don't have to hang around that place with her if Buddy doesn't.

I get the sweats whenever I first fold the phone-booth door shut. I guess that means I'm in love. Like if the pay phone has a hard time swallowing my dimes. And when I cram my dimes in the slot my tongue dries up and all I can taste is dime. And the phone is already warm like it just came off another person's ear. Then I hear both those dimes in the phone and it feels like they caught in my throat. I hear the phone ring. Five times.

"Hello."

"It's me."

He doesn't say much. He's usually up by now, because he wants to have a little bit of daytime before he goes on second shift.

I say, "Are you busy?"

"Gettin' ready to go."

"I've been needing to call you since way back last month. I thought I better let you know I can't be seeing you anymore."

He doesn't answer me. That's one bad thing about him. Sometimes he doesn't answer me.

"The law got after me on account of me not going off with Momma. They put me on probation. They said I can't see you. Tina either."

"Why?"

"Just because I decided to live with Daddy and be near you."

"Who said that?"

"That woman at the courthouse. Jetts. She's going to violate me."

"She got any proof of me and you?"

"Blue Chevelle, was all she said."

"She can't do nothin'."

"Well, I just thought I'd better call you up and tell you why I can't see you anymore. In case you might be interested."

He doesn't answer. I've wound my neck up good and tight in the cord, and the metal bands are pinching. "You don't care I didn't go."

"Go where?"

"Chicago, with Momma and them. Maybe I should if you don't care and everybody's got to make a federal case out of it."

He cusses something awful on the phone. He says, "Cain't nobody make you stop seeing me, unless you get ready."

I can't think what to say.

He goes, "What are you doin'? You bawlin'?" He says it like I better not be.

"No."

"Say tomorrow night, same as always. You're my sweet thing. You my sweet thing?"

"Yeh."

"Miss me?"

"Yeh."

"Take your hand and feel of somethin' and let me hear about it."

"Rosco, hush. Not over the phone."

He's laughing. He says, "You think I'm concern about the phone? Who you think is list'nin'?"

I use my other dimes calling Tina. She says, "How was that Jetts and that shrink and those peers?"

"I didn't stay. I walked out too."

"Watch out. You getting brave?"

"They gonna do something to us?"

"What they gonna do? We was there on time. Listen here, I want to know one thing. You brave enough for adventures? Under the cover of night?"

"What time?"

"Midnight or after."

"What about now?"

But she can't come out. Colored people they get grounded too.

PART TWO

MARTIANS

J

I asked Tina did she ever dream some crazy stuff at night because I didn't know if colored people dreamed like us, and she said whenever Martians come to Earth your brain waves go berserk like television when the mixer's whipping a banana pudding. And I said that's the truth, because I had this dream with Judith in it, and it's not like my brain to let her in when I'm asleep.

In this dream about Judith, Tina was waiting for me but I couldn't sneak out until Judith went to bed and Judith wouldn't go to bed. She was standing in the kitchen chewing cupcake off a yellow paper cup, and she was ready and waiting for somebody's funeral. She was wearing her short black dress that hits her where it did in high school, except it rides high in the front on account of her showing a pot. So you can see her swole-up knees. She was pissed at my daddy like always and feeding her face on account of him not coming home when he needed to take her to church or a funeral. So she kept chewing cupcake crumbs with teeth like a horse and mashing cupcake cup against her nose until it changed itself into a yellow flower, and the more she chewed on that flower the bigger she got. And her belly kept swelling and Judith kept chewing and licking the petals and I thought she was going to break water and have a little green kid right there in the middle of the kitchen floor and keep me there waiting all night.

The reason I dreamed about Martians was Tina. Tina said we were the Martians. Then it came true.

She didn't make it all up. This woman predicted in the paper how Martians were coming to Earth. And the paper said this woman sees ahead of time when movie stars are going to die. And one time she saw a vision of a man without a face and it wasn't long before this famous person burned his face clean off with acid. Except they didn't show a picture of it in the paper.

Anyway, this woman she predicted that the first Saturday night in November there was going to be an invasion from outer space. It would be at midnight. She said how these space invaders would be after teenage girls, and the girls would all have to be virgins, and the space men could tell whichever bedroom had a virgin in it by shining brain waves through the windows, and if they found a virgin they would beam her out the window. Then on Christmas Eve the girls would all come back to Earth like their regular selves and ask their mommas for some eggnog, even if they hated eggnog up till then. And every one of those girls would have a little baby with her. And the baby would be kind of green. But the babies would cry like regular babies, and eat like regular babies, so nobody would feel like killing them off around Christmas. And pretty soon the green would fade so people didn't notice. So all these babies they would grow to be adults and show all the rest of the regular people how to fly around in outer space and not be starting wars up all the time.

All the normal people just said, Sure. They said, Right. But there's this eighth-grader named Theresa Hedgecock and she's a moron. She is a pitiful excuse for a virgin. And she had a hissy when she read in that magazine about green babies. She started bawling in school for no reason. People said she set a bunch of muskrat traps around her house in the bushes, and got her daddy's shotgun out, and found a pair of hand-cuffs she could use to lock her skinny ankle to the bed when-ever brain waves started shining through her window. And she starts getting people shook up all about these Martians. So guys start coming up to girls and saying they could Martian-proof you free of charge. And some of these girls who are such big Christians and think they're so perfect started seeing who could act like the biggest virgin, and have the biggest nervous breakdown, and Friday some of them were in the bathroom throwing up. Plus my teachers thought they had to bring the Martians up in class and make a lesson out of how it wasn't realistic.

Tina said, "Amazing." She was ecstatic and thrilled half to death. She starts talking Martian talk and telling Martian jokes. She can start a Traveling Martian joke and have it go all over school in just one day. She goes:

"There were these two virgins, and they lived up so far in the sticks they took their baths together outdoors in a washtub. So here they both set in the washtub, buck nekkid, when this Traveling Martian comes around there sellin' Martian cam'ras. Them virgins say they never seen a Martian cam'ra before. So he gets one out and aims it at 'em, and the first one asks him, 'Whatcha doin'?' So the Martian says, 'I've got to focus.' So then the second girl, she says, 'What's he say?' and the first one stands up, dripping soapy water off her boobs, and hollers back, 'He says he's gonna focus.' So the other one, she thinks on that awhile and then she claps the suds and scatters up a mess of bubbles in the air and she says, 'Bofus? Ahh-*maaay*-zin'.' "

Tina stayed all fired up about the Martians. Like on Friday we were in Eberhardt's social studies class and he was blaming Martians on the news media. He kept pacing up and down between the desks and preaching yellow journalism. He cut that story out of the paper, and stuck it on some yellow paper by the door. And the yellow paper stood for yellow journalism, according to him. And the headline of this story said

VIRGINS AWAIT SPACE INVADERS

Finally I guess Tina got fed up from seeing him pace so she stuck out her elbow. And Tina can block a whole aisle with her elbow. So Eberhardt turned around and squeaked his stupid loafer on the floor and started up the other aisle but Tina stuck her other elbow out and Eberhardt just stopped and thought about that arm because he doesn't like to mess with Tina. On account of if Tina got irked she might take all his chalk and then not give it back. She might start up with some Traveling Martian jokes in the middle of social studies. You can't predict what she'll do.

Finally he pushed on her arm with his hand, and people laughed.

Tina goes, " 'Scuse me, Mister Eb," and lets him go through.

It was time for the bell, but Eberhardt he went right on and wrote our homework on the board like he had all the time in the world. We had to *Define Yellow Journalism in One Page*. Then he asked us who wanted to try for extra credit. Tina raised her hand. Which is just like Tina. She hasn't done her homework once this year.

Eberhardt tried to act like Tina didn't raise her hand. He said if we took some initiative over the weekend we could write an extra page on how come Martian babies were "implausible." That's the way a lot of teachers think they have to talk.

Tina asked him what was "implausible," and he acted smart like always. He said, "I'll tell you what's implausible. Advanced intelligence squandering itself on teenaged girls. *That's* implausible."

Tina said, "If they can find a virgin anywhere around this place then they deserve her."

Which made him plenty mad because the boys went to snorting. Eberhardt said, "Can you afford another blue note, Tina?"

Tina dropped her arms like she was shocked about it. "Wha'd I do?"

He was looking at his watch.

Tina said, "I can't help it, Mister Eb. It's because of all them butter rolls." Tina blames a lot of different things on food.

He knew better than to ask her, but he did. "Butter rolls?"

"They're giving me brain damage, Mister Eb. I can't stand to smell 'em. Every day at lunch the same old greasy rolls. You can smell 'em cooking downstairs every morning. Smell! Do you smell it?" She stamped the floor and it shook. "Right down there! The smell comes through the wood. It's rotten. That's why all the walls smell greasy. It's the butter rolls. They're steamin' up the place. I swear, don't you white people ever eat something else besides butter rolls?"

Eberhardt said white or black didn't have anything to do with it, but people didn't listen. They went to sniffing their books and their desks and their sleeves, and Tina goes, "Make it stop! I mean it! If I smell one more stinkin' butter roll I'm goin' nuts. I used to make the honor roll, you know it? Then the butter rolls start eating up my brain and I start—"

"That's enough—"

"The rooms stink, the walls stink, the teachers stink. I bet when you go home at night your wife says, 'Oh God, here comes Mister Butter Rolls.' "

The bell rang then, and everybody ran outside, saying, "Mister Butter Rolls! Mister Butter Rolls!" and from now on that will be his name.

Tina took her time and ripped the Martian story off the wall like it was a wanted poster and she was off to hunt some bounty. And she looked at Mister Butter Rolls like maybe he would like to make something of it. So I got out of there. And halfway down the hall I heard the Ticket holler, "Lampert! You monkey!"

So I looked back up the hall and she was waving that paper like a hankie over everybody's head. I said, "What?"

And she said, "You and me. The virgins are awaiting."

And I said, "Bofus?"

And everybody in the halls—I mean seventh-graders same as eighth and ninth—was slamming lockers up and down and screaming loud enough to where old Mister Butter Rolls and Cunningham and all those other teachers had a heart attack and died: "Ahh-*maaay*-zin'."

Tina said meet her outside of her spaceship at midnight. That meant to go around back of the fish camp and find that potato-chips truck her and Chuck keep on trying to fix. That thing is halfway as big as a house. Most of the paint is skint off. It looks like somebody took and rolled it off a mountain. Chuck said his boss at the fish camp was cool and would put up with having that truck on his place until Chuck got it fixed up to run. Tina won't care if that truck ever runs. All she cares about is spreading a piece of shag carpet in back, and ripping out shelves, and spray-painting obscenities to metal. Tina named it Chuck and Tina's Charles Chips House of Love.

Tina the Martian was waiting for me at her spaceship. She

spit tobacco juice at me and missed. She stuck a pouch of Red Man under my nose. I asked her what in the world. She said, "This here is Martian food, monkey. What you and me like to eat on the spaceship."

I took a chaw and tried not to drool it.

Tina slipped around behind my back and wrapped me in a choker hold. I said, "Turn loose of me, so I can spit."

She tightened down on my neck, and then turned me loose. I tried to spit and got some on me.

I said, "Where's Chuck?"

She said, "In the cargo bay, asleep. Landing wore him out. You should've watched us in space. All of a sudden I see the firmament dividin' from the waters, and I say, 'Hey, big Chuck, that's *Earth*. Man, check it out.' "

She climbed inside of the truck. My cheek was all swole up with Red Man. I tried to spit far enough so the juice wouldn't land on my shoe. Tina sat sideways and leaned on the wheel. She said, "How come you keep hangin' around me?" Tina is all the time looking me over, whenever we first get together, like I'm a different color every night and she needs to get used to me all over again. She said, "You look peculiar. How come I let you keep hangin' around me?"

"You just like beating me up." Tina likes to start me off rough and then gentle me down. She keeps a tight hold on a person. Which I like.

"I never hurt you, monkey. Hey, that paper said virgins await us. You about ready to roll?"

Sometimes it seems like I landed on some other planet with Tina and we have to stay there for good. Like I went up in space with this Martian and she got her brain waves inside me. I can't decide if she'll kill me or keep me alive.

Tina said School Hill was where the virgins were awaiting, so here we're running down like fiends through yards and sticking close to places that were dark and keeping on our tiptoes so the cold dew wouldn't soak our shoes. Mostly we could tell which bedrooms to invade, by checking out the curtains in the windows. They were always something you could match with pink. Tina squatted down and I would climb up on her shoulders. When I tapped, a head popped up and I could see whatever girl it was go to flopping around in her covers like a fish in some weeds. I kicked Tina and she let me down and lights would flash on, but we would already be running and hearing the screams of the virgins.

We invaded Martha Tims, Holly Beachum, Penney Moore, Sebrina Holderfield, and some girl I can't remember. Then Tina let me have another chaw of Red Man and we went to Sharon Poole's. It was colder then. Tina heaved me up and I tapped, but Sharon was a sound sleeper. So I kept on pounding till my knuckles hurt. Then I blinked and saw the lights come blazing on and Sharon's mother she was standing looking at me. I don't know if she could see me, though. It was bright in there and dark outside. I kicked Tina but that maniac she wouldn't move. Sharon's mother hiked her nightgown up and sat on the bed and tucked that virgin Sharon in and touched her hair. Sharon's mother's legs had freckles.

I said, "Let's go." Because I didn't want to sit there watching Sharon and her freckle-legged momma all night.

We ran up Valderee Drive to the corner and took off up Valdera Lane just as fast as we could. We heard car and saw lights and shot clean off the road and dodged back through some yards, and then Tina tried jumping a hedge and tripped, but she kept going. Lights came up fast on our heels and we're seeing some shadows of legs running crazy ahead on the road and they're ours, so we jump us another big ditch to a bank and half fell down the bank and then made for a gully and Tina said, "Dive!" so I hit the dirt rolling and swallowed my Red Man complete.

I sat in the weeds feeling poisoned and then here comes Tina waddling down the bank just grinning at me. She chased me up the gully in some woods and we circled the football field to the gate and scaled the fence and ran two steps at a time through all the empty seats. We could stand on the sill of the concession-stand window and reach the ladder screwed to the press-box wall. We made it all the way up to that little roost they use for making movies of the games. You can see a long ways down from there.

The wind blew a good bit. We were high up in the air. I said I was cold, so Tina set me on her lap and wrapped me up in her goose-bumpy arms and squeezed. Through the railing we could see the lit-up windows down where all the virgins they were crying to their mommas. A cop car was cruising and shining his spotlight all over School Hill.

Tina said, "Don't he know Martians are implausible?"

I said I sure wished that we had us some stuff to go with the rest of this excitement.

"I'll get you some tomorrow."

"Promise?"

Tina squeezed me. I was warmer. We were up high in the air, and that's not a very realistic way to look at a high school. Because the roof was flat with pipes and hoods and chimneys poking through it like avulsed parts. And all around the building there was half a million flakes of ratty notebook paper plastered everywhere like dandruff. So it was hard getting up some school spirit. But Tina said we better try, since next year wasn't all that long.

The cop was working School Hill better than he ought to. It got on my nerves. He would turn and roll real slow a ways and disappear behind the trees. Soon as I could settle down, his lights would kind of spill across another street and here he comes so slow inside his car that's black with gold shields on the doors. It made my stomach knot the way he stopped dead still and washed the road good with his lights and sprayed his little spotlight on the yards and bushes like he was hosing them down. He was bad as Judith for keeping your guts in suspense.

It got worse and worse. The cop was creeping up and down, appearing and disappearing. And I kept thinking of Judith chewing that cupcake I dreamed. It made me sick. My tongue was half drowning in spit. Then Tina opened the Red Man and stuck the bag under my nose and said, "Want some?" and I dived for the railing and held with both hands and heaved my guts enough to fill the grandstand. It was running down the press-box windows. Tina prized my fingers off the railing and sat cross-legged and stretched me out on my back with my head in her lap. She combed my hair back with her fingers. They were big pillow fingers and warm. "Poor monkey," she said. "Swallowed some."

I could see the stars around her hair. Then it seemed like Tina's kinky hair was soaking up the stars. The stars didn't twinkle. They just kind of floated and danced on Tina's hair. Every now and then they stopped dancing and stood real still, then all of them moved the same way at the same time, down, and up. They curtsied. That's how bad I had the quakes. I really thought I saw them curtsy to me. After a while I got a little bit more steady. Tina felt like talking.

"People are es-scared of me," she said.

"I'm not."

"You better be, you monkey."

"Chuck's not."

"Chuckie baby. I rock Chuckie and he go sleepy-bye honey-tight." She pulled some hair around my ears and smoothed it down. "Daddy is and Momma."

"No they're not."

"They are. They're expecting me to do like Darrell did."

"Who's Darrell?"

"My brother."

"Oh yeh. What did he do?"

"Missing in action."

"Oh."

"He was a corporal or a sergeant, one of those."

"You can't be a soldier."

"If I want to"—Tina the Terrible—"but I don't."

"I'm sorry about your brother."

"Okay. I was too." She might've meant "two." I looked up at her neck and it bulged out and made a pillow for her chin. She looked down at me and pulled a hair out of my eye. It was very gusty there. She looked up again. "One day I came home after school and Momma had Daddy draped over her shoulder like a rag. His head flopped and his arms were limp. I thought they finally knew Darrell was dead, but they didn't. They were missing him, was all."

"What did you do?"

"It was my fault for letting things get too quiet. Whenever it gets quiet Daddy lets hisself be mournful. I can't stand it quiet, when I'm home. Whenever there's a quiet minute it reminds you how there used to be a brother. I make Daddy sit and read to me, or talk about the world. He can read a whole book every week."

"That's perverted."

"His heart's not really in it, though."

"Oh."

She shakes her head. "He's always fooling around with his words. That's where I get it from. Like when I was little he didn't beat me or nothing whenever I would act up. He wrote prescriptions for words. And I'd have to go look 'em up. Like 'ingratitude.' I remember that word something awful."

"He's not a real doctor."

"He can tell as much for fifty bucks as any doctor can for a hundred. You don't have to go to some medical school to learn how a heart's s'posed to sound."

"Real doctors live in nice brick homes."

"He gives people their physical when they need to buy insurance."

"Oh."

"He's a insurance doctor."

"I never heard of that before."

"He don't like you, monkey."

"Why not? What did I do?"

"He says I've got plenty of trouble already, without running all over the place with a white."

That got me mad.

Tina said, "I tried to tell him you weren't that kind of white."

"What kind of white did you tell him I was?"

"Monkey white."

I can't ever stay mad at the Ticket. I said, "You ever lived in the same house with a pregnant woman?"

Tina said, "No."

"Daddy can't handle her, now that she's starting to show. He thinks we're all s'posed to act like a family. He claims I'm never at home. She's the main reason. People like her shouldn't ever have babies."

"You be its momma. Be its little monkey momma, like ol' Tarzan the Ape Man had."

I started laughing but then I felt sick and it seemed like my head tried to fill up with air. I could feel my head float up and bump real soft on Tina's fingers. I said, "Now you're quiet."

"I am? Sometime I would like to go someplace where nobody's missing and it's okay to just be still."

"Where's that?"

"Sometimes in the truck, when Chuck's asleep."

"Where else?"

"Like this. How come that is? How come I start feeling quiet with this little white monkey around me?"

"I don't know."

"Maybe it's 'cause you're not in no rush. You got no good place to go your own self."

I thought it over and that was the truth. "Where else are you quiet?"

"No place."

So I told her, "Not me. I like action. I like Rosco."

She walked her fingers on my ribs and made me squirm. "Rosco doesn't love you, monkey."

"Yes he does."

"He's got another item."

"I know it."

"She's a sister."

"I know."

"I saw her one time. We're talkin' clothes, we're talkin' chest. You ain't got neither one."

"I know it."

"How long's he gonna keep you hangin' this time?"

"He calls me all the time at night. I keep the phone in my bed. I've got this really long cord."

"When you gonna learn, girl? He's just bein' big bad Rosco."

"You don't know."

She held my face between her hands and stared me down. "Are you a liar, Libby?"

"Sometimes."

"When?"

"When people keep on pushing."

"Like now?"

"No."

"You like to lie?"

"Maybe. Sometimes."

"When?"

"When it has a better sound to it. When it sounds more realistic."

"It's a filthy habit. Makes you squint."

"Sometime I would like to go someplace where you can tell the truth and not have people go all to pieces."

"Where's that?"

"I don't know."

"Where do you think? Hollywood? New York? Africa? Heaven?"

"Probably hell."

"Here on Mars?"

"Maybe."

"Here on Mars."

2

Lampert drove up on the mountain one night to a porch where the price of a hound could seek its natural level, with the necessary breadth of space and altitude around, and dickered his way through a pint of Tennessee whiskey and most of three hours, until the figure was fifty, which still didn't feel like a buy until the seller, a man named Bledsoe, sweetened the deal to his liking. The sweet was a story. Bledsoe withheld it past midnight, until he saw that they were closing on a figure, because, having years ago pitched to his catching, he knew Lampert well enough not to squander such things on preliminaries.

The hound was called Rooster, a redbone. Bledsoe let him go cheap because the dog had alligator in him. Rooster's right eye looked at the world through a notch in his eyelid. He was young but so bunged-up and welty he carried himself like a cat with a hide full of wire. He would turn mean on a trail and attack any hound that ran with him. Bledsoe acknowledged as much, as they settled a price, but held that fifty dollars was the least a man could pay for anything with teeth. He handed Lampert the last of the whiskey and said, "Polish the bottom."

Lampert turned up the bottle and swallowed. He returned the empty to Bledsoe and said, "I reckon for a man that never runs but one a fifty-dollar hound is plenty."

On the following Saturday afternoon, when Bledsoe arrived with the dog in a plywood box that bounced in the bed of his pickup, Lampert made him come inside and hear the whole thing told again, as if the story-telling rights attached to ownership and were best affirmed and exercised at the moment when money and redbone changed hands.

As Lampert told the story, Judith made iced tea and glanced out the window at the dog, which was temporarily lodged in the Fairlane, asleep on the very seat where Judith liked to sit the afternoons when Buddy played his drums. "I would like to know who you think is going to feed him," she said, pouring the tea.

But Lampert kept telling the story to Libby and Buddy.

"Bledsoe here came home from church one Sunday and let the dog in the yard to play with his kids. Came time to set dinner on the table and he hears this beautiful bawling windup, so he looks out his kitchen window and Rooster's lunging at the cherry tree like coon is strutting every branch. Trouble is, the coon is Bledsoe's little boy, who's scared so bad the pee runs down his leg. Now whether Bledsoe ever got that young-un down from there, I just don't know. He's not said, that I've heard."

Bledsoe said, "Todd was up that tree before the dog barked. Eating cherries. I'd done told him twice to get on down before he spoilt his lunch. Durn dog just took a notion to howl."

"Spoilt his lunch," Lampert said, grinning.

"Spoilt his lunch," Buddy said, nodding and drumming his thighs.

"Boy'll learn, I reckon," Bledsoe said, getting up to go. "Got my doubts about the dog."

When he was gone, Judith said, "I would like to know if you think I am going to have a dog like that around my baby once it's born."

Lampert trained the dog to voice commands by teaching him that words had impact. He brandished the heavy ash bat—the one he called his niggerstick. "See this?" And Rooster kept a nervous eye on the bat, though Lampert never hit him with it. Lampert did, however, conceal a short length of chain, a choker collar, in his right fist, and when the dog ventured off beyond reach of the bat, Lampert called out his command and threw the chain. He was very accurate at a range of fifteen or twenty feet, and the chain didn't injure the dog, he said. It taught him to listen. The dog learned that words were steel knuckles that rapped on the back of his head.

Buddy and the dog took up. Many afternoons, when Libby came home, she would find Buddy sitting in the Fairlane with the dog. Judith was constantly trying to make Buddy understand that Rooster was a hunting dog, that hunting dogs should not be overpetted. So Buddy had better just keep that in mind, whether he liked it or not, she said. "Don't you know why your daddy wanted that dog? Don't you? He wasn't giving you a pet. He thinks if he turns you into a hunter, you'll be closer to his kind of man."

Buddy shook the chain at her and snarled, knowing she hated the sound of the chain on the head of the dog.

The evening after she had been raiding the virgins, Libby was out in the yard with her father. They were training the dog to her voice. She commanded, he threw the chain. There was no grass to cover the ground, and the weather had tooled the red clay into long, fanning ribs. The dog trotted hip-sprung and yawed like a skiff over swells. Libby and her father walked over the slope to the spot where the collar lay curled on the ground like a bass clef. The night was cold, and the swerves of red clay were bristling with pink feathered crystals of ice.

She watched him squat to pick up the collar, bracing himself on the bat. She turned away and looked down where the cold had been brazing the lights on the bottoms. Nothing twinkled, not the vapor lights around the mills, or the headlights of cars, or the incandescent yellow of shade after shade across Baughtown. They were all fixed and waiting. And the question she asked him surprised her as well as her father, because it didn't seem native to her mind. It was one of that assembly of misfit impressions that had gathered all week toward this dusk: Buddy's naked toenails as he pestered a pile of stiff, laundered clothes for his socks; a monogrammed spoon by a gouge in the table; her hands on the rim of an iced-over dog pan as she came to the kitchen where Judith was bathing her wrists under cool running water; and now this suspension of time and surroundings and her tongue on the flavor and substance of tin, as if the night had seized up, frozen and waiting, while the ground slipped and buckled beneath her.

She did not think the question through before she asked it. The cold in the air seemed to bleat it, just as her father was rising. She thought the sound was demented, like the rest of what tracked through her mind.

"Who was better-looking when you first saw her, Momma or Judith?"

He straightened, and looked at her over one shoulder to see if she wanted the truth. "Judith."

"Who looks better pregnant, Momma or Judith?"

He thought about it, shaking the chain like a rattle in his loosely cupped right hand. "Your momma."

"Who do you think's going to have a better baby and be a better mother, Momma or Judith?"

"Go on in the house, if you're cold."

"I don't want to go in there. I can't stand her around me."

He put the chain in his pocket and called the dog. "Whooo, hound," he said.

"That's the reason I'm not ever home. You're always saying how I'm not ever home. Well, I just thought you might like to know the reason."

His stomach rumbled and they glanced at each other. His digestion proceeded while around him the world froze and waited for something to budge.

"I must be hungry."

She kicked at pink crystals with the toe of her shoe. "You're always hungry."

"Trying to keep up with this fast metabolism. My metabolism never slowed down once I was grown."

They stood around. He lit a cigarette and let her have the first tug. Judith's silhouette appeared at the window. He said, "Let's go find us a pizza, at least, and get out of this cold."

The place where they ate was familiar and warm. They sat facing each other in a booth, and curled back their lips when they bit the hot pizza, stretching the cheese to great lengths from their teeth. It tasted so good to them both that they knew what had passed was excused. They could simply go on as they were.

Rooster's training progressed, and later that month they made him a bed of feed sacks stuffed with cedar shavings and spread it under the trailer, where, surrounded by sheet-metal foundation skirts, he shivered and squirmed to the thud of their walking, the vibrating hum of their voices. He would poke his nose out through his hole in the skirts and whine when he heard them come home. He didn't answer to "Rooster" anymore. They called him Daddy's Hound.

3

I started thinking way back to when Buddy and me were just little. It was Red Man that did it. I kept that pizza down all the way home, but as quick as we got to the trailer it came right on up. Anyway, when I've been sick to my stomach and weak I want Momma and miss her a lot. Sometimes it feels like I'm stranded and Momma is wondering where in the world I could be. She tries to find me but I am long gone. She has to give up her search. She has to go back to being herself in real life, never to even imagine her daughter ate Red Man and made herself sick.

One time when Daddy was a baseball player, Momma she took us to one of his games. I was just a little girl and Buddy was a little boy, but he was more than a whole year older. Momma climbed up in the grandstand. Buddy wanted money for a drink. She gave him some and said he had to share. We ran down through all the people who were stamping for a homer and bought a drink. Buddy wouldn't share it. We stood over by the fence where we could see in the dugout. Daddy and the men were in the dugout spitting. Daddy was the one with shin guards. I ran up the steps through all the people who were yelling. I asked Momma could we go down there and spit with Daddy. She said not. Daddy's team was losing. I told on Buddy and she said for me to get him. I ran down through all the people who were quiet.

Buddy had to pee first. He went around behind the grandstand in the buttercups. Then a foul tip hit the grandstand roof and landed in the buttercups and shocked him and he wet his leg. I ran and got the ball. It was heavy and it had a real good leather smell and all the little pores were white. There was just a little smooch mark from the roof. My finger went around and around the stitches. The stitches were red. I looked up and thought the grandstand wall was leaning over top of him and me. Way, way up the people's teeny heads stuck out in blue sky screaming at me, Give it back!

I said, No! I ran in a back door in the grandstand wall. It was dark as night in there. Buddy ran up to the door and stopped. Buddy had a wet place sticking to his leg. Behind him were the buttercups and sun. I ran farther under. It was sticky dark and wet in there. It was like the biggest place that I was ever under. It was like a night in there.

Come back! Buddy screamed. Come back!

No! I ran a little ways until I couldn't see him. There was some of Daddy in the smell. My hand was sweaty on the baseball. I was scared I'd drop it in the dark and have to stay until I found it. I was going to have to run through there and give the ball to Daddy in the dugout so that they could play the game. I didn't know they had some more baseballs. Daddy! I said. Daddy! I ducked a beam and looked up and the sky was black and tilted. It thundered off and on. It was full of teeny cracks and holes like stars. I would run a little more and see a piece of crescent moon and in the beam of it was something floating down like snow. I caught some in my hand and it was peanut skins. Daddy's smell was stronger. I was scared. I thought it was a night in there.

Buddy called me. *Liz*-beth! *Liz*-beth!

The gravel under there was gooey black. I walked on the edges of my feet. Up above my head it thundered. I ran down a hall that had a ceiling and a cement floor. All the walls were cement. I spun around and skinned my elbow and ran down the long wet hall and skidded on some puddles. I remember I could see a little bit, so there had to be some light, but I don't know how it got in there. My fingers felt across the wall until there was a door and I went through it to a cement room. The floor was sloped. There were bent pipes poking out of the walls and broken metal on the floor, and I kicked a stob of pipe and stubbed my toe bad and hollered, Daddy!

—addy, addy, it echoed. I was lost. Another room was full of benches. I fell over one and dropped the ball.

No! I said.

Oh! Oh! it echoed. I stood up and listened for rolling. It was still. I climbed the benches by the way they felt. They were clammy. I saw a pond of scummy ink and it was all around my baseball. I was on my belly on the bench. I reached in the water and it shocked me. I cried. I had to get the baseball. I reached in the scummy shocker water quick and got the ball and dried it on my shorts. It was smooth and stitched up good and tight.

I had the quakes. I climbed over the benches and found another door and saw a little patch of daylight far away. That's where I headed. There were pieces of fence under there. I had to zigzag around in the dark. I squeezed myself past a post and some fence and there he was, between me and the light. Daddy!

But it wasn't. Daddy's hat was blue and backward. This man was a red-hat. He was peeing on the gravel, and his head was swinging back and forth so slow like he was tired of saying no. When his face went one way he spit out a stream and I could see it splatter on the ground. When it went the other way he said, Gawdamighty, little girl. Then he spit again and said, This ain't no place for you. He stopped peeing and shook it in his hand and squatted a little and tucked it back and stuck his tongue out and a wet round ball fell off the end of it and splattered on the gravel. I could barely see it.

The red-hat kicked his spikes and walked into the light and I was looking at the wad and there were more wads down there—more!—and I stood up on my tiptoes, shaking with the quakes. Everywhere I saw the wads. I was prancing on my tiptoes all around the wads and Down! Down! Down! it thundered on me. Something grabbed my elbow. I screamed, No!

It was Buddy. He said, Stupid! He dragged me by the elbow past the posts and fences through the dark and out the door into the buttercups, where I was blind and squint-eyed. When I got my eyesight five big boys ran up and one of them pushed Buddy down. Another one grabbed me and took my baseball. I said, No! and pulled it hard but he wrenched my wrist and yanked the baseball loose.

It's mine, he said, and they ran off.

Buddy got up from the buttercups and didn't cry. See what happens? he said. See?

I'm the one who cried.

4

"This ain't right," Lampert said in the middle of dinner on his birthday.

Buddy stopped eating. He laid his wrists on the table edge.

"What ain't right?" Judith asked. Libby knew what; Judith didn't yet. "Here's your family at the table. It's your birthday. This is your spaghetti dinner. Later we've got pie."

"The one dish I want special. Give you three years now to get it right. This here tastes like soap. Did you put soap in here?"

"No." Judith mashed her napkin into her sauce. Buddy shoved back from the table and left the trailer. They heard him kick-start his motorcycle. "You know he's got a nervous stomach," Judith said. "Why'd you start this up at mealtime?"

Lampert balanced his plate on his palm. He flipped it over Judith's head against the wall. The plate bounced on the floor. Spaghetti hung on Judith's shoulder. Some of it was on the wall behind her, where the plate had hit, the sauce sticking, red as Judith's face.

Judith said, "You damn bastard. Clean that up."

"It's your mess, not mine."

When Buddy came home, he wiped up what he could of the spaghetti. Judith made him leave the oval on the wall. Bits of meat were in it.

Libby went out late that night to meet Rosco at the car wash, but Rosco didn't show. This was the first freezing night of November, and one of the wash bays was icy, its wand dribbling water. She believed Rosco had been there and left for some gas or a coat and would circle back for her as soon as he could. She tried to skate where the concrete sloped down to a drain, but the nubs of her running shoes snatched at the ice.

When headlights spilled into the car wash she thought it was Rosco's Chevelle, but as she stepped to the apron she saw that the car had a shield on its door. She turned and half skated the bay to the opposite side, ran out of the lot, leaped a ditch, and ran deep in a field full of tall, browning fescue. Crouched in a cold nest of stems, she hoped the cop would not leave his patrol car to chase her.

She watched the car turn and pass the near side of the car wash, the spotlight playing over the field. After a moment the car crept away to the bypass and traveled southwest into town. Libby stood up and was wading the fescue toward home when the cruiser came back up the road. She dropped belly-down in the grass.

The cruiser kept tending that half-mile of bypass for most of an hour. The passes were irregular but frequent enough that she didn't dare try dashing across to the long, steep embankment she needed to climb. Except for that small swatch of field there was open terrain on all sides. She had to stay in the fescue for cover. She drew her jacket around her, but she was wearing the one she looked best in, and it was not very warm. She became numb from the cold. The tall brittle stems of the grass flailed and rattled whenever she made the least movement. She could not think why the deputy wanted to hound her. Did he think she had come to steal quarters and dimes?

At first she worried that Rosco would come to the car wash while she was pinned down in the grass. But after a while she stopped looking for him. The fear and the cold were encroaching; they closed on her mind like a fist. After some forty-five minutes, more afraid of the cold than of the deputy's light, she stood and walked stiff-legged out of the grass and onto the bypass. The headlights were distant and tiny, but coming. She set her sights on the woods at the top of the embankment. There was no panic or urgency in her, only the faintly electrical tingle of muscles resuming their work.

She stood on the stoop of the trailer. The plating of the door handle, scarred from the stabbing of keys badly aimed, stuck to the tips of her fingers like ice. Then she remembered the latch would be locked, and she had forgotten to smuggle a key from the kitchen. She couldn't climb into the trailer the way she'd climbed out because the window was too high in the wall. She pounded the door with her open hand. She waited and pounded again. Almost that instant the door swung open. Her father was wearing a T-shirt. His trousers were beltless and low on his hips. His biceps and forearms were tense. The bat seemed alive in his fist.

He didn't move from the doorway. "Where in the world have you been?"

She edged past him, her eyes watery in the warmth of the room.

He closed the door and said, "Come here."

She didn't turn. "Just let me go to bed."

"I said, 'Come here.' "

She faced him. "What are you going to do? Beat me with that niggerstick? You and your wonderful niggerstick."

He tossed the bat on the sofa. "Sit down."

"I'm cold."

"Well, sit and get warm."

She sat on the edge of the sofa, the bat behind her. He squatted before her, so that their faces were at the same level, some two feet apart. His wrists rested on his thighs; his fingertips touched. This was his natural stance when the ball was approaching the plate, his attention approaching the crux.

He said, "I want to know where you've been."

"Out of this place. Anywhere away from you and her. Just look at that mess on the wall." She pointed to where the spaghetti sauce had been staining the paneling. He didn't look away from her face. She said, "I went out walking. I was just walking around by myself. Anything's better than here. If I didn't get cold I wouldn't never come back."

"Who are these people you're seeing? Who's so important you have to go sneaking around?"

"I already told you. I was all by myself. You think I'd freeze if I had me a ride?"

"I think you're seeing some people. That Jetts woman had something on you. She said Chevelle."

"She is a liar."

His upper lip curled. She glanced up and saw the tobacco stains tracing his gum line. "You lie to me and I'll—"

"What? You gonna whip me? I'll go to Momma. I mean it. I'll go and tell her what living with you and that woman is like. I'll go and tell Ramona and whoever else I need to tell."

He shook his head, looking down through the disconnecting tips of his fingers. "I got a temper and Judith does too. We don't aim it at you."

She said, "Why did you marry that woman if you hate her so much? Why don't you leave her?"

"We've just been having this rough spell. People can't pick who to love. When you get older you'll see what I mean."

"You hate her cooking. You hate how she acts. You hate how she sounds when she talks. You hate how she's pregnant. Did you act like this when my momma was pregnant?"

"No."

"Then why don't you leave her? She's the whole trouble. I wish that woman was dead."

He was shaking his head, as though all of this ground had been covered, as though he had already tramped it and searched it and there was no use doing so again. His voice was low and calm. He looked into her eyes. "Listen, babe. You and me have to be on the same side together. We need to wear the same colors. You know what I mean? Nothing means spit if you're turning against me."

She was afraid she might cry. She half turned on the sofa. The knob of the bat was in view. She said, "You and that wonderful niggerstick. You think as long as you've got it we'll all be so safe. I swear. Nobody's bad as that woman. She's worse than all of the coloreds alive."

He laid his hand on her knee. "If you don't like me having

that bat out I'll shut it back up in the trunk of my car. Is that far enough away?"

She cried. The moisture was warm on her cheeks, where the numbness had been.

He said, "I never meant to scare you with it. Okay?"

She nodded.

He said, "We don't aim it at you."

5

Momma came back for Thanksgiving. Buddy and me went over to Aunt Betsy's and ate. He let me ride on his Harley. That was a shock, knowing Buddy. I love to feel when that Harley hits fifty. Part of my face like to froze.

I wasn't nervous till right when we got there. Buddy said I better try and be nice. I never liked my Aunt Betsy except when I was little. She used to take me and Momma to church. Really the only thing I ever liked about her was the seats in her Buick. They were as soft as a cloud. That was way back before Betsy had Annie. They traded in on a Mercury wagon. I never saw why they needed a Mercury wagon to haul around one little kid.

They have a brick house that sits on a hill, and their driveway is cement and it's plenty wide. You have to climb a good ways up some steps from the driveway. Annie came out on the stoop with her brown fuzzy bear. She started jumping and screaming, "It's Libby! It's Libby!"—on account of her being just five. She is so pretty and little. Betsy likes dressing her up in a velveteen dress. I started feeling so grungy for wearing my jeans.

Momma was back in the kitchen or somewhere. My Uncle Bob came and opened the door. He never says the first word when he sees me. He aims his finger at me like a gun, then clicks his tongue in his cheek for the sound and pretends he is blowing the smoke off the muzzle. I like his smile while he's pretending to blow off that smoke. One thing I hate is when people rush up to the door and start yelling hello.

Buddy came in behind Annie. We were lined up like some kind of parade. I smelled the turkey and dressing and decided I needed to pee first. I shut myself in the bathroom till Momma came back to the door and said, "Libby?" I had to look at myself in the mirror right quick. Some of my face was still trying to thaw. Some of my hair was mashed flat on my head from the helmet and some was still wild where the wind had got to it and whipped it around. Momma said, "Libby?" I let her in.

One thing that's good about Momma is, she doesn't grab you and hug you the very first second. She likes to see how you look. She likes to add you up slow in her mind.

I washed my hands and got used to how pretty she looked in her Thanksgiving dress. It had some white and some yellow wove in to make cream. Momma said I was so thin. I could tell she was more nervous than I was. I started drying my hands on a towel and got both of my hands in the towel and it seemed like they wouldn't come out. Momma came over and kissed me and gave me a hug. It was a good time for her to do it.

I tried to be as polite as I could all through Thanksgiving dinner and eat something of everything. We had to listen to Aunt Betsy get Momma caught up on the people that died or got sick or divorced. Momma was trying to act like she cared. Betsy thinks Momma should one time grow up. It's wrote all over her face. Betsy says Momma had children too young. Betsy says, "You should've waited till you had a home and some hope for the future."

You wouldn't think they were sisters. Betsy is bigger and thicker and looks like a Whitley. All of those Whitleys have cheeks that look slapped. Momma is pale with some freckles and hair the same color as mine, which is brown if I'm not in the sun. Except Momma has wave in her hair and I don't. Buddy got all of her wave.

I saw a picture of Momma and Betsy when they were both little. Most of the picture was blurry except for Aunt Betsy. Momma was wearing a one-piece and sitting in one of those round little pools that need air. Betsy was washing her off with a hose. Betsy was standing with one foot in the pool. She had ruffles all over her bathing suit. The water hit Momma right under her neck. Momma looked up at the sky. I couldn't see her expression because water was spraying her face.

All of the time we were eating I'd catch Betsy looking me over, and then I would look and see Momma was catching her too. It's hard to chew up a mouth full of turkey when that's going on. Momma looked worried about it, but then she calmed down. One time we all three caught each other and Betsy turned red.

Momma just smiled. She can say something true and make people relax. How, I don't know. She said, "Betsy, you remember when we were just little?"

Betsy looked down at her salad real bashful. I never see Betsy bashful except when she eats some kind of holiday meal with my momma. I'll never figure them out. Betsy will all the time boss and look down on my momma, but once they sit down at a table that woman will sweeten right up.

Momma said, "I would stop playing and lay down my doll for one second. And here would come Betsy, all ready to snatch it away."

They were both smiling and laughing. I couldn't believe it.

I drank some tea and ate sweet-potato casserole. I didn't see what Aunt Betsy would need with somebody like me when she already had her a doll of her own. She doesn't know the first thing about me anymore. Of course, neither does Momma. I could be Martian for all either one of them knows.

Betsy said we could digest all that dinner and then she would serve our dessert. She started clearing the table with Annie and Bob. She said how Momma and Buddy and me were excused.

We sat down in the living room. One thing I'll say about Christians is, they keep their living rooms clean. Buddy kept picking up books off the tables and putting them down like he wasn't quite ready to read. Buddy said how was Chicago. Momma said fine. She said how Miles liked his job. Momma said she got a job in a drugstore, working the cash register. I asked her how did she like it and Momma said, "Oh, fine." She said, "Right at first all the people kept staring at me when I talked. I never had any idea I sounded so southern. I had to learn how to say certain words. And you know what? It worked. Now people just pay me and never even look up."

I said, "I want to hear some."

Buddy said, "Yeh."

She sat up straight and said, "That'll be one eighty-five."

Me and Buddy couldn't hardly believe it. She didn't sound like Momma one bit.

"Four fifty-nine, please."

I started laughing and Buddy kind of smirked like he does.

"Nine twenty-one."

Aunt Betsy came and stood by the door with a frown on her face, like what did we think was so funny. Then she went off.

Momma said her and Miles both joined a club that went dancing on Saturday nights. I tried to picture them dancing like people in Chicago but I couldn't do it. I asked her how she got down here, and she said she flew on a plane because she only had one day off from her job. Bob picked her up at the airport. She said Grandma Whitley won't fly on a plane and so Miles had to stay home and watch her.

We talked some more about things we were doing. Mostly we went over everything and said it was fine, same as we do on the phone. Momma said she wished that Buddy would try to be home when she called. Buddy said he would do better. That's what he always says—he will do better.

It aggravated me to keep going over and over things just like we do on the phone. Seems like people ought to have more things to say when they are together in person. That's why I started acting so hateful and bragging on Daddy and Judith. I said we had a good home and we all got along. Buddy just stared. I said how thrilled we all were about Judith expecting. Buddy said, "Shit," but Momma didn't fuss at him about it. I said, "Judith and me have been picking out names." She lets you keep right on lying until you get done.

Momma said, "Is that right?" She looked at me and then Buddy.

Buddy said, "I don't know," real irritated. Buddy was staring at splotches on his boots, the same greasy ones he wears to the motorcycle shop where he works.

Momma said, "Things settling down?"

Buddy acted like he didn't see any point in her asking that question. He said, "Ever'body I know that's married, they just fight all the time. So what?"

Momma looked at me. I said, "I know I'm feeling more and more settled and I'm not planning to ever leave Daddy." I was acting so spiteful. I felt like hurting my momma as much as I could. Sometimes that's just how I am.

Momma said, "Well, if you say you're happy, I guess I'm relieved. I wish you weren't looking so thin, though."

Betsy poked her head in the door. "Dessert?" Then she went off.

I can be the worst two-face. I was so mad at Momma for not even trying to get us to come back with her. I was just aching to stand up for Daddy against her but she wouldn't even try. I said, "Anyway, you go off to Chicago and change."

"I didn't change. Seems to me you're the one trying to change."

I said, "You're the one left."

Buddy said, "Shit."

Momma said, "Libby?"

I said, "Maybe I'd like to at least see what it was like. I've never been anywhere except here. Maybe you ought to at least ask."

Momma said, "You can come visit. You want to visit? We've got it planned for next summer. You want it sooner? I'll find the money. At Christmas?"

I said, "What, for one day, maybe two? Is that all you can stand to have me around you?"

Momma got mad and that shocked me. I shut up. She said, "Now listen. Who was it wanted to stay with her daddy? Who raised that fuss about Miles? You come with me, and it's final. You know I love you. You know I want you to come. But if you come home with me, then it's final. You're not going to bounce back and forth when it suits you. You're not going to keep playing your daddy against me. You hear me?"

I looked her straight in the face. I tried to hate her as much as I could. I said, "I'll stay with Daddy."

Buddy and me couldn't look at her face. We were so quiet. Seems like my momma and me were both trying to calm down, and Buddy was getting more nervous. He started drumming his fists on his legs. I didn't say a whole lot after that. I didn't want to provoke her. It was already such a short day. Seems like she got there, and we had to eat, and I acted hateful, and we had to make up as fast as we could. I didn't want her to hate me when she went to get back on the plane. I tried to think what to say to make up but then I gave up. It seemed like we'd never have time.

Betsy came all the way into the living room. She said, "Pie's on the table. You ready?"

Daddy says people can't pick who they love. I know he didn't pick me. I know my momma didn't either. I keep on piling these horrible things on my conscience. I keep turning against Momma and Daddy, either one or the other. People can't stand but so much. Sometimes I figure my Momma would die if she once ever knew me down deep. Rosco and me on the roof, for example. Feelings I've had with him up there. Momma has never been places like that in her life. Momma is not a big Christian like Betsy but she lives clean in her heart. Sometimes I'm glad she is so far away. People can't tell much about me, long-distance.

I've had a hateful side to me since I was a kid. Probably since I was born. One thing I did I can't ever forget. I was eight, maybe nine. I thought I was so perfect, going to church and singing the hymns, and all because of that I didn't stand by Daddy. It was after he quit baseball and stopped chewing. He said every time he chewed he thought of playing ball, so he would have to smoke and get tobacco in him that way. Momma didn't like it. She said his smoke got in her hair and stunk and made her carsick on a trip.

Daddy promised Momma he would quit for Mother's Day. He said he'd quit and stay quit. You could tell how proud it made my Momma. Every week he didn't smoke she made a yellow cake with sticky-chocolate icing and said how he deserved it. He would eat a bite and say, "Now I know why people get so fat when they quit smoking." Daddy he's not ever been the kind to put on weight, though.

We had our summer revival. Daddy didn't use to go to church but that time they had a basketball coach preach revival. Daddy came just for the coach.

After the preaching I ran down to push a low note on the organ. Momma said for me to stop that. I ran out the side and saw my Daddy standing on the gravel driveway. He was sucking on a Camel like he barely made it through the preaching.

When we got home I laid on my bed. I was a baby about it. I thought Momma would divorce him, if I told her, so I would have to keep it all a secret to myself. I kept seeing Daddy with his suitcase getting on a train and leaving. Me and Buddy weren't allowed to even wave good-bye. Which is so retarded it's not funny. We don't get the kind of trains you ride on.

We were having ham and cold potato salad. Everybody watched me try to eat a green bean, all but Daddy. He was busy bragging how he'd eat his plate of food and everybody else's. Momma said for him to save some room for sticky-chocolate cake. That's what made that bean turn over in my belly like a lizard rolling underneath of something, licking out his tongue. Buddy couldn't keep his mouth shut. He said, "She's not eating. Make her drink her milk at least." We still had our milk rule. Daddy said, "Shut up, Buddy."

Momma started feeling of my head and asking was I sick. I said I would like to leave the table, but Daddy went, "Look here at this dinner." Buddy started up again, and that's when Daddy saw my face and froze up like he knew or something. Then I got so scared and mad at Buddy I couldn't keep it a secret for one second more.

I said, "I saw Daddy smoking."

Buddy laughed at me real hateful. "So?" he said.

Momma got quiet, her and Daddy.

"Everybody knew he started up again but you, you baby," Buddy said. "Look at that baby, she's crying."

"Shut up, Buddy," Daddy said.

I said, "Momma didn't know."

She said, "Yes. I knew that he would have one every once in a while. I guess it's hard to cut right back to nothing."

"Everybody knew that," Buddy said.

"Not me."

"So what."

"He said he stopped. He ate the cake." I ran off like a dunce and hit my bed so hard it knocked my breath out.

Daddy came back after while and said how some man ought to take a strap and beat him for the way he did sometimes. He sat down beside me on the bed and combed his fingers in my hair like always. It was his same fingers. I couldn't see why he wanted to touch me.

Sometimes the Ticket says, "What color you gonna be if there's trouble? Whose side you gonna be on?"

I can't predict how I'll act in the future. I barely know what I'm doing right now. Momma and Daddy keep trying to love me but they never see me deep down. Tina knows everything bad. She can see through me right quick. She doesn't give a good shit how I am. All Tina knows is, you cross her you die.

I know we put in a lot of cold nights on that chips truck. We kept a kerosene heater in back so we had us a place to get warm. We had to scrub rusty parts with a brush and a bucket of kerosene. I've still got kerosene smell in my clothes. I've still got blisters from filling those tires with a bicycle pump.

Sometimes I figured that truck wouldn't ever get put back together. Pieces were busted and strewed all around. One time I thought it was useless. I was so tired from not sleeping. None of the parts would fit back like they should. I started running off at the mouth. I said we needed my Daddy, because one thing he knows is his engines. Chuck dropped a wrench in his toolbox. He doesn't talk when he's pissed. Tina just stared. She said, "Why don't you go on home and ask him?"

I didn't blame her, because of that truck being theirs and not mine. It was Chuck and Tina's Charles Chips House of Love. I never had any right to that truck.

I started walking away. Tina said, "You runnin' home to your daddy?" I didn't say. Tina said, "You're turning whiter already."

But all the next day I was desperate to get to the fish camp. I was scared they would get that truck running and drive off and leave me. But they never did. Tina said, "You back again? You act like you done been adopted. We adopted this monkey, Big Chuck?" Chuck didn't say. He is the quietest person. He wants some tools in his hands all the time.

He got it cranked and she runs. The pistons go wham-a-ka-wham like a shootout and second's tore out of the gearbox, but we got her running at least. First time Chuck cranked her she sat there and shook. Me and Tina stood back a good ways. The metal was quaking and buzzing all over. I thought those rivets would pop but they stuck to her hide tight as ticks. We ran and jumped in the front. Chuck smiled, and he never smiles. We had to grab holt of Chuck because everything shook. We couldn't talk for the racket but we didn't need to. He shoved the clutch and the gears were all gnashing and we about fell over backward when he hit the gas.

If we get money for gas then we all go to ride. Sometimes they let me steer if I sit on their laps. I wish I knew how to drive and could reach. Some nights when Chuck is asleep in the back me and Tina go off down the road, just us Martians together up front. We never know when we start off where we'll end up. We found a place in some woods. It's like a world in the future where all of the people died off in a nuclear war. Like there's all of these overgrowed streets and nobody to use them. Tina, she drives like a maniac fool. So the branches are busting and pine cones are spinning back up in your face. She goes to whipping us sideways and screaming, "Oh shit, man, oh shit, where the fuck is the road?"

I can't explain why we put so much work in that truck.

Nobody normal would do it. All I know is, it seems like the Ticket and Chuck and me have a deep secret between us because of that truck. We kind of smile when we pass in the hall now at school. Tina says, "Smell of my hands. I get the kerosene smell off my hands?" I tell her all I can smell is her soap.

6

At ten in the morning her father arrived. Libby sat up and said, "They kept me in here all night."

"I decided it might wake you up if you had to stay in there a while."

"I need a cigarette."

"Can't do it."

She stood. "They took my Winstons and my lighter and my rings and eighty-something cents."

"Hold on to your receipt."

"I'm in jail, Daddy."

"No, you're not. This is just juvenile detention. Doesn't put the stigma on a person jail does. If it did, I'd of put a stop to it."

She stood two feet behind the bars, her arms folded on her chest. "Why'd they lock me up in here?"

"You've been violating your probation. There was property damage."

"Did you hear what I did?"

"I want to hear it from you."

"Let me have a cigarette first."

"No."

She sat down on the cot, facing the cinder-block partition between her cell and the cell where Tina had been put.

Libby watched the deputy take coffee to Cassie, the dispatcher, who sat at a switchboard a few yards down the corridor, and then to her father, who stood by the cell. The deputy didn't look into the cell at her. He was handing out coffee as though this were some kind of entertainment, and his job were serving refreshments.

"Hadn't heard anybody call the name Lampert on this switchboard for close to a year," Cassie said. She had a big, hearty voice that carried to them without strain. "I was about to get lonesome for it."

Libby saw the deputy grin. She could tell he was the kind of man who grinned when he was nervous.

Her father drank coffee. His hand was steady. Libby was afraid of that steadiness. She was afraid of what he might already know, of what he might have already resolved to do.

The deputy chattered on as if she were not in jail but merely on exhibit. "Durn if them kids hadn't rooted a creosote post out the blacktop, then set the post back so you can't tell a thing. Place out past the country club, where some people come in from out of state and paved some streets through the woods and went under."

"Anybody could've told them they would," Cassie called. "They were from Bluefield. Not even Virginia."

Libby was seeing in her mind the parade coming out of those woods. She had been first, then Tina, then Chuck, then the deputy. Tina had whispered, "Keep your mouth shut. Don't be doin' like no white girl." The deputy had loaded them into the car. She remembered the artificial sound of his voice when he lowered its pitch for the radio: "I have one black male and two females, one black."

Now the deputy stood in the middle of the corridor. His skin was unevenly colored. "It took a good while to find. They drove a-way back through the woods. Soon as I got there I seen the fairway was plowed up right smart with some ruts. And here was that truck, on its wheels, with its nose in the sand trap."

Libby felt her father's gaze search her, as though for the traces of sand on her jeans. She was afraid. Her father seemed to be trapped, momentarily, at the edge of her confinement, neither inside with her nor outside with her captors. She didn't know which way his anger would turn.

Cassie laughed.

Her father said, "What are you laughing at?"

For a moment Libby thought he had meant these words for her. But they had been aimed in the other direction.

Cassie said, "You at that age!"

"I managed not to get stuck in the sand with two niggers."

Libby felt the temperature of her skin invert—ice, then fire.

The deputy shuffled his feet.

Lampert said, "You see this deputy here? I never even knew he had a regular name until he got him this uniform to wear. Harry. If you call that a name. We called him Smiley. He figured our slugging percentage. Like we needed for him to keep up with our slugging percentage."

She listened to him with the same disbelief as she had the night when they had first gone to dinner with Judith, when he had suddenly enlisted her as an ally, as if against a common opponent, a scorcher of chicken-liver drippings, worthy of ridicule only. She knew, now, what this meant. It meant that he was ashamed.

"Even paid his own way on the road trips. Finally got him a uniform. One that comes with a gun. So here's this boy named Smiley, that couldn't make anything happen without help, so he got him a job where all he had to do is drive around and wait for things to transpire on their own."

"And me to call him up and say when they're transpiring," Cassie called from the switchboard.

The deputy was nodding, the grin frozen tight on his face.

Libby stopped thinking or wondering how this would go. She slouched on the cot and considered the wavering line of a mortar joint in the cinder-block partition.

Her father went on. "Never had his own slugging percentage to figure, so now he starts getting revenge, staying single. If he ever got messed up with marriage and kids he would be in the same shape the rest of us daddies are in. Worse shape, I reckon. And wouldn't be lording it over us now."

The deputy's feet made a shuffling sound.

Her father said, "Way I look at it, single is cheating."

Cassie said, "You want to see her alone, Jake?"

"Her and the other two both."

Libby looked up. The deputy was shaking his head. "Just her. Not them other two. Their daddies both come in and got 'em. When we couldn't get you on the phone at home, Ramona said to keep her in detention till tomorrow. You can see she's just fine, like I said on the phone. Not a scratch."

The cot where Libby sat was hung by two heavy chains from the wall. She grasped one of the chains, feeling its tension, her weight a slight trembling in the links.

The deputy said, "Sure was a soft place to land, in that sand trap. Boy in the back of the truck never even woke up. Shined my light in his face and said, 'Hey here, wake up.' And he opened his eyes and looked at me like I'm a bad dream he was dreaming. And them girls were still shoving each other around in the sand trap, not even hurt."

Cassie said, "Couldn't be too awful bad if a colored boy slept through it."

"It was just enough property damage to where you couldn't overlook it," the deputy said.

Cassie said, "Not enough to bother his sleep."

"But they couldn't move the truck. I said, 'Here's what you do. You manage to move that truck, so we don't have to call in a wrecker, and kick some sod back in them ruts—' They gave it a good, hard try, I'll grant you that. Thought for a minute the colored girl would heave it out by herself."

Cassie said, "You should've left it in there long enough to spook some fancy golfers off their game. I would like to see their faces when they bounced one off that truck."

To Libby, these people were only the outermost ring in her compounding confinement: the bars and her father and them. She heard the deputy slurp coffee. "Jake, I wouldn't never have brought her in if the truck wasn't stuck. If there wasn't that damage."

"Don't worry about it."

The deputy began breaking off pieces of foam from the lip of his cup. "When I was their age I missed it. You know it?"

Cassie said, "Harry, you sound like TV! You sound so sincere. Don't he, Jake? Just like TV?"

Libby heard the deputy walk off down the corridor. She looked and saw Cassie get busy with the phones. Her father was standing near the bars.

Libby said, "Are you getting me out?"

He said, "Come here."

She was so tired of being afraid that she was ready for him, for whatever he intended to do. She walked over to the bars. At least they were getting on with it, now.

He said, "I got here late and didn't get a look at the man. Who's the man, babe?"

"He's not anybody."

He punched the bars with the heel of his palm. Libby ducked. The bars settled down. She cried a little, not because she thought it would do any good, but because there was a new kind of distance between them, a distance involving his shame. She wiped her eyes and said, "He's not anybody. I swear he's not. This was just some people with a truck. They were together, not me."

They stood there awhile. He said, "Got in a truck with some coloreds and tore up a golf course. Where was this Chevelle I been hearing about? Couldn't you get but one wreck to a sand trap?"

She didn't respond.

"I brought Buddy with me, but he's hanging back."

He was standing at the end of the corridor, watching. She could tell by the way Buddy looked at her, by the half-glance with bitterness in it, that he was ashamed of her also.

Lampert said, "He doesn't have the stomach for this. I just barely do myself."

She watched Buddy walk along the row of cells. He leaned on the opposite wall.

She said, "Make him stop looking at me."

Buddy said, *"Stupid."*

"Make him shut up."

"There's no way she'll worm out of this," Buddy said. "They'll send her off."

She looked at her father.

He nodded. "If that woman has it in her power."

Buddy said, "Stupid."

Her father said, "Shut up, Buddy. You're not much of one to talk. Only thing you ever beat her to was training school and birth."

Buddy's face went blank.

Her father said, "We haven't settled this other."

Libby looked up. "What other?"

"This other car."

She thought about it. "I never rode in but one. Just to see how it was. If Ramona said it was a colored car she's a liar. I mean it. It's just a car."

"He been around you lately?"

"No. I can't stand him. I told him to leave me alone."

"You going to tell me if he comes around you?"

"Yes."

"Liar."

Her father said, "Shut up, Buddy."

Libby said, "He was just somebody with a license. And all because of just one time she goes to accusing me. And you take her side."

"Am I going to have to lock you in the house to make you act right? Answer me."

"You can't make me stay in there. It makes me sick being around there. I wish I was living with Momma. Maybe that's what I better do, go and live with Momma."

"Do it," Buddy said.

She hadn't been looking directly at her father but she flinched and stood back when he reached for her shoulder through the bars. He withdrew his hand, and stood away from the cell. Buddy was walking down the corridor. Her father turned to go. He said, "You better think of some words for that judge, or you won't have a choice where to go."

She began thinking of words for the judge. She already knew what her father would say if she were to remain silent, if she forced him to make her excuses. He wouldn't blame it on her. He would blame it on somebody else. He would blame it on Baughtown or color or both. Or worse, he would take all the blame on himself.

At ten forty-five a woman in uniform came to her cell and led her up to court. It was the room where her family had gathered for the custody hearing. Ramona laid papers one by one before the judge, reciting the words and statistics she kept in her file drawers. When each paper hit the bench it seemed to rise and float a little sideways, weightless on the polished veneer, until the judge laid his index finger on it and grunted. Libby hated him for grunting.

Her father said that if they let her stay with him then he would see she got all the punishment she needed to straighten her out. There was another spreading and amassing of pages, from which emerged more nodding and questions and at last the word "delinquent." She waited. The judge looked down at her and asked if she would like to have a lawyer. She watched her father and said no. The clerk gave her a waiver to sign. She wrote "Elizabeth Corey Lampert." The judge said, "Young lady, why can't you do as Miss Jetts asks?"

"I believe I can now."

"Why haven't you before?"

She said, "I got to running with the wrong element. They were a bad influence."

She was aware of Ramona beside her, stiffening.

The judge said, "Will you associate with them again?"

"No sir."

"Why not?"

"Because it woke me up, being in jail."

The judge regarded her with a slight hovering of eyebrows. "Madame Clerk," he said, "let the record show that Elizabeth Corey Lampert is a delinquent child; that she has violated the terms of her probation set—enter here the court date, Madame Clerk—by remaining away from home past curfew; that she has been a party to the destruction of property valued at nine hundred and thirty-seven dollars; and that she has failed to comply with the directives of her probation officer. The court's judgment is that the period of her probation be extended to twelve months. She will be released from detention into the custody of her father."

When he dismissed them, Libby and her father followed Ramona down the steps, where a beam of sunshine slanted from a skylight and half filled the stairwell, the surface of the pooled light running perpendicular to the rise of the stairs, so that it seemed the walls themselves and not their contents were tilted out of plumb. As Ramona waded down into this light it simmered on her pumps, her stockings and pale-blue corduroy skirt, submersing last her hair in a fine, foaming broth of illumination.

Downstairs, her father stopped in the corridor and lit a cigarette. He gave Libby a long drag, took the cigarette back, and left her with Ramona in a narrow, smoke-tinged space framed by the doorway of Ramona's office. Libby stepped into the room and watched Ramona maneuver the door shut, swinging from the hips. Libby toed the loop-pile carpet, waiting. Ramona filed her sheaf of papers and left the drawer standing open. She raised her arm to the level of her shoulder and dropped her ballpoint pen like a spike to her desk.

"What I want to know is, where do you get off, Miss Cutie Pie? 'It woke me up to be in jail, Your Honor.' Let's get realistic here. We're not blind to you, dear girl. What happens when he's on the bench the next time you decide to sashay in there?"

Libby shrugged.

"What I want from you is realism," Ramona said. "You think you outsmarted me? Made me look a little dense? Get real. What you did was fool yourself, got yourself elected to the opposition. *My* opposition. That means trouble."

"What did Tina get?"

"Tina got what you should get: sent off. Training school. This little caper was the big leagues. Nine hundred dollars' worth of green and fairway, ripped to a fare-thee-well. Do you know how many judges play that hole?"

Libby stared at her, snagged on the words "sent off." She said, "What about Chuck?"

"Cute little vehicle, that truck of his. No inspection. Phony plates. Nonexistent registration. Chuck was very gallant. Said he'd work the whole nine hundred off waiting tables. He's a sullen bastard, is he not? Restitution and probation."

"I was driving. It was me."

"Too late now, dear girl."

Libby knew what "too late" meant. "Too late" was another, even greater confinement: the sound of her words in the courtroom; the moment when she had determined that white versus black was the issue, and that she would be white.

Ramona said, "His momma cried. Tina's people didn't cry, though; they're a proud bunch, aren't they? Chuckie swore it wasn't Tina who was driving. Said that he was. What I asked him was, 'How'd you drive the damned thing from the rear, flat of your back?' So Miss Tina's gone, gone, gone. When you're big and black as she is, it's a little harder putting on your Little Miss Innocent face."

Libby turned her back and reached for the door handle. Ramona didn't move. The latch clicked open. Libby said, "Can I go now?"

"What I want to know from you is this, Miss Cutie Pie: Is it worth it?"

"Is what worth it?"

"What you're getting, is it worth it?"

"What am I getting?"

"Is it hotter than that blue Chevelle?"

"What?"

"It better be."

"What better be?"

"Get real."

PART THREE

ONE WHITE FEMALE IN TRANSIT

]

Rosco knows where he can get this stuff that makes a cold night spin until it's warm. Flies me through the sky and flaps my jacket out like wings. Lands me on the roof and makes me screech from parts of me I never had before.

Spins me, hops me, sails me, twists me, shakes me, over and over the roof. Gives me jailbird wings, so here I swoop and tiptoe on the edges. Rosco grabs me when I'm red and asks me would I like some rough stuff. I start sagging on his belly and nibble-nibble at his lips, and nibble-nibble little puffs of breath off Rosco's lips. Then Rosco's fingers go to rambling on my back. I use my tongue on his neck and his lips and I bite his old jaw till he screams. He punches hard. In my belly. He punches hard and it caves me in double and I have to fall on my knees. He locks my head in his legs and tries cracking my skull like a nut. He drops me hard like a flat broken rock and climbs up on the ridge, giving me his red side.

I can't get my breath. I try, but it won't come back. He's coming after me again. He hooks his toe under my chin and flips me backward on the roof and straddles me. Over him I see the stars are gone, the moon is gone. The sky is thick black fur, and when the M lights up it's like a branding iron and I can hear it scorch. And then my breath is never coming back.

It's never coming back. But something slower is. This is not the breath I'm used to. It's the kind that scorches when I use it. Mine and Rosco's.

The first night when we fell in love we did it. I was fairly drunk by then. We drove somewhere to a field. It was dark and there was one tree in the middle, black as a busted umbrella. We got out at the tree. I was cutting up. I climbed a little ways

up and straddled me a low branch. Rosco spread the blanket
out. It was army green. I was laughing at the stupid way a man
spreads out his blanket, squatting in the middle on a wrinkle.
Whenever he would push a wrinkle out it made a wave that
kept on getting bigger all the way across the field. That's how
drunk I was, in this big old dewy field with just that one big
tree. Just that one little blanket.

When he got his blanket fixed he looked straight up at me.
"Come on down," he said. I peeled a piece of tree bark off and
threw it at him. He was standing by the blanket. In the middle
was a low place where his feet had tramped the grass. It
seemed like that was where my body was already, on the blanket, mashing down the grass. I thought I would sit there in the
tree and watch us do it. That's how drunk I was. "Go ahead,"
I said.

He took his clothes off. I laughed. It made him mad, if I
remember right. He said, "Come down." I shook my head. He
said, "Take your clothes off." I had to turn loose with my
hands and hang on tight with my legs. First I took my shirt off.
He was watching me. "Take your pants off." So I had to swing
my leg across the branch and grab a higher limb and wiggle
off my jeans in little hops, kicking them down with my feet. I
was staring at him. I thought I would like to stay up there
forever, watching him. He was this fantastic color I had never
seen before. I'm so white at night.

But I couldn't stay up there. He stood on the blanket under
me and grabbed my feet, rubbing my arches with his thumbs.
I began to stir my legs like spoons in soup. "You're making
me crazy," he said. He yanked. I had to jump or fall. We
landed on the blanket. That was the time it hurt. On the
blanket it hurt me some. I got scared and crawled off in the
wet grass. Then he went a little wild and got me from behind,
I think. I remember a weed up my nose. Sometime in there I
cried. I was such a baby. He said he loved me. He slung the
rubber a long ways off in the field. I thought that meant we
could relax and be in love now.

He went to sleep on the blanket. I had the quakes. I was
looking up at branches in the tree. All the leaves were twitch-

ing bad as I was. A million zillion leaves, all twitching. I stopped looking up and studied him. Finally I got used to how it hung across his leg. He woke up and wanted me to pet it. When I did it got as heavy as a roll of quarters, only bigger. I pushed him off and ran to the car with my clothes. He knocked on my window, wrapped in the blanket. I made him sit in the backseat, and I put my clothes on. I sat there a long time, watching the field. Way, way off at the edge of it sat a little house without a single light. He said, "You're my woman, ain't ya, baby?" I looked at him right quick in the rearview mirror. "You expect a little blood, the first time," he said. "Then it feels good, after that." I shook my head.

"Look in the dash and get me a cigarette," he said. I opened the glove compartment. He flicked on the dome light. Inside I saw a necklace like a movie star would wear. It was this extremely fabulous gold neck chain with three little gorgeous pearls. He didn't say anything. I got his cigarettes and handed them to him and closed the glove compartment. "Punch the lighter." I did. After a long time it panged. I thought, Rosco doesn't love me. He leaned over the seat back and I lit his cigarette. His shoulders were bare and they had a smell like peeled tree bark. He sat back.

He said, "One time I had this girl who was always dying for it. I could be just walking down the street and she would grab it. We would go to watch a movie and with all these people around she would throw her sweater in my lap and pull my zipper down. But you know what I said?"

I shook my head.

"I said, 'I don't love you. I'm going to wait for when I find my one girl in particular.'" He smoked the rest of his cigarette and told me to look in the dash again. The neck chain was still there, more gorgeous than ever. He said, "Put it on."

I said, "For me?" like a retard.

He said, "Well, ain't you the foxiest little white girl in this part of the state?"

The latch didn't work right. He cussed the place that sold it to him and said he'd have to send it off and get it fixed. It would cost him plenty too, since he had to pay insurance on it. I told him I didn't mind waiting awhile until he got it fixed. I said, "It'll give me something to look forward to."

He calmed down. He said, "Now are you going to come on back and sit with me, or what?"

So I did. We picked at each other—pulling hair, tickling, stuff like that. I ended up squatting across his lap, trying to pin his arms back on the seat so he couldn't goose me. And that was when it started feeling good, along about the time the sky turned off a little gray behind that toy house a long ways off across the field, headed for morning. And I was kind of bouncing easy on his blanket. It was loose. He unzipped me and my shirt rode up from rubbing on his chest. It felt good. How his belly was towel-scratchy on my belly. How his mouth was, on me. It felt better than I need to think about right now. It felt fabulous. It was just like I heard Daddy say one time. He said, "Loving's just the opposite of chewing gum. The longer it lasts, the sweeter it gets."

One time in the middle when the tip-top of the sun was just grazing the mountains, we stopped a minute to rest. Morning didn't matter. It was foggy. I laid my chin on the seat back and let myself go limp and felt his belly pressing, pressing, pressing, pressing, every time he breathed. And for a second I dreamed up the craziest thing. I thought I saw somebody throwing back the blankets in that little house across the field, and tramping downstairs, and flipping on the kitchen light, and rinsing last night's grounds out of the pot, looking way out through the kitchen window at Rosco's foggy car. And she was thinking, Aren't they cold out there? They've been out there all night long, all by themselves, ever since I perked this Maxwell House last night. And now it's time to perk another pot. Wouldn't that taste good? Wouldn't it?

We've got a better place now. But it's cold. Rosco says this isn't nothing for February. He claims we're having false spring. I know I'm freezing up here on the ridge. I have to sit with my back to his belly, and him wrapped around me. We've been here a good long time, and either the wind's turning colder or we're not stoned anymore. His chin's on the top of my head. Daddy used to kiss me right there where the bone's not too thick in the middle. He called it my sweet spot.

Rosco and me haven't been here since right around Christmas. He gave me a giant box of chocolate candy. We ate it all to keep warm. I can still see all those round paper cups blowing off of this roof. They floated down over town like little black parachutes.

I say, "I know you've got another woman."

Rosco's Adam's apple moves on the back of my head. When he talks I can feel his chin digging into my sweet spot. "You're the only one I bring up here, though."

"I can't ever call you."

"Black and white is risky."

"You don't love me."

"What's this 'love' stuff? You're my baby."

I don't say anything. There is a strong gust of wind.

He says, "I'm making some arrangements with a man to plant some Christmas trees. Then it's five or six more years until the money rolls. Firs are good as money. It's time a man like me invested. I can't whittle wood forever."

"Can I call you, if I need to?"

"If you have to, you can call me. Just be sure, okay?"

"Sure of what?"

"Sure you have to."

2

"Where did they take you?" Judith asked, gazing out a window in the trailer's front door.

From the sofa, Libby could see Judith's pale face, the diamond-shaped glass, and the snow flurries swirling like summer insects around the porchlight. "Out for pizza."

Judith crossed the room and stooped for a bottle of whiskey

she'd left by the recliner. When she sat, she seemed to cringe, as if the upholstery pained her. "Where did they go?"

"Drinking beer. I tried to tell Daddy I could drink better than Buddy, but he said for me to get to bed."

"Do it then."

Libby swung her legs onto the sofa, and lay with her head on its arm. Snow melted on the laces of her running shoes.

Judith said, "There's not a bit of room for secrets between you and them blue jeans."

Libby ignored her.

Judith poured George Dickel whiskey into a smoke-blue glass. "See how puffy?" She tugged at parts of herself through the emerald nightgown. "This is why he spurns me, Momma says. 'Spurns' is what she means by cheatin'. He's been spurning me all over the county, Momma seems to think. She says that when a pregnant woman gets puffy right away, it means she doesn't want the baby. It means she's tryin' to deny it room to grow, so it swells her up all over."

Libby closed her eyes.

"I don't think it hurts to take a drink, do you?" Judith's questions all began with one shrill, nasal note. They dropped word by word into her throat to the caesura, rising to the original pitch. "He don't want this baby, Libby, you know it? He's got his two kids already, what's he want with one of mine? I tell him it's just water weight. Would you like a sister, Libby? He just better let me have some nice things for this baby. Today I seen a set of pretty dolls in town. They come in flavors. Flavors! That's George Dickel talkin'. What I mean, they come in scents. One is cinnamon, I think, and one is peppermint. One is sour apple. They're so cute. Ever' one has got a little comb, and you can tell which comb to use from smellin' of it. I should buy them, shouldn't I? In case I have a girl?

"I'm just not a pretty woman like your momma anymore. She's got pretty things now too, I bet. We need so many things around the house. I imagined I would have a pattern—you know, china and some flatware. We don't even have a vaporizer. How can we expect to have a baby? They dry out. But he says everyday is good enough for dishes. He won't buy a thing for me, you know it? Just you kids—Buddy and his drums. Does he complain about me, when he's off with you?"

Libby didn't answer.

"Only fun we have is once we're drunk. Monday night he pinched my chin and called me puffball. I was holding a hot hamburger pie. I set it down on his other hand. We were drunk enough it didn't matter. I know he goes out on me. Done your momma that way too, when it was me in this same trailer over in Sinksboro. He used to hide his car in Milo Gentry's driveway. See those spots on the carpet? By the door? All of that is mud he tracked from Milo's driveway."

Libby looked. The carpet was in the gold family—maize. The spots were maroon.

Judith dropped the blue glass on the floor and drank straight from the bottle. "I admit I knew he was married. Momma was sayin', 'Judith shoulda thought of that before she fell in love.' She wouldn't shut up until she seen a miracle happen, and he was giving up his wife and kids to marry me."

Libby said, "He never gave us up. Momma kicked him out."

"The point is, my momma said he wouldn't but he did. So now she's sayin', 'Judith's gettin' spurned. Judith shoulda thought of that before she let herself get pregnant.' Next she'll hear I've got the baby sleeping in my dresser drawer. She'll be sayin', 'Judith can't afford to furnish; shoulda thought of that before she had that baby.' Once you think of something, it's too late."

Libby rubbed her eyes.

Judith said, "Why don't you go to bed?"

"I might. Let me have some licker first."

Judith sipped at her bottle. "I knew one teetotaler. She had a baby girl and it was borned without a valve inside its heart. George Dickel might've fixed that."

"Let me have a drink, then."

"You're just testin' me, young lady, seeing what I'll do. I've got him. I can't stand it. How your momma stood it so long I don't know. Lord, we fight like roosters. I'm so jealous. He will pick that time to look at me and say, 'Your frame's too small for bearin'. Shoulda thought of that before.' "

Judith was quiet. It was dark in her corner. After a while she said, "Nothing in this trailer's like it was. Everything's been tore or broke or scratched or slapped around. I keep diggin' broken glass out of my carpet."

"He wouldn't fight like that with Momma. She won't stand for it."

"Can I help it? I might leave him. Every time I try, the thing that stops me is, I can't see what comes next. I can't fix it in my mind. I'm only twenty-three, and here I'm five months pregnant. He's the only man I ever knowed who changed a room for good as soon as he was in it. Whatever you've got pictured in your mind, he'll erase it. I'm a blank. I didn't use to be. What am I supposed to do? Haul this trailer home? He'll be standin' in those muddy footprints now till doomsday."

Judith pulled a lever and the footrest sprang up, tilting her into the corner. Her slippers were a fuzzy aqua. "You know what he used to say when he was tired of fighting? He says, 'You're the one to start it, I'm the one to end it.' Did he say that to your momma? He didn't? The first few months, when he would say that, I was scared to keep it up. Then I wasn't. After that, he wouldn't say it. He just cleared his throat. That was his idea of a threat. It scared me too. But pretty soon I argued my way past his throat-clearing. Then he took to ballin' up his fists and squeezin' till the blood veins stood up on his arms. It meant, That's enough. I'm supposed to think he'll hit me. Then I went on fighting past those balled-up fists. You know where he's up to now?"

"No."

"He'll go back and open his dresser drawer. There's at least one or two pistols in there, loaded. He believes in loaded guns. He brings the black revolver in here. Breaks it down. Spins the cylinder. Shows me he's aware it's loaded. Lays it down between us on the kitchen table. Leaves it layin' there, all loaded. Not a word."

Libby craned her neck to see if there was a pistol on the table now. She didn't see one, but she sat up and said,

"Watch it, then. I mean it. Don't keep pushing, hear? Don't get on him when he acts like that. Okay? God, you're stupid. Stop before he gets the gun out. Just stop. Don't keep pushing. Hear?"

"I don't argue past that gun yet. Can you imagine what my momma's going to say if she hears what he's been doin'?"

"Work him back to balled-up fists, you hear me?"

Judith tucked the bottle under one arm, pressing it against her side. "How can I do that?"

They sat for a while without talking. Judith poured another drink. "You're the only one who ever suits him, you know it?"

"What are you talking about?"

"I feel sorry for Buddy—his daddy always after him to be a man. You know what your daddy says? He says if he could put Libby's nerve with Buddy's frame he'd have him a ball-player, sure as the world. Plus he's always after Buddy to get him a girlfriend. Your daddy don't know what galls him worse—you runnin' around with the opposite sex or Buddy not."

"You don't know. You're just drunk."

"How come you think he took Buddy off the other night in the snow with that dog? And a gun? I knew as soon as they come back that it was weighin' heavy on Jake's conscience. On account of he told me what happened. He never tells me nothin' unless he's tryin' to justify hisself in his own mind."

"Just tell me what he did."

"Told Buddy he knowed of this girl livin' wild in the woods by the name of Blest Be. Took him way off up the mountain and went in the trunk of his car for that Winchester rifle. Buddy ast him how come he needed a rifle, and you know what Jake said? Said he was gonna be off out of sight in the woods, in case Buddy needed him to hold that rifle on her. Buddy ast him, 'You mean it takes a gun to make her do it?' And Jake says, 'I mean it makes a gun to make her stop.' But you know what I figure, Libby? I figure most of that statement was aimed right directly at me. Don't you?"

"Just tell me what happened."

"He says all he wanted was for Buddy to have him a breakthrough and stop takin' girls so dead serious. So they walked a long ways up a cold, windy holler, where a crust was froze hard on the snow. And they come to a little log cabin way up in a cove. And Jake told him go to that cabin and knock. But nobody answered, and the place was all dark and shut tight. Then about that time they hear that hound dog split the creek and go bayin' uphill. So Jake says, 'There she goes. Follow me.' And they clawed up the side of that mountain and come to a tree. And that hound dog was havin' a fit. And Jake said, 'Gimme that flashlight,' and Buddy did. And Jake said, 'Here, take the gun,' and Buddy did. So Jake shined the light up and down in the branches and Buddy kept aiming along with the light till these two little eyes flashed a bright flaming red. Then Jake said, 'Fire,' and Buddy did."

Libby met Judith's eyes. There was a silence, then Judith went on.

"I ast Jake what in the world he was tryin' to accomplish. He says all he ever had in mind was takin' Buddy on a snipe hunt, like his buddies used to do whenever Jake was in the 'coon and gun club. And the new boys would stand by that cabin and yell, 'Blest Be!' while the rest was all watchin' and laughin'. Says he never expected to tree a big 'coon. But here's the part that concerns me about it. Buddy still thought they was chasin' a girl. Buddy just fired on account of his daddy said 'Fire.' Then he stared at that 'coon bouncin' down from them branches and hittin' the snow, like he thought it might still be a girl. And Jake claims it wasn't no harm, and this might be Buddy's breakthrough. But I really wonder, don't you? I really wonder if your daddy ain't done somethin' he's ashamed of, and got hisself down in a hole, so he's tryin' to talk hisself out."

Libby leaned forward. "Stop pushing him, you hear? Stop drinking around him. Stop stirring him up."

Judith's face soured on a swallow of whiskey. "I ain't stirrin' him up tonight, am I? He's off stirrin' his own self—or somebody else. The bastard."

Judith got up and went off down the hall. In a few minutes, Libby heard the toilet flush, and Judith staggered back to the kitchen, bracing herself on the table, the muzzle of a pistol in her hand.

"What's the gun for?" Libby asked her. "Are you insane?"

Judith's face was florid. "This is mine," she said. "Not his. *Mine.* I'm gonna lay it on the table."

3

The smoke alarm goes off and wakes me up and I wonder what Judith's been burning in the middle of the night. Daddy says he would yank out the wiring if Judith had another way of telling when the food was done. Judith thinks the smoke alarm's just sensitive. At night when I've been having one last cigarette I go down the hall with a mouthful of smoke and blow it at that little red eye on the ceiling. It goes beep, be-beep, saying good night.

But now it's crowing like a rooster with his crower stuck wide open. That means Judith's scorching meat or bubbling-over some macaroni and cheese. I climb out of bed in Buddy's sweatshirt and switch the lamp on, and step barefoot in the hall with Momma's old hand-mirror. It's a yellow plastic mirror with a handle like a paddle. One day I was wising off and Momma whacked my bottom with it. I said, "You can't spank somebody with a mirror." That just cracked us up. Now that Momma's gone I keep it handy for whenever it's my turn to fan the smoke out of the wiring.

The living room lamp is on. I can barely hear somebody talking, low and steady. Buddy, maybe. I decide we've got a trailer full of morons tonight. He was playing his drums in my sleep, that moron, ka-wham, ka-wham, ka-wham, ka-wham on the snare drum. Buddy, he's a mess.

I fan the smoke alarm until it coughs and settles down, but when I stop, it crows again, wide open. There's a bitter kind of smoky smell with liquor in it. I decide we've got a trailer full of drunks tonight. I follow my phone cord down the hall to the living room door.

What I'm seeing stops me. It's not real enough. It's more like a tilted picture of some people on a floor. Buddy's hunched there—over Judith. Daddy's on his knees. "What's he doing?" I ask Buddy.

Buddy says, "Get out." I am mashing Momma's mirror on my chest.

"What's the matter with Judith?"

"Get out," Buddy says. *"Get out."*

I run back and slam my door and my face is tilted in the mirror so my chin is gross and bent and not my chin. I throw the mirror at the floor and it bounces. What I see's that tilted picture of some people on a floor. In the picture Daddy's face is turning up to me. It's the face he had that day a long time ago. When I was Honorary Batgirl, standing by the dugout. The man came sliding home and Daddy tagged him. Then all of us, we heard the umpire yell, "He's safe!" and Daddy ripped his mask off. What I saw was not his face. It was something from a cage. It turned to the ump and said, *"The hell you say."*

That's the face I see again, in this picture of a floor. I can't make it stop. There's a soaked place in the carpet, down by Judith's head. Guns are in it. Two guns. Judith, she's as crooked as a hook slide. Buddy says, "Get out. Get *out.*"

I jump sideways on my bed and quake and grind my knees into my eyeballs. Yowling like a cat that heard the smoke alarm.

I am half out the window. Then I hear feet. I hurry too fast and get hung in the window. I am stuck belly-down with my legs kicking out in the cold going nuts.

It's just Buddy. He says, "What are you doing?" He makes "you" sound so hateful.

I don't say one word. My belly is mashed in the window.

He keeps on like I answered. "No you're not. Get back in here."

He picks up the phone and listens to it for a second like he's not for sure he's got a dial tone. My rib bones are stuck on the windowsill. That's how tight it is, even with me being skinny. At least I don't have a lot of chest to keep me in there. Buddy sits on my bed. He acts like maybe he can't remember how to dial a phone.

He says, "What do you think I'm doing, stupid? Calling the law. I swear."

He's acting so smart, like he knows what I'd ask him. I wiggle a little ways backwards. My coat bunches up in the window and makes a tight squeeze. I'm scared I'll have to climb back in there to take off my coat. The worst part is thinking how Buddy might snap out of it and drag me back in there, so he can squeeze his own self out the window first. It gives me the quakes. I try to squirm without making a noise he will notice. My sweatshirt rides up in the coat and my back feels like some kind of ice. Air goes to leaking down my pants and freezing my butt.

"Get back in here."

I'm not about to. My pitiful brain is just thinking how if he stays in there and dies then I won't have to stay in there and die. I'm just relieved it is him and not me. Which shows exactly how I turned out. It just proves a lot of people right, is all.

I drop on the mud where the snow has been melting. It's just like me to land in some mud. At least we are having a warm spell. But it doesn't feel much like a warm spell whenever I first get outside. More like a cold snap. Warm sometimes and cold sometimes, like the weather's not quite stirred together real good.

In a second he comes to the window. For a minute I think, I'm a goner, because I'm not for sure it's just Buddy. It's a shape, is all. But he is still holding a part of the phone. And he talks to me like I am this idjit, as always. That's how I know it's just Buddy.

For a second I want to say, Hurry and come. I picture him tossing me stuff out the window. I would catch it before it hit the mud. Just stuff we need to have. Maybe his canteen with water in it, since my mouth is dry. And some towels to wipe off the mud. And some dry socks and maybe a blanket. And I wonder if he could sneak us some cheese or something like that for our food, that wouldn't go bad for a while. And he could drop all this stuff to me through the window and climb out in time. Maybe if he stripped off everything else but his shorts, he could make it. And he could hand his clothes down to me, and I would be careful to catch them. And they would be warm still. And then he would drop in the mud same as me and get dressed. And I would hurry and wrap all of our stuff in the blanket and run for it with him.

But Buddy says, "I don't have time to be fooling with you. First I've got to call the law. Then I've got to get some coffee in him. You can't leave or it looks bad. Get in here and make him some coffee."

I keep walking backwards, shaking my head. Buddy ought to know I never perked a pot of coffee in my life. And Judith can't perk it. I am watching his shape in the window, watching to make sure there's not but just one. I've got four other windows to watch in that side of the trailer. Plus the front door. A whole slew of windows. I am staring them down like a pack of bad dogs. I try to back-pedal slow as I can and not trip while I'm staring them down. Except I can't really stare at but one at a time. And the rest can start coming. Which is just how my brain wants to work, like a dog could be close to the same as a window.

"You don't know nothing about it," Buddy says.

I turn around and walk faster, not looking back. Not saying a word.

Buddy goes, "He didn't do it. It was her own stupid self. I can't go to chasing you down right now. Get back in here."

I start running. I'm just praying my two stupid legs won't lose all their strength like they do when I dream. Whenever something gets after me I try to run and the strength will run out of my legs. So I die or wake up when it grabs me. At least I can finally run.

Buddy is yelling a whisper as loud as he can out the window. "You liar. You don't know shit. You baby. You traitor."

I am running like somebody losing her mind. Like people whose clothes catch on fire. And they've not got the sense to drop down in the mud and roll over.

4

The route she tracked followed bottoms past Baughtown and crossed Messer's Creek on a timber-framed bridge which surrendered the road to the bypass and finished it off. Across the bypass, Highway 50 rose crookedly north along the river, deep into rugged terrain. On the west bank of this highway stood a dense swatch of bush and small trees, dropping away to some low-lying ground where the creek and the river entwined. On the east stood the barbecue place. The spell of mild weather had fogged the land over and melted the snow, laying a mist on the bottoms.

When she had come to this place in the dark, after walking and hiding for most of two nights and a day, it had seemed like the limits of town, like the bounds of a region she couldn't explore until she had rested. So she wedged herself under one end of the bridge, drew her coat around her, and slept.

She had not slept a wink before then: not on the roof by herself, the first place she went from the trailer; not in the crawl space of their old rental house, where she escaped from the wind later that morning; not in the toolshed she found on School Hill. The world was too new to be slept in. As she walked she was weak but unbothered by hunger or cold. She was too busy posing and testing that scene from the floor against angles of structures or mountains, against smooth painted metal or windows she passed, as though by imposing that picture on constant and knowable forms she could prove it was false. But when she reached the bridge, and the limits of town, she had walked around in that world long enough to accept it as hers. She could say it then: "Judith is dead." After that, she was ready for sleep.

The first truck across Messer's Creek that morning woke her. It was dark when she crawled out and stood, stiff and hobbling, and looked across the bypass, down Highway 50, which seemed to be worming its way into the fog. The dark, tangled masses of growth on one side of the highway, the square-windowed cinder-block building of Messer's Creek Bar-B-Q on the other, seemed waiting for balance like parts of an unsolved equation.

The delivery truck was parked, with its engine running, in front of the restaurant, blocking one of the windows. Another window showed a woman sitting on a stool behind the cash register, wearing a cap. A man filled the newspaper vending machine by the door, and drove away, winding first gear. The woman came out and bought a paper and went back to her stool.

Libby wanted one of the papers. She crossed the bypass to the vending machine and read a line of boldface type:

MAN HELD IN DEATH

A frame hid all but those words and the top fraction of a photograph. She had no money to open the rack.

The restaurant was empty except for the woman behind the cash register, who was watching her. Libby looked down and was surprised at the grime on her jacket.

"You okay, honey?" The woman's cap advertised a bait-and-tackle shop.

"I'm a little bit cold."

"There's a bathroom back there where you can wash up in time for school."

"I won't be going to school."

"Now why's that?"

Libby had been alone with the fact of Judith's death long enough, and was ready to say it aloud. "I just got through seeing a woman killed."

"My God, honey, where?"

"Between here and Baughtown."

"Do the police know it yet?"

"They should. She was pregnant."

The woman set down her cup. Its rim was scalloped with a shade of frosted pink where her lips had been.

"You've seen enough for one morning, then," she said. "Jules will be here in a minute. That's my husband. He's just out in the smokehouse getting the barbecue on. Jules!"

No one came. Libby saw the unopened newspaper by the register. She wanted it. The woman rolled it up and smacked the counter with it.

"It was down by Halliburton's, in that bad curve, wasn't it? Seems like every week somebody new slides off that hill and lands in the hospital. Was there any more hurt?"

"It wasn't an accident. It was deliberate."

The woman gazed at her through pink-rimmed glasses, as if she thought Libby might have lost her senses, as if she wanted to come around the counter and give her a good looking-over, but thought better of it.

"How's your head? You cut anywhere?"

"I'm okay."

"Well how far along was this woman? Might be a chance they can save the baby. I'm just relieved you weren't in there with her."

"She was pretty far, but—"

"Then there's a slim chance, if they get her in time. Now, what do you mean by 'deliberate'?" The woman spoke rapidly, and Libby was dizzy.

"I mean 'on purpose.' "

"Self-inflicted? You mean she just drove her baby right off the road with her? Honey, you better sit down in that booth."

Libby obeyed and took a seat near the window, looking out. Dawn had brought the wooden bridge into soft focus, and it seemed nearer than she remembered it. The woman couldn't understand her. She wondered if this meant that nothing had happened, if crossing the bypass was all she must do to go on as she'd been.

The woman carried her newspaper like a club through a door at the end of the restaurant. "Jules! Come in here a minute." She came back and sat down behind the register and said, "He can just let that barbecue cook itself for a minute. It's pit-cooked, you know. Now, what about that car? I expect it's a total loss."

"What car?"

"The one she died in. Honey, are you a little woozy?"

"There wasn't a car. He took a gun and did it."

"He?"

Libby didn't answer.

The woman shouted for Jules again. The sun cleared the pine tops and lit the chrome-plated legs under the dining tables. Libby rubbed her temples.

A man came in, untying his apron.

The woman said, "Jules, this girl's been going on about some accident. First it was a wreck, then it's a suicide, and now it's got a gun in it. I don't know what to make of all this."

Jules took the newspaper away from her and read it for a minute. "It was right there in your hands," he said. "Here's the man's picture, when he played baseball."

"Well, you never told me about it." She read aloud. " 'Man Held in Death of Pregnant Wife.' But Jules, that was night before last."

Jules folded the apron on his way over to Libby's booth. "You're the little Lampert girl, aren't you?"

"Yes sir."

"You been missing all this time?"

"Yes."

"You must be half starved."

"I'm a little hungry."

Jules came over. He smelled smoky, like barbecue. "Martha, fix this girl some breakfast, while I think what to do."

The deputy raised a microphone to his mouth. "I have one white female, Elizabeth Lampert, in transit."

Libby sat in the back of the patrol car, watching the pavement rush past. This was the same man who'd taken her into detention with Tina and Chuck. Now she slumped on the seat, resigned to whatever role was waiting for her: the victim's stepdaughter, the accused man's daughter, the witness. One white female in transit.

The deputy said, "Maybe I can work it out so you and your daddy can talk before they hit you with their questions." When

Libby didn't respond, he went on. "Because your daddy's not this kind of person. He might have a fair amount of devil in him, but not enough to where he'd do such as this on purpose. So I'll see what I can do."

Libby squinted into the glass, watching a landscape she'd crossed at a sprint only two nights before.

"Then whenever I can get you two together I'll go up and see about Miss Jetts. Maybe I can keep her out of this. Because I figure you've got enough on your mind, let alone her. I know myself, I like to keep her off my back if I can. Her and her memos."

They were passing the trailer. All she could see was the crest of the hill and the herringbone pattern of ribs in the TV antenna.

"So I'll do what I can," the deputy said. "Seein' as how I knew your daddy. But he sure never once needed no hand in the past—you know it? People grow up, though, and need different things. Like you might need a break or some luck, and that's all."

After a few minutes, the deputy said, "You want somethin' out of that trailer? Some clothes?"

"I need some clothes."

"I'll drop you off at the courthouse and go back for some. Reckon your brother will know where they are."

When they arrived at the desk near the juvenile lockup, Libby was already clutching her rings, necklace, bracelet, cigarettes, and four pennies—prepared to surrender them up to the woman in charge.

" 'I don't know.' Is that all you can say?"

Both of the city detectives were in her cell. For the last ten minutes she had been sitting on the bunk, puffing at her clenched fists as if blowing on a burn, answering "No" or "I don't know" with every third or fourth breath, until finally she screamed at them: "I don't know, I don't know, I don't *know!*"

The deputy came down the hall with a grocery bag full of clothes. "Is that the way you city boys like to work, bullying young-uns?"

The detectives let themselves out of her cell. One of them said, "She's a sweetie pie, all right. Her daddy's little girl."

The deputy set the clothes inside her cell and stepped back. As soon as the door was closed, the men began to talk as though Libby no longer existed, as though she were not in plain view.

"No offense," the deputy said to the detectives. "I'm a little short on sleep."

One of the detectives swore. "Boy says suicide; girl says, 'I don't know.' Daddy says all he knows is, he's an innocent man. Seems to me like him and his wife both got drunk and waved their guns around. Happened it was her head with the hole bored through it. Maybe that's murder, maybe it ain't, Harry. What do you think?"

"Well, whose gun killed her?"

"Waiting on ballistics."

"Then I don't know."

The second detective was laughing. "Sounds like a member of the family."

When they were gone, Libby washed, dressed, and lay down on the bunk. When she opened her eyes, her father was standing outside her cell, wearing a blousy white shirt with open French cuffs. One sleeve was rolled to the elbow; the other cuff flapped on his hand. He spoke in a low, steady monotone.

"Are you okay?"

She was not entirely awake. When she saw his face through the bars, she thought for a moment that he was the one in a cell.

"I made bail this morning. My lawyer is letting me borrow this shirt. You like it?"

She turned her face toward the cinder-block wall, but could still see his hands on the bars.

"Talk to me, babe."

She was rigid on the bunk.

"What's it going to take?" he said. "Apologies? I apologize. I'm sorry. I wish to hell it was me lying dead and not her. Is that what you want?"

Libby did not respond. Her father took a swipe at his hair.

"I need you, babe. This is hell for me."

Nothing. He mumbled a curse at the floor. Then he said, "So that's what you're willing to believe about me? That I killed her? That's the worst part. What you're willing to believe." He waited a long time. The other sleeve unrolled on his arm. "Not even drunk, I couldn't," he said through his teeth. "Not even drunk."

The deputy walked up the hall and said, "Come on, Jake. She needs some rest. The state boys came and hammered at her, wore her out."

Lampert ignored him. "Listen, babe. *Listen* to me. Lightning can't keep striking us over and over. Once I get this mess straightened out we'll be a regular family again, I promise. It might be this will draw us closer. I expect it will. Tell yourself this is bad as it can get. If we can get through this, we've got it made."

He turned away. When he was midway down the corridor, Libby spoke—not a word but a raking of consonants on teeth. He stopped. "Yeh, babe?"

"Get me out of here."

5

I told them I wanted my momma but they wouldn't listen.

I was stuck in a room at the courthouse because nobody knew where to put me. Buddy came in and they told us to sit at this table and left. They kept it cold in that place. I tried squeezing a sack full of clothes between my knees under the table, to see if it warmed up my legs.

Buddy said, "Keep on like you are and see where it gets everybody."

He sat where I'd have to look through him to see out the window. He took his toboggan off his head. He started wiping it back and forth on that end of the table. The tables they put in this courthouse are close as you can get to wood, except they have a lot more reflection. Whenever I laid down my arms on the table it suctioned my pores so they stuck. When I raised up my arms they left prints, and the prints shriveled up like your breath on a window.

After while the social worker came back. Her name was Trish. I told her and Buddy I wanted my momma. They claimed she was notified. I tried to call her from somebody's office but nobody answered the phone where they live in Chicago. Buddy had her number on him. But the paper was purple from his billfold, and limp. And two of the m's had got smeared from the way he'd been folding them tight over top of each other so long in the middle of "Momma." I sat down at the table and accused him of carrying the wrong sweaty number around.

He said, "That's the right number. I called it this morning."

The social worker likes to gallop her fingernails back and forth on the edge of the table. They weren't even a shade. She said to me, "Your mother might be on her way here right now."

Buddy said, "I told you twice already I called her. She was getting off work." You could tell he was talking to me by how disgusted he sounded.

I asked the social worker, "What if she was notified and didn't feel like coming? Does she have to? Does somebody make her?"

They both stared at me like there might be some ants crawling around in my eye sockets. Like my brain was infested with ants and if you poked around inside you'd stir up a lot of those white ones, the ones that are blind and just lie there.

Buddy couldn't think up something spiteful enough to call me that second. He said he'd better go on back to that trailer and see about things. But he didn't. The woman got irritated with us two and stood up like she'd wasted enough time on us already. She said, "Maybe I'll step down the hall for a minute."

When she left, Ramona Jetts came in there and braced both

her hands on the table like she was about to shove it up against me. Her reflection came all the way across to my hands. She said, "We don't know yet exactly how this changes your picture. We are looking into the legalities. And we are in touch with certain members of the family. I won't go into that now. Suffice it to say this is just the sort of thing I foresaw all along. And now somebody's got to pick up the pieces."

I could feel her looking me over. She said, "Do you need medical attention? Are you injured or ill?"

"No."

"Wait here until somebody tells you differently. Do you understand?"

I said yes. I hate that woman. I hate her for Tina and I hate her for me.

She left and Buddy said, "What did they ask you?"

"If I needed some medical attention."

"Not her, stupid. Them others. Them cops."

"What I saw."

"What did you say?"

"Nothing. I said I didn't know."

The only time your brother looks at you straight in the eyes is when he needs to see if you're insane or lying.

He goes, "You don't know shit," like that settled it. He goes, "Just stay out of it, since you can't be on our side. Maybe you would know how to act if you weren't off running wild in some car all the time. Maybe he wouldn't always be so aggravated to start with."

That's when a baby like me goes to bawling. I had plenty of chances to cry by myself for a day and two nights, and here I go holding it back till this exact second. Buddy felt of his toboggan. He spread his fingers around in it. He picked at the yarn where it pilled, like somebody checking real careful for ticks on a little kid's head.

Trish stuck her face in the door and said, "Just in case, we're looking into a place for you to stay, temporarily. I'll be right down the hall."

She couldn't tell anything about my eyes being wet, because of the hair in my face. She went away.

Buddy said, "I gotta go." His chair gave him trouble when he first pushed away from the table. He stood around for a second, thinking up some way to make me stop bawling. He decided to get me as mad as he could.

He goes, "If it was me I would stand by my daddy."

I yelled at him. I said, "What happened, then? What happened, since you know so much?"

He had to act so dramatic and grab holt of his chair.

He said, "She shot her own self. I told you already."

Maybe he did tell me that from the window. I don't remember. I said I'd wait and see what Momma said.

Buddy said, "How does *she* know? She was thirteen, fourteen hours away. I swear. You see something after it's already over, and run off and think like however you want to. You make me sick."

Buddy walked out, with me trying to think what to ask him. I knew better than to ask him "Why?" like a baby. He would say "Why?" was for babies.

I know my brother's a liar. He tried to lie out of everything, when he was living at home. He tried to lie out of F's on his report card. He tried to lie out of stuff he would hide in his room. He's trying to lie his way out of what happened. Just so he won't have to face up to Daddy.

That's how he does. Momma asked him one time did he have Grandma Whitley's darning needle. And of course he lied about it. He said, "What do I want with her needle?" I knew he lied. That was the same day he went out for basketball and blistered his feet. He had to walk everywhere on his heels. Buddy has such bizarre feet. His arches are so high his footprints come apart in the middle. I knew he lied about that needle. After supper I popped the lock with a bobby pin and swung the door open. I could smell alcohol where he was pouring it on his foot. The washrag was bloody. His foot was all bloody. The needle was stuck underneath his big toe. He was draining his blisters. He screamed bloody murder. I ran.

Momma said don't ever make ugly faces because one might freeze so you're stuck with it all of your life. Daddy's face froze when he looked up and saw me. Nobody's lying that look off his face. Nobody's lying that blood and those guns off the floor. Judith is bent like a fishhook. She never bent her own self in that shape.

After while they put me in this home for delinquents, which I deserved because of being one. On the way we were driving as slow as a hearse in this sorry old car like a Plymouth or something. I couldn't see anybody decent riding in one. Trish said, "Where did you sleep? Were you cold?"

She didn't act mean, just busy and easy to irritate. She asked where I'd been sleeping those nights I was gone. I told her I slept sitting up in a toolshed. I don't know why I told her that. Nobody made me. My fool brain was just in the mood to be cramped up somewhere like a toolshed, where it's dark and you can't budge an inch. I spent a long time awake in that toolshed. I tried to tell what things were by their shapes. I felt all over some metal and pipes for maybe an hour before I guessed it was a kitchen sink sitting upside down. I guessed a paint can from feeling how some of the color sets up in that slot by the rim. It makes a dry rubber O. I tried to pull out the O but I couldn't. It came apart. Clippers and hoe blades and jars were all easy to feel of, and chains and bent nails. There were some smells that came off on my fingers. I touched some oil on a lawn-mower motor and reached under the body and pulled out some dead, scabby grass that was stuck underneath. I thought the smell was my daddy. That was the smell I got sick on.

I said to Trish, "If Momma comes, don't tell her I slept sitting up." I grinned and made it sound queer, like a joke. She looked at me like, You're so bizarre.

When we got to the home it was old and all brick like a mansion. And there was this giant-size fire escape coming down from the roof of the porch. You can burn people up in a hurry, in someplace that old. The wiring goes bad and it's all the time catching on fire.

We pulled in the driveway and tried to park behind a van. It was blue. All of a sudden it started to roll back toward us.

I thought, Dead in a Plymouth. The back-up lights came blazing straight for us. Trish screeched us back in the street. Here comes the van bearing down. Trish tried to stand on the gas. We almost got mangled. The van turned around in the street. It bounced off the curb and tipped sideways a little. You could see it was full of delinquents. When the van slammed on brakes, all the heads leaned and wobbled like bottles of Coke in a carton.

Trish pulled over and said, "Get out and wait." I despised her for making me stand by myself in the yard with a sack full of clothes like a fool. Everything kept on turning just as unreal as it could. It was sickening. People go nuts when you were one of the ones in a killing. They put you someplace where nobody can recognize you. They try and make it look like a regular street where somebody normal could live. Then they go to swarming like a bunch of hornets when you knock down their nest with a broom.

I figured Trish would just dump me and leave me. She drove off a ways down the street and turned around, came back and parked by a tree. By then the van was backing up crooked. They just barely fit three of the tires on the driveway.

Patsy Edwards, the poet, was the first one to hop down from out of that van. I guess Ramona got sick of her poems and decided that Patsy belonged in a home. It was creepy how quick Patsy got up in my face, just like always, running her mouth. She was trying to peek in my sack.

"Are you the new girl, Libby? Are you going to tell me what happened? You're gonna hate it here. All but Fun Night. Fun Night's not bad when it's pizza. Are you gonna share my room?"

I said no.

The other girls acted so fierce walking by me. They carried the grocery bags as fierce as they could. At least they had food in theirs. They were talking so I couldn't hear what they said. Trish was a long ways away, walking fast. A woman got down from the van. She was little, with ringlets all over her head. She had a baby squirming down from her arms. She said,

"You've picked a good week to come. I've been to the store."
Like she was a regular mother.

Patsy said, "She can share my room."

I said, "I'm not going to be staying that long."

Nobody happened to be paying attention, though. They
were all watching Trish, who finally got there.

The woman said, "I told the girls, 'Hey, there's Trish! Let's
run 'er down!' And they said, 'Sure, why not?' So! How are
ya, Trish?"

Trish said, "Linda, you owe the county three bucks for the
gas we burned up parking."

Linda's shins were shaking. She was laughing all over. She
goes, "That van. If I forget to leave it headed out, I'll be sitting
there tomorrow morning in the pitch dark, late for the school
run, with a van full of sleepy girls, trying to back my way out
of a driveway I can't even see to a road I can barely remember
in this bomb I can't steer."

She grabbed hold of my arm. She said, "My goodness.
Come in."

The baby squirmed loose and took off up the yard. Nobody
even tried to stop it, which was a hideous way to act. Because
of how cold it was turning. And the grass was froze to a crisp
and the wind was that kind that goes down in your ears and
causes infections that rupture your eardrums. That baby fell
down in the grass, and its backbone was showing. I could've
told her. Its skin was so white on the backbone. That woman
went running to pull down its sweater.

6

Ruby had called ahead to the home, and when she parked in the driveway behind the blue van she found Libby and her grocery sack full of clothing sitting on the red-tile floor of the porch, hard by a stout wooden column, as if moored there. Without hesitating even long enough to remove the key from the ignition, she loaded Libby and the sack into her car, so that Libby sat watching her mother face Linda in the drive, both of them earnest but smiling, as though negotiating their respective jurisdictions.

Then Ruby drove them out of town. She drove with both hands high on the wheel, her shoulders squared to the seat back, and Libby saw from this rigor of posture and steering that she would not be expected to talk until they had put a lot of highway behind them. For more than an hour they climbed among mountains, into gorges and dark funnels of stone, where seeping striations of granite had layered the ice into delicate fringes. From the cuts they swung out onto balds and the shoulders of ridges, where the mountains compounded before them, toward the horizon, the great blue tumbling of earth and distance. The embrace and abandon of space made her feel she would always be winding her way among mountains, as a child knows she will always be dwarfed by adults, that she and her mother would never emerge, that they would wander forever, adrift in grandeur, lost.

At dusk they began to descend, yawning to clear pressure from their ears. In the foothills they stopped at a diner and ate buttered grilled-cheese sandwiches and sweet gherkins in a booth. An odd kind of time operated in the diner. An obese man began moving down the aisle between booths as they waited to order. Libby finished her sandwich in the time he stood shifting his weight in his aqua jumpsuit, holding his wallet open beside the cash register. He was a fixture for the course of their supper. They ate without talking, as though time hardly passed. Libby saw her mother staring toward a hall at the back of the room; her gaze rallied through pillowed, immobilized lids. Ruby said, "I haven't been this tired since you were born."

Long after dark, the highway turned north and the first ropy remnants of unmelted snow appeared on the shoulders. She closed her eyes and opened her eyes, and the snow patches grew into light throws and coverlets. The approaching headlights flickered like needles; impressions of snow—and of her mother steadfastly driving the car—knit and settled like quilting around her.

7

Rosco would answer and love how mature I can sound on the phone since I've been to Chicago. He would come get me and we'd go to ride. He would say, "How was Chicago?" I'd whisper "Big" in his ear so he can't even steer.

Maybe I act like a shithead. So what. I've been to Chicago and look where it got me. The first day I ever woke up in Chicago, here's what I heard. I heard something that sounded like dogs that were gagging and puking up grass in the bedroom. So I climbed off the sofa and went back to see. It was Grandma Whitley, clearing her throat. That's how I knew I woke up in Chicago. She gives me her look, like I need a good kicking, like she could get a sharper picture off a decent television set.

Here is the first thing she says to me in Chicago. She says, "Eat some of that oatmeal in the kitchen, before it sets up in the pot."

I go, "You eat it."

"You ought to learn how to eat oatmeal."

So I asked her where was Momma, and she acted like it was all my fault Momma drove herself to the point of exhaustion. She says, "Gone on to work without hardly shutting her eyes. What she's going to need is hospital bedrest. Where exactly did he shoot that woman? More than once, I imagine."

I said, "In the head."

She opened her gruesome mouth and showed her monster teeth and made a noise like a dog gagged on grass.

Momma told me we could go into the city on Saturday. She wore a skirt, but all I had with me was jeans. She said our limit could be forty dollars, which seemed like a plenty. We couldn't drive to the store, so we rode on a bus. Momma said, "It's strange to be going someplace without driving. I keep thinking we'll run off the road if I don't put my hands on the wheel."

I said I wished I could drive.

She said, "I didn't use to enjoy it that much. Now I'm taking to it all of a sudden. I never had to drive a car such a long ways before. Sort of piddled at it once in a while. Now I'm all broken in. My fingers keep remembering the wheel, you know it? I guess you never really learn to drive a car until you wear yourself out on one."

I said maybe so.

She goes, "I wonder if that's true for anything else." She was baiting me. Momma doesn't ever act as old as you expect her to act.

I said, "I don't know," but I did.

She said, "You better not." She yanked at a string of my hair. "I hope, anyway. Not yet, anyway." She was combing my hair with her fingers like I was somebody she wished she could tell.

Maybe one reason some people get married is so they can talk about sex with their mommas. But you can't imagine her face if she got wind of Rosco, and how he's been spelling my name on the roof with used rubbers. He's up to LIBB. Which proves how I'm living a lie.

Momma said, "I've got choir practice tonight. You want to come? You've got a pretty voice, Libby. You ought to use it."

I said we'd see, but we won't. I figured quick as I open my mouth in her choir they would know I've been living a lie.

She took me into this store that covered a whole city block. Forty dollars went as far as a handful of fingernail clippings. I couldn't get over how tremendous their selection was. It was a complete selection. I rode the escalators up and down, just to see it all, and wandered around in Lingerie. At first my eyes were popping out, but then we got silly. We broke out laughing. Momma said, "You look like a girl who woke up in the Garden of Eden," and she started me dreaming stuff up in my brain as usual. I had us pictured in there by ourselves, walking around naked where everything had that new smell to it, and we weren't sure what to call it, or what we were supposed to do with it, or what was safe to touch, or why there needed to be so much, and we kept being amazed that somebody made everything, and wondering why they would, and then this woman whispered very sexy in our ears and cordially invited us to attend a complete makeover on the mezzanine level, and for a second I thought she was talking like God, which shows how sacrilegious I can be when I feel like it.

And every place in this store they had special boutiques. And Momma said, "Let's go in this boutique," but I walked past a full-length mirror and saw how revolting I looked beside everything else. My jeans were so baggy, and my sweater was one of those cheap, sorry colors like you buy in a regular store, and my face was a fish face, and my hair was so stringy, and my feet looked like they had a smell to them. At first I thought somebody invented a mirror that makes people pathetic-looking so they have to buy clothes. But that's how I honestly look. I just don't have to face up to myself that much.

There were all of these girls who were my age, except for being a lot more mature. They were so fabulous. They had the most fantastic clothes and that fresh-looking kind of makeup. If one of them ever showed up at my school, all the regular girls would be eating their hearts out. Gorgeous girls are crawling all over Chicago. They don't hang around with their mothers, either.

Momma pulled me over to a mirror and stood behind me

and raised a sweater up to my shoulders. She said, "That's a good color on you."

It was copper with silver-looking threads running through it. I looked at the price. I said, "Are you serious? We've got *forty dollars.*"

She said, "Maybe we'll cheat on our limit a little."

I said, "Right. A whole forty-five. I'll still have to wear these same pants, and these shoes, and no makeup. One sweater's not going to make any difference. *Forty dollars.* Are you serious?"

She folded the sweater so careful, like it came off a baby or something. Her cheeks looked hot. The woman in the store took the sweater off her hands, like Momma didn't have any business with it in the first place. I started walking away. I rode down the escalator. The sides of it were chrome. Everything was chrome or one of those up-to-date colors, to prove how dinky you are. Then I stood by myself on the sidewalk, waiting for her to catch up, and it took me about thirty seconds to annoy a whole sidewalk, because you're standing around where everybody's trying to walk, and the horns sound so infuriated.

All the way back to the house we didn't talk, and I just stared out the window, watching different places I was probably too stupid to go, and at least that was a halfway realistic way to ride on a bus with my momma.

I'm sitting in that same cushion chair with my legs stretched out on the ottoman. I'm feeling the same little pills on the cloth under my arms. But I'm not looking out through our old kitchen door to the broom closet Daddy built custom. I'm looking slantways down a hall where Miles is coming out of the bathroom, combing his soggy black hair so it sprinkles his shirt.

He says, "Thought we could eat on the way. How's that sound?"

Momma says fine. She says a chicken pie is always better the second day anyhow, because the flavors have more time to mix. She's already dressed in her square-dancing outfit. It's a gingham dress that fits tight to her body and flares out in the skirt. Not many people look decent in gingham but Momma. Plus she's got the slim kind of ankles that do right in black slippers.

Grandma Whitley is back in her bedroom hoping out loud for some lucky number, and it wins and that really galls me. I figure we'll sit down to supper tomorrow night and try to eat warmed-over chicken pie and find out Grandma Whitley ate all but the crust while we were off at the square dance.

I don't want to go to a square dance because it's so country. Plus having zero to wear. I can feel myself start getting quiet—I don't know why. Momma hears me turn quiet. She says, "You doing all right?"

"No." The pills on the chair start feeling like ticks crawling under my arms, finding a good place to bury their heads. I mash my arms down as hard as I can, so they can't move around anymore.

"What's wrong?"

"How can you go off dancing after everything that's happened?"

She says, "Do you want to talk about it?"

"No."

"Are you clear on where everything stands? Your father was charged, and they've hired a lawyer. Buddy says first there will be a hearing, to see if the case goes to trial. He says there is a good chance the lawyer can show it was suicide. He thinks it might not even go to trial. They're going to try and keep you from having to go to court, since you weren't in the room when it happened."

I say, "You don't even care what happened."

"Of course I do."

"I've been here two days."

"I know that, Libby."

"And you haven't cared yet. I was in jail more than he was. What do you care."

She spreads the hem of her dress on the sofa. Whenever Momma gets dressed up, she sits like a little girl.

She says, "I've been allowing you some time. Yesterday I

thought you came close, on the bus. I just figured it was something we had to work up to. Sometimes when a person has a serious shock—"

"I wasn't shocked. I knew it would happen."

She says, "What do you mean?"

"I knew he would go nuts if he ever found out."

"Found out what?"

"Because he turns mean when he's jealous."

"What are you telling me, Libby?"

I try to say it sincere as I can. "She was going behind his back and everybody knew but he was blind to her. Then somebody saw her ride off in another man's car and told him about it, so he said he had proof but she denied it. She made him believe her side of the story. I guess because he was so much in love. Then after that he was driving someplace and he saw her in a car with his own eyes. He came home so jealous. I know you don't believe me but you haven't been around him lately like I have. He had it worse than you ever saw in your life. He wouldn't've left that woman in a million years."

I can't tell the first thing from Momma's face. She says, "Then what happened?"

"By the time he got home he was that close to killing somebody already. He made her admit she was living a lie. She said she was sick of living a lie, and she was in love with another man and she didn't care who knew it. He tried to make up with her and put his hands on her, but she said they were through. It sounded final, the way she said it. She said she had to follow her heart. He swore that if he couldn't have her nobody else would either. He loaded his gun to her face. After that he shot her but I didn't see it. But I heard a loud noise like a gun, and the smoke alarm went off, so that's how I knew to come out in the living room and look. By the time I saw her she was already dead. The only thing I know is, he did it for love. He didn't ever love anybody that much in his life, and that was the reason he did it."

I look up to see if she's crying and shocked, but nothing is wet on her face, and her eyes are both sorry for me instead of for her, which gets me confused and disgusted, and I cry so much worse when I'm like that, because if I could ever once tell something realistic maybe somebody would believe me and stay off my back.

We sit there so long I can't stand it. I say, "Why don't you just go on to the square dance."

She shakes her head. We sit there a little while longer. Miles comes back. He's so stupid he stares like a mule. His shirt is candy-apple red with pearl buttons. His pants are those stiff kind of Wranglers that need to be washed at least twice by theirselves. He says, "Y'all ready?" real country.

Momma says not quite. Miles stands around acting stupid for a couple of seconds and goes off in the kitchen and I bet he's eating chicken pie because it sounds like he's blowing on something hot like a crust. I can't believe she won't stop him from eating ahead of the rest of us.

She says, "Why don't you start again? If you want to."

I wait a long time, till I have a sick stomach like I always get when I'm telling the God's honest truth. I figure she's got to believe me for once.

"Really it was him that was cheating."

"That sounds about right. Then what?"

"She found out about him."

"What did she do?"

"She got drunk on some licker and fired off her gun. They got him for shooting his gun, but really he was just trying to scare her and make her stop. Like Buddy says. She went crazy, was all. She probably went crazy because she didn't want her own baby. But really a lot of people who used to be good-looking go crazy after while and commit suicide. Like Marilyn Monroe. Even if they're not having a baby."

"What did you do?"

"I acted like it was his fault, but really it wasn't. I don't exactly know why I acted that way. You can ask Buddy."

"I did."

I look at her feet and they're flat on the floor. She claps her hands on her knees and straightens her back like somebody who already had her picture made too many times and she doesn't want to sit still and smile anymore.

She says, "Maybe we'll talk some more later. Maybe some fiddle music will loosen us up."

I go, "You don't even believe me. I swear. I told you the truth. I can't help how it sounds."

"What scared you so bad that you ran off and stayed gone two days?"

I don't know what to answer. Who knows.

"Libby?"

"I don't know. Just get off my back about it. I wasn't lying. It was her own stupid self."

"You afraid and Buddy not—it was always the other way around. You agree on what happened, but you're acting just the opposite. If that made any sense I would know what to think."

"Buddy is not afraid. Who said he was always afraid?"

"At Christmas, he was. I could tell. I could just about see his daddy's grip on his shoulder. When this first happened, I was more scared for Buddy. I had a feeling he might be in trouble."

We sit there, waiting for her to stop thinking about Buddy. Christmas was the last time I saw her, before now. She came to Aunt Betsy's. Really the only thing that happened was, Aunt Betsy and Uncle Bob and my cousin Annie had their own separate Christmas together, then Buddy and Momma and me had our own separate Christmas together. We went ahead and used their same tree. Most of the presents were gone before our turn. Momma made out like she liked what I gave her. It wasn't worth shit, though, this thing that I gave her. It was plastic was all, not even china. The wrapping was cruddy besides, and Buddy's was better. I was acting so tough all through Christmas. Buddy said, "Don't act so tough about everything, you baby."

Momma starts talking again. "But I spoke to him on the phone and he was already in charge, arranging the bail, keeping his daddy sober, seeing to lawyers. The last time I knew Buddy to be that sure of himself was that time when he was just seven or eight and shined all our shoes. You remember? He lined them all up on a newspaper, and sat down behind them so I could take a picture of him with shoe polish up to his elbows, and streaks on his face like war paint, and all of our clean, shiny shoes. You don't remember that. You were too little."

"I saw the picture of him and the shoes."

"I wonder how long it will last. You think it will outlast a shoeshine?"

"I can't stand him thinking he can order me around."

She comes and sits on the ottoman and lays her hand on my legs. She's looking at me like I might be running a temperature. She goes, "What was it, really?"

I don't know what she expects. I wish I could move out from under her hand. It's so heavy, like secrets I don't want to tell on my daddy. But I go, "He was guilty and Buddy's a liar. I don't care what the law says. I don't care what anybody says. He can put on his regular face and act same as normal. But I saw how he really looks. He wanted her dead and she is. She was the one on the floor but he was looking at me, like why wasn't I dead. I might as well be. Something will turn him against me and then I'll be dead, same as her."

Then I start bawling, because anybody normal would know they were making things up and just shut up. That's how you know when you've used up your conscience and there's not any left. You can't tell the truth from a lie.

She waits a long time, holding my leg like it was a kitten or something with breakable bones.

She says, "I know, Libby. I've seen that face."

"You have not."

"Yes I have."

I am waiting and waiting. She stops holding my leg and lets her hand lie there. Then she stands up. She walks around the lamp where it's dark. She says something vicious to herself that I can't hear. Then she says louder, "That jackass. I know what he's guilty of. She lets him bring home his guns and his booze and his grudges, and wave them around. All of his instincts."

"I hope they electrocute him."

"Libby—"

"I mean it."

She lets things turn quiet. After a second she says, "The first time I saw that face, I thought he would murder me. It was like this invisible snake, one of those jungle snakes like a boa constrictor, used to crawl out of his pants pocket and wrap him up tight from his chin to his ankles, and start crushing his bones, so his face swelled up vicious and red. I ran straight to Betsy's and locked myself in. Later I stopped running to Betsy. It was such a big strain on her, trying not to gloat."

"Why did you keep going back to him? That's what I don't understand."

"I couldn't stay gone. It sounds funny to say it, but there was a time I didn't know who I was without seeing myself in his face. You know what I mean? If he ignored me, I didn't exist. If he showed me his ugly side, I was giving myself up for dead. But then if he smiled, I was so happy and proud. I just kept going back to him. I had to *know.* Is that how you're feeling now, Libby?"

"No."

"Are you sure?"

I don't answer. She stands in the dark for a while, and comes over. She sits on the ottoman beside me again. She sounds tired like a mother. "I've got plenty against him. But the truth is, the whole time we were married he never once hit me or handled me rough. Libby, he loves you. He might not do the right thing, but he wouldn't hurt you. It won't help anything for you to be afraid of your father."

"You don't know. I've done all kinds of stuff. You never did anything."

She laughs. I can't believe how she can just go ahead and laugh in the middle of everything. She goes, "What do you think, I was perfect? There is nothing you could possibly do to make him hurt you on purpose. Just try to forget how he looked. You're not the outlaw, Libby. It wasn't your fault."

"You don't know. Maybe I did something worse than you think."

"Like what, for example?"

I start acting hateful. "If I told you, you wouldn't believe it.

I'm a lot worse than you think. Besides, I don't have to tell you. He's the one who's got custody."

At least I can move once I start acting hateful. I head for the door. She comes up behind me and grabs ahold of my arm. I jerk it hard, but she won't let go. She tries to hug, but I won't let her. She turns me loose, and I sit on the sofa and make myself stop bawling, the same as before, when our sofa was home. I start feeling for stuff that goes in between cushions, like raisins or popcorn or something that Buddy stuck down there to hide. And that's how I make myself stop. At least I can stop. My hand is way deep in the sofa, feeling around. It's fairly clean under there.

She sits down near the end of the sofa. I don't look at her face but she blocks out some light from the lamp that was stinging my eyes. After a while she says, "We'll call off our square dance, tonight."

"What for? You're already dressed."

She watches me. "You want to go?"

"I'm not going to sit around here and listen to Grandma Whitley all night."

Momma is quiet, like we ran off the road in the dark and busted our heads and she doesn't know where in the world we wound up. Which is bad because neither do I. She says, "Miles? Did you already eat?"

I'm sitting on the washing machine, smoking, knocking ashes off behind the dryer when Momma comes back here and opens the door and stands with her back to the kitchen. Momma won't crowd in on top of a person. Momma can see when there's not enough room in a place.

I spit in my palm and put out my Winston. It sounds like a cuss word. I jump down, drop the butt in a bucket of garbage, and heave myself back on the washing machine. I never in my life weighed enough to dent something in, and she knows it. I'm the only person Rosco allows on his hood. I really miss that man. I miss him worse around my momma than anyplace else. I wish I knew why that was.

Momma doesn't say the first word. She just stands there in

her square-dancing outfit. Momma's not one of those people who want to rush home and change clothes.

I go, "Are you needing to put something in here?"

She says, "No."

I sit and stare at some shelves full of boxes and cans. It's the kind of food like people give to their church so the needy can eat on Thanksgiving. Food they're sick of looking at.

Momma says, "This is the first time I've ever had my own utility room."

I can't tell if she's proud or what. She sits down on the floor in the door, stretching her legs out in the utility room.

She says, "I'm glad you went to the square dance—and we finally got you out on the floor."

"That place was so country. I swear. How did you manage to move all the way to Chicago and find a place country as that? Why do you have to keep right on living in the past?"

"Am I? I kind of like it here. Seems like I know who I am here."

"Who's that?"

She grinned. "One of the best square-dancers in Chicago."

"Well, I'm not."

"What didn't you like about it? You did just fine after Miles showed you the sashay and bird-in-the-cage. He's a good dancer. Admit it."

"You know what I couldn't stand? That man who was calling the dances. He looked like the kind of person who's probably got a bunch of paper boys under his house, sawed up and buried in green plastic bags."

Momma laughs.

I go, "I mean it. And the other thing was you and Miles, the way you acted, like everything was going so perfect and you didn't have a care in the world."

"That was the music, Libby. We were just light on our feet."

"Then you sat there in the car on the way home and ate two separate Butterfingers just exactly alike. It reminds me of these couples who all the time wear the exact same T-shirts, like it proves they're in love more than normal."

"Libby." She says it like I'm being silly.

I study how the broom and the mop handle lean over top of each other back in the corner. When I look back, Momma's laid a white envelope down on her lap. She says, "I want you to listen all the way through, before you jump to conclusions."

"What?"

"I don't want you to leave us. Okay?"

"I never said I was leaving."

"I've been afraid you might try, later on. You're just as fretful and anxious—the same as you were when I said we were planning to move. I keep hoping that whatever possessed you to stay there is all in the past. Is it?"

I don't answer or look at her face. She turns the envelope over and over in her lap. The envelope has a thick look to it. She says, "These are some tickets back home. One is the bus to the airport. Then two for the airplane, on Piedmont. First down to Charlotte, then Winston. Don't lose them. You've never been up in an airplane. Knowing you, that wouldn't faze you. Your daddy carried you down to Winston that time so you could see a plane taking off on your birthday. Remember? The bus would be cheaper, but there are so many stops, and the waiting, and things that could happen. These are good anytime. You would have to call somebody you know from the airport, and wait a few hours. I put in a map with instructions and money for food. I'll show you where this envelope goes in the side-table drawer."

I look for her face.

"Libby, I told you, I don't want you to leave. This is in case. We can fix you a room. They have a good school here, and you would make friends in a hurry, knowing you. These tickets are my last resort. If you can wait till summer, you can use them to go for a visit, go and see Buddy or something. But if you can't, I don't want you hitchhiking or beating around in the city. Okay? Go on to Betsy or Buddy or even your father, where I know you're all right."

I keep looking at these wood shelves that are painted on top but not on the bottom, and the little drips stuck to the edge like dead bugs.

She says, "I hear all the time about girls who run off and

don't tell anybody where they're going because they're afraid somebody will try and stop them. Maybe if they had a safe way to travel they wouldn't be missing."

I don't answer.

"Is that too much to ask, since I paid for these tickets?"

We sit there long enough to get good and quiet, except for the backs of my running shoes, bumping on the front of the washer, not loud. Sometimes you don't feel like stopping your feet, once they start making noise.

She says, "Your grandmother is going to die."

She says it so desperate it stops me from kicking. It sounds like somebody had to hold a razor blade to her throat to make her talk.

"She is not." Momma keeps nodding until I say it again— "She is not."

"Why would I say such a thing?"

"I don't know."

"Not soon. Not this spring. But she is."

I start bumping my heels on the washer again, hearing that tin-metal sound.

She goes, "You don't really remember her, do you?"

"What are you talking about? I've been in the same house with her."

"You don't remember when she was more like herself."

"I'm sick of having to remember how all of these people used to be. When I get old I'm going to take poison. Old people ruin everybody's life."

"You came down sick when you were a baby and coughed and cried for three solid nights. The next night I was so tired I called Momma at eleven o'clock and she got out of bed and came over and rocked you all night while the rest of us slept. It was the best night's sleep I've had since I was a girl."

"I didn't ask her to hold me."

"I'm in between. You have your whole life ahead. She hasn't got but a little bit left."

"People deserve what they get."

"What are you talking about?"

"I said, 'People deserve what they get.' "

"Who told you that?"

"She spies and acts like a witch and look at what happens. Judith stole Daddy and look at what happened. I accused Miles and look at what happened."

She stands up fast. "You stayed with your father. Which is what you were dying to do." She walks past me and taps the envelope on the door glass while she stares at the carport. I wish I had her kind of hips, so a skirt would flare decent. I might wear a dress if I did.

I go, "Why are you getting so ticked?"

"Having it cross my mind when I saw you two dancing."

"You should've known I would lie."

"Where all have you been, since I left?" She counts off the places, and her fingers come out of her fist one at a time and touch the glass. "That trailer, and running away, and in jail, and that home, and where else? I've never been to a single one of those places. I've never seen anybody who was shot. I can't even pretend to imagine, and I'm supposed to be your mother."

She keeps looking through the door glass. "When you were little, I thought if I couldn't see the top of your head in the bathtub you would drown. Tonight I felt silly for keeping my eye on your head over top of his shoulder."

"You called me common, that time I accused him. I don't care. So what if I am common?"

"I said it was common to tell such a tale."

"Same difference. You said it about me."

"All that proves is, a person falls back on her raising the second she loses her temper. When I was your age, people called a girl common if she used that kind of language. At the time I didn't have any way of knowing what a useless word it was going to turn out to be."

"I'm sorry I ever went to that dance in the first place. I wish I never came."

"I wish I could've gotten you sooner. The first thing you needed was loved ones around you, not wandering off by yourself, letting it work on you. I was afraid to imagine you out there alone, at night, in the dark—"

I'm not going to tell her. Banging my feet's a lot better. When I went on the roof by myself I was peeling up pieces of tar paper. I kept seeing his face and her dead. It got stuck in my brain so I smelled it and felt it, all black and peeled off like old roof. No matter how many pieces I peeled off and scattered around, there was still all these layers and layers. Which proves how my brain turns perverted and freezes on something when nobody stops me.

Momma says, "Now that you're here, we're not exactly sure how to act, are we? All I thought about was getting you out of that place, away from that—that mess. Mothers are made so they come to the rescue, you know it? But I can't be driving you up and down highways the rest of your life."

At least I don't have a bunch of wet clothes lying inside of here, all tangled up with the rest of their washing. It's gross to think about all of their soaking-wet underpants touching and twisting together with mine. My feet make a good empty sound on the washer.

"Why don't you stay long enough to get settled? Give yourself time. That little town and your father—it's not the whole world. You hear me? It's up to him to make all of this right, not you. Okay?"

Like a horse on a tin-metal bridge—bongety-bongety-bongety-bong.

"I wish there were maps for where we are going from here, you know it? I will do the best I can, though, I guarantee you that. If all it takes is hard work, we'll be happy day and night. Like driving or keeping awake, I can manage. When I was driving, I might have been a little too proud of myself, though. I thought, This proves I can do without sleep if I need to. Nobody has to take over."

8

On the plane from Chicago an elderly couple offered Libby a ride up the mountain. "We're headed right past there," they said when she told them the name of her town. "We can just take a detour."

Now she was glad to be sealed in their late-model Buick, touching its wine-colored plush. She was glad to be somewhere cleanly and recently made.

As they rode through the foothills, the woman, who sat in the backseat with Libby, opened her purse and extracted some Polaroid pictures. The first one she laid on the cushion showed a dark strand of buildings at the margin of cornfield and sky. "That is my home," the woman said.

Libby liked seeing the world in this way—indirectly, and at considerable distance, the neatly squared pieces appearing for only a moment on the fine, cordial plush of the car.

Soon they were climbing the mountains, the Buick beginning to labor. The man pressed a button; his window whirred open. Libby looked up from the photographs and shivered. The compartment had filled with the odors of humus, rhododendron, and cold, moistened rock.

The man inhaled. "I love that good smell of the mountains," he said, pushing the button and sealing them off again. To Libby, the odors remained like a taint on the air and the plush.

The woman said, "Here's my favorite." She laid another picture on the cushion. Its background was dark, almost black. The flash had surprised a small crowd of exuberant faces. Libby tried to imagine herself in the dark with those people, smiling and feeling the flash light them all up at once.

"My children and some of their cousins," the woman said. She retrieved the photograph and replaced it with another: a

small boy and two girls. There were many arms reaching into
the frame from above. There were hands on the heads of the
children, hands on their shoulders, fingers at play on their
sleeves. The children were smiling. Libby could not imagine
whose hands were attached to these children. She could not
imagine herself connected at so many points to the people she
knew.

"Those are my grandchildren," the woman said. "I am their
grandmother."

Libby glanced at her, trying to reconcile the look of this
calm, gentle woman with that word, "grandmother." She
could not. The woman put the photographs away and began
working with needles and thread on a cloth. The pattern was
stitched and established: a horse jumping over a fence.

Libby looked out of the car into afternoon shadows. The
road rose through gashes and cuts in the granite; it seemed
to be gouging and boring its way through the earth, explor-
ing the source of what drew her back home. She couldn't
explain why she was leaving Chicago, couldn't fashion her
reasons in words. She had felt only the necessity of escape,
of being engaged in this journey—her tickets all ready and
waiting, her course all laid out. "I need action," she had told
herself, riding the bus to the airport. "I need Rosco. And
Tina. I need to *go*."

The note she had left for her mother was simple: "Momma,
I'm not like you think." Libby believed this was true. In the
strange, remote place called Chicago, she had found herself
drawn more and more to that scene on the floor of the trailer,
intrigued with the notion of what she'd become: the dead
woman's stepdaughter; the killer's favored child; the renegade
outlaw; the chaos come down from the roof. This was the role
she could see herself playing. How could she ever live up to
her mother? Or sing in her choir? Who would she be in that
household? She couldn't think of her clothes in their washer,
couldn't spin and entwine with those dancers. She knew she
couldn't come clean.

Later the Buick swung down through the passes and blind,
darkened curves to the bowl where the town lay in wait. They

reached the bypass at three forty-five on a Monday, the first day of March. Libby asked them to drop her at an Omelette Shoppe on the bypass. The woman said, "Are you sure this is the right place to leave you?" The man left the Buick running, got out, and lifted her grocery sack full of clothes from the trunk. He said, "Good-bye and good luck." The woman said, "Are you sure we can't take you home?"

When they were gone, Libby used a pay phone inside the restaurant. People at the counter watched her set her sack in the corner and dial the phone. She realized that some of them were staring at the airline's ticket folder, which protruded from the seat pocket of her jeans. She pulled the folder from her pocket and turned away from them, under the privacy hood of the phone. Rosco answered. She said, "You miss me?"

He said, "You go off?"

"Yeh."

"Where to?"

"Chicago." She opened the folder and picked at the staple attaching her boarding pass. "Can you come get me on your way to work?"

"You know what time it is? Where am I gonna take you 'tween now and then?"

"I just need to see you a minute. I've been gone to Chicago, is all."

He said, "I'm in a hurry."

"I came on a jet."

"Unh-hunh."

"You know if Tina is back?"

"She been gone? I ain't heard tell of her lately."

"When can I see you?"

"Maybe Sunday night."

"What about sooner?"

"Don't be putting this pressure on me. I put pressure on my ownself. Don't you be putting it on me."

She hung up and walked into town. It was cold. She was sick of being out in the cold. When she reached the home, the blue van was in the driveway. She walked to the porch and pushed the doorbell and heard it chime deep in the house. She heard feet bounding down the stairs inside. Linda opened the door, her ringlets escaping her scarf on all sides. "Libby?"

"I decided to turn myself in."

PART FOUR

PROBABLE CAUSE

J

The swelling on Judith Shreve Lampert's right temple was the size of a fig, purple except for a scorched black corona surrounding the hole and a luminous, transparent pink on the skin, a blush from the carbon monoxide discharged from a muzzle. The bullet had angled back down through her brain, punching a small, stellate plug from the bone just behind her left ear. Both the entrance and the exit were small, but the brain was badly cavitated, the effect of a bullet speeding through soft tissues, setting up a partial vacuum that oscillates with diminishing amplitude, leaving a long, funnel-shaped void.

The deputy stood in a kitchenlike room, where the coroner, Timmons, was telling Soffit, the district attorney, that the wound was ambiguous.

"Don't count on much from her," Timmons said.

The body lay on a table before them, exposed as the root of a turnip.

"Give me what you've got," Soffit said, folding his arms.

Timmons pointed his pencil at the swollen right temple. "This big ol' lump. It's what you'd expect from a suicide," he said. "A tight seal from the muzzle forces discharge up under the skin and gives you a gas blister. But there's no muzzle print. And you'd figure on more of a burn 'round the wound, if the muzzle's that close. Judging from the powder burns alone, I'd say the gun was ten, maybe twenty inches away. Too durn far for suicide. And the swelling, well, there's a lot of blood in there—a hemorrhage—and that might explain it."

"So it's murder, then, V.J.," Soffit said. "That's what you're telling me."

Timmons shook his head and tugged at the small tuft of soft

white hair that grew in the hollow just under his Adam's apple. "Nossir, not necessarily."

Soffit shook his head, stepped past the deputy on his way across the hall. The deputy followed him into a tiny office, where Soffit picked at a thin strip of loose veneer on a corner of Timmons's desk. " 'Don't count on much from her,' " he muttered.

Timmons and Soffit were in the habit of working on each other—two men so similarly fat and unpleasant that they could neither like one another nor leave one another alone. They were a fixture at the drugstore every Wednesday morning, drinking coffee together. They grumbled into their cups about the town, the government, the sports page—never meeting one another's gaze. They were outsiders who had followed professions sure to keep them that way, Soffit because he prosecuted the hometown folks, Timmons because he delved into their victims.

Timmons appeared in the door of his office, his hands hanging open at his sides. "You know what gripes my ass about this town?"

He was looking at the deputy but addressing the district attorney. He often advanced his arguments through a neutral transmitter.

"It's the way you have to get here," Timmons said. "You have to come low-gearing-it down that damn straight drop, riding your brakes, and then when you finally get to the bottom, where are you? You go squeezin' through that blasted shady curve between the creek and the cliff. You come out of the shade, half blind from the sun. And what do you see first? Three creosoted poles and three old sheet-metal signs. 'The Elks Welcome You,' 'The Lions Welcome You,' and 'The First Baptist Church Welcomes You.' They are exactly the same sorry signs that stood there twenty years ago, the first day I ever saw 'em. Same number of rust spots. Even oxidation is not required to attain the level of proficiency here it does other places. What's a man supposed to make of rusted welcome signs? Been living in this town for twenty years, I'm still not sure if anybody ever intended to welcome me or not."

"What about this murder case of mine?" Soffit said, irritably.

Timmons turned to the deputy. "What are you doing here, Harry? You on this case for some reason?"

Soffit said, "I brought him with me. He's got his own reasons. Maybe he'll see what we miss."

Timmons slipped sideways past a filing cabinet and sat behind his desk, filling his cheek with tobacco. "Not necessarily murder," he said, chewing. "She did fire the thirty-eight, the one that killed her, at least once. The lab found its powder and metal traces on her hands. Hairs were clubbed and singed."

"Then it's suicide," Soffit said.

Timmons tilted his head and spat into his waste can and made a clucking sound in his cheek.

"What, then?" Soffit said.

"There were traces of powder and metal from the thirty-eight on his hand too. Not much, but it was there, along with signs of the other gun, the forty-five."

"You mean they both fired the same goddamn gun?"

"It would almost look that way."

"What are you telling me? Do I have a case or not?"

"It's inconclusive."

"You believe he killed her?"

"Yes."

"Why?"

"The angle of the bullet. It was not your typical suicide. She would have had to hold the gun like this"—he lifted his pencil and pressed its point against his right temple, just above the brow—" and that's awkward. Do you see how high my elbow is, high and forward? How clumsy that would be, squeezing off a round? It just ain't your natural suicide."

"Then that's my murder case, the angle of the bullet. Should be about the right angle for murder, him being taller."

"Medically, though, it's still got to be inconclusive."

Soffit counted points on his fingers. "The angle of the bullet, the traces on his hand, the fact that pregnant women don't blow their own brains out—"

Timmons laughed. "Where'd you hear that?"

"They don't in this county's notion of things, Doc. The charm of motherhood, you know. It'll play real sweet. Give me the details. Boy? Girl?"

"A girl, sixth or early seventh month, I'd say."

"Healthy?"

"I didn't work her up, Link. But my guess is, likely no. Not healthy."

"How do you know?"

"The alcohol in that woman's blood. She was dead drunk. If she'd been drinking thataway long, that little young-un didn't ever have much of a chance."

"But these—birth defects—did you actually see them? Were they actually visible? I mean, she wouldn't have known about that yet, would she?"

Timmons shrugged. "You know, a defect doesn't mean a hill of beans in utero. Ever think of that? It's only after we get born we get the bad news, learn we ain't perfect." He snickered and spat in his waste can.

"Next you'll be telling me he did the kid a favor."

"That would be a cynical view, Link. I don't take the cynical view. You want my view, it's case to case. This case, I'll say inconclusive. Where's that leave you?"

"Nowhere special," Soffit said. "On my own."

Later that week, the deputy showed up at the trailer, and Lampert stood out on the stoop with him.

"Jake, I seen a truck I didn't recognize and no lights on in the place," the deputy said. His flashlight was aimed at their feet. "Thought I better stop and look see."

"Old Lady Shreve had the power shut off. Thinks she wants her trailer back."

The deputy played his light over cartons and bundles in the bed of the pickup. "Guess you're not carting off nothing of hers—I mean your wife's."

Lampert wiped his mouth with the back of his hand. "How do you mean, Smiley? Hers that she came with, or hers that was mine that she took, or hers that I paid for, or hers that was ours?"

The deputy snapped off the light. "You had that bottle out long?"

"You want some? Come on in and sit down."

The trailer swayed as they walked to the kitchen and sat at the table. Lampert poured whiskey into two sticky glasses. "Take a drink," he said. "Whiskey goes down better in the dark."

They drank quietly. Then the deputy said, "Was down to the coroner's office with Soffit. They didn't have what he wanted. Timmons said medically speaking it would be inconclusive."

"You volunteering this news for me, Smiley?"

"It's nothing your lawyer can't get for hisself."

Lampert stood and jarred the table. The deputy grabbed for a handhold on his chair.

Lampert was moving around in the kitchen. "You kind of like having this knowledge about me. Something you figure I need."

The deputy hesitated. "I just seen that truck full of boxes and bedclothes and reckoned I might better stop."

"Oh." Lampert set his glass in the sink and tried the tap, which was dry. "Old lady shut off my water. Need to leave her some piss in the toilets."

The deputy heard him kick a box on his way to the bathroom, heard his stream in the bowl, his zipper and feet in the hall.

Lampert sat down at the table again. "What I need is a character witness. You like my character, Smiley?"

"Ain't doing yourself no good, showing up drunk at her funeral."

"Buried my wife today, Smiley. Remember?"

"If people seen you like this they would say you can't live with your conscience."

Lampert stood by the table. "You representing the county here, Smiley? You come to straighten me out? Why don't you teach me to hit, while you're at it? You ever ache for a woman? You know what it looks like on a man? I doubt it."

"Hell—"

"Looka here, Smiley." Lampert laid his right hand on the table—fingers cramped stiff and clawlike toward the palm. "Still got the feel of her in there. Right there. Your hand ever done you that way? You ever had one mashed permanent into your guts?"

The deputy didn't say. The topic was over his head.

Lampert removed his hand from the table.

The deputy said, "Hell, there's not a man I know who don't wish he was eighteen or nineteen, so's he could act like a kid."

"Except you. You like 'Deputy' better than 'Smiley.' I better look someplace else for a character witness. You might rather convict me, see if that squared us for what you missed out on."

"That's a bunch of durn drunk talk."

Lampert shoved his chair against the table and the deputy's glass fell on its side. They listened to it rock. Lampert's breathing calmed. He sat down and poured more whiskey into the deputy's glass.

"Lawyer says what I need is a couple of character witnesses. Maybe a female."

"Where you aim to get one of those?"

"I can think of one already. She's a widow."

"What kind of widow?"

"How many kinds do you know?"

"I meant to say 'Who?' "

"Miz Gregson. One of the recent kind."

"Don't know a widow by that name."

"Ice storm hit her, back two years ago. Big spruce keeled over flat 'cross her driveway right as she's trying to go see her husband. Man was dying of cancer. All the neighbor men working. She looked under 'Saws' in the yellow pages and wound up with me. Wanted to know would I bring her a chain saw and teach her to use it. It tickled me she planned to saw up that tree by herself. So I drove up and took her a Stihl and we stacked nearly half-cord of spruce on her porch."

"Least it was spruce and not heavy."

"Set us some lunch on the table. She was admiring her wood pile and that put her on the subject of her porch, which Gregson was meaning to close in with glass, so they could use it more days of the year. She said it looked like he wouldn't get to it. I saw she was going to cry, and looked for a way to get up and leave her alone, so I went out on the porch and paced it off and sketched it all out on my napkin, so I could show her where all the studs and sills would go. When she stopped crying she came out to see what I was drawing. I told her to figure on casements. A casement will give you the best kind of seal, because wind wants to push the sash back to the frame. You aware of that, Smiley?"

"Don't believe I ever was."

"She asked me if I wanted the job, but I said I couldn't work it in, right then. That showed some character, Smiley. It's against my nature to turn down a handsome woman."

"I heard."

"She might make a fine-looking character witness."

The deputy sipped at the whiskey. He said, "What're you doing for work? I don't see you back down at that garage."

"Early to say. Might get back in the horse business."

"Horse business. What do you know about horses?"

"Hired on with Robey, when I was eleven. Currycombed up on my tiptoes. He taught me to ride. Now Old Man Robey's got old. Needs a man for his gaited stock, take 'em around to the shows. Horse shows play all the same parks I used to, Smiley."

"Draw the same loudmouth drunks too."

Lampert laughed.

The deputy pushed back his chair and stood by the table a moment. "You know a reason the angle was funny?"

"What angle's that?"

"How she held the gun, so the bullet went down at an angle."

"I'll have to ask my boy. Buddy saw more of what happened."

The deputy began groping his way toward the door.

"Here," Lampert said.

"Yeh?"

"Take that flashlight and piss in the toilet back there, 'fore you go. Don't hold back. Let 'er fly."

2

Betsy the Christian says, "Here, take a jar lid and sit on the steps." She keeps me shut in this basement when I need to smoke. She doesn't want any smoke where she breathes. I have to wash out my jar lid whenever I go back upstairs.

All that woman cares about is church and birds. She's got feeders stuck to half her windows just so she can have some birds around to bicker over seeds. It's revolting how her high-heel shoes keep banging dotted lines across the kitchen. She won't even take her high heels off between preaching Sunday morning and preaching Sunday night.

Bap, bap, bap. Like Buddy used to bounce marbles off my head. Bap, bap, bap.

She comes and sniffs at the door to the basement. Maybe I'm trying to burn up some boxes or high chairs or Grandma Whitley's mahogany. Betsy hollers at me through the door. "Ten minutes." She goes bap-bap-bap and starts banging her pans. Babytalking some of her birds.

She's so high and mighty on account of having her the only basement in our family. But she had to marry into one. And whenever some of her relations move, they put what they can't use down here.

This is what I wish. I wish we had some more people down in this basement. All of the different kinds of people Betsy the Christian couldn't stand to have my cousin Annie copy after. I'd like to look over there in that corner that's dark and see somebody sitting around in that chair, the one that's got arms like a throne. I'd like to see a big grin and hear Tina say, "Get up from there, monkey."

One time I saw in this movie how these colored people went to live in the jungle. And they all drank poison. Pretty soon they died. After that it got so hot their bodies bloated up and turned this dead-black-purple color I could almost smell by looking at it. They were piled all over. There was a fly on one eyelid.

I can't stand to have this jungle wood around me. Somewhere in here is a circle I made with a tea glass when I was a kid. It left a little round ghost on the table. Grandma Whitley whacked me with a hairbrush for it.

I heard her cough all the way from Chicago when they called on the phone. Betsy said for me to pick up in the kitchen. I picked up and near about went deaf from the old woman hacking right straight in my ear. I said, "Who's this?" Like I didn't already know.

After a while Momma came on the phone, and at least Momma's voice was down low. I mainly told her stuff she didn't need to hear. Like Cousin Annie tagging after me. So Momma asked me was Annie like having a sister. And I said not especially. She said, "I remember how you used to want one."

When I was little I decided I would die unless I got a sister.

On the phone Momma said, "Here you'd come with all your pockets sprouting Green Stamps."

That's because of me not having sense enough to know that Daddy was just talking when he said that you could get sisters with Green Stamps. Suckers who fool easy always deserve what they get.

Like for example I would fatten me up some stamp books just as proud as could be. And whenever I would get one full we ate ice cream. Daddy always likes to celebrate with something sweet. I would hang around the filling station and the store and beg for stamps until the workers ran me off. I licked stamps until I got addicted to the taste. It was like wanting a sister so bad I could taste it. Grandma Whitley says I got brain damaged licking all those stamps and that might be some of my problem. Which is just how she treats me.

When I got up twenty books, Momma finally said you can't buy a little sister with Green Stamps.

Betsy starts screeching at me through the door. "Five minutes!" Betsy loves putting a time limit on me. That's how she is about Daddy and all. It just drives her so nuts for me to be thinking things over. She says, "Reach some decision." She says I can't keep on putting him off when he wants to come see me. She's getting fed up with making excuses for me on the phone.

She screeches at me through the door. "Elizabeth?"

"I heard you."

I guess that kind of horrible voice wants to run in a family. For example, Aunt Betsy sounds just like her mother the witch-face, who thinks she has to yell whenever it's long-distance. I said hello in my regular voice and Grandma Whitley went straight in to hollering at me.

"How do you like it at Betsy's?"

I said I had my own room and the house had a whole lot of space.

She goes, "Well, I thought I would speak for a minute. You left off from here and nobody around to tell you good-bye."

I didn't say much. Betsy came in the kitchen and picked that second to unload the dishwasher.

Grandma Whitley said, "I was gone to a get-together that morning."

"Okay."

"Well, I told Betsy you could stand a few sweets if you clean off your plate, since you turned out so skinny. And see to it she doesn't sell off my furniture. Likely you'll want it whenever you've got your own home."

"Okay."

"Well, I better go on. You dress better and pay attention in that school. Hear me?"

"Okay."

"Well, good-bye, here's your momma."

That's when Momma first came on the phone, while Aunt Betsy was lining her glasses up straight on the shelf. Like always, I turned just as mean as a snake. I don't know why I always turn mean on my momma, and make out like I'm better off she's not around. We said hi and she wanted to know how we were, me and Buddy. I said fine. She said how did I like it at Betsy's. I said they sure had a nice house and all, and how my room was air-conditioned, if it ever got hot. I said there was plenty of room for my stuff.

Momma didn't say much.

I said, "I'm sorry I had to use up those tickets."

She said, "Long as you're fine."

I said, "It was a hard decision."

"I guess it was."

Aunt Betsy turns her glasses so the monograms all face out the same way. Why, I don't know. People can't see how the glasses are facing when Betsy shuts the cabinet.

I go, "But I knew they had all of this room, and a bigger house here close to the rest of my family. And my friends and my school. And the main thing I was worried about was you-all not having much room."

"I guess."

"Plus I really needed to live where I don't have to make all these huge decisions. Because really I guess I'm too young to be making all these tremendous decisions."

"You are?"

"So this way I can live someplace strict where I have to act right, and that way I'll probably build up my conscience some more so I stay out of trouble."

"If you think so."

"Plus Aunt Betsy doesn't have to go to work, so she can be around in case something happens."

She didn't say anything.

"You said I'd wind up here and I didn't believe it. But I did, and I guess it'll be for the best, once I get used to it. Like tonight we had scalloped tomatoes, and I found out you don't have to eat those with sugar because they taste fine without it. Did you know that? We always put sugar on ours."

"Libby?"

"Hunh?"

"What about your father?"

"What about him?"

"Did you talk to him yet?"

"No."

"Are you?"

"I don't guess."

She waited a second. Then we talked about Annie and stuff and Momma said, "Let me know if you need anything."

"Okay."

"When you see Buddy, tell him to call me collect. I have a time getting up with your brother."

"Okay."

She said she missed me and all, then she wondered if Betsy was handy, like she couldn't hear Betsy stack plates all the way to Chicago. I gave Betsy the phone and looked in the dishwasher for some excuse to hang around her and listen. There wasn't much left to unload but the silver, so I got all the knives out as slow as I could, and laid them as neat as I could in the tray so the cutting sides aimed to the right. Betsy stood off to one end of the room by herself and said, "How is she?"

It's amazing what-all I could tell from one side of a phone conversation. Like Momma gets money from Betsy for keeping my grandma. Like Betsy sure wishes she knew what became of that money. Like Betsy would save in the long run to take us all in at one time. Like maybe I need a firm hand for a while. Like no she is *not* talking *down*. Which is just like two sisters, to fuss all the time. When Aunt Betsy hung up she stared at the spoons for a while, and took them out one at a time, like maybe I left all my fingerprints on them.

Betsy should drill her some holes in Grandma Whitley's mahogany dressers and make her some places for birds. She could nail dressers to both of her trees and start some hotels for her birds. The birds could be perching on handles and building their nests in the drawers. Then if the Ticket was here, she could reach up and hatch her a Bud. And Tina would see me climb up in the tree and say, "Get down from there, monkey."

Betsy says, "Tweetsie eatsie seedsie weetsie?"

The basement door opens and Annie comes down. These steps are steep for a kid. Annie holds onto the rail with both hands and comes sideways. She can't talk because her mouth is full of bear's ear. That's the way she carries him when she needs both her hands. Halfway down she stops and takes the bear out of her mouth.

"Hi," she says.

I say, "Hi."

"What are you doing?"

"Having a cigarette."

"Oh." She pulls a little bear fuzz off her tongue and sits on the step. Betsy'll croak when she sees dirt on Annie's tights. Annie goes, "Are you coming upstairs?"

"Yeh, I guess so."

"Do you want to see my farm set?"

"Sure."

Betsy comes to the door. She says, "Annie, come up here, right now," and goes away. Bap, bap, bap.

Annie gets up and puts the bear in her mouth and starts climbing. She closes the door. I can hear Betsy start straight in to griping at Annie for getting so filthy down here in the basement with me.

Betsy is working herself up to sending me back to that home. She holds it over my head day and night. Like it's any worse than this place. She's only had me three weeks and she's ready to send me back. I know she's already dreading my Easter vacation. She doesn't want me around her all day.

Betsy says I've got a choice to make: her place or back in that home. Some choice. And Linda—the woman who works in that home—said they can't accept me for longer than one or two nights at a time on account of me not being sentenced to a permanent placement. And Betsy the Christian can't stand me around her unless I act perfect. So it looks like I've got to either act better or worse. Those are my choices.

Bap, bap, bap. Betsy says, "Supper," and listens. I take a drag on my Winston. She opens the door to the basement. "Elizabeth?"

"What?"

"Supper!"

"In a minute."

"Now!" She slams the door.

I stub out my Winston and set my right foot on the bottom step. Every time I climb a step I call Betsy something filthy to myself, until I get the steps all named.

When I get upstairs of course she stares at my face to see

what my attitude is or whether I came to some kind of decision about Daddy while I was out of her sight. Then of course she orders me to wash my hands. So I come on back to the bathroom and run the fan so I can have another cigarette. What I hate is how she orders me around and thinks I need to be so perfect. There's about a zillion things I'm not allowed to do but just three things I am: go to church, go to school, do my chores. And of course those are the ones I'm never any good at.

She's not anything like Momma. Momma, she would let me use her makeup. She would slip me money for a magazine or something. She could tell when I better go off by myself. But Betsy and Grandma Whitley, they think they're supposed to keep me busy all the time. That's something else that can run in a family. If I'm off by myself one second, they get so bent out of shape. Betsy claims I needed some closer attention a long time before. I knew she was trying to blame me on Momma. She figures Momma screwed up and so now I am all up to her.

Betsy starts pounding the door. "Elizabeth!"

"What?"

"Supper!"

"I'm on the pot."

She stands there a minute and goes off.

I wish Uncle Bob was home this weekend. Bob's not bad, if he was ever here. Mostly he's off selling furniture. Sometimes he's so far away he can't come home on weekends. At least that's what Aunt Betsy says. Betsy says that wherever he is, he always finds a way to go to Sunday service. I'll just bet. I bet he eats a lot of cabbage too.

Last weekend he was home. He needed to string a wire across the attic for a ceiling fan. He was going to crawl around up there himself but I said I would, since I'm little. He said okay. Betsy didn't like it one bit. She takes everything so serious. She kept saying I would stick my foot down through the ceiling. Bob boosted me up through the trap door and I crawled around on the boards in the dark until I found the light cord. There's this insulation piled between the boards and it's the kind that's light and crumbles up like snow. It stuck to my hands, and my hair was dragging in it. Bob called me and I crawled over to the trap door and looked down. He started telling me about the wire but when he did some insulation fell out of my hair and landed on his face, and that just cracked us up. Every time I shook my head it snowed on Uncle Bob.

Finally I crawled off across the ceiling and found the little wire wiggling up through a hole at the end of the house. It tickled me, seeing it wiggle. I said, "Boo." He said, "Boo you." I pulled the wire and started crawling, trying to balance and not fall through. He was telling me the way to go by tapping at the ceiling with the end of a mop handle. But when he tapped I felt it tingle in the boards and that just drove me nuts. It was like the boards were giant ribs and they were my ribs and he was goosing them with the mop handle. I would crawl two feet, and bap, I got another poke. I had to stop and hang on with my hands and feet to keep from falling through. I could hear him laughing too, and Annie was racing around the house squealing. Betsy yelled at her. The more he tapped, the harder I laughed. I thought I would croak up there, and fall down dead through Betsy's ceiling.

All through supper it was time to treat me like somebody's scabby disease. Annie didn't dare talk to me, mad as Betsy was. Annie's bear was in her lap. She had her napkin spread over it. Pass the ham and piss on Libby. All because I didn't want to go to church. Betsy sat there in her white dress with the gray pinstripes and her black patent-leather belt and the black-and-gold earrings, and got a rash on her neck from despising me so bad. She kept scratching at it. She had church wrote all over her.

I said, "I ain't going."

"Yes you are."

"You can't make me."

"Yes I can."

"You're not my mother." I scraped my spoonbread back in the bowl.

She got up from the table and grabbed my elbow. "You're coming with me, young lady." She pulled me up and dragged me down the hall. Annie didn't dare leave her seat. She held onto her bear.

Betsy hauled me back to her bedroom and sat on her bed and tried to heave me over her lap. I jerked away. She hung on to my wrist and yanked. I yanked back and hurt her some. She swung her hand at me and grazed my hip. I jerked hard and she turned loose. We stared at each other. It was a very weird stare. I've been thinking ever since they left for church how weird it was. It lasted a long time. First she looked spooked, like if somebody snuck up on her under the hair dryer. Then it was like she was waking up from a sound sleep, trying to recognize me or something. Then she started going blank and dreamy, like I wasn't there. After while she stared at me like she had rancid meatloaf in her mouth and she was looking for a place to spit it. I have stared a lot of people down, but not like that. Not somebody in my own family. It's fairly scary.

She got up and went over to her dresser. She said, "I should have known." She leaned on her dresser. "I feed you, clothe you, carry you back and forth to town, doing what your momma can't do. Your momma and her looks. Where have they got her? In return you sulk and pout and sneak around and smoke and give my little girl ideas. Don't you know how she looks up to you?"

"So?"

"Typical. That's just typical." She shook her head. I thought she might cry but she didn't. She went, "Maybe you better go back to that home for a couple of days. He's got a right to come visit you there. They won't prevent him like I do."

I let on like I didn't care what she did. Which of course was like slapping both sides of her face.

"Now I can see what you're doing. You don't have the first notion of trying to fit in with us. You just want to stall until you find out what his verdict's going to be. Then if he's not guilty you will run straight to him. And if he's found guilty, you will act like you don't even know him. Right?"

I chewed my tongue in one side of my mouth and that griped her butt. She went and stood by the window.

She goes, "To think we were planning on setting a little aside for your college, assuming your grades turned around. To think we had even been thinking of custody, maybe. You've got a long ways to go if you're planning on living with us, in our home. We need to see some improvement in attitude, right off the bat. Maybe you'd rather go back to that home, or your father or Ruby. Maybe your father and mother won't mind if you bounce back and forth, playing one off of the other. But I won't allow it. You have to reach some decision. You understand me?"

I didn't answer. She grabbed aholt of a bedpost. They are these tall, skinny bedposts like candles with pine cones on top. Maybe they're meant to be flames but they look more like pine cones. Besides, they are carved out of wood. Wood looks too solid and thick for a flame. I never thought that these pine cones would turn, but Aunt Betsy turned one like it was a glass on the shelf in the kitchen. Then she went, "What do you *want?*"

What a stupid question. I don't ever think I heard a dumber question. I should've said, "I want something fast enough to get me out of here. I want a silver Trans Am with a five-speed and white-letter tires." But I just said, "Out of this hole," and went to my room.

I predict that tomorrow I'll be back in that home.

Tina would peek in my window. She would say, "Get out of there, monkey." She would be ready for action. She would be ready to roll.

I ought to be in that training school with her. That's where I really belong. Daddy said, 'Think of some words for that judge,' and I knew he meant put all the blame for that truck on the coloreds and stay on his side with the whites. So I did. It was the worst thing that I ever did. I never deserved her. I still don't. Because I still can't decide whose side I'm supposed to be on. Sometimes I think how it better be Daddy's. Anybody normal would stick by her daddy when he was in trouble. And here I am wishing for somebody colored while he's standing trial. Two coloreds: Tina plus Rosco.

One thing I know is, I never did have the right feelings like most people have. For example, one time when I was thirteen I fell in love with this guy before Rosco. His name was Gary and he used to like me. I got in pitiful shape. I didn't have any stomach for eating to speak of. Then my brain would confuse me. I felt like doing a whole bunch of things, like just sitting and watching him eat and then punching his arm and then kissing his mouth a long time. Except I didn't feel like doing it with him yet because I never did that before last year. But then he broke up with me and went with Terri Hinshaw. I told all these people how heartbroke I felt, and how I hated Terri Hinshaw, but that was a lie. I just felt these big holes where I used to feel like doing one thing or other. Which proves how I don't have the same kind of feelings like most people have. I am just full of these holes.

3

Linda had told her to sit in plain view. There was a clear line of sight from the kitchen at the back of the house, through the central dining room with its facing doors, across the parlor—which they called the den—to the window, which framed that part of the fire escape where Libby sat.

It was windy there. She wore a zippered jacket and no hat, and felt the cold metal treads imprinting wafflelike dents on her bottom. She watched the Mustang float past on the street, their faces searching the houses. Buddy wore his white toboggan, Jake his Twins cap. They stopped the car a block down the hill. The sound of them winding reverse gear was like the first sluggish moan of an air-raid siren.

They parked on the street. Buddy got out of the car and

came around to the curb. Jake rolled his window down and Libby heard him say, "Bring her out here to the car."

Buddy turned and said, "If you want to see her so bad, why don't you come on in?"

"You go on in and get her. I don't need to see a lot of people right this minute."

Buddy limped up the sidewalk. Jake rolled his window up.

"Up here," Libby said. Buddy looked up. He stepped off the walk, came around to the foot of the fire escape, and propped one boot on the second step. They both looked at the sky. It was gray and faintly pink. The air was not bright but the cold seemed to give it a hardened clarity, except where their breath was fogging it.

She said, "You want a tour?"

"A what?"

"A tour of the house. Do you want me to give you a tour?"

Buddy thought about it. "Did they say to?"

"I'm supposed to ask but you don't have to."

"I don't guess."

Libby watched the bill of her father's navy-blue Twins cap turn a few degrees and point at them. The cap seemed black in the gray-pink light.

Buddy's toboggan nodded at her. There was a small red knot of yarn at its top where he'd snipped off the pom-pom. "He wants to see you."

Libby shook her head. She heard the far-off clacking of pans in the house, dinner getting started.

"Why not?"

"Buddy, he killed somebody pregnant. He went crazy."

"No. I told you twice already. She killed herself." He turned a minute to see if his father seemed to be listening. "Do you know what a probable-cause hearing is?"

"I don't care. I saw him. On the floor, and—Buddy, all that blood." Libby's arms were crossed, elbows clamping her fists to her ribs.

"It's where a judge says, If you don't have no better proof than that, let him go. He's a free man, as of yesterday. Hear me?"

"He's a drunk. Buddy, you know he is. She wouldn't ever be dead if he wasn't."

"He's your daddy and you better stand by him. Hear me?" She shook her head.

"You better." Buddy looked at the car. The cap's bill rotated the other way, toward the street. He looked at Libby. She pulled her hair back and exposed her ears; they were red from the cold. Buddy said, "Are you going to go down there and see him?"

She glanced at his face and then down to his feet. "I can see him just fine from right here."

"Baby."

She bumped the toes of her running shoes together. "Where are you living at?"

Buddy shrugged. "Down at Granite Motorcycle. In the back on the sofa. I'm looking out for a place."

"Momma said for me to look after you."

"She did not."

"She said you needed a lot of looking after."

"That's a laugh."

"You do, too. You're not even clean. You've got dirty clothes on."

"You're the baby, not me."

"What about that time the yellow jackets got after you? You were howling like a little-bitty baby, flapping your hands—" She swatted with both hands at an imaginary swarm around her head.

"Thirteen stings. You'd run too."

"I've been stung before, and I didn't cry."

"That's because Daddy dabbed tobacco on it right quick. Drew the poison out."

"It still hurt."

"No it didn't. Tobacco draws the sting out."

"Not that time it didn't. It didn't draw nothing out." She sat for minute, thinking about tobacco. Grandma Whitley called it a failing, which was right on the verge of a sin: the failing of tobacco. "Where is he living?"

"I can't tell you. He wants to tell you about it himself."

"What are you talking about? Is he living at home— Is he still living in that trailer?"

"No, stupid. The trailer was Judith's momma's."

Libby watched his boot, rocking on its heel on the tread. A few inches of polished white shin showed above his sock. "You think you're so tough. Why don't you just get out of here?"

"Why don't you shut up? You're the one in a home." He said "home" a way that made it sound shameful.

She sat a long time, watching his boot rock. "Tell me where he's living at."

Buddy tilted his head toward the car and said, "Go ask him."

She didn't move; she looked him over. He seemed thinner. "When you get a place, what kind of place is it going to be? Is it going to be a house or something?"

"Yeh, something."

"Brick?"

"You think I'm rich?"

"You've got drums and stuff you can sell. I can get a job somewhere." Buddy laughed at her. She turned her face away and watched the girls tending pots on the stove, deep in the house. The kitchen lights were on. She heard someone, probably Patsy, squealing in the kitchen. After a while she said, "Well, I ain't got no drums to sell."

"Say 'haven't got.'" He watched her head, the uneven trail of the part in her hair. He climbed the steps. "Move over." She slid toward the house. The tread was very cold. He sat down beside her. "Let's just go on down there, so he'll be satisfied."

She shook her head.

They both looked at the car. The bill of the Twins cap was turned their way but pitched forward, hiding Jake's eyes. Buddy looked away. She rubbed her palms on her thighs. He straightened his black belt by its buckle. The belt was imitation leather and very slick; it slipped clockwise in the loops. He had a runny nose. Libby watched him wipe it on his jacket sleeve. He said, "What do they make you do around here?"

"Dishes, homework, shit like that."

"Not bad. Better than training school."

"You don't know."

"What's so terrible about it?"

"We have to act a certain way."

"Well? You have to do that anywhere."

"Just never mind." She watched one of the girls in the kitchen stuffing a new plastic liner into the garbage bucket. Then the girl gathered the neck of the full bag and lifted it like a dead goose. "I won't be in here much longer anyway."

"Why not?"

"I'm temporary. They're sending me back to Betsy's tomorrow. Ramona Jetts and that social worker are going to take me back to court and sign me over to Aunt Betsy. And if she gets custody, that's where I have to live. Forever, Buddy. I'm not kidding."

"What's wrong with Aunt Betsy's?"

"Are you kidding? Church all week? And her all the time thinking she can boss me? Momma said this would happen, said Aunt Betsy would try to get me, and—and no cigarettes?"

"It won't be so terrible. She'll buy you some nice clothes and stuff. We'll all be right here in town."

She mocked him. " 'It won't be so terrible.' You go and live there too, then."

"Well, at least it's someplace."

She looked at him. The cold drew moisture to her eyes. "It's not no place. I ain't got no place." She saw the cap's bill turn toward the street.

Buddy's face was very pale except his cheeks and ears, which were all the same alarming red. He jumped up as if there were something swarming around them, or fire in the house, and grabbed for her elbow, trying to drag her away. Her fist gripped the railing. Her knuckles were marbles, milk-white.

Buddy stopped pulling her elbow and stood one step below her. "Libby," he said, looking down.

"What?" She still held the rail, unwilling to move.

"He got fired. He lost his job. He's trying to do better."

"Why'd he do it, Buddy? Look at all the trouble. Look at where they put me. Why'd he do it?"

"He didn't do it. She did."

"Liar. You're a liar."

He grabbed her jacket shoulder and shook her. "Who's a liar, Libby? Who?"

She waited until he let go. "Why did she?"

"She was drunk."

"That's no reason."

"She was drunk and got confused. People kill themselves all the time."

"Why did she do it, though? She had to aim and get the nerve and steady herself and pull the trigger and—why?"

"I don't know!" Buddy screamed. She looked at him, startled. He almost never screamed. He seized the back of his head with both hands, lacing his fingers over the fabric of his toboggan, trying to be calm. "You have to talk to him at least. He's your daddy."

She turned loose of the rail and reached through it to touch the window glass. She peered inside at the light in the den and peeled a shred of loose rubber from her shoe and slumped and brushed some grit off the step and wiped her nose on her sleeve and rubbed her palms together, very rapidly, but nothing helped. And then Buddy said the word again, "Daddy," pressed it like a boot into the idly spinning spokes of an upturned wheel, stopping the blur of motions and textures and sounds. And she knew what it meant, that word. It belonged, had a place. And it was the word itself, familiar and fixed in her mind as surely as "up" and "down" and the other words of orientation and position, that enabled her to get up. Not the fact of that man in the car. The word itself made it possible for her to allow Buddy to lead her down the steep steps by her arm, down to the cold, solid ground, over the long, stiff grass to her daddy.

Jake got out of the car. As she drew near, but not very near, and stopped, he lunged forward and swept her up in his arms, against his windbreaker. She let him squeeze her and squeeze her, over and over. It had been a long time since he'd held her, long enough for him to change smells. She didn't remember the windbreaker. She felt the cold air on her back, where her jacket rode up in his arms.

He set her down. He looked at her and gripped her arms, her shoulders, stroked her jaw, the back of her neck, moving in a controlled panic, as he had done once when she had fallen down the back steps; checking the soundness of her bone, comparing the sizes of her retinas. "It's okay," he said when he'd finished. "You're going to be okay." She stepped backward, eyes on the ground, and he asked her, "Did you hear the good news?"

She glanced at him as if he'd lost his mind.

"I beat the charges," he said. "The judge looked it over, all the evidence, and he said, far as the facts were concerned, I'm an innocent man."

She nodded. The way he spoke was different from the way she remembered; what he said didn't seem to matter to him. He was searching her with words in the same way he had with his hands and eyes, searching for the tender places, the pain. The tempo and pattern of his speech were the same, but the voice was thinner in the lower ranges, strained in the upper, hemmed, and a little frantic. He looked tired. She thought he must've had it pretty bad, after all. "That's what Buddy said."

"I told Mo Sedge, 'Let's keep Libby out of this mess. She's shook up enough already.' So we did; you didn't have to testify. Buddy did, though. Told 'em how it was. Now it's a clear road. Listen, babe. Did he tell you I'm getting back on my feet? We're going to be a family again, just like before"— she looked at him so fast he knew he'd phrased it badly— "before all this trouble. I've put the guns and bottles away. I'm a changed man. Ask Buddy, he'll tell you."

"He hasn't been drunk since that night," Buddy said.

She couldn't understand why she was the center of this, why they were so anxious to persuade her. They were acting as if it mattered what she thought.

"Listen, babe," Jake said. "Are they treating you right in there?" He nodded toward the house; she shrugged. "Hey, aren't you gonna talk to me? Here, listen. Did you hear about my visit from the magazine man? Look here, Buddy's crackin' up already. It was that first day I got out of jail, and hadn't moved out of the trailer. Buddy was over there with me, and we were scratching around for something to eat. Shook up, not knowing how this thing was gonna turn out. All we had was some old cans of soup, and no crackers, not a cracker in the house. Finally we gave up on eating; we weren't hungry anyway. Then we hear this knock on the door and I open it up and there's a man standing there like this—"

He hung one hand fingers-down at a sharp angle from his wrist and swung his right knee awkwardly across his left, twitching. She blurted a small laugh, like a hiccup.

"—and he was trying to ask us did we want to buy some magazines. But he said it like, 'Numont oo-my nuh mag-naneen?' He was shaking this wore-out old catalogue at me. I said, 'What?' and he does this same number again, 'Numont oo-my—' "

Libby laughed, watching him, her foot kicking at the grass.

"So I said, 'What?' and he goes through the same routine again, worse than ever. Finally we figure out he's selling magazines. So I say, 'We can't use any,' and try to close the door. But he yanks this ragged old card out of his pocket and sticks it in my face, and it says he's a certified member of the alliance of handicapped magazine sales representatives."

Buddy's laugh was like a quiet panting.

"So I said, 'No thanks; we don't need any magazines.' But he wasn't giving up. He was what you call determined. So he says something else, and I go, 'What?' And durn if he doesn't say it again. But I still don't have any idea what he's trying to tell me and I don't care, so I go, real loud, thinking maybe he's deaf, 'No! You hear? We don't want your magazines.'

"And so then he says—and I'll swear this is what he said; Buddy heard it too—he goes, clear as a bell, 'Well, yuh don' haff tuh be suh damn dumb abou' it.' "

They all laughed together. Buddy said the last of it again,

twice, punching his thigh with his fist, " 'You don't have to be so damn dumb about it.' "

Jake opened a new pack of Camels and passed them around. They lit up and leaned on the car, smoking without talking, watching the girls carrying food to the dining room. It was getting dark. After a while Libby said, "Daddy?"

"Yeh, babe?"

"Where are you living at?"

He dropped the cigarette and left it smoking on the curb, without moving his foot to crush it. "I've got this new arrangement now, babe. I think it's going to keep me out of trouble. I've already been to church one time this week, ask Buddy."

"Where are you living at?"

"Well, see, temporarily I needed a place that wasn't too steep. Judith's momma, she took the trailer, did you know that?"

"Yes. So where are you?"

"Well, babe, it turns out there's this lady I know, this widow lady, and she lives by herself in this big brick house—" Buddy looked at him, anxious. "Well, anyway, there's nothing wrong with it, babe. She's just a good friend, and she's had kind of a hard time too, and so she understands what I've been through."

He watched her smoke the cigarette. She was looking down, her hair falling over her face.

"And she's going to keep me straight, babe. That's the best part. She won't stand for any booze or guns around. And she's mature, this lady is. She's not some little thing that needs a lot of looking after, burning the food."

Buddy walked a little ways up the street and turned, facing the house.

"She's just glad to have a man around the house," Jake said. He straightened the cap on his head. "But we're not married or anything, so it's not right me bringing children in with me just now. But it's just temporary, and I'll still get to see you, and there's nothing wrong with what we're—"

She flung her cigarette at him and sprinted up the walk, crossing a distance of ninety-odd feet in one held breath, hearing him calling behind her, "Libby, wait, for Christ sake," and "Babe!"

She slammed the door and blew out her smoke in the half-dark hall. It drifted, waiting for currents of air.

4

I guess the bitch decided not to handle last night this morning after all, because they went ahead to church and left me in the bed. I guess the bitch is scared of me by now. Picture this bitch in her curlers, and wearing a robe that has mushrooms for buttons. And mushrooms are poison. She got a shock on the stoop with the lights blazing in the yard. Then while she's being in shock she could see I was already coming right straight for the house, but she still had to order me in. She goes, "I'll handle this tomorrow morning. Get to bed." Like I had a lot of staying up to do.

She's always asking me what do I want. I want to see her eat mushrooms and pokeberry root. That time when Buddy fed me pokeberry root, I had to puke up my lunch and get all the way empty. That was when Buddy was little enough to still cry. Momma, she sat on my bed with my head in her lap and sung me a song. Then she cooled off my face with her hands.

Maybe I did give her cause, but what of it. She can't prove one thing on me except being inside that car. For one thing she can't even prove I went out of the yard. If I'm still in the yard then I'm not really out after curfew.

He said he'd come to the roof. I called him up and he said he'd come. And I went to the roof but he never. So last night I had to sneak out and go find him. I went to Vass-Baugh's and that's where he works. I found his car where it was in that long gravel lot by the tracks. I could tell it was his by the shine and those Super-Sport S's on his grille. He won't leave a bug on those S's for more than one second.

It took a while for the whistle to blow at the plant. Then he came out with some others and saw it was me. And I said how we needed to talk. He told me not right that second in public and said to go get in the car. Then he stood facing his back to the car and the others were looking at me through the window and hearing him talk. Then he climbed in the car. All of my bones turn to slush when he cranks up that engine. That's how I know I'm not over a person.

He didn't head for the roof. I wondered where in the world we were going. Rosco said back to my aunt's. I wouldn't say where she lived but he already knew on School Hill, since I told him before. He drove around on School Hill awful slow past the houses and said, "That one?" over and over, like it was a lineup and I was supposed to be picking out killers. He said if I didn't tell he would just set me straight out in the road. Which I didn't care but I wanted to talk to him some so I finally told him which house and he stopped where their sidewalk starts up by the light post. The house it was dark, up that hill. I could tell how aggravated he was when he looked at the house. Like me and the house were both ticking him off with our looks.

I punched his lighter and got me a cigarette out. I told him we better talk but he squeezed on the gearshift impatient and said, "I told you don't be putting this pressure on me."

They're home. You can tell by her heels she goes straight for her room. Annie closes herself in her bedroom and says, "Well!" to her bear. Uncle Bob beats on my door. "Open up."

"Just a minute."

"Now!"

"I'm not dressed."

"Get your clothes on and open this door, right now."

I pull on my jeans and a sweatshirt. I open the door. He comes in. He's a wide man. He's got these thick kind of hands that look choked when his shirt cuffs are buttoned.

"If you lie to me I'll wear you out," he says.

I must be nervous to laugh straight out loud. He whips off his belt and that stops me from laughing right quick.

He lets the belt hang down beside of his leg. "Do you see what you're bringing me to? Here I am ready to whip my own niece." His hand tries to loosen his tie but the knot just gets worse. "Do you know who is back in her bedroom, upset? Your aunt. Who did right by you and gave you a place in her home. Not back from that home but two days and now look." His left hand is clawing the knot. "Who was that man in the car?"

"Nobody."

Uncle Bob doubles the belt.

I go, "He was somebody wanting a date. I had to go out and tell him to stop coming around here." I stare at his shoelaces. They look waxy and twisted like pitiful lies coming out of my mouth.

He says, "What a picture that was when she turned on the light by the sidewalk and looked in that car. What a picture that was."

The lighter it panged and I jumped and the cigarette jumped right out of my mouth and I found where it rolled on the floor but the lighter was already cold so I punched it again and he still wouldn't talk. He was tapping his thumb on the wheel awful slow like he's counting to ten. He said what did I want and I took the cigarette out of my mouth to say to him, On the roof, but the lighter it panged and I stuck the wrong end of the cigarette back in my mouth and tried to light the wrong end that was wet and the lighter went cold so I punched it again. I said, "Can't we just go on the roof like before?"

He said, "I told you I'd be the one to say when."

Then there's light in the car on his face and the lamp by the sidewalk is blazing and Betsy comes out on the stoop in her robe staring down and she sees us and it looks like she's fixing to pop five or six mushroom buttons off her chest and the lighter it pangs.

*

Uncle Bob goes to twisting his belt in both hands.
I go, "You going to whip me?"
"I guess I better."
"I want to call Daddy first."
He turns his face to the door and says something starting
with "God." His Sunday shirt's stretched tight on his back like
the front of my brother's bass drum. He says, "No," after
while. He says, "No, I won't whip you. But things have to
change. Here I thought we were buddies."
Then he goes out of that bedroom and leaves me alone.

So I yanked out the lighter and got out of his car and threw
the lighter down on the sidewalk so it rolled in a slow shiny
curl and then slowed up and stopped. He sat in the car and
said, "Pick it up. Give it back here."
I headed on up to the house.
He got right out and came straight up the walk for his
lighter so Betsy could see him full-size and his slow kind of
walking and then she was ready to bite through her teeth to
the nerves. Then when he bent down and picked up his lighter
he stood up and looked back and pointed at me and said,
"Don't you ever be ringing my phone or coming around me
again. You hear me? You're too damn much trouble." Then
he got in his car and drove off, and I climbed for the door,
where she waited for just the last possible second to order me
straight in to bed.

If I open the door to my closet and sit on the floor by my
shoes, I can hear Annie talking to Bear through the wall. "Bad,
bad, Bear," she says. "Momma's got to whip you." Her voice
is like a little mother bear would have. I just sit in the closet
and listen until she stops talking to Bear.

5

The terrier trotted a circuit of rooms. As his feet left the dining room carpet his nails clicked and slid in the kitchen. His water dish rattled. The sound carried back to the living room, where Trish, the social worker, said, "What do we want to see happen here?"

Trish occupied one end of Betsy's oyster-white sofa, Libby the other. Bob and Betsy sat in matching teal chairs by the fireplace, engrossed in their hearth of white brick and their andirons of brass. Ramona Jetts adjusted her skirt and settled into a maple captain's chair between Libby and the door.

The sound of Trish's question surrendered the room to the sound of the dog lapping water.

Bob said, "Annie, our little girl, was upset when we told her what was up. She's been wanting a sister. We thought a puppy would take her mind off it, but she hasn't shown much interest in him yet today."

"She will, soon as all this is over," Betsy said. "She'll love that little dog for all she's worth." Betsy was not watching the hearth now. She seemed to address a run of crown molding over Bob's head.

"What exactly's been decided?" Trish said. "I thought we had something workable here. Now I'm hearing it's finished. Something's final."

"Based on what we feel right now, it is final," Bob said. "I just can't see any other way."

Libby heard the dog panting impatiently beside her knee and then going away. She had turned, bracing her ribs on the arm of the sofa, and was studying the lamp table. Its veneer had been sliced from a flitch of pecan and laid open like pages in a book, so that one face exactly mirrored the other along an invisible joint. She could almost feel the two plates pressed together under force, each strand of fiber permanently set against its likeness. By inclining her head slightly, she could alter the focus and see the cranberry color of Ramona Jetts's blouse tinting the gloss, like a sunset reflected in ice.

"You have to understand that there are very few options open to us, now," Trish said. "This was our permanent placement. Foster homes are out. They're full and she's too old to suit them, anyway. What's left? This is the best we've got. You have to expect a period of adjustment. We all do."

No one responded. Libby saw the dog approaching Trish and pricking his ears expectantly, his bottom hovering near the carpet. He yipped once and ran back to the kitchen.

Betsy said, "I remember when she broke my mother's gravy boat one Thanksgiving. Dropped it on the floor, when she didn't have any business with it in the first place."

"It probably won't be very productive to dredge up the past," Trish said. "Let's focus on the future."

Ramona Jetts sighed deeply, as though under the weight of a grave responsibility. "The reality of this situation is that, number one, we have a time factor. Her father is seeking to regain custody from Social Services, as Trish well knows. My best anticipation is that the court will see this as a realistic outcome in, say, two or three months. His case was dismissed. His living situation has apparently stabilized. So if the mother is out of the picture, what I see is her father. Trish? Am I wrong?"

"No."

"Now I don't know what kind of deal he's cut with the mother to keep her out of it, but she says it's all between him and Elizabeth. There's something going on behind the scenes there, I suspect. Is there not?"

Libby kept her eyes on the steady convergence of grain in pecan.

"Number two," Ramona said, "we can't afford to lose another opportunity to involve her with the right community-based resources. My feeling is that, as things stand right now, her situation indicates training school, but I'm still open at this moment."

Libby could feel the cool flow of air from the picture window behind her. She knew who she was in this room. She was an alien creature among them, profaning their clean, ordered place. She knew this from their postures: They sat as though arranged for posterity, their hands and feet firmly and solemnly placed. And she knew it from the sound of their voices: They lashed her and bound her with words she did not understand. Words from the Bible, words from the dying, words from the law—these could be neither explained nor repealed. They could be only eluded, escaped.

"We know her people live scattered around," Bob said. "We had our hopes it would work."

"Yesterday she came out of the bathroom smelling like a cigarette," Betsy said.

"The way it is," Bob said, "I've got my immediate family to worry about first. My wife's been upset. She can't enjoy a meal. And our little girl is old enough to pick things up. And it looks like Lib's father will be back in the picture."

"Maybe if we deal with one issue at a time," Trish said.

There was silence again. The dog came in and poised himself near Betsy's stockinged legs, which were crossed at the ankles. This seemed to make Betsy self-conscious. She uncrossed her legs and set her feet flat on the floor. The dog leaped, wrapped his forelegs around her calf, and began pumping his hindquarters.

Libby was pleased with this action of dog-against-Betsy. For the moment the focus of the room had miraculously swerved from her to the dog.

Betsy leaned forward and shoved him away, powerfully, with both hands. The dog staggered backward on his hind legs, yipping and wagging his tail. Bob rolled a blue rubber ball with white stars along the rug. The dog pounced and tossed the ball with his mouth.

Betsy glared at the oyster-shell carpet, the red fading slowly from her cheeks. "She'd be better off someplace where they don't have impressionable children."

Trish said, "What if you spelled out exactly what you expect of Libby, then hold her to it? She can decide to stay and live by the rules, or leave. We would have some room for compromise."

Betsy sighed and shifted her feet. Libby saw the warp of Betsy's shoe reflected in the andirons. The toe of the shoe seemed to curl and elongate—like the shoe of a witch.

Bob said, "I'm not a man to compromise himself. It would have to be how Betsy says."

The dog returned the ball to Betsy. She pinched it with the nails of her thumb and first finger, as though to prevent his saliva from touching her skin.

Bob said, "I guess it looks like we gave up. We've done some soul-searching over this."

"We carried it to our minister," Betsy said. "He said we certainly had to consider our immediate family. His message to me was, 'You can tell yourself you tried.'"

The dog lunged for Betsy's right leg. She shoved him away with her left foot and flung the ball overhand against the floor. The ball caromed off the ceiling, struck the back of Ramona's chair, and rebounded from the window casing, narrowly missing a glass shelf of African violets. The dog bounded after the ball, leaping and tumbling toward the kitchen.

Bob said, "He's just a puppy."

Libby laughed—a sound like a half-stifled sneeze.

Ramona said, "You find this amusing, young lady?"

Libby didn't say.

Ramona leaned forward. "What precisely do *you* think we ought to do with you, anyway?"

Libby looked at her. "Don't do nothing with me. Just let me go."

Ramona hissed a short, chiding breath through her teeth. "I have three words to say to that: 'Delinquent. Minor. Child.' They sound familiar?"

Libby stared into the fireplace. It had never been soiled. It was white as an igloo inside.

Ramona said, "This attitude is the thing that concerns me, Elizabeth. It's becoming clear from this meeting that things have decayed to the point where they can't be resolved in a community context. What did we say from the beginning about that blue Chevelle? And Tina Triplett? Which is another issue. If she gets home time for Easter, I have two words for you, young lady. Are you listening?"

Libby looked at her. Yes, she was listening. The sound of the name seemed to rampage through the room, hot on the trail of the dog.

Ramona said, "And those two words are—'No contact.' "

Libby was listening to the ecstatic clawing and skidding of nails in the kitchen. In a moment the dog came racing back to the living room, dropping the ball from his mouth. It rolled, wet and foamy, toward Ramona Jetts.

Betsy said, "Bob, will you please do something about that dog?"

Bob got up, lifted the squirming terrier in his hands, and carried it back through the kitchen. He returned without the dog and sat down. After a moment Libby heard a low, steady croon from the basement.

Ramona began ticking things off on her fingers: "Mother to father. Father to mother. Mother to Linda's to here. Blow a good chance with your uncle and aunt. What next? What are we supposed to do with you next?"

Libby didn't say. She listened to the howl of the dog, his pawing at the basement door.

Ramona said, "I think we have to look at a very structured environment, at this point. We have a curfew violation and a loss of placement; that's all I need to adjudicate."

Trish leaned forward over the coffee table, laying her hand on a copy of *Furniture Down Through the Ages*. "I don't see training school, Ramona. I'm sorry, I just don't."

Ramona seized her purse from the floor and shouldered its strap. Trish said, "Just let me try for a thirty-day placement at the group home. I'll try to make it renewable, maybe. Of course, we'll still have to deal with her father."

Bob and Betsy were standing erect by their hearth. They seemed to be out of the picture, forgotten, immobile as stone.

Ramona stepped forward and stood over Libby. "What does he know about this? Have you made him aware of what's happening here?"

"Who?"

"Your *father*. Who do you think? Don't you think he'd be interested?"

Libby looked up from the gray in Ramona's wool skirt to the black in her eyes. She was sick of this woman and ready to hate her head-on. She said, "What the shit do you care?"

Ramona's lips clamped shut, as though on a row of pins.

Trish took Libby's elbow in her hand. "Don't you know when to shut up? Go pack your clothes. I'll come and get you at five."

Libby got up from the sofa and walked through the kitchen. When she passed the basement door, the dog sniffed and whined at the jamb. She went to the laundry room, opened the dryer, and fished out a small load of staticky clothes. They crackled. She was hearing the sound of Ramona. Ramona had brought her two electrical words: *Tina Triplett*. Libby tucked her clothes under her arm and walked to the basement door. The dog whimpered. She opened the door. He burst past her leg and sailed clawing and skidding on the clean, waxy floor of the kitchen.

---

§

I was way deep in the grandstand and couldn't see down to the road in the dark, so I didn't know who it was driving that Plymouth. I figured law again, maybe. Then I saw rust spots like scabs on the hood of that car and the door went ka-whomp. And then here she comes up the steps behind third and she sits on the first row of benches. She didn't say word one. She was just looking where all of the water was standing at home. This place is low and stays wet.

We kept our distance like that for a while. I sat and looked at the back of her head. I couldn't see that much change in her

hair. I smoked a Winston. I couldn't think what to do. I tried
to see from her back was she ready to kill me. Her blouse
didn't have any sleeves. Both of her arms looked so huge. I
figured the longer I sat there, the worse off I'd be.

I walked the benches and rattled some boards going down
so she'd hear. She didn't move. She knew all the time I was
there. I stood behind her right shoulder. I said, "Hey."

She turned and looked. She grinned and jiggled her keys in
my face. I couldn't tell from that grin and that jiggle if the
Ticket was hating my guts.

I said, "You got your license?"

"Yeh." She took my Winston and smoked it.

I said, "When did you start smoking?"

She gave it back. "Just now."

I said, "Whose car?"

"My daddy's."

I said, "Where'd you take driver's ed?"

"In that place where they put me."

She turned and looked at the infield again. There was a scar
on her shoulder. It was a little pink minus sign. I said, "What
happened?"

"I got stabbed."

I said, "What stabbed you?"

"Something sharp."

I couldn't tell if she meant to be hateful. I said, "Chuck like
you driving?"

She said, "Who?"

"Chuck. Your man Chuck."

"I wrote him a letter and gave him his freedom. He never
wrote me back."

I couldn't think what to say. I said, "You miss him?"

"No I don't miss him." She got up from the bench and
grinned at me. "I just miss something *about* him."

I said, "Oh."

She took aholt of the front of my jacket and twisted a little
hard knot in the cloth. She stared me straight in the face and
said, "You know where I been?"

"Where?"

"You know where."

I didn't say anything.

She said, "This here's my Easter break. I have to go back and stay in there another five, six months."

"So?"

"I don't belong in no training school. It's like a prison."

"I never once said you did."

"Nobody puts me in prison."

"Let go of me."

That's when she shoved me back down on a bench.

I said, "This why you called me? And said to come down here? So you could whip me?"

She pinned me down by my arms and she mashed down my guts with her knee. She held me down in her death grip and didn't talk any. She was staring me down. I said, "Get off."

She said, "You never went to that place, did you, white girl?"

"Get out of my face. You're not any better than you were in the first place. You're worse."

She mashed her knee in me deeper and hurt my insides. I couldn't talk like myself. I had to grunt. I said, "I got put someplace too."

"Where, in that home? You see some fences around you? You see some guards? You see some lines to go eat?"

"They put my brother in one, same as you."

"Not you, white girl."

She stared me down like she dared me to make up some kind of excuse for myself. I tried to keep staring back just as fierce as I could.

She said, "I bet you blamed that whole truck on me and Chuck, didn't you?"

"No."

She pushed harder. It hurt. She said, "Don't lie to me. I bet you acted like it was our fault, not yours. Didn't you?"

I was scared. I said yes.

She dropped my head on the bench and walked off down the aisle. I stood up and got to where I could breathe halfway normal. I started crying, like a baby. I cry so easy and act like a baby about half of the time. I said, "I'm sorry. Okay?"

She didn't answer. I climbed about three benches up from the aisle. She came back up the aisle. I couldn't see in the dark how much she hated my guts. She climbed a few benches and sat on the next one down. Her shoulder was right in my face. She said, "What am I gonna do about you?"

I said, "I don't know."

She said, "What am I gonna do about that place? Easter be over next Monday. Just got three days left."

I touched her little pink scar. I didn't mind how it felt. It was raised up like those letters the blind people read with their fingers. I said, "What really stabbed you?"

"Dreama Parrish sunk a number-two lead in my shoulder."

"What for?"

"I called her Scabies. She had these canker-sore eyes."

"What did she do?"

"Tried to keep being in charge. Thought she better have the best cue stick, and all the time breaking in line. People said, 'Dreama's so tough.' And she chewed on this pencil and carried it back of her ear. And soon as she woke up she smoked her cigarette real desperate outside by the door. And nobody better interrupt her."

"She die for stabbing your shoulder?"

"They pulled me off her too fast."

"Oh."

"One time she cut up my sheets with a pop-top off a Dr Pepper. Said a sheet cut hard compared to skin like mine. I pushed her down and told her which of her parts I would start to avulse. I said from then on her name would be Scabies. Later on somebody told her how scabies was some kind of a scabby disease. Then after that I'll be standing in line for my breakfast and feel something stab me. She breaks the lead off and pulls out her pencil and sticks it behind of her ear, all bloody. Some girl said, "You had it. You lead-poisoned."

I said, "Maybe there's two kinds of lead."

She said, "That doctor was cute. I said, 'I got lead in my blood, and what's the prognosis?' He said, 'Tell me the second you want to start in on a sketch.' I said, 'You funny bastard.' He asked me what was I planning to do with my future and I said, 'Be a surgeon.' I just said that. He rubbed me with alcohol and made the neatest little incision. He said most people flinch and don't look when he cuts on their shoulder. He pulled the lead out with tweezers and cleaned me all out."

"Maybe there's some kinds of lead that's not poison."

She didn't act like she heard me. I smoked another Winston. We talked some more about what-all they did to her shoulder but I forget all of the medical parts. She asked me how about Rosco, and I told her I broke off with him because he was causing me trouble.

She said, "You liar."

I didn't talk back.

She said, "You miss him?"

"Who?"

"Rosco, mole brain."

"No."

"You liar. Tell me the truth."

"Sometimes."

"I know when."

"When I need something to happen right quick. You know, *something*. He was good for going places."

"You monkey. I know what places he was good for going."

She leaned her head on my knees. Her neck was so smooth, like a chocolate neck. Not the sweet kind, the cooking kind. Her hair was right there in my face. It's the black kind of hair that will kink and not go any certain direction. I shoved my hand in her hair and felt of the top of her head. I said, "I'm glad I'm not a bug in that frizz. I couldn't ever escape."

She said, "Like me in that place."

We sat around there and looked at the moon in the puddles. I said, "I'm in a home for delinquents, you know it? That place you called? It's a home. How did you get my number?"

"Momma had it. She tried to get me put in there instead of that training school."

"Oh." I couldn't tell if she hated me for getting in and her not. I said, "I've been going back and forth to my Aunt Betsy's. She's the one broke us up."

"Broke who up?"

"Me and Rosco. She caught us out front of her house in his car."

"How was the look on her face? I need to see."

"Like she had a yard full of dead rotten bodies and she couldn't breathe on account of the smell."

Tina said, "Whoo. Wha'd she do then?"

"Kicked me. I figure she'll tell my daddy. Soon as he hears who it was in that car he'll decide to go kill him or me, either one."

She looked at me squint-eyed. "What kind of mess are you talkin'?"

I said, "It's the truth."

She said, "No it ain't. He won't do no such a thing."

"I don't care what he does. I'm sick of worrying about it. I wish he'd just go ahead."

"Listen at you and your mouth. You don't know shit from tomatoes."

We both acted a little spooky. We looked around in the grandstand, like there might be somebody sneaking up behind us. I said, "You don't know how my daddy is. You hear about my stepmomma?"

"Wha'd she do?"

"Got killed."

"She never! What killed her?"

"They thought my daddy."

She stared at me and whistled through her teeth. "Wha'd they do to him?"

"He got off."

"How'd he get off?"

"It was self-inflicted. She self-inflicted herself."

"With what?"

"A gun. In the head."

"You get a look at her head?"

I made a hole with my thumb and one finger.

She whistled again. " 'Spect she was dead 'fore she hit the floor."

I didn't say.

" 'Spect there's a whole sight of blood."

I didn't say.

"Least you could see for yourselves and won't hold out no hope."

"What do you mean by that?"

"You see the body, things settle down after while. At home we never had us a body to bury."

"You don't know. People don't die like you think. Most people pick some fool way to die, so it causes you more aggravation."

"Now you and me can both sympathize together."

"It's not the same and you know it."

"Why's that?"

I didn't answer. I couldn't think of any good reason. I was just being dumb about it.

She stood up and walked back and forth. She started acting like something was funny. "I bet your daddy 'bout dies when he hears of that truck in the sand trap."

I grinned.

"I bet he goes all to pieces when he hears who-all's with you in that sand trap."

I said, "He near about stuck his fist through the wall."

She grabbed me up by the neck, and lifted me off of the bench with her thumb underneath of my chin. I didn't move. Tina can snap off your head. She said, "That why you first hung around me, 'cause of your daddy? That why you hung out with us, me and Chuck and Rosco? You been slappin' his face with us?"

"Let go."

"Your daddy, he hate black people?"

I didn't look at her face.

She turned me loose. "Explain something to me. I need to figure this out. How come he's like that? He just naturally hateful?"

I said, "I don't know." I never once wondered about it before.

She said, "Listen at you. You just like him. You like bein'

against. You and Rosco and me against him. How come you people are like that?"

"Shut up."

"I 'spect you'll be about ready to go and be back on his side, after this."

"No."

"You lookin' whiter and whiter."

"Shut up."

She looked at me some. "You the most confused little monkey I ever did see. You all confused on the outside. But deep down, you a daddy's girl."

I said, "You liar. The only thing like him is my nose."

She hooted, which pissed me off. Then she looked my face over real good, seeing was I worth a damn, which I'm not. She said, "Just your nose? Maybe I'll fix it." She punched my nose with her fist but not hard. Just a tap on the end where there's not any bone. It made me mad as fire. I jumped back and got ready to fight. I didn't care if she killed me. I was ready to fight.

She grinned as big as she could. She said, "Whoo, look at you."

I wish I knew why I can't ever stay mad at her.

She said, "Whoo, don't hurt me. No, you ain't like him a bit. Not one little bit. Matter of fact, let's change your name. You want to change your name? Want me to find you a new one?"

"Maybe I will change my name."

"Change it to Triplett. We can be sisters."

"Right. And get whipped all the time."

She grinned and looked me over some more. She set me down on the bench and took hold of my leg. She said, "Still not much meat on that leg." She bounced her fist over my heart. "You got a shade more up there, though. You trying to be a girl, finally?"

I didn't say.

She smiled at me nice as she could. I never deserved it. Sometimes I can't understand why she's quick to forgive me. I wish I knew, I swear I do.

I was relieved and I wanted to say something nice and make up. I knew she wanted to hear more about Judith. Tina likes hearing the facts of the case. I said, "I was asleep."

"When's this?"

"You know. My stepmomma."

She listened.

"I heard these noises, like *bam,* except louder. I thought my brother was waking me up with his drums. It sounded just like his rim shots."

She sat and straddled the bench.

I said, "So I tried to go back to sleep, but I heard the smoke alarm and got up and came in the living room and Judith was lying there crooked and Daddy was squatting beside her. And all of this blood was around. And her hair was stuck in it. And two guns were lying in some of the blood."

"You saw all that?"

"Plus his face."

She said, "What did his face look like?"

"My daddy. He has a bad side."

"Look at you shaking. You think he done it?"

I kept staring at the puddles. I started picturing wild, crazy things in my head. I was afraid to look around me in the grandstand. I had this feeling that hundreds of people were sitting there hearing me tell on my daddy. I had this feeling that he was down under us both in the dugout, spitting where I couldn't see.

Tina said, "Hey, don't shake." I tried not to. She said, "You gonna ask him about it?"

"I don't know."

"He gonna really be pissed about Rosco?"

"I don't know."

"Maybe you just blowing all of this up in your mind. Maybe you got it all cockeyed and it's working you up in a state."

I didn't know what to say. I had the quakes. I was shaking so bad there was hair falling down in my eyes. Tina just sat there and waited till I got some better control of myself. She said, "What are we gonna do about this? Me in that place and you being scared all to pieces? We just been together ten minutes and here we are right back in trouble. What are we gonna do?"

"I don't know."

She said, "I know one thing we can do."

I looked up. She was grinning and jiggling her keys.

7

Linda said, "I think you have a guest," but Libby didn't leave the house until she saw from the window that it was Buddy, not Jake, who stood in the drive by the Mustang. When she reached him, he was leaning butt-first on the fender, swigging a beer.

She said, "What are you trying to prove?"

Buddy didn't answer, so she headed back toward the house. He said, "I heard how you got kicked out of Betsy's."

Libby stopped but didn't turn. "So?"

"She told me what for."

"Who?"

"Betsy."

"That witch."

"Stop changing the subject."

She faced him. "All because of this guy I don't like. And he tried to get me to go in his car, but I wouldn't. But he kept after me, so I had to come out here and tell him to leave."

"You're a liar, Libby. Why are you such a liar?"

"Where are you going in that car?"

"Somewhere."

"Buddy, you've got a *date*."

He didn't respond.

"How come you're here, if you've got a date?"

"I can't be tending to you all the time, from now on."

"Who asked you to?"

He gestured with the beer can. "Girls start all of this up and the men have to stop it."

"Shut that crap up."

"They mess it all up. You messed it up. Here I was planning to see about getting a place. And letting you go in with me on the rent. Then here you go in that car."

"I didn't do anything."

"You make me puke." He drank the beer.

Libby said, "You were just lying about getting that place."

"No. I had one in mind. Now I can't stand the idea."

She thought a moment and said, "Listen, if I get a job, they might let me move in with you because of how you're my brother. And Buddy, listen, I can almost cook now. I mean it."

Buddy drained the beer and wiped his mouth with the back of his hand. "Maybe before, but not now."

"You just came here to brag about having a date. Who is this wonderful date?"

"Listen who's talking to me about wonderful dates."

She looked away and stepped toward the back of the car. "Why's the trunk standing open?"

Buddy didn't answer. She leaned under the lid and saw the contours of rifle and bat where they lay side by side like two sleepers under the fold of a blanket. The red-and-black check had been eaten by moths.

She stepped back quickly and said, "Buddy, you're crazy."

"I know who it is, and I know what he drives, and I know where he works."

"Shut that trunk and go take back his car."

He shook his head.

She headed for the house.

Buddy said, "Where are you going, you baby?"

"I'm gonna call him and tell him."

"Go tell your boyfriend I'm coming to see him."

"I mean *Daddy*. I'm telling what you're gonna do with his car."

"Right, and see what he does. Tell him what Betsy told me."

She came back and pointed. "You act so tough but you're

not. Daddy's not stupid as you are. He wouldn't show me his trunk if he planned to go do something with it."

He swung his open hand and missed the finger she pointed. "Stupid. I came here to show you this trouble you've started."

"I'm not doing anything else after this, so just stop."

"No, it's too late."

Libby cried.

Buddy fidgeted. "Stop bawling. I already made up my mind."

"Go on ahead and just do it. I don't care. I should've done it myself."

"You liar."

"Go on. What are you waiting for?"

Buddy didn't seem ready to give up the argument. "He'll just keep after you, till I do something. That's how they are."

"You don't know."

"Listen at you. You never used to talk like that. You never used to like running around with something that crawled out of a hole. All I know is, you changed, and I know who changed you."

The person she thought of was Tina.

Buddy said, "I know his name."

"Whose name?"

"Your boyfriend, stupid."

"I don't have any boyfriend."

"Shut up, you liar."

She stood with her arms entwined across her chest and her gaze on the distance, like an umpire who's made the wrong call but won't ever admit it or change it, no matter how many furious players and coaches come charging and whipping their caps off their heads.

He drained the beer can and dropped it, mashing it flat with the heel of his boot. "It's Reginald Henry Dupree."

At first, she didn't know whom he was talking about. Then she laughed out loud, thinking that she might at last be ready to get over Rosco—now that she'd heard his real name.

Buddy was angry. "Go ahead and laugh. I'm gonna find him and kill him."

"Who, Reginald Henry?" She laughed again.

Buddy said, "If you think I won't you're a fool."

Libby stopped laughing when she saw he was scared. She knew he would be even more afraid of backing down. And if she said, "Go ahead, kill him," Buddy would probably have to try. So she lied.

"Buddy, I learned my lesson. I swear it. I won't go near one, or sit in their cars. Buddy, I swear it."

He behaved as though she hadn't suffered enough. This made her angry, but she covered it up. "Buddy, you *can't*. You do something and Daddy finds out—then what?"

"Maybe he better wake up and see how you are."

"He'll land in trouble again and you know it."

She saw him consider this.

"Just forget it, Buddy. Okay?"

It galled her to see that he thought he was doing her a favor, but she didn't let on.

Buddy said, "You just better watch out from now on. I can't be tending to you all the time."

She didn't argue.

He went around the car to close the trunk, but Libby said, "Wait." They ducked inside the trunk together. Buddy pulled all of the blanket away and wrapped his hand around the bat, showing her the vicious way he could squeeze the handle. He laid it back on the blanket and showed her how his finger would crook on the trigger of the rifle. She ducked farther into the trunk, smelling the gun oil, an odor like her father's, and tried to imagine the future, to see who might be holding the gun and the bat. She said, "Who gave you that name?"

"Ramona Jetts. I asked her straight out."

"That witch. She'll tell Daddy next." They were quiet inside the trunk. Libby touched the bat; its sweet spot still showed the white, ghostly prints of the balls. She touched the rifle, tracing the grain in the stock, feeling the light coat of oil on the steel. She liked the heft and the hard, solid fit of the bat and the gun in her hands.

Buddy said, "Hey," and she jumped. He said, "You want a beer?"

There were four cans in the trunk, sweating on a corner of the blanket. Buddy and Libby each pulled a can from the clear plastic rings and backed out of the trunk, closing the lid. They propped side by side on the fender. Libby didn't want to worry about who might be watching from the house. She didn't want to think about her father or what he might do. She wanted only to lean on this car with her brother and drink a cold beer.

After a while she asked him when he would look for a place of his own.

He said, "I can't be making these plans till things settle down."

"If you're thinking Daddy, forget it. He won't let things ever get settled. Not ever. Let's just go do for ourselves."

"You just remember whose side you're supposed to be on."

"I told you already."

"They treat you okay in that home?"

"I reckon."

He took a swallow of beer. "Maybe sometime I'll come get you out and take you to ride."

"Yeh. Why don't you come on your Harley? Wear a clean shirt like you are. All of these girls will be eating their hearts out."

"Maybe I will later on. Maybe we might go to ride."

"Yeh, we might go to ride."

8

Sometimes I looked in the mirror and Tina was laughing. Sometimes I looked and she stared out the back of the car. I got better and better at driving, and Tina got closer and closer to jail.

I learned as fast as I could and Tina said I passed my exam. She said, "Look out, this monkey is loose on the road."

I asked her where I was going and she said to find us a good place to go and praise God for our lives. I took her up on the roof.

We had a time getting there. It was rainy, and everywhere we tried to set our feet it was sopping and rotten. And here we came falling around on these rocks that come out of the mountain as slimy as fish.

Soon as we got to the sign, I said, "Don't look down," but she wouldn't listen.

She stepped out on the edge of the wall and said, "Whoo."

We couldn't hardly see for the rain. I said, "Hush. We can't be up here laughing."

She said, "Oh shit. Is it worth it?"

"I reckon."

"You *reckon?* It better be worth it."

I said, "What if we slip off and kill our fool selves?"

"You care?"

I said I might later on.

She said, "You don't believe I can make it."

I jumped. It was slick on that moss in the rain. Then I looked up and this gigantic monster comes flying through all of the red from the sign, yowling and clawing like somebody cast her in the Lake of Fire.

She landed straight on me, of course. She knocked me flat on my back and was digging her claws in the roof to slow us both down but we slid for the edge. Tina grabbed holt of a pipe sticking out of the roof and we stopped. She said, "Fuck." She laughed so deep in her body she buzzed every one of my bones.

I said, "Get off me, moron."

Tina said, "You're about slick as a little white dick."

Then she flopped on her back and looked up at the sign and said, "Whoo."

It was O she was talking about.

There's not a person alive that can make me forget where I've been except her. Seems like my brain just erased about Rosco and me being there, and needed to have new adventures and look all around at the world.

After while I took off my shoes. I needed to hold with my toes where it's slick. I walked the ridge to the end and walked back.

Tina said, "Maniac!" She crawled up real slow on her knees to the peak. She was covered all over with mud.

We sat beside of each other and looked at the town for a while without knowing the first thing about it to say. Tina sat still for me picking the leaves off her head. It was just misting a little, not much.

She talked in time with the letters. She said, "Look at this little-bitty town. No wonder I been feeling too big."

I said, "You are too big."

"Hey, I see my house where I live."

"Where?"

She pointed. "See there? Our lights are all on."

"I can't see any such thing."

"Because you're half blind."

"Nobody can see that far. You're just making it up."

"It means they're both up. Daddy wonders where in the world is his car."

"So? You knew they'd catch you. You think he wouldn't see all of those miles on his car?"

She shrugged like she didn't much care.

"What will they do?"

"Try and bear up."

"That doesn't sound all that bad."

She looked at me. "Your momma and daddy the kind to bear up? Or they grab holt and do something to you?"

"Momma is one way and Daddy's the other."

"Which one you rather?"

"I don't know." I was standing a little ways down from the peak. I said, "I'll be down here with my momma, and look up, and Daddy looks better." I walked up to the peak. Tina was watching. "Then when I get there, me and my daddy start sinking." I waited for M and walked down the other side. Tina was grinning. "And then I look up at my momma." I waited for O and walked up to the peak. Tina was laughing. "But then me and Momma both sink."

She grabbed me after the L. She caught both my knees when I got to the peak, and said, "Then stay in the middle, you monkey. Where it's still."

I never figured there *was* any middle.

She let me go and I sat down beside her on the peak, facing town. Later they turned off the sign. It was late in the night.

She said, "I'm going off." She sounded steady and quiet.

"Where?"

"I need a change."

"What are you talking about?"

"I'm not going back to that training school. Besides, this town is too little. Somebody always be watching. I'm too big, I stick out. I need to go be someplace bigger than this."

"Where's that?"

"I'm gonna be a surgeon."

"Do what?"

"I'm gonna be a surgeon. I'm gonna cut on people."

I thought for sure it was one of her jokes. I said, "You can't be. Surgeons have brains."

"I got brains."

"If you're a surgeon, you can't be all the time beating people up."

"Sure you can. Then you get their business."

I said, "It costs money."

"I'll get money. I'll save up."

"You can't ever shake. You need a steady hand."

"I got one." She raised her hand in my face. A water drop hung off the end of her finger. It never even jiggled. That pissed me off, how her hand was so steady, like she meant it. It pissed me off how she came on that roof and acted like she'd already planned out the rest of her life.

I said, "You're crazy."

"Listen who's talking. Look at this place. It's the hatefulest place I've ever been. Listen at that. It's like a war going on, like a war over nothing but rooms. This where you pick to be in love?"

"It's better than some beat-to-shit snack truck."

She grinned like her gigantic teeth were too hot for her mouth. "You better keep it, then. Find you a white boy."

I said, "I don't care what you do."

"You better. You're the one slapping that scalpel in my hand when I say, 'Scalpel!' "

"Crud."

"Your little monkey nose will be so cute poochin' out the mask."

"Get real."

"Nurse Monkey. That sounds real to me."

"When did you decide all this?"

"This morning. And I decided again, just now."

I tried to get up and leave but she jerked me back down by the arm and got me in a full nelson. She talked up close to my ear, from behind. "I'm telling you the truth, monkey. I can't go back in that place. I hate that place. Even if I make it out of there they'll just put me back in, if I stay around here. That Jetts, she'll be violating me again, that pigsucker. I ain't going back. I swear it. My aunt Leitha, she lives in California. She's a schoolteacher. She got the best education in the world. She used to like me. I'm gonna live in her house. I already called her, after supper. She's gonna let me be in her school. They don't ever eat butter rolls in her school. I know for a fact. Some days they eat tortillas. Sometimes they don't eat bread at all. I'll get all A's. Aunt Leitha, she told me she'd help me do things with my life if I needed her to. And she wasn't just saying it, neither. She's like that."

She turned me loose and we sat. She said, "I told my momma and daddy already. And they were sorry I need to be gone. But they hate me being locked up in that place. So I said, 'When I'm rich I'll get me a great big ol' house. And you can come live in my house if you ever once cheer up.' "

I said, "You didn't really say that."

She said, "No, but I might." She said, "You can come too, monkey. If you cheer up."

I said, "I don't care what you do. Just go."

"Won't be long 'fore I write you this letter and say come ahead. Then watch out, California."

"Shut up."

She squeezed me hard in that full nelson. I felt her stretch-

ing the back of my neck. Whenever I spend any time around
Tina I come out stretched.

I tried to picture her heading out West. I tried to picture
me with her. I said, "Won't they catch you, if you try to escape?"

"They can't touch me out of state. Once I sneak out of this
state, I'll be free."

I tried to picture myself leaving town. All I could get in my
head was more questions. I said, "What about my daddy?"

"What about him?"

"What if he's really not guilty? What if my brother was
telling the truth for one time in his life?"

"You think he was?"

"I don't know. The law said he was. But one thing I know
is, the law don't know crap. The law says something, you can
just about figure the opposite. I need to know for myself."

Tina said, "What for? What good it ever do you?"

"I don't know." I looked around and the mountains were
steady but all of the little white lights were just jumping and
twitching like bugs. I couldn't really believe myself saying
what-all I was saying. Things that won't ever sound right in a
house come out making some sense on a roof. I said, "Everybody says I'm about half Daddy. What if I'm really a killer deep
down? You can get that from your daddy. I know for a fact.
It was in this magazine."

She hid her face in her hands and peeked out through her
fingers, like she was afraid to look straight at a killer. She
covered one eye, then the other. She said, "Which half is
which?"

I said, "I mean it. And another thing is, I don't know
whether he did it or whether I was just ready to hold something ugly against him. I have this huge imagination. What if
it's all in my head? Sometimes I figure he'll kill me for Rosco.
I did a lot worse than Judith. And he used to love that woman.
I mean it. He loved her a lot."

Tina was listening to me.

I said, "What if I'm the one guilty? You accuse somebody
of something real ugly then maybe that just proves you are

ugly yourself. That's what Momma always says, anyway. Maybe I *wanted* my daddy to kill her. Maybe she really did kill her own self."

Tina said, "What if she did?"

"Well, maybe he could forgive me. Then maybe we could make up and go back like we were."

I saw the roofs stepping down, down, down, and felt ready to blow off and bounce. I said, "Except now he moves in with some woman. Moves right on in with some woman. Just like he don't care what nobody thinks or who's dead. And he's the one free and I'm the one stuck in some home. And that's what I really despise. That's what really sucks."

Tina was watching and listening. I never saw her so quiet before in my life. She was smiling just like she was happy and proud we were having this talk. Just because I finally told her the truth, and nobody made me.

She said, "You are such a confused little monkey. What are you gonna do?"

"I don't know."

She said, "You es-scared?"

"I reckon. Are you?"

"Of what?"

"Leaving your momma and daddy. Going to California."

"Who, me? It's the Sunshine State."

"Right."

She touched my knee. I like the size of her fingers. I like the color her nails really are. She said, "You figure all of this out. You stand right up to that daddy of yours and say, 'Boo!' Use some words on that man. Try 'consternation'—that's one of my daddy's favorites. Try 'mortification.' Tell him to go look 'em up. And then come right ahead, if you need to. We find a good place for you at Aunt Leitha's."

I watched her fingers come off of my knee. I didn't want her to go out of state. I'm such a baby.

I started putting my shoes on. She said, "You come see me, you hear? Just stay the same way as you are but cheer up. You hear?"

I walked to one end of the roof, where the top of the wall

comes down level with the edge. I jumped and landed in leaves.

She yelled at me, "Wait!"

"What, Tina? *What?*"

"Get me down from here!"

9

She hooked her thumbs in his belt loops and they rode double, leaning ear-first into turns, agog in the ratcheting thrust of the engine, his hair whipping into her eyes. They coasted School Hill, through the curve at the school, took the bypass and looped the whole south end of Baughtown, weaving their way to a ridge where the road lay as flat as the top of an anvil and gave them a glimpse of the way they had come, the curves of gray pavement embedded like horseshoes, hammered and shining.

Buddy turned in at a three-gabled cottage whose glassed porch commanded a long view of ridges and peaks. He set the kickstand. "Get off."

Libby said, "No."

"Get off."

"That's his car in the carport."

Buddy hopped one-legged away from the bike. "Come on," he said.

"You liar."

"I never said he wouldn't be here."

"You said we were going to ride. You said we could go someplace different."

"You ever been to this house?"

"No, but that's his Mustang, and we're at that woman's, right? That's not someplace different."

"Daddy said for me to bring you. He's got a surprise."

"What is it?"

"I don't know. He said surprise."

Libby balanced over the Harley, bridging from the toes of one foot. "You got some idea."

"It might be something to do with living here, or else he wouldn't say to come and call it a surprise."

"No way. Take me back."

"What for?"

"Because! Once he starts his mess you can't think straight your own self. He gets rid of Momma, then he gets rid of Judith, then he—"

"Shut up, Libby."

"Then he thinks he can just go right on with some other woman, like nothing ever happened."

"Shut up."

"No!"

Buddy said, "I thought we had all this settled, but you're just the same as before."

"That wasn't him we were talking about. That was separate."

Buddy kicked pieces of turf. "You don't know. You're a girl. All you have to do is not show him trouble."

"You're crazy."

"At least I don't turn on my daddy. You think you're better than he is. You're crazy. He's better than all of these people around here. He can whip any man in this county. You don't know half of what-all he can do. He can train dogs and build rooms and make people laugh and hit doves on the fly and fix most of what needs it. And all of these people respect him, and women go after him too, because they can see he's a man. But they get him in trouble, is all. But you wouldn't know. You don't know shit about what kind of pressure he's under. Men have to take on these pressures you don't know the first thing about. Like in business and everyday life."

"Like what?"

"Like for one thing raising his own self up and bettering his own self. Like he bettered himself past his daddy, and got out of Baughtown, and didn't let people walk over top of him all of his life. Like he proved to that foreman at Baugh's. He showed him he wouldn't do work they could give to a nigger."

"You don't know."

"Yes I do."

"You're such a big shot whenever you crawl off that Harley."

"Shut up, Libby. Whose side you on?"

"Why can't you just leave him be for a change? You gonna tag after him all of your life? Why can't we do for ourselves for a change?"

"Daddy said to bring you and—"

"He just cares what he wants. He just cares about him. I hate him, Buddy. I mean it."

Buddy wheeled and she flinched, lowering her gaze. "*Okay,*" she said. "You don't have to get mad."

She followed him up to the house. He set his foot on the first brick step, and looked at his boot, listening. It was as though he had pedaled a drum. They were feeling and hearing a thudding percussion. They stepped back and glanced to the porch, where the casements flushed sorrel then emptied. A horse cleared the end of the house into full view and shied, dancing sideways over spring onions and dead thatch with its white-stockinged forelegs mincing and two swirls of foaming saliva coiled at the ends of the bit.

Their father chewed a cigar set in the corner of his mouth and lightly slapped the rein of the snaffle rig on the neck of the horse and nudged its flank with his heels. The horse stepped forward then sideways, rolling its eyes at Libby and Buddy.

"What's that?" Buddy said.

Lampert took the cigar from his mouth and considered the lit end. "This?" he said. "A cigar. One like you smoke when you climb on your five-gaited gelding and ride."

Libby sat on the bench of a picnic table, watching her father ride the horse around the yard. Buddy stood holding the nozzle of a garden hose, water seeping down his arm.

"What does he want with that water?" Libby said.

"He just said hold it and aim."

Lampert called out, "Get that water hose ready." He was riding toward them, posting with the jouncing, earth-bound trot. He pulled the reins side to side. The horse shook its head. Lampert said, "Now!" Buddy twisted the nozzle. The horse seemed to stagger and bolt through the spray; he shook off the trot and was churning a single-foot drum roll of hooves on the lawn.

"Rack on!" Lampert said. He rode with such calm that his body seemed not to engage in the riding, as if all he required to be perfectly tranquil was an engine of maximum motion, of pistonlike forelegs and camaction shoulders, of frantically kinetic muscle and bone.

Libby said, "Buddy, you can turn off the hose now. He doesn't need it anymore. He's not going to need you around to be holding that hose every time."

Later Lampert dismounted and called Buddy over. "Hold my horse." Buddy took the bridle in his right hand, his arm stiff as if to repel an attack. The horse yanked him sideways.

Lampert sat on the edge of the table beside Libby. She was facing the other direction—west. The sunset was staining the sky gradations of nicotine-yellow and brown.

Her father said, "I promised Annabelle your eyes would light up. That's why we spent all this cash on a horse and a barn and some work on the fence. I told her Buddy and you would both come on the weekends and ride and we'd go to the shows. And that's how we'd get back together. Back like a family."

Libby didn't say anything.

"If you're nervous about her, relax. She's at her mother's. I thought we'd all better take this a step at a time."

The horse towed Buddy sideways and began to crop the thatch.

"Don't let him chew on the onions," Lampert said. He stubbed out the cigar and left it lying on the table like an animal's dropping. She could smell it.

He said, "You want to ride him?"

"No."

Her father waited a couple of beats and got up from the table. It seesawed a little under her elbow. He walked across the yard and snatched the reins from Buddy. "I told you to keep him out of the onions." The horse tossed its head. Lampert flicked the tail of the reins on Buddy's shoulder. "You want to ride him?"

"I don't guess."

"You at least going to sit on his back?"

"What for?"

"What a question. I reckon I should've known your sister wouldn't stoop to ride a horse of mine. What's *your* excuse? You scared?"

"No."

"I don't care if you're scared."

"I'm not scared."

Lampert flicked the reins again, but Buddy only stared at a crescent of bent thatch slowly recoiling from the print of a hoof.

"Then get on."

"You go ahead."

"Get on."

"You go ahead."

Libby said, "Leave him be."

Lampert kept slapping the reins on Buddy's shoulder.

She said, "Just leave him be."

He kept slapping the reins.

Libby untangled herself from the picnic bench, shouldered past Buddy, and lunged for the saddle. She kicked her left foot at the stirrup and missed. The horse shied and laid back his ears.

"What are you doing?" Buddy said.

"Get back," Lampert said to her.

"You satisfied?" she said. "I'm riding your horse."

"Get out of here, stupid," Buddy said.

Libby grabbed the saddle and muscled herself onto the horse, which stamped and laid back its ears. She managed to catch the swinging stirrup with her toe.

"Get down," Buddy said.

"No." She swung herself across the saddle.

Buddy said, "I swear." He limped around the house. In a minute the sound of his Harley had sunk down the opposite side of the ridge, out of earshot.

Her feet wouldn't reach the metal, so Lampert tucked them under the stirrup leather and led the horse once around the yard. She rode with one hand on the hornless pommel and the other behind her on the cantle, her thighs stretched tight over broad leather, feeling the horse yaw beneath her like a mountain collapsing. She could not remember ever looking down on her father's head, seeing the crescent-shaped hollow in the bone just over his ear, hair thinning on his crown, his neck so exposed in his shirt. She had never before thought of him as having parts, and now as she caught herself so brutally appraising them she became nauseated over the rocking withers.

He led her out of the yard through a windbreak of white pines, stopping at a strand of charged wire that was strung in the gap of an incomplete fence. He lifted the wire at a junction by a plastic grip to let them pass. He replaced the wire and led the horse down a steep bank. At the foot of the bank, he lifted her down from the horse and set her on the clay apron of a small, shed-roofed barn sheathed with galvanized steel.

After he unsaddled the horse, it pranced head-down into the open stall and stood snorting into a trough. Lampert opened the wooden door of a small tack room, hung the leather, and came out with a coffee can full of grain. The horse nosed his arm away from the trough and began to chew. Lampert tossed the can through the tack room door, among the feed sacks and tools, and said, "I built this," with no particular inflection. She studied the finger-length of wood he used to close the hasp, and saw the mark of his whittling on it. They stood around in the dusk a few minutes. They were on the northeastern side of the ridge, in a shadow laid down by a crescent of pines. The sheet metal drew light out of the sky and lorded it over them. She could smell the perfume of saw cuts in the wooden frame of the barn.

"Not going to give me a chance, are you," he said. There was no question in it.

Libby didn't answer. It seemed to her she had come to a place where words all had edges and could not be taken up without bodily harm.

"Over and done with in everybody's mind but one. Not guilty in every durn mind but one."

His voice sheared a sliver of metal from the barn and coiled it up tight in her chest. She felt the sweep of his shoulder in motion as he flung a small stone at the barn. The horse stamped and flung its head as the stone rang on the sheathing. His voice held the quaver of metal: "It was the man. It was that man you stayed for and came back for, not me and not Buddy. Him, whoever he is. Go on and find him. *Go!*"

The "*Go!*" was what moved her. It shot through her trunk to her legs. She turned and was walking, then running uphill in the dark. She was running on steep, gullied ground toward the windbreak of pines, which was black at the edge of the yard.

He called, "Look out! *Stop!*"

The wire in the fence lashed her hips and she recoiled and fell on her seat. Her first thought was, *How did he do that with words?* but then she remembered the wire. She crawled underneath toward the windbreak, stood, crossed the yard, and went on past the house to the road and the switchbacks toward Baughtown.

There were splotches of light on the southwestern slope, and she looked up and squinted to bring into focus the flickering highlights of amber and gold on his clothing. He was just two road embankments behind her, on foot. This did not startle her. He was always behind her, one way or another.

At the bypass, she sprinted across, but he loped, in no hurry. It angered her she was so easy to chase. She looked into Baughtown for places to hide. She vaulted the guardrail and plunged down a weedy embankment into a yard of Vass-Baugh, picking her way through a slum of stacked hardwood, through a fibrous and cottony darkness, over low, rutted ground where the strips of still water were glinting.

Then she was climbing a slope through the litter of impro-
vised nests, among bottles and wrappers and clots of damp
cloth, veering north into fresher, green lumber, whose smell
was acidic and keen. He snagged her arm and said, "Come
on."

"No!" She yanked herself away.

He snatched her elbow again and she lunged with a fury. He
let go rather than disjoint her arm. "I'm not in the mood to
take crap off of you. I'll take and whip you right now."

Libby wouldn't look at his face. She stared broadside into
sandwiching layers of lumber and air. "Leave me alone."

"Where are you going?"

She didn't say.

"Running to some of your buddies from Baughtown?"

With this she turned and walked, speaking as though words
came in long, leggy strides: "You talk about Baughtown so
much you must really love it."

His voice was behind her. "You never sassed me like this in
your life."

"Maybe I learned."

His hand was on her shoulder, pulling her around. "That's
right, you did. And you wouldn't learn you a mouth like that
if it wasn't for all of these people between us. These coloreds
and government people."

"I did what you wanted me to, and look where it got me. I
stayed here and look where it got me."

"Yeh, you stayed. For a nigger from Baughtown."

She had been turning away when he said it. Now she
glanced up to see what he knew. The dark was a single dimen-
sion, a plane, his face like a pucker on velveteen fabric, a place
where the blackness had winced. He spat, as if to expel something green and unripe from his mouth. His spitting restored
the dimensions of lumber and landscape around them.

His voice was low and monotone. "I didn't know it for sure
until now."

"Why don't you kill me like Judith? I did a lot more than she
ever did. I did whatever he wanted me to. I rode around in that
car doing dope like you wouldn't believe. So why don't you kill

me? Then Momma can hear about what-all I've done and despise me and I will already be dead."

"I never heard of such crap in my life."

"Go ahead, nobody's looking down here. You can claim it was niggers from Baughtown."

"How long you planning to put us all through this?"

"Through what?"

"All of this wild talk and freezing me out."

"What do you want? You've got a horse, and a house, and another new woman. And Judith won't get on your nerves with that baby."

"Here we go into all that. Why are you so determined to hold out against me?"

"Just because." She stood with her arms crossed over her chest.

He smoked a cigarette, as though calculating the risks of pressing for her answer. "Because what?"

She faced him. She was ready. She had the words. "Because I saw you. I saw how you looked. And that blood. And the way she was lying. You didn't love her. You didn't want any part of that baby. You wanted them dead and they were."

His hand stabbed the cigarette at her. "Nobody treated her hateful as you did. How many times did you tell me you wished she was dead? So I reckon that makes you a killer just like your old man. Don't it?"

She froze. Her gaze did not budge from his neck, as if moving so much as an eyelash would finish her off. He held the Camel midway between them, waist high, like a dagger withdrawn from her breast, as though astonished to find that the dagger was his.

As soon as she cried she could move. She pitched herself at the side of a stack. He laid a hand on her arm. She spun away. He said, "I didn't mean it was you. She didn't die about you."

Libby looked at the soil, a curtain of hair in her face.

He said, "Don't pay any mind to all that. I'm not myself."

She didn't respond.

"You hear me?"

Then she was glaring at him, squeezing a "Why?" in each fist like a caliper brake: "Why did she, then? Why?"

His hand and his shoulder were in motion. She saw the starburst of lit cigarette as it fell. She heard the slow twitch of his boot on the soil. She heard him say, "Because I told her to."

She blinked, still listening, as though the sense of this message were too long for its sound. The dark settled into the stacks like a stupor, and they were both in it.

"You want to see the whole picture? That what you want? That all the choices I've got?"

She didn't answer.

He seemed to nod, or to bow. "Maybe you do need to hear it." He laid his hands on her shoulders, trying to steer her around in the aisle. She resisted, but he fastened his hands on her shoulders, and planted her, saying, "Stand there. I need to get us arranged."

His body was moving in the near-dark, stepping off the dimensions of the scene, the width of the aisle like the width of the trailer, the stacks a bit higher than walls. He seemed to place pieces of furniture, then to toe his own mark in the middle, half the room's width from her side. His tenor came out of the lumber around her, a humming like carpenter bees in the wood.

"We were having a fight about something like always. At the end we just fought all the time."

His hand seemed to brandish something imagined, a weapon.

"We had the guns out. Both daring each other. She fired one off, at the ceiling. Surprised me. She never dared that before. So I fired off one round at the wall." He pointed to the base of the stack, just behind her, and waited, as if they might both hear the slug splintering wood.

"She was drunk and fell back over something. Hit her head. And Babe, I hope you never wind up in such sorry shape to where you laugh at a woman who's bumping herself on the head."

He waited. He gestured to his left, palm open as if introducing a phantom. "And Buddy was standing right here in the room. Seeing how sorry his daddy turned out."

His hands burrowed deep into his pockets, his shoulders

hunched up to the base of his skull. He was bracing his ribs with his elbows. She looked in another direction and waited.

"She got up from the floor. She aimed that gun at her head. Like she thought that was the next step up. I said, 'Go right ahead. You never did have the guts. *Fire!*' I saw both her eyes glaze over. And stare at the lamp." He came to Libby and carefully, tenderly cocked her arm, bent her elbow, aimed her hand at the side of her head. His body began to recall for him, in slow motion, the way he had lunged, the point where his wrist struck her arm, raising her elbow out of position.

When he finished with her hand it dropped to Libby's side.

He said, "I tried, babe, I swear it. I tried to knock it away from her head. But I just caught a piece of her elbow. She was already pulling the trigger."

The ribboning sense of this message lay quietly heaped at their feet. Libby looked there and remembered the sound of the guns, the sounds she had taken for rim shots while she was still coasting the edges of sleep. She heard the smoke alarm. She saw him again on the floor, saw the guns and the blood, saw the odd, crooked curl of the body. She felt herself clutching the mirror, and all of it—what he said, what she saw in her mind—suddenly seemed of a piece, not ribboning now but all solid and whole, as though from the same flitch of wood, sliced and laid open like truth in a book.

Libby began to walk.

Behind her, he said, "So there wasn't any part of it you. You hear?"

She kept walking. He followed her, two or three paces behind. He said, "What was I supposed to do? Plead guilty? That make you happy? What about Buddy? That make him happy? Even if cops and the judge and the jury had all been inside of that trailer, watching the whole blessed thing, no court of law would convict me. You can't convict a man for daring his wife."

His palm touched her shoulder. She ducked away and stood back. "Leave me alone."

He lit another Camel. She heard the match and backed away, dreading the smoke.

After a while he said, "Listen at me. Whining around after you in this yard like a durn yellow dog. Like I ought to just move into one of these shacks here in Baughtown and lay on the bed all day long."

"Why don't you? Since you love it so much."

He swore and kicked off a length of oak sticker protruding from one of the stacks. "You didn't go with this nigger from Baughtown because of what happened to Judith. You've been out riding around in that car since a long time before. Picked the one kind you knew would just gall me the worst. The worst kind you could."

"You think they're all the worst kind."

"You getting even with me? You getting even with me now for leaving your momma?"

"You think everybody acts like they do to get even with you. Maybe I loved him. You ever think about that?"

He shook his head. "You can't tell me anything worse than I've already dreamed up to blame on myself."

She was so angry she bent. The anger was folding her up at the knees, at her hips, at her waist. "I hate you."

Libby bowed and waited, stared at his torso, his strike zone. The blow didn't come. There was no flex or motion. His body was rigid, a stob. She might have thrown ringers against it. She backed away, watching. The stob of her father remained, as though hammered in deep there and left. She stepped away, letting the darkness consume him. She knew that he needed some word or her touch to go easy. That was all he required. She would not. There were too many audible horrors between them, too many ringers on the stob. She turned and walked on through the stacks. Later she heard him behind her, his feet in the mud.

They emerged from the yard in an alley that dropped off a short, rutted slope to the rear of a propane distributing company's lot. The slope was still sopping from rain and he slipped and fell back on his seat. She heard him cursing and she stopped, turning among the empty propane tanks that lay scattered in the weeds like blunted missiles or exaggerated bullets. When she saw him get up she went on.

He overtook her again on an oily dirt road, under the greenish glow of a vapor lamp lighting one side of the mill, and said, "I guess some man should take a whip and beat me for the way I raised you both."

Libby was dragging the tips of her fingers on the chain-link fence, feeling the metallic grit in its galvanized coating. Its mesh seemed to strain from the huge mass of brickwork behind it. The mill was a fortress, a region of masonry; the black sky's reflection seemed mortared and stacked in its windows.

When he spoke again, his voice was low and quiet. "I asked Miz Gregson to marry me. She said she would."

Her hands gripped the links, rattling the fence.

He said, "That all you've got to say?"

"Call Momma and tell her."

"Don't know her number."

"You've got it."

"I'm not one to talk on the phone."

"You have to call her."

"All the telephone's good for is connecting a mouth with an ear. Women don't listen to men with their ears. A man's voice goes direct"—he struck his breastbone with his knuckles—"not the long way around through her ears."

She stared at him.

"It's true. A woman can listen to some other woman or kids on the phone, but a man's got to tell her direct or it won't come across. When he gets on the phone she'll be hearing things he never meant."

"Call her. I mean it."

Libby didn't know why he said what he said, after that. It almost seemed as though he had begun to regard her as someone apart from himself. He might have been trying to come clean. He might have been looking for sympathy. She didn't know, and so she listened, reserving the words for sometime when she might have the wits to decode them, when they might be of use.

"I guess I'm as worthless as you seem to think. Maybe when you've got a kid of your own then you might change your mind. Because I'll tell you what, and this is a fact: Kids make a change in your life. Before a man's got kids, all he wants is one thing."

For a moment he let her wait, suspending them both in that time of wanting, before children. She rattled the fence.

"He wants to be the kind of man who never wishes he could swap and be somebody else. He wants to hang onto that feeling—like when he connects with a homer. Like when he is watching that ball clear the creek. Except he wants it permanent. He wants that feeling in his fingers, that tingle. He wants it to last. Then a day comes when he has to face himself and know that it's not going to last."

Libby stopped shaking the fence. Her father flipped his Camel away and said, "There's plenty of reasons. Not lucky or accurate, maybe. Some kind of a shortcoming—could be a number of things, I don't know. Then after that he has kids, and he wouldn't trade places with anybody else, on account of his kids couldn't still be his kids if he did. So then all he wants is to be the kind of daddy his kids wouldn't swap for the world. That's all he wants."

What she wanted was a drink in a can. She wanted to hold something cleanly and recently made. She began walking away.

As she passed from the vapor lamp's humming green glow, his voice seemed to press at her back. "I know one thing for sure. You got me in you."

Libby was walking in darkness, shaking her head.

"Because if you didn't have some of me in you, you wouldn't show all of this nerve."

She left him and walked through a grid of dirt streets, streets designed for people filing back and forth to work, through a mazelike replication of houses with shallow verandas and triple-A gables—one house many times over, multiplied as if by the mill, as if by some trick of reflection in the tiny square panes of its windows, like an image in the eyes of a fly. She walked past the boarded-up school, past the pipe-metal swing sets and chin bars exposed on the playground like plumbing uprooted, through ranks of newer, meaner houses, where a dog yapped and voices entwined with the odors of food in the dark. She followed the tracks past the finishing plant, to a road that hooked into the bottoms and down to the bend of the creek. At the edge of the fairground she turned and walked on toward the high, jutting brow of downtown, a breakerlike crest of foamy, bright haze and remote, faintly promising sounds. The ground in the bottoms was spongy. The cold in the weeds was a serrated edge at her legs. The grandstand was looming and hooded, a sentry alert on the edge of an alien land.

PART FIVE

NEW PEOPLE SING

]

First I was Undisciplined, then I was Delinquent, and now I'm Emancipated. Next I'll be gone.

The Omelette Shoppe where I work puts a map on their placemats, and all of the franchise locations are eggs. I draw a star on the egg for Chicago, that's Momma. I draw a star on the egg for San Diego, that's Tina. I draw an X, and that's here, Rapid Falls. I draw a line up the middle. I need to see a good map of those roads. I need to see where to put me a star.

I know that doesn't make sense in real life. People aren't nothing like franchise locations. It's just a feeling I've got that gets stronger. I'm headed out of this place. I need a year, maybe less.

Daddy leaned over the counter last Sunday and asked me, "How long you planning to live by yourself and handle other people's dirty plates?"

I told him, "Just till I get up the money to leave."

He asked me, "What would leaving accomplish? You put this counter between us already. Ain't that accomplishment enough?"

I told him "ain't" was ignorant.

Sometimes he acts like he wants to come back of that counter and grab me—hug me or shake me, one or the other. He has to keep to his side of the counter. This side's for workers. I am a worker.

I never thought I would see Uncle Bob. I figured Betsy and him were relieved I was out of their lives. But one day the week after Easter he came to that home for delinquents and got me. He didn't say what about.

He drove me back to his house and we parked. He marched me back of the house to his double garage. There for a second I thought he would cut him a switch but he didn't. We went around to the back, where those steps run upside his garage. He said, "Go ahead up," which I did.

He used his key to that room and he told me to go on inside. I didn't want to go in, on account of that room being musty and slanted from sitting up under the roof. But I did. The air wasn't anywhere near room temperature in there.

I could see all of this dust on his desk and his chair and some boxes shoved up to the walls. That's when I figured he might be a pervert. It looked like a place where a pervert would lock me—nothing but wood and off-white. Betsy could turn any man into a pervert right quick.

Uncle Bob's one of these men who will whip out his knife at the drop of a hat. He scratched a drop of off-white that was dried on the light switch. Then he pointed his knife blade at parts of the room. Men point their knives upside down, with the palm of their hand underneath, so the knife doesn't slip through their fingers and drop and get blunt. So Daddy says, anyway.

Uncle Bob said, "These boxes can all go to the basement. I don't need an office that much, now that I'm traveling. Already got a shower and toilet in there. Maybe there's room for some kind of a kitchen along that side wall. Plumbing's roughed in. Run about ten foot of baseboard electric along that far end. Center it under that window." He shut his knife and he rattled it up with some change in his pocket. That's all my fool brain could figure, that money sound down in his pocket.

He goes, "Betsy needs to be able to look your momma in the eye. That and do the good, Christian thing. I just figure you are my niece and you need you a safe place to live." He put his hands on the ceiling and pushed like he needed to check it for give. He said, "But this would be business only, not family. You hear me? You won't come down to the house unless Betsy invites you. You act like company then, if you come. Rent will be thirty-five dollars a month. You won't bring people up here unless they're approved in advance. If you tear something up, or get crossways with us or the law, or make noise, or don't keep up with your rent, or we catch you with somebody up here, I'll kick your behind off the place. And that's it. You hear me? It's simple as that. You better just make up your mind."

So I did.

Some nights that deputy Smiley comes into this restaurant and eats when he's going to work. He needs a thrill of some kind or other. I guess it has to be boring to spend every night in this one little town, just riding and shining his light. He wants to figure me out. He wants to hear what went on in that truck. He says I seem a lot older to him. He says I've aged past my years. I told him that's not surprising. I've been stoned past my years, and screwed past my years, and scared past my years. Smiley is easy to shock.

One night he started on Judith. He said, "Let's see, wasn't you home when it happened? I 'spect it shook you up bad."

I wiped the counter and leaned over close with my palms planted flat on both sides of his plate. I said, "You want to know how it happened?"

His little eyes like to pop. I figure sometimes it pays to give law what they want, just as long as I get something back. I figure if he won't leave me alone then maybe he'll leave me a tip. Which he does.

I started whispering to him. I was so quiet I sounded like steam in the dripper before there is coffee. I said, "We had a Fairlane he kept in the yard. He came home late in the night and caught her in the backseat with a soldier. He told her to go in the house. He had his Winchester ready. She watched him order that soldier to lie in the trunk and then shoot him and slam down the lid. That's why she went berserk and shot her own self through the head."

That deputy swallowed some egg he'd forgot was still lying around on his tongue. He said, "What kind of make-believe story you telling?"

I said, "You want to see in the trunk of that Fairlane? Too

late. He had it dragged to the crusher. Once it was crushed then they melted it back into steel. So that soldier is part of the steel. Next time you buy something metal you'll wonder."

He cocked his head like a chicken that's hearing a spook owl at night. He asked me what in the world I was trying to prove. I said some grape jelly dropped off his toast on his chin. He wiped his chin and looked down at his napkin to make sure the jelly was real. He leaves me five-dollar tips. He weighs them down with the edge of his plate, like they might blow away.

Daddy says we'd be a sight better off if the law hadn't got itself mixed in our troubles. I guess he's right about that. He says it's better to keep everything in the family. I said fine, but where was this family? I don't see any family. I see a dead body and all of its parts are avulsed. Just because some of the people are living don't mean you've got family there.

Daddy takes his time using up his breakfast. Then he drinks a hot refill on coffee. He says, See you, Babe, and I say, See you. When his car pulls out, the space stays empty for a while, but not too long. Then somebody else pulls up and parks there long enough to eat. Then somebody else, then somebody else. But it seems like his space a good while.

I met this woman named Willie. She likes to sit on a stool and eat blueberry waffles. She doesn't need all those blueberry waffles. She is so heavy and country. Her hair's a bright silver, the same as those buttons and studs on her shirt. After Daddy and Smiley, she is my third best tipper.

Daddy started umping this summer. He claims he's just picking up a little bit of side money, but I know the truth. I know he likes being ump. He says, "When a league needs an umpire, they go look for the meanest son of a bitch they can find. They don't want no sweethearts calling balls and strikes." I'm supposed to admit he can face his own faults like a man. I'm supposed to see there's a good side to him underneath. He wants to hear me take back that whole night when I told him I hated his guts. He wants to hear me take back that word "hate." Maybe I should, but I won't. That's all I've got between me and him taking me over—this counter and one little word. Somebody shows me what else I can use and I will.

Last night he came in with Buddy and they took a booth by the counter, so I had to serve. Daddy was wearing all black, so I guessed he'd been working home plate. There was a ghost in the dirt where the mask had been stuck to his face, and his hair was mashed down on the top of his head where the strap had been tight.

Some of the workers from Baugh's like to come in that time of the evening. Two guys came up to the counter to pay and they recognized Daddy. One guy said, "Called a fair game tonight, Jake. Fair and square."

Buddy swelled up, being proud. That's all he wants to be doing: tag after Daddy and swell. He'll never satisfy Daddy. Daddy wants Buddy and me to both stand on our own but still be on his side. Maybe there's people alive who know how to do both, but not me.

Daddy turned halfway around on the bench and looked back at those two guys from Baugh's. People will stop what they're doing and listen whenever he's fixing to talk. He said, "All I needed to do was remember the strike zone: between a man's knees where he crawls and his armpits where he sweats. That ain't hard, is it, Swifty?"

Swifty was grinning at Daddy. All of the people around there were grinning, except me and Satch. We were both too busy working. I do the counter and Satch does the grill.

Daddy thinks I'm just determined to prove things against him. He can't believe I would ever act separate from him. Maybe he's right. If I wasn't his daughter, maybe I wouldn't have all of this nerve to begin with. Maybe I ought to just thank him and never be like him. He put a creek between him and his daddy, and that was as far as he got. I'm headed off a lot farther. Durn if I'll live right beside of a place and look down on it all of my life.

He says, "Babe, do you need anything?" I tell him I need a year, maybe less. I need a license. I need a car that can move. I need a console to keep stuff from rolling around. I need to cover my steering wheel up in that extra soft leather that's kind to your hands. Then I'll be ready to roll.

After we buried Grandma Whitley, Aunt Betsy had all the loved ones over to her house for covered dish. Momma said come ride with her and Miles because we better talk. That was the first part of May. But I refused to set foot in that house, so we stood in the driveway a minute, with all of the cars of the loved ones. Momma wore everything black. She said wouldn't I come to Chicago and live. I said, "Sure, in a dead person's room." Probably once I get old I'll be sorry for all of this stuff I've been saying. There is no telling how many people I'll have on my conscience by then.

We stood around in the driveway some more. Annie's face kept popping up in her momma's African violets. Uncle Bob looked out the window and went away. Daddy looked out the window and went away. Then Buddy of course had to copy after them both. There were people in that house who don't belong together. That happens when somebody dies.

Momma said, "Where do things stand between you and your daddy?"

"He's getting married again, in case you don't know."

"Have you met her?"

"I've been to her house."

Momma shaded her eyes. There was a good bit of glare off those cars. She said, "Have you settled what happened?"

"Settled what?"

"I mean, are you settled in your own mind about it. Have you settled it with him in your mind?"

"Sure."

"Good."

"He finally saw he needed to tell me the truth."

"Good."

"You know that Fairlane he kept in the yard?"

"Yes. It was red."

"What really happened was, he came home and found her in back of that car with a colored. So he ordered her back in the house. And he had his bat. So he took and whipped the colored. And she saw him whipping this colored she loved out the window and shot herself clean through the head."

Momma just stared at the lies flying out of my mouth. She stepped around somebody's bumper to get closer to me, but I stood back in the edge of the yard. Seems like the first thing I always do when I get around Momma is try hard to hurt her, and I don't know why.

After a while she said, "Bob said he offered to rent you a room."

I kicked at somebody's tire. "I'm moving in there if I get a job and some money."

She said, "I'll help with the money. I'd rather see you over his garage than staying in that home. You would have family close. Unless you will come to Chicago with us."

I was too gutless to look her in the face and tell her once and for all. She walked around to one side of their Fairmont and leaned on the hood. After while she said, "I can stay maybe till Monday. We'll fix it up while I'm here. We'll make it nice as we can."

First off we cleared it with Trish. Trish came and looked the place over and said we could see how it went. Momma drove over to that home and got me on Sunday and carried me over to Betsy's again. Betsy and Bob were at church but Momma had a key. We ate banana sandwiches and went down in the basement. We were up to our necks in the furniture. It's always dark in that place on account of the wood soaking up all the light. Momma tried shading her eyes and turned this way and that. She said, "Pick what you want. Miles and Uncle Bob will move it."

When I went to pull out a drawer, or sniff of a mattress, Momma would tell me if it belonged to Bob and Betsy, or her and Daddy, or Grandma Whitley, or some other relation. She didn't care whose I took. Mostly I tried to find metal or cloth. Seems like you can't look at wood without scratching it up.

Miles set my bed up and Momma found bedclothes and washed them. She tested my kitchen to see if it worked. I have an all-metal kitchen. It's this little combination stove and sink and refrigerator. She said, "You be okay here tonight?"

I said I would.

She set a sack full of cleaning supplies on the floor. She said, "I'll come back first thing in the morning and cook you some breakfast and we'll clean everything and see where this furniture belongs."

I said, "Okay."

Soon as she left I shoved the furniture around till I got it arranged halfway right. Then I decided I wanted my bed against that side wall, where the ceiling slopes down, because I wanted to set me a table and chairs at the end by the window. So I had to shift everything over and mix things around. It took me until way after midnight. Then I started cleaning. Seems like I had all this energy left. I scrubbed the bathroom and stretched out on the floor and looked at everything upside down. I scrubbed underneath of the sink. I wiped the bottoms and tops of the lights. I mopped around behind the toilet. One thing I learned is how much needs to shine in a bathroom.

I did the same in the kitchen. I washed the dishes and glasses and stacked them by size. I put a shine on the faucet and dried all the water drops up off the sink. I didn't leave any dust on the furniture, or dirt on the floor. I worked till three in the morning. Then everything I could think of was clean. I was so tired about then. I curled on top of my bed in my clothes. Right when I'm going to sleep I remembered a Scot-Towel dropped by the stove. I thought, That one thing can wait. I was so sleepy. I closed my eyes, but my brain was eat up with that wadded-up towel. I saw it gradually open and swell. I was determined to just let it wait. Plus being too tired to move. I closed my eyes for a second and woke up and hurried and threw it away.

Next thing I knew there was somebody climbing the steps. It was morning already. I smoothed my bed and she knocked. I said come in and she did. She was all set to clean in her scarf and her pink rubber gloves. She had some curtains hung over one arm. They were tapioca.

She didn't say the first word after "Hey." She walked around and just touched with a couple of fingers to see if it wasn't a dream. I wished she'd look underneath of more things but she didn't. One time she reached for a lamp shade. I thought, "Shit, it's cockeyed." But she didn't change it. She stood in the door to my bathroom and stared at how spotless. I watched the back of her head for a while. She peeled her gloves off and shoved them both down in her pockets. She turned around and said, "You like these curtains?"

I said, "Sure, if they'll fit."

She said, "You want to hang them yourself?"

"You go ahead. Unless you mind."

She slipped the rod into one. I like to look at her hair when sun's coming through it. She has such heavenly hair. She started singing. She sang "He Leadeth Me." She didn't sing it to shame anybody. She just naturally sings when she gets down to work. She wasn't trying to turn me religious either. Momma can't help she was born with a voice that goes perfect with that kind of music.

She sang the verses except the one about "nor ever murmur nor repine." She stood back and looked at the curtains and said, "What do you think?"

I said, "Those are fantastic curtains."

She said when she came back for my birthday she would bring me a bedspread to match.

Willie eats all of her blueberry waffles. She says, "Who are you trying to be?"

I can answer her questions as long as she's leaving me tips. I tell her I'm just a girl who lives all by herself over top of a double garage out behind a brick house on School Hill, and I'm working and saving my money to leave.

Willie says, "Where are you going?"

I show her one of these maps with the franchise locations.

She says, "West? Hell yeh, I like West. I been to Nashville and Memphis and Columbus, Ohio. They was all pretty places, and lively. I been a waitress all over. It's just a livin', though, sweetheart. It's not a life. One of these days, you'll need to come around from back of that counter."

Daddy got married this summer and wanted me back. He tried to prove he deserved me because of a wife and a brick house with plenty of room. Buddy moved up there but I said I wanted to keep living out all by myself on my own. Trish said she could stall Daddy a couple of months, but he might get me back if I liked it or not, since a judge usually wants to side with a blood relative. Then she said there was a slight chance she could get me emancipated. I never heard of that before this year. It's whenever a judge decides a person's ready to live out on her own before she's a legal adult. He passes this verdict that she can be an Emancipated Minor, and not anybody's child, and can't anybody get custody. It's for somebody who knows more than her age.

But Trish said we had to get me out of that home for delinquents and set me up in my own independent living situation, or I'd never stand a chance. I didn't know of a place till my uncle came through.

Trish said that living out back of some Christians was perfect. She said it looks mighty good to the law. So I figured if Christians could help keep the law off my back then at least they were good for something. And Trish said if I did right, and took some responsibility, and kept my job and paid my rent and stuck to my budget and maybe went to church sometimes, she could go to court and prove on paper I deserved to be emancipated. Plus I was getting ready to turn sixteen, which sounds twice as mature as fifteen.

So I did all this stuff we could prove on paper. Then Trish took me shopping on money Momma sent down from Chicago, and we bought a tan skirt and a white blouse and hose for court. I borrowed some heels from Linda, who's little, and she put my hair in a bun. Everybody said how old I looked.

Daddy's lawyer said Daddy needed me and had a place for me and he had always been a loving father. Then Trish said she'd been watching me set a fine example of a young woman, and how I went to church sometimes. She spread some papers out that showed how much money I made and how I stuck to my budget and how my grades started coming up after I got put in that home. She said some pressures that used to be on me were out of the picture. That meant my daddy and Judith, I reckon. She had a letter from Satch that said I was a prompt employee doing fine, and how pretty soon I might be learning the grill. Linda said I could have their support and come over for Fun Night sometimes.

Ramona Jetts said that she had bent over backward for me and nothing worked and if all these experts thought they knew better than her what I needed she would just as soon not have to fool with me anymore. And the judge asked me would I know how to act if Ramona wasn't around to keep me out of trouble. I said she'd already helped me enough, and I said it with a straight face and acted sincere. I thought Ramona would slap me, but she didn't. I'm so relieved to be out from under that woman. Then the judge asked me was I ready to live by myself in the world and take responsibility for myself, and was I ready to be treated like an adult if I ever broke the law. I said, Yes sir, I am. Then he sentenced Elizabeth Corey Lampert to be an Emancipated Minor Child.

Daddy caught me by the elbow and asked me, "You happy, now?" I didn't say if I was or I wasn't.

I fixed the place how I like it. My socks are in a drawer beside my underwear. My pants are in the middle with my tops. My sweaters and stuff are in the bottom, and my uniforms are hanging in the closet. Once in a blue moon, if Uncle Bob is home, I'll go to church with them and eat Sunday dinner at their house, which tastes good after all those dinners at the Omelette Shoppe. Sometimes it's roast beef or maybe fried chicken. I found out I can put up with church and Aunt Betsy for a couple of hours if I like what they're having for lunch. For example, it's a relief to eat anything without eggs.

I keep my tips in a sock until Friday, and that's when I normally count up my money and roll up the change and go down to the bank. Annie likes hearing me jiggle my sock. Sometimes I get home from work late at night and I'm tired so I turn out my light and lie down on my bed and I'm waiting to sleep when I see how this light goes to playing around on my ceiling like a giant moth flopping around to get out. Annie is shining her flashlight around in my window again. So I pull on my robe and go barefoot outside with my sock down the steps to the grass, which is dewy and itches my feet. And she will be beaming that flashlight all over my legs while I'm walking. She'll sit cross-legged up on the top of her dresser in one of her nightgowns and whisper at me through the screen. She says, "Hi." I say, "Hi." She says, "Hold up your sock." So I do, and she touches how solid it feels through the screen. I jiggle it for her to hear. She says, "I can't believe all that money." She thinks you're rich if your money is heavy.

Sometimes she shows me a picture she drew or she sings me a song that she learned. And some nights I need me a Winston before we get done. But I always try not to seem like my cigarette's got a good flavor around her. And I make her promise not to copy after me. And she says she won't. So maybe I'm not the worst thing that happened to her in her life.

I've got a hundred and eighty-some dollars saved up in my passbook so far. I wrote "CAR" at the top of my passbook and underlined it twice, and that's where I put all my tips and any money I get from somebody I can't stand, like when that woman Daddy married sends me a check for twenty-five dollars in the mail, like I was some kind of orphan. That way I don't exactly spend it on myself. I mean, I don't need their money for my food or like that. But they can help buy my car, because they'll be paying for a car they can't touch or ride in. I can see it.

I never knew anybody who got emancipated before, so I didn't know what to expect. Right at first I felt funny about being loose on my own. Like if I didn't keep right on my path straight to work or I would wander around and not know where to go. The first day or two I kept thinking people were staring like I was some kind of ignorant kid on her own. I even got the creeps from walking by that man they welded together from pipes and mufflers and chained to a post in front of Budget Exhaust so nobody would steal him. It was like his lock-washers were watching me.

But I kept going and now I am used to my freedom and love it a lot. I like to walk into work by the car place and see what they parked in the showroom. They keep the floor waxed and all of the colors reflect. Canyon Red and Laser Blue and Star-flake Silver. I like all these modern colors. And the tires, they're so new you can just about feel of those goose bumps that come on the tread. They make the tires seem excited and ready to roll.

People say once you get out on your own you'll have heavy burdens and responsibilities, but I feel so light. I feel lighter than I ever felt in my life. I forget all about him, except when his Mustang pulls up. I'll be working and kidding around with a customer, like I don't have the first thing on my conscience, and then he pulls up and it's just like you slapped me or splashed me with water to make me think back. I do a lot better job when I don't have to ever think back.

People who live in a brick house don't know, but a wood house is not very solid. Noises go all the way through one. Somebody prizes the lid off a tin box of crackers and it'll go *boing* through the walls. I could be all the way back in my bedroom at midnight and still hear our Frigidaire come open. Because how the door would be suctioned up tight to the box. Like my lips want to stick against something that's froze and it hurts to yank loose.

Then I heard milk through the walls and him chewing and swallowing milk with the cracker sound in with the milk. And sometimes it seemed like I'd still hear his crackers and milk with my pillow shoved tight to my ears. That's how I mean by "not solid."

Grandma Whitley who is finally dead said that licker burned holes in his stomach like acid and that's why he needed those crackers and milk. But that woman always was one to blame everything in the world on a sin, you can't ever trust what she said. Maybe he had his own reasons.

Anyway, I would be right on his way back to bed. I was supposed to be sleeping already. I would play 'possum and wait and he wouldn't be wearing his shoes. Here came his heels smooching wood down the hall. Then when the door to my room starts to open, the air goes away like I'm losing my breath. I'm peeking out from under my eyelids. And I thought how my room was as dark as can be. But he was blacker than anything else. And he comes with the rest of his milk. And he leans over closer and kisses my cheek. And his glass it is tilting but milk never spills when I think every night it will spill and I wait and I wait but I never get wet. I just get a sticky, damp place on my cheek where he kissed me and left me some cracker crumbs in it. And it would dry slow. And it felt like when somebody broke open part of a Camel and spit in the pile of tobacco to get it to stick to my skin. And he dabbed it on top of a bee sting to draw out the poison but that didn't work.

Sometimes the lie part will drop in my head like a picture and swell. Sometimes I see myself hop out of bed and go run to the bathroom and scrub all of that cracker and milk off my face. I dry my cheek just as hard as I can. Soon as I lift up my face from that towel he's standing there squinting his eyes from the light. He looks ashamed of himself and not me.

Maybe that sounds like I hated my daddy, but really I loved him and liked him to kiss me good night all the time he was living with us. Maybe I always had some little part of myself that was wishing it wouldn't get kissed. All I know is, soon as I think up this lie he is gone. I can forget him and go back to working the same as I was.

Buddy says one of these days some guy will pull up in the right kind of car and come in here to eat. Buddy says this guy will claim me and carry me off. I tell him I'll never need to get claimed. I tell him he's the one wishing that he would get claimed. I tell him he keeps on trotting around after Daddy: "Here I am! Here! Claim *me*! Claim *me*!" Buddy says over and over: Shut up. But I like to talk. I'm learning more and more words in this restaurant. I'm turning into a talker.

Daddy says I'll never leave here. Daddy says I will stick close to this county and spite him till I have a back-talking kid of my own. He says we're both the same person down deep, but we're not. He never met up with Tina. He never saw a way out of this hole. She is the difference in me and my daddy. She was the best thing about this whole year.

I am half Martian like Tina. I know she's gone and that's final. I know she has her own future and she will forget about me before long. People can try and remember a person but they will still change if they move and stay gone. But I've got her grip on my body. She took and twisted and stretched all my bones. She jerked a knot in my tail. I've got enough of her in me to last.

I'm going off like my momma and Tina. I need to start something up for myself. I need to see where I fit in the most. And what kind of people I like when I get there. Someplace where I can live cheap on my own. Warmer and closer to level than this. Maybe I don't know the name of this place where I'm going, but I won't stay here. I'll never be like my daddy. I'll never lay all my troubles on Baughtown. I'll never lay all my troubles on blacks. I love my daddy but I'm keeping him in my rearview mirror. I'm headed out of this place. I need a year, maybe less.

2

We ate some three-layer cake at my table. It was yellow with chocolate icing. Momma said how about coffee. I made some instant. I used a whole spoon of coffee; it was regular strength. Me and her sat on the steps by that steep, weedy bank where the bulldozer chewed out a flat place to set this garage.

Momma said, "Look at those weeds. Does Betsy have any idea?"

I said, "She wouldn't dare come in back of this place."

She said, "You know the names of these weeds? They're like flowers."

I said no.

She said, "I know just two. Those yellow-and-black ones—those are black-eyed Susans, aren't they? And pokeberry, there in that pile of old stumps, with those berries and thick purple stalks? Let's name the rest."

I drank some coffee and waited to hear what she'd say.

"See those little orange ones there? I'll call those 'orange shenanigans.'" Which was perfect. She said, "You next."

I said, "See those that are lacy and white?"

"Yes."

"Frost-on-the-Chevy."

She laughed out loud. "On the Chevy?"

I was thinking how one night I came down the mountain with Rosco when it was so freezing and late, and the frost was all over his paint like these small, silver patches of lace.

She said, "Did you start school?"

"Yes."

"And still working?"

"My boss said he'd juggle my hours around." I leaned over to pick up my coffee, and Momma saw my necklace fall out of my shirt. She said, "How pretty. Can I see?"

I said sure.

Her thumb touched the little white face. "It's a cameo. Where did you get it?"

"From Daddy."

"Oh." She tucked it inside of my shirt. "Well, it's pretty. Rough as he was, he always had beautiful taste."

I guess I figured everybody's daddy could pick out a present, but maybe they can't.

Momma said, "Did you ask him for it, or did he think of it himself?"

"He came in where I work and said what did I want for my birthday. It was the first time he ever asked me." She looked at me. She knew I was driving at something. "I mean, last year he gave me a necklace and he never needed to ask me. And it was just perfect. And that was just *last year*."

"Which did you like better, being surprised or being asked?"

I didn't know how to answer. I had to wonder about it.

She smiled at her coffee. "It's a hard choice to make. It's a woman's choice, Libby."

"I don't see why you can't get surprises sometimes and some choices the rest of the time."

"Who's supposed to keep track and decide?"

I didn't know.

Momma said, "I guess I was thinking of Betsy. She's never had any peace in herself. She wants surprises, but she wants them all to turn out like she'd choose. Maybe that's why she's religious. Maybe she thinks God is the one with all the best surprises."

"I don't doubt it. That's how Betsy is."

Momma bumped knees with me. "Like you—you didn't turn out to suit her one bit."

She laughed about it. I didn't see all the humor. I started wondering how Momma could sit on the steps to this place— this place that was mine, up beside of her sister's garage—and still be exactly the same. I said, "Which way are you?"

She smiled at something a good ways away, like the tips of some houses out over the trees. "I like surprises."

Momma would. Momma is ready to love whatever people give her, as long as they give it sincere. I'm not that way. Maybe I'd be better off if I was, but I'm not. I said, "I'd rather be asked."

Momma looked at me like I was a person she needed to study about for a while. She said, "Then I hope you find a good man someday who knows how to ask. And I hope you can learn how to answer."

I wasn't ready to think about men. I've had enough of those for a while. Right now, all I want off a man is a tip.

We sat around till the coffee was gone. Then we sat there some more. She said, "Libby, please tell me the truth about you and your daddy. Not Judith and all of that other—just you and him. I want to know you're okay."

"He can't force me to go back with him. If he does, I'll just run. I can't stop him if he comes where I work and buys food. But I'm not going to let him take me over."

"Take you over?" It didn't sound like a question, exactly. She asked it like she already had her own answer, and needed to hear me come out with the words.

I said, "He gets inside of your head and you do what he says. Just like Judith. Doing whatever he says. And everything I do is either for him or against him. Nothing is me, my own self."

Momma looked down in her cup at the last little puddle where most of the sugar winds up. "He was always fighting and striving. You don't know how he fought to get out from under that bitter old man of his. He fights it every single day. All that hate and resentment and anger. I suppose he accomplished something. I guess your daddy's some improvement."

"But he's never happy."

She said, "He was happy with you, Libby. Sometimes he was happy with me. And he was happy when he could connect with a homer. You remember? That ball would come sailing, and he would connect, and *smack* went his bat, and the ball would be clearing the creek." At first she was seeing that ball clear the creek, and then she was looking at me. "Except now it seems like you're doing it over, the same. There's no improvement in that."

"No. I refuse to be like him one bit."

She watched me to see if I knew what I was talking about. She said, "I guess I don't worry after you as much as Buddy. How is he, Libby? Do you know?"

"He's all right."

"How is he, really? I mean, is he calmer?"

"I don't know. Buddy and me are just different. Seems like before, we were going along fairly close to the same. But ever since Judith it seems like we split. Like I took a sharp turn and he went straight on ahead."

Momma smiled. "That sounds about right. Buddy always wanted to find something fast and hold on for dear life."

We sat and looked at our cups, like we wanted them both to fill up on their own, so we'd have a good reason to sit there.

"Your daddy wanted a ballplayer. I guess I wanted a girl to sing all of those beautiful hymns I grew up with." She smiled and bumped my knee. "And I had one, there for a while."

She didn't say it to spite me. Momma was just in the mood to think back.

Momma said, "I wish you could've met my momma and daddy when they were both healthy and younger."

"Don't get sad, Momma."

"I'm not. I was sad at the funeral, I think. Anyway, it's kind of a relief. She's been a lot to look after since she started to slip. What will I do with this freedom?"

She stared away at the weeds for a while. She said, "We had such a nice home. We had our music, we had our neighbors, we had our church. I guess somewhere in the back of my mind I knew my daddy had his troubles, but they didn't spill out on us. I guess he did pay a price for his pride—him and his mahogany—but I didn't see it. Maybe Betsy did, but I didn't. He protected us from every kind of trouble. Maybe that was the wrong thing to do, I don't know. I know we weren't always striving and fighting. We didn't hate poor people. We didn't hate black people. We didn't hate rich people. We just didn't have any contact. I guess that's not the real world. I guess I never exactly knew what the real world is like. I guess I wanted a dose and wound up with your father. And he was enough."

I couldn't argue with that.

She looked at me. "You've done a lot, haven't you? I mean, a lot I don't know."

I was scared. I didn't know what she was fixing to ask me. I didn't look at her face.

"You've been places, and done things, and felt things, and seen things that I'll never know. Haven't you?"

I couldn't tell her. I didn't have any words.

She said, "It's like you've been off in a different world. And you know what bothers me about it? I don't know anything about where you are when you're off in that world. What if you get into trouble? How can I come to the rescue?"

I was looking away at the orange shenanigans.

She said, "Are you glad you did all of those things? Did they help? Are they doing you any good?"

I couldn't answer. She was looking at me so close and curious, and I was afraid if she kept looking she'd see something awful about me. And there was no way I could tell her. I couldn't lie and I couldn't find any words for explaining the truth. It was like I was out over the edge of a wet, freezing rock in the dark with some roots pulling loose in my hands, and I was just falling and waiting to land.

But Momma said "Libby" and everything stopped. She said,

"Libby, I don't need to know." She even laughed a little. She said, "Gracious, what in the world would I do with such knowledge? Take all the credit? Take all the blame? If sometime you did want to tell me, just come and surprise me. I wouldn't mind having a glimpse here and there. Like 'frost-on-the-Chevy'—I like that. But I won't expect it, not even one word. Just look at me and say you'll be okay."

I looked her right straight in the eyes so the words would go quick and straight as they could. I said, "Momma, I'll be okay."

She started smiling like I gave her a present she wanted and never expected to get. She said, "Thank God."

She set her coffee cup down on the step right behind me. That way her chest was turned closer. I leaned my cheek on her chest and she let me. I didn't cry. I just remember my ear to her chest, and how soft, and that sound off her shirt like a wind, and her fingers so light on my shoulders. And I could keep going and going, like flying that never comes down.

She knows I'll never go live in her house near Chicago. She knows I need to be out on my own. She'll never hold it against me. She'll mail my rent every month with a few dollars extra. And sometimes she'll call me and ask me if I am all right. Which I am.

I figure Tina is down by the ocean. Tina is sandy and happy and wet. She's saying, "I wonder what little monkey is doin'? I 'spect she's lonesome for me in that town. I better send her some kind of a friend."

She sent this woman named Willie. Something like fifty and heavy. Bunchy and thick and sawed off. She comes regular to the Omelette Shoppe. She wears a burnt-orange skirt and some cowboy boots.

I never liked her the first time I saw her. She was so noisy and I didn't care for her looks. But we got to talking. She's been a waitress all over. She can predict who will give me a tip, and come close to how much. One thing about her's exactly like Tina. She is easy to thrill and hard to shock. That is the best thing about her.

Willie says, "You got a mighty big voice for such a wiry little body. And it rings like a spoon in a good china cup. You like to listen to music?"

"I reckon."

"What kind of music you take to?"

"Most any kind except country."

She laughs. "Hell, honey. That's the only kind there is. Listen here, some of my buddies and me get together. What time you finishin' workin'?"

"Midnight or after."

"Well come listen to me and my buddies. I'll pick you up."

"I better not."

"We been friendly here lately?"

"Yeh."

"And talkin'?"

"Yeh."

"I been leavin' you tips fairly reg'lar?"

"Yeh."

"You want me to keep it up?"

She can smile and mean business, the same as the Ticket. Turn Tina white, saw her off about eight inches, ugly her up a good bit, put about thirty years on her, and Willie is close to what Tina is like. They've got the same kind of look in their eyes. They've got that *hell yes* look in their eyes.

Willie says, "I ain't above a good bribe, honey. And I won't bite."

That's how I know she's got Tina behind her—how she says "bite." I know that doesn't make sense, but it's straight from my brain. It would be just like the Ticket to send me a heavyset white woman who's country and not a bit pretty and say, "I hope you like her. This is the best I could do." It would be just like the Ticket to come back undercover and have her some fun in this town.

It's about ten after midnight and Willie is driving. She drives a 'sixty-five Cadillac coupe.

She says, "You ever been to a city?"

"Chicago."

"Mercy me, that *is* a city. I been to Nashville, Columbus Ohio and Memphis. I met a mandolin picker in Memphis. He was ugly and usually drunk. I let him take me a ways out of town. He got finished doin' whatever it was he was tryin' to do to me. Then I finally got what I come for. Hearin' him pick that ol' Gibson A-Five. That was as close to the fireworks as I've ever been with a man. When he got through, I was weak. I sat and stared at the city. We could see all of them untold lights of Memphis. I ast him how did he come by such music. He reached and walked his skinny fingers on the windshield. He said, 'I like to sit around here, in the dark off a rocky dirt road in some weeds. I like to reach out and feel of them twink-a-lin' lights from way off at this distance.' " She looked at me. "You know what he meant by that, honey?"

"Yeh."

"I knew you did." She smiles, and here we go climbing the side of some mountain. "You got a family, honey?"

"They all live scattered around. How 'bout you?"

She turns the car up a steep, rocky road. She has to stretch out her neck to see over the wheel. Willie says, "When a woman makes country music, she makes her own family."

This Cadillac smooths out the road.

Willie pulls up at a hill going up to a two-story house. The porch light is shining. There are these godawful pickups and big, rusty Dodges and Lincolns and wagons that needed a wash before now. And nobody took any trouble to keep them all straight. Willie parks down by the road. She has to get her guitar from the trunk. She heaves a heavy black case with both hands. She grunts, "You get the lid." It goes ka-whomp—very solid and heavy like Cadillacs are.

We pick our way through these cars up the hill to the house. It's a good ways and the hill is right steep. The ground is chewed up a good bit from the tires and the weeds are bent over and smeared. The closer we get, the more we can hear of this hillbilly music. I don't enjoy country music.

Willie says, "Racine plays banjo. I better warn you ahead of time about his face. Chain saw kicked back and near killed him. Took part of his jaw, about half of his teeth. So he sings a mite stiff, but he's a good man. Now Sabe is the fiddle player, and this is his momma's house. Sabe holds his fiddle real tight like a grudge, and saws it right bitter, on account of him losing his boy. But he's a good man. And Albert sings tenor, plays bass. He does the talkin'. Albert's wife left him last summer, and sometimes it seems like he wanders off after Charlene on that bass, but there never was a sweeter man at heart. And they'll be others around there. Most of them broke and half ugly. Sittin' around the front room, and back in the kitchen. Not a one's gonna care if you come in amongst us. We're all here for the same kind of reason—to get next to some good country music. Get some *on* us."

She's grinning and swinging that giant guitar case. It bumps against fenders and doors. We pick our way through the cars. I hear the fiddle and banjo and bass. It sounds like a whole crowd of people is in there, stomping for a homer.

We climb those splintery steps to the porch. The house is all wood and the paint is popped off. We squeeze ourselves in this room where the people are rung all around us and packed in the corners and close to the walls. Willie starts naming some names. Clayford and Maxton and Linda and Alton and Rosa and more. They are all grinning and nodding. I don't know what they are grinning about.

Willie pops open her case and pulls out a tremendous guitar. It is bright orange and rusty red-brown with a beautiful dove on the pick guard. She says, "We've only got this one rule: New people sing."

I'm by myself in the middle. I'm in a trap with these people around me. I'm so scared I can't run. It's just like that night in the grandstand when Tina came in from the rain soaking wet. I was cornered and hurting for some kind of action. She heaved me up and I opened my mouth. I bit her and got a good taste.

This Albert, the bass-fiddle player, he names the song. He says, "You know the words?"

I nod my head. I've been hearing that song all my life. People can't live in this place without knowing that song.

Willie starts strumming and I try to sing. Albert says,

"Whoa," and we stop. He looks me over. He says, "Okay, let's start again. Now just relax, sweetheart. Try to remember you're amongst desperate cutthroats and thieves."

He makes me laugh.

He says, "That's right. Now open your mouth up a little. Loosen your jaw and breathe deep, from your belly, right here. Racine, work that banjo lick *under,* not *over,* when she hits that high part in the middle. Now seems like she scraped bottom once or twice in G. Willie, slip your cheater bar up there a couple of notches. Let's kick this puppy off in A."

Quick as he says it the banjo breaks out on my skin like the chills and the fiddle is anxious and straining and bass has gone deep in my bones like a curse. And all of these people around me connect with this music, and words that were always so ugly and country are all of a sudden so modern and fresh, and I'm in the middle, where all of the words and the music take hold and go up in the same kind of fire. But what is so perfect and scary is how I can be smack in the middle one second like fire and the next second flying away by myself in the cold. Fire and then cold and then fire and then cold. I can feel all this heat on my cheeks from the fire while I go catch a long, frozen hill by myself. And my runners smack down on the snow where the cars have been packing some hard, icy ribs with their chains. And my hands grab the ends of that wood where I steer. And the bones in my chest beat the wood in my sled but I'm flying and flying and little froze pieces of gravel shoot sparks off my runners like sparks shooting up off a bonfire and all of these faces are on me and with me away to that hill where the road levels off and turns up at the end and I stand and look up at the glow on their faces and see where I am. And all I can see are those red, fiery faces around me. And that's when I know what I want. I know exactly what I want. I want to do that again.

The words and the music burned up but the fire is still hot on my eyelids and cheeks and the back of my neck. Albert turns loose of his bass and it falls back against him like some kind of brown, swooning girl. He says, "Gawdamighty, little girl. You hit them notes like you *belong* there."

Sabe jabs his fiddle bow over my head like he's pointing to one of the planets. He says, "Looka here's Momma—up outa her bed."

All of us look when we hear him say "Momma." We see a skinny old woman perched high on the steps in her lavender nightgown. She is stoop-shouldered and bent. Her feet are so bony and blue. She sits all hunched, like a buzzard with lavender feathers and wings, her toes curling down on the edge of the step. She is looking at me. She smiles like an angel who's grateful I bothered her sleep.

Racine he doesn't have lips on one side of his face. There's a sunken place dug from his jaw to his cheek like a little pink ditch. That side of his face doesn't move when he talks. He says, "Where in the world did you get such a *voice*?"

"From my momma."

Racine starts grinning, and it seems like his face will split open both ways where the chain saw connected. "From your *momma*?"

All of the people around me are grinning. I can't see what's so funny. Maybe I sang the wrong words. Maybe it's some kind of joke they played on me because I am new. Maybe I only imagined these people were with me. I squeeze my way through a hard knot of people and stand on the porch. Willie comes out here behind me. She is so near but not touching.

"Sweetheart, don't you know what was funny?"

I feel so weak, like my bones will be coming apart on the porch, like a puzzle I can't ever work back together. I stumble down in the weeds near the cars.

Willie hangs back on the porch. That's the right distance between us. If she goes back in the house I'll walk off and catch my own ride into town. If she comes closer I'll run. She says, "Listen here to me, sweetheart. Maybe you got them dark eyes from your momma. And maybe you got that soft hair. But you never got such a voice from your momma. And you never got it from your daddy, neither. You took and grabbed holt of somethin' that nobody's momma and daddy would wish on their young-un. I seen you squeezin' your fists on them high notes. I seen your knuckles turn white. One fist on love and

the other on hate. One on this snaky old mountain, and one
on the free, empty air. And all of them words and that music
shot through you like lightnin', like fire through a tinderbox
house. Now listen here to me. We got some work to do on you.
We need to smoothen you out a good bit. You come on back
in this house with these big ugly men and older women. It's
where you're ready to be."

The porch light's behind her. The fiddle goes wild like a
dog after something that lives in the woods. Willie is feeling
that music all over her clothes and her heavyset body. Her
shadow crawls flat in the weeds like it's itching for action and
ready to roll.

I need to stand in this yard for a minute. I need to think to
myself what to do. I've got some questions for people who
don't have the slightest idea where I am. I need to put this
whole night into words. I need to go ask my momma: What
was it happened to me and those people? Is this my surprise
or my choice? Is Willie my friend or the devil? Is this my way
out or a trap?

Both of my hands have a tingle. All of my fingers are jumpy
from squeezing those notes. I need to go ask my daddy: Is this
like connecting with homers? Is this how it felt when you
kissed one good-bye? If it is, then I can come out from in back
of that counter and never be scared of you ever. I can look
straight in your face and say, "Boo." Because now I can see
the whole reason you've never been happy since baseball. It
wasn't Judith. It wasn't Momma and Buddy. It wasn't me. You
had to be in the middle. You had to kiss one good-bye.

Willie is dancing and whacking that porch with her boot like
she's trying to drive home a nail. Her shadow is stretching and
twisting and jerking this way down the steps, through the
weeds. It wants to break loose of her and turn solid. It wants
to grab me. Tina, I wish it was you in that shadow. I wish you
could hear me this second. I wish this could reach all the way
to the coast: I can *sing*.